NEVER NEVER

BRIANNA R. SHRUM

SPENCER
HILL
PRESS

Copyright © 2015 by Brianna Shrum

Sale of the paperback edition of this book
without its cover is unauthorized.

Spencer Hill Press

All rights reserved, including the right to reproduce this
book or portions thereof in any form whatsoever.
Contact: Spencer Hill Press, 27 West 20th
Street, Suite 1102, New York, NY 10011

Please visit our website at www.spencerhillpress.com

First Edition: September 2015
Brianna Shrum
Never Never / by Brianna Shrum – 1st ed.
p. cm.

Summary: A re-telling that starts when James Hook, the
boy who only wanted to grow up, meets Peter Pan, the only
boy who didn't, and follows their journey from innocent
friends to the fiercest rivals in all of Neverland.

This book is a work of fiction. Names, characters, places, and
incidents are used in a fictitious manner. Any resemblance
to actual persons, living or dead, business establishments,
events, or locales is purely coincidental. Use of any
copyrighted, trademarked, or brand names in this work of
fiction does not imply endorsement of that brand.

Cover Design: Hafsah Faizal
Interior layout by Jenny Perinovic
Author photo by Taylor Whitrock

ISBN 978-1-63392-039-2 (paperback)
ISBN 978-1-63392-040-8 (ebook)

Printed in the United States of America

For Dad.

Hope your big adventure is everything
we dreamed it would be.

PART ONE

In Which the Hook Meets the Pan

ONE

ALL CHILDREN, EXCEPT ONE, WISH TO STAY YOUNG. James Hook, however, wanted to grow up. At twelve years old, James was mostly happy with the state of things, in the way that most twelve year olds are—he had parents who loved him very much, a dog that loved him even more, and a pantry that never emptied of sweet things for him to eat. But there was an older-than-he-really-was part of him that had always recognized this happiness as fleeting, and it was because of this that the boy James could not wait to become a man. As the summer drew to a close and his first year at Eton School loomed in the not-so-distant future, he found himself very much looking forward to the next chapter in his life.

As he packed his things neatly into his suitcases two weeks early (always early), he had a sort of wistful look on his face. The kind of look that was generally reserved for men on their wedding days or women when they first beheld the tiny faces of their newborns. James was beholding a future untainted by foolish youth and silliness—a future filled with the hopes and dreams that only a man could ever begin to accomplish.

This sentiment, however, did not stop him from grabbing stray hangers here and there and swishing them through the air, stabbing at bodiless articles of clothing with the flat end, slicing at them with a makeshift hook between his fingers. Even while he was packing for adulthood, a piece of him clung to the dreams he'd had every night this week, and several nights per week before that. Dreams in which he was a pirate captain, vicious ruler of a wicked, gleaming ship and a dark and horrid band of pirates. The *Spanish Main*, his sleeping self had christened the ship. Between the folding of his shirts and the mating of his socks, he pretended his little bed was his ship and his bags were driftwood on the ocean until he could almost smell the water and feel the damp chill of the sea on his skin. It was only at this early hour of the morning that he could recall those stolen fragments of his dreams, so he thought it was probably all right to waste a bit of time until they inevitably disappeared again.

He wagered that even adults dreamed sometimes. He grinned, wondering if his father ever dreamt himself to be a pirate at night, bigger even than the sailor that he was. Perhaps he did. Really, what was so childish about playing at piracy every now and then?

But he could only justify so much of this to his mature half, so he allowed himself mere seconds of play from hour to hour.

Mostly, he stood stick-straight, kept his hyperactivity to a minimum, and held his mouth in a solemn line as he packed.

James's mother was downstairs, rustling around in the kitchen, banging pots and pans together with such vigor it must have been on purpose. James grinned. She had always been a particularly good mother, but in this one skill, she was woefully deficient. He frowned then, wondering why she would possibly trouble herself with cooking, unless she had forgotten about the plans he had made to go to Kensington Park today. He left his suitcase open on his bed and bounded down the stairs, taking them two at a time.

"Mother," he called, sniffing at the smoke in the air, "are you cooking for me?"

She waddled out of the kitchen, massive pregnant belly coated with flour along with the rest of her.

"Yes, James. Why are you carrying on?"

"Well, it's just, Father and I were going to lunch in Kensington Gardens this afternoon."

Her face fell as James's father walked into the room, hoisting a bag over his shoulder and looking every bit a sailor—neat, light-colored pants that would come back from the other side of the world all dark and frayed, layers of blues and browns over his shoulders, hazel eyes shimmering with the call of the sea.

James furrowed his brow, and his fingers jumped to the back of his neck and fiddled with the ends of his hair. "Father?"

The sailor smiled and rumpled James's hair. James frowned, looking him slowly up and down, and shrank back from his hand.

"What's the bag for?" he asked, more than suspicious, but forcing himself to deny what he knew was coming.

His father raised a dark eyebrow. "I'm heading out on the Thames today. You knew that, didn't you?"

"But I…"

"You what?"

He opened his mouth, intending to say something entirely different, but shrunk at the question instead. "Nothing."

James's father eyed him hard, sharp jaw set. "Don't lie to me." James mouthed the next line along with him: "Good things don't happen to boys who lie."

James felt his mother's long fingers brush the back of his neck, and he swallowed hard, past the knot in his throat. "I thought…"

"Out with it, boy," his father boomed.

"You said we would go to Kensington Gardens today," said James, focused on a burled spot in the floorboards.

"I said no such thing."

"Father, that's a lie!" He was unable to contain the outburst; his emotions were threatening to explode from every bit of his skin.

His father furrowed his brow deeply, bringing a blush to James's cheeks. "Bad form, James. Bad form." His ridged nose twitched, the way it did sometimes when he was frustrated.

"Edward," his mother said in her gentle voice, reaching toward her husband, but he simply ignored her, hard gaze trained on James.

The boy struggled to compose himself, humiliated when small tears crept their way out of his eyes and slid down his face. He rolled his gaze up to meet his father's. "I leave for boarding school in two weeks. And my birthday's in half that time!"

"Come now, James. I've been 'round for most of your birthdays, and I'll be 'round for fifty more."

Smoke began to drift in from the kitchen, and James's eyes stung more than they already did, so he blinked hard, wishing desperately for the tears to go away. His mother wrinkled her nose and wiped at her reddening eyes, then left them alone, dashing off toward the kitchen. Presumably to stop the house from burning down.

"What about Kensington Gardens?"

The other man softened then and pulled the boy into a hard embrace. And James breathed in the smell of salt and earth, memorizing the feel of his father's smooth, hard face against his cheek. "Come now, boy. It's not as though you'll be gone forever. It's only a few months at a time."

James refused to pull away even when his father did, afraid that if he did, his father would disappear from his sight. Finally, though, the larger man won and the hug was broken. He knelt and wiped a calloused thumb across the tear on James's downcast face.

"I promise, when you return on holiday and when I come to shore again, we'll lunch in Kensington Gardens."

James sniffed and slowly looked up into his father's face. It was kind and smiling and a bit sad. There were little wrinkles there, lines from smiling that James rarely had the opportunity to notice. He looked away again, trying once more to stop the rogue tears from coming.

At that moment, James was sad that he wouldn't be able to see his father when he first came ashore. He liked him best then, cropped hair grown long and wavy, face full of trim stubble, smelling like the sea.

His father grabbed James's chin, harder, probably, than he intended, and turned it toward himself. James screwed his mouth into a firm line, resisting the urge to shift away from the man's bruising affection.

"I'm proud of you, boy," he whispered. "Off to Eton, off to become a man. What a brilliant one you'll make. One a hundred times better than your father, better than a poor, dirty sailor. You're exceptional, James—remember that."

The boy threw his arms around his father and hugged him as tightly as he could. The battle against the tears was altogether lost, and they dampened his father's jacket. But James didn't have enough room in his heart to feel ashamed.

His father kissed his head, and said in a low voice, "It's not forever, son."

Then, he stood and strode over to the entry to the kitchen, staring at James's mother, whose cheeks were bright and round, grey eyes shining. He rubbed a smidge of flour off her face and kissed her cheek, and James turned away when he kissed her mouth, fearing that he was invading a moment that should've been private. His father whispered something to her, and he knelt and kissed her stomach. Then he shot James a parting smile, and breezed out the door. His mother sighed, looking tired, and headed back to assault some more kitchenware.

James's lunch was dull and tasteless and he ate it solemnly, just picking at it here and there. His mother screwed her lips and eyebrows up, and reached for his hand, which made him feel slightly better.

"Come now, James. He'll be back not long from now."

He sighed. "He won't come see me for my birthday—he can't even send a card. Or take me off to boarding school and say goodbye before I'm gone forever."

"It's not forev—"

"It may as well be," said James, aware he was acting like a spoiled child. He hardly cared. He stole a glance at her belly and shook his head quickly. "He won't even be around when the baby is born, will he?"

His mother's lips parted, and she started fidgeting. "Well, of course he'll be back in time for that."

James flinched. "What do you mean, *of course?*"

"Just that the birth of a child is a very important thing, and of course your father will be here for it."

Hurt flashed across his face; he felt as though he'd just been punched in the gut. He pursed his lips and pushed himself back from the table. "I'm not hungry anymore. If you need me, I'll be up in my room," he choked.

His mother reached out to caress his shoulder. "Oh James, that's not what I—"

That was all he heard, for he'd jerked away, slammed his door, and thrown himself on his bed before she could finish.

HIS MOTHER NEVER DID COME UP, AND HE WAS GLAD. Probably the effort of propelling her body up the stairs was just too much without the promise of reward. He sat on his bed, stroking Meggie's smooth golden fur, wishing that the next two weeks would be through by tomorrow, and wanting more than ever to be gone from this place. Wishing that the bits and pieces he could recall from his dream were true and that he was a pirate captain of a dreadful ship, the—whatever it was called. He couldn't quite remember. It had been quite a while since this morning, after all.

If only he was a sailor, a pirate, he could follow his father out to sea if he wanted, and he'd only come back to London if he pleased. Meggie laid her large head on his lap and he knew she could feel his problems.

"You'll be there when I leave, won't you, Meggie?" he cooed, scratching her head. "You'll help me blow out the candles on my birthday cake."

She just lay there and groaned. He took it as a "yes."

"But you can't take me to Kensington Gardens, can you? And I can't very well go alone, especially not at this hour."

The sky was dark, apart from the moon and a couple of twinkling stars. There, looking out his window, his mind on the blurry edge of sleep, James got a wicked idea. One his father would almost certainly regard as "bad form." He grinned and hopped off his bed, startling Meggie, who rolled onto the floor with a resounding *plop*. Then, he pulled a decidedly too-large, faded red jacket he'd stolen from his father out of his half-packed suitcase and slid it over his shoulders. He fit the matching cap, which he'd also nicked, onto his head as well and tiptoed out of his room into the hallway.

Usually, the floor creaked beneath the weight of footsteps, but tonight, it screamed. Somehow though, his mother didn't wake up. Small victories. The front door loomed above him like an omen, daring him to open it. He shut his eyes tight, waiting for the squeal he knew would come from its hinges. But it opened for him silently, and he let out a giant puff of breath as he made his way into the foggy streets of London.

They were empty, save for a few errant wanderers and stray animals, and that gave the night a sort of eerie quality. Fog pooled around his ankles, sinking into the little cracks between the cobblestones and snaking its way up his calves. It smelled like nighttime out here: like earth and damp and dark. He curled his fingers into tiny fists in his pockets and kept his head down, trying his hardest to ignore the mist and the steady *clop-clop-clopping* of a horse and lonely carriage rolling down the middle of the road. It didn't contain anyone of any malevolent kind of importance, he was sure. Certainly no mates of Jack the Ripper's or psychopaths or anyone interested in kidnapping him. That was ridiculous. He barked out a laugh, breath clouding in the humid air, then shrank back against a brick storefront, lest he'd inadvertently drawn the Not-Kidnapper's attention.

The closer he got to Kensington Gardens (and the further he got from home), the eerier and darker the night became, until he was hugging his jacket around himself tighter than he thought possible, and was very much regretting his choice of rebellion. The Gardens were just up ahead, though, and it seemed silly to turn around now. His footsteps echoed as he drew closer to the Gardens, sounds running together as he quickened his pace. He thought that maybe he would simply step inside Kensington's perimeter, so that he could say he'd gone today, and then turn straight around and go back home. When he reached the edge, however, he found that that was not what he wanted to do. He wanted, more than anything, to venture into the greenery and sit for a while by himself, pretending his father was there with him.

He took a deep breath, made his way farther in, and stopped by the pond in the center of the garden. He looked out over it for a moment, stretching and quietly watching the mist rise from the water. Blades of grass wrapped themselves around the boy's calves and he fell back into them, relishing the soft feel of the lawn on his neck and back, the distinct smell of water in the air. He lay there for quite some time, not allowing himself to cry, and, to his surprise, not really needing to. Crying was a crutch, the reaction of a child, and James fancied himself to be transforming into a man already.

A brilliant man, his father had said. *A man a hundred times that of his father.*

He didn't believe he would really be all that, but it felt good to play the words in his head over and over. Besides, being near the body of water made the dream feel all the more real. Like he was just waiting, waiting to sail out on a grand adventure. It wasn't a pond; it was the sea. And he wasn't a schoolboy; he was a sailor. Perhaps a pirate, even. Sometimes he pretended that that was what his father *really* did on his missions at sea—pirated, had marvelous adventures. He hoped he'd accompany him someday and find out. He began to feel glad that he had made this foolish decision as the silent, private minutes stretched on.

"Are you lost, boy?"

A voice, smooth and commanding, but young, sliced through the quiet and jerked him into a sudden panic. James leapt straight from lying on his back to standing on unsteady feet, and he adjusted his little cap nervously.

"Stay back!" he shouted, stepping slowly backward.

The person in front of him hopped easily toward him until James could make out his features. He relaxed a bit when he saw that the hopping person was not much older than he, fourteen or fifteen at most. His little smile was disarming, and he looked rather like an elf—sharp features, laughing eyes, ears that almost *pointed* back at the water.

Even his clothes made him look as though he'd just popped out of a tree. Moss draped about him, hanging lazily over his shoulders, leaves of all sorts of shapes and colors inexpertly stitched together, wrapping around his thighs and torso.

"Did I frighten you?" the intruder asked, laughing.

"No, of course not."

James bristled and stood taller, desiring to look more mature than he was, especially in front of this peculiar boy, who gave James the distinct, odd impression of being older and younger all at once.

The lake behind the boy glimmered and pulsed, and James swore it hadn't been doing so before, which was entirely strange, and made him feel that perhaps he was overly tired or going mad. One or the other.

"You're lying, I think. I'm sure you nearly jumped out of your skin," the other boy crowed.

James scoffed and raised his chin. "Well, I think I've had quite enough of this. I was just going home."

The other boy stopped laughing, then, and furrowed his brow. "So you aren't lost?"

"Not at all. Being here was quite intentional. Are *you* lost?"

"Yes," said the boy, raising his eyebrows, "but I know exactly where I am."

James frowned and then rolled his eyes. "Who are you anyway?"

"Peter," said the boy, a near-laugh in his voice. The sort that made James feel absurd for not knowing who Peter was already. "Peter Pan. Who are you?

"James Hook," James said, trying unsuccessfully to match Peter's mocking tone.

"That's a funny name," Peter said, wrinkling his nose.

"No funnier than Pan."

Peter squinted, considering. "Yes, it is." Then, he turned around and darted off, lightly illuminating the trees and the grass wherever his feet landed.

James blinked hard and shook his head until the glowing had worn off, and regarded Peter for a second, part of him wanting to go home, the other part wanting desperately to follow the strange boy further into the park. He chewed on his cheek, gaze darting from the boy back to the edge of Kensington Gardens, and the comfortable, boring familiarity of home. In the end, the desperate half of him won out. James darted off in the direction of his new companion.

"What are you doing in Kensington in the middle of the night, Peter Pan?" James asked, running, stumbling in an attempt to catch up to him.

"Nothing. Just chatting with the fairies, looking for Lost Boys. It seems you're not one of them."

"Fairies?" He slowed to a stop beside Peter. He set his hands on his knees and leaned over, self-consciously trying to catch his breath. "What are you going on about?"

"Surely you know about fairies," Peter said, that condescending chuckle back in his voice, too-large eyes lighting up, eyebrows drawn together. He may as well have laughed and pointed at James.

James's jaw twitched. He hated cockiness. It was horrid form. He particularly hated it when it was directed at him. He was compelled to answer Peter's question anyway, because, well, he couldn't figure why. Either way, he still wished to impress him. "Well, of course I've read about them in stories, but those are only for children."

"And you aren't one?" said Peter, looking around, distractable, touching all the leaves and twigs in his reach.

"A what?" asked James.

"A children," replied Peter, looking back at him.

James raised an eyebrow. Pan was certainly no Eton man. Somehow, that mattered less than it should've, as James found himself opening his mouth to say that of course he wasn't a "children." Then an image of him several hours ago, blushing apple-red and struggling not to cry, flashed in his mind. He pursed his lips. Then, glumly: "I suppose I am a child."

"Good." Peter let out an exaggerated sigh of relief.

"I don't see what's so good about it."

"Well, I couldn't speak with you if you weren't a children." He said this as though it were a given, as though no one associated with people who weren't children, of course.

James huffed and shook his head, black hair flying about, and tried to make some sort of sense of the situation. He wondered, for a moment, if throwing one's lot in with someone like this was a very obvious way to get oneself chopped up and splattered all over the front page of *The London Gazette*. Pan the Ripper. How would he even explain himself to St. Peter at the gate? "Yes, sir, I'm afraid I got myself rather murdered, following an obviously deranged fellow wearing the guts of a tree into the dark in the middle of the night."

But there was some pull inside James that whispered at him to ignore the alarm bells. That no one ever got an adventure without giving up a little sense first.

So, against his better judgment, but in accordance with his adventuresome half, he followed Peter further and further into the park, past the pond, past the open, manicured grass, and into the trees. James had never been this far back before, back where the tree branches were more fingery, the shadows more shadowy.

"Where are you going, Peter?"

"To see the fairies."

"Well, that's foolishness," said James, warning bells ringing louder and louder in his mind, but his legs disagreed, following Peter all the more quickly into the grove.

"I don't think so," said Peter, and James huffed.

"It is, though."

Peter stopped and stared at him, then cocked his head like James was the lunatic, and not him. "What's so foolish about it?"

James blinked several times in rapid succession. "I don't believe in—"

All of a sudden, Peter barreled into him and clapped his hand over his mouth.

"Sssssshhhhhh." James's eyes widened and he just stood there, frozen. "Don't say it. Never say it. When children say they don't believe, a fairy drops down somewhere, dead. And you *are* children, aren't you?"

James nodded fiercely.

"Then never say it, James Hook. Promise me." He removed his hand from James's mouth.

"I promise."

Peter did an about face, expression shifting to a pleasant blank, then bounded off again, and James followed him and disappeared into the trees.

Suddenly, James stopped and stood completely still, mouth agape, staring into the leaves. He stumbled backward and his eyes darted back and forth, and a shocked smile spread across the whole width of his face. There were little lights flashing and bobbing about, darting in and out of the shadows. Peter hopped on his toes, and they swarmed around him, glowing on his fingers, his nose, shining on wisps of his red-gold hair.

One or two came within a couple centimeters of James, and he forced himself to stay put, not to back away as his entire perception of the world shifted around him. He laughed brightly as the faint sound of tinkling bells echoed in his ears, and he spread out his arms and fingers.

Perhaps he was insane. Perhaps his companion was the mad one. But it didn't matter in that moment. For he was spending tonight among the fairies, and he was absolutely certain that he already wished to do it again.

TWO

MOST NIGHTS AFTER THAT, FOUR IN THE COURSE of a week to be exact, James found a way to meet Peter at Kensington Gardens. He learned how to avoid all the creaky spots on the stairs quite quickly, and always managed to make it home before his mother had had a chance to realize he was gone. Pregnant women tended to be oblivious to most things.

One particularly dark night at the week's end, James was lying on his back next to Peter, shadowed by the trees, lit by the fairies, when Peter asked him a question he never had before.

"How old are you, James?" Peter ran his fingers over the long blue-green grass between them, absently.

James rolled his head over to have a look at his companion. "I'll be thirteen tomorrow."

Peter turned toward James and furrowed his brow. "You will?"

"Yes. Tomorrow's my birthday."

"How awful," Peter said, misery coating his words.

James sat up and frowned. "What do you mean, *awful?*" Blood rushed to his cheeks, and he was glad for the shadow of the trees around them.

"You're growing up, of course," said Peter, sitting up with James. Peter shook his head, clearly disappointed in something.

James furrowed his brow. He'd always feared he was rather too young to be hanging around with a boy so much older and more interesting than he as Peter. Of course, when he was young he was too young, but now that he was old, he was too old. "I don't understand," he said. Growing up was something everyone did, whether Peter wished it or not.

"It seems a terrible thing to have to grow up. To have to be a man." Peter shuddered at that last word, and stared away into the stars as the fairies lit the darkness around him.

"I don't know about that. I'm rather looking forward to it."

Peter leapt nimbly to a standing position and looked at James with horror in his eyes. "Are you mad? Why ever would anyone want to grow up?"

James shrunk back, ears burning. He had never considered this question. Growing up was something he'd wished to do for as long as he could remember, so he'd never had reason to consider why. He just always had. "Well, I, um, I should like to think it would be a wonderful thing to be a man. To have myself a wife and children and to explore the world and conquer the sea."

Peter looked at him, then, as though he'd never seen him before. A long shadow fell over the little wood, and James hugged his jacket around him.

"That's all nonsense. Being a man means you're trapped forever. I'll never be a man. I always want to be a little boy and to have fun." He nodded decisively, a lock of stick-straight hair flapping down over his eyes.

James laughed and hoisted himself up from the dew-sprinkled ground, sending a smattering of fairies flying all about. "Well, that's all well and good, but you've got to grow up someday, Peter. We all have."

"That isn't true."

"Yes, it is. Just look at yourself. You're half a grown-up already. You're at least an inch taller than I am and your voice is going to get all low and rumbly any time now. How old are you, anyway?"

"I'm not sure," Peter said, waving his hand and rolling his eyes.

James shook his head, used to Peter's particular brand of peculiarity by now.

"Anyway," Peter continued, hands on his hips, "I'm hardly 'half a grown up.' I'm a boy, and I'll always be."

James scoffed and focused on the fairies bobbing overhead, making the green oak leaves glisten.

"You think I'm joking?"

James snickered and fingered a purple flower in one of the beds nearest him. "I think you're daft."

Peter narrowed his eyes and peered at James, a half-smile quirking his mouth. "I can prove it to you, you know."

"Oh, can you?"

"Yes, I can. I'll take you there. To a place where you never have to grow up."

"Sounds brilliant," James said, sarcasm dripping from his lips.

Peter dug his fists into his sides at this, cleared his throat loudly, then his feet left the ground, and he began to float, until he was nearly three feet in the air. James sprang up, breath fleeing him, and stumbled backward. "Wh—what are you—what is...?"

"Oh, this?" Peter asked, resting his chin on a massive tree branch. He grinned, clearly terribly proud of himself. "I do it all the time in Neverland."

"It can't be true." It wasn't. James blinked hard once, twice, a third time. Each time he opened his eyes, he was faced with a flying, grinning Peter Pan. James considered the very real possibility that he was perhaps a nutter. Yes,

James would be spending his thirteenth birthday in the loony bin, which was rather unfortunate.

"Well, it is," said Peter. The fairies clouded around his head, and James simply stood there on the ground, staring up, cool air dampening his curls of hair.

A probing sort of fear burrowed into James's chest when the reality of it all hit him. He could barely breathe for a moment as he watched the boy before him very clearly floating and flying about. It was no stranger than seeing a real live fairy, really. But it had taken him days to come to terms with the existence of those little beasties alone. However would he possibly work out the science of a *flying* boy? He sat in the grass, knees suddenly too weak to support him.

After several minutes in which James was nearly catatonic and Peter was doing backflips and zig-zags and all manner of other acrobatics (because simply floating wasn't impressive enough in its own right), James stirred. "Neverland, you say?" he whispered.

"Neverland. Where you never, never have to grow up."

"Where is it?" he asked, feeling extremely foolish and extremely curious all at once.

Peter pointed up at the sparkling sky, to something James couldn't see. He wondered if it was due to the clouds overhead, or the spider web of branches, or his own incompetence. "Second to the right and straight on 'til morning."

James stared up at the stars, lips just slightly parted in a deluded, lazy state of wonder. "Is it a good place?" he said, still lost in the blackness, wondering which star was the second to the right. "I mean to say, is it somewhere a boy should like to live? Or at least to visit?"

"Of course!" Peter shouted. "Full of fairies and mermaids and adventures and pirates."

"Pirates?" James exclaimed, gaze jerking back down to meet Peter's. It was on this last point that Peter had him. Pirates were, after all, the boy's only childhood tendency.

"Oh yes. The *Spanish Main*. Full of bumbling, stupid, grown-up pirates. I've killed at least a dozen of them."

"*Spanish Main?*" said James, head cocked. The words felt more familiar on his tongue than they should have. And James felt a slippery, wriggling sort of disquiet in his gut at the term, but he couldn't recall why. Like the reasons were grey and blurry and he couldn't quite grasp them.

"Yes," said Peter, and James ignored his gut, worrying instead about the obvious disapproval in Peter's voice.

"Yes, of course. I thought I'd misheard." He shifted uncomfortably, wringing his hands. "You say you killed them?" James's face wrinkled into deep, concerned folds.

Peter rolled his eyes. "Pirates, James Hook. It's not the same as killing regular folk."

James chewed his cheek and thought. Peter *was* rather older than him, and he seemed to know a great deal about things James knew approximately nothing about. Perhaps pirate-killing was one of them. "Killing, though? I don't think I could kill a person, even if that person was a pirate." *Especially if that person was a pirate*, thought James, but he figured it wouldn't be wise to admit aloud.

"Well, I'd never trust you to kill a pirate anyway. There's too much London on you."

James recoiled, not sure what that meant, but quite certain it had been an insult. "Well, I hardly think—"

"Like it or don't. It's how we do." Peter waved his hand and leaned up against the nearest tree, flicking little fairies off in every direction.

James frowned, trying very hard to focus on his morals. He knew Eton men had to have codes against killing. But every time his mind got close to refusing the venture, his heart got all twisted and distracted by the flying and Peter's sparkling smile and the fairies.

"Is it somewhere you can come back from?" he said.

"Of course. I was born in London, you know. I go back and forth as I please."

James raised an eyebrow, and took a step toward Peter. "Born here? In London?"

Peter looked past James's shoulder, over to the beginning of the pond. "Grew up right here in Kensington Gardens with the fairies. 'Til I decided to stop, that is."

'Til he decided to stop. James bit his lip. He wondered if it was really all that easy, deciding to stop. For the first time, James wondered if growing up was really something he wished to do.

"That's when I dreamt up Neverland. Been flying here and there whenever I please ever since."

James considered this boy and his offer and his promises of flight and pirates and adventure for what felt like an age, but it was more likely no longer than a minute.

"And you could take me there? To Neverland?"

Peter regarded him carefully, pinching his chin and piercing through him with those mesmerizing green eyes. "Perhaps."

The early morning started to become a sort of chalky grey-black and James rose to his feet, though he found they were stuck to the ground. He was torn between staying in Kensington Park like he wanted and going home, like he ought.

"I've got to go, Peter."

"Well, go, then. But I'm going home tomorrow. Find me or not."

With that, Peter flitted away and James trudged to his house, head filled with fantasy and foolishness. His brain was so full of clutter and distraction that he barely even knew when he was through his bedroom door and crawling under the covers. Somewhere between sleep and waking, he could think of nothing but this mysterious magical place where boys stayed boys forever and battled pirates and frolicked with fairies and swam with mermaids. Eventually, slumber overtook him.

His last thought before waking, as it nearly always was of late, was of his pirate ship filled with ruffians—a man with a golden tooth, a fat one with a quiet little smile, another with orange hair, a big one with tattoos. And a grand room for him, filled with golden goblets of things he most certainly was not allowed to drink.

His first thought after waking, however, was of an entirely different variety. He awoke wondering if it were possible to change his black curls of hair to red-gold, straight ones. That was foolish, he figured, and so he resolved not to consider it at all. Thus, his second thought was not of Peter. It was unintelligible, but pleased, as the smell of baking cake filled every corner of the house. He padded down the stairs in his nightgown and into the dining room, where his mother was putting the finishing touches on a cake he couldn't believe she had made. She beamed when she saw him.

"Happy birthday, James!" His mother set the pretty cake down before him.

His cake-related happy mood dissolved.

How—what? Awful? Wonderful? He couldn't puzzle out how he felt about it anymore. But his mother didn't seem to notice the rather forlorn look on his face. His mood did brighten a bit when he came to the realization that, since it was his birthday, his mother was allowing him to have cake for breakfast. That was certainly a spot of luck. So, he found a reason to smile and ate his birthday cake and pretended that it didn't mean he was a year older, a year closer to manhood. Before, he would've thought this a good thing, but now, well, Peter wouldn't talk to him if he wasn't a children.

For the rest of the day, James was distracted and conflicted. On the one hand, Neverland sounded like an awfully grand place to live, and Peter made being a little boy sound like the best way to be. On the other hand, James really did want to grow up and become a man and do all the sorts of things men did. He desperately wished he didn't have to make the decision tonight.

He trudged up to his room and sat heavily on the bed, laying his head on Meggie's warm stomach. He would so miss Meggie if he left, and Mother and Father. He was quite certain they would miss him, too. Forever was an awfully long time to miss a person.

A thought struck him, then. Peter had never explicitly said it *was* forever, had he—this relocation to Neverland? Peter Pan went back and forth, after all. Perhaps he could just go there on holiday, before his term at Eton started. That seemed reasonable, didn't it? Now, Mother would have a conniption, but that would be forgotten soon enough. Honestly, a week or two of being grounded was more than worth the big adventure he would certainly get if he were to take Peter up on his offer. So he sat straight up, which set Meggie to barking, and leapt from the bed to stare out the window, waiting for darkness to fall, more eager than ever to go to Kensington Gardens.

WHEN HE GOT THERE, HE FOUND PETER QUITE EASILY, retracing his steps as he had every night before, to the Fairies' Wood.

"Peter! Peter, I'm here!" he said, running toward the boy, breathing in the damp, earthen smell of their spot in the Gardens.

"So you are." Peter nodded, not giving much away in his expression.

"Are you leaving tonight?"

"Yes. Quite shortly." The fairies bobbed and wiggled around Peter, playing in the fog and on his hair and lighting up the blackness. James wished, as he often wished, that the fairies would pay him some attention.

"I should like to come with you, I think," James said, turning his head to smile brightly at the lone little fairy that had landed on his shoulder.

Peter cocked his head at him. "You're sure?"

He rubbed his arms over his threadbare white shirt, attempting to soothe the cold from his skin. He was shifting excitedly, avoiding Peter's eyes. "Well, I thought that maybe I could just go there on holiday. Just for a little while. If that's all right with you."

Peter was quiet for a minute, and he pinched his chin between his thumb and forefinger, batting a fairy away from his face as he thought. James bounced nervously before him.

"Yes, all right. To Neverland, then."

James thought he might faint from excitement.

"How do we get there?" he asked, inexplicably out of breath.

Peter threw his head back and laughed. "We fly, of course."

James grimaced, for he had no idea how he would manage that.

Peter stopped laughing and raised an eyebrow at him. "You *can* fly, can't you?"

James found that he was suddenly, unreasonably embarrassed. "I—I don't think I can."

"Anyone can fly, James." Peter crossed his arms and leaned back against a tangle of low-hanging branches and greenery.

"I can't!"

Peter shook his head and rolled his eyes at the sky. "You Lost Boys can't do anything by yourselves. Not a brain among you."

James wanted to say that he wasn't a Lost Boy, but chose to be quiet. He was much too busy watching Peter to be protesting. Peter then floated up to the tip-top of a nearby tree and whispered something into its branches. A little light popped out and fluttered its way over to James, who just stood there, having nothing else he could possibly do. The little light was a fairy, of course, and as it bobbed and hopped, a smattering of fairy dust fell onto James's head. He sneezed and wondered if it were possible for someone to be allergic to fairy dust. That seemed a stupid question. He chose not to be so foolish as to ask it.

"Now what?" asked James, hands hanging lamely at his sides.

"Now, you think of the happiest thought you've got. Get a running start. Then, you just float up into the sky."

"That's it?"

"That's it. Anyone can do it."

James scrunched up his face and set his chin upon his fist, trying very hard to come up with a happy thought. Not just a happy one, the happiest. He was loath to disappoint Peter in any capacity. Then, a face popped into his head. It was that of his father, just returned from a voyage at sea. Rough, tired, smiling, the creases around his eyes and mouth making themselves apparent. Low, rumble-scratch of his voice lulling James to sleep with a story of an adventure on the waves. Then, like it was nothing, he found that he was face to face with a treetop.

He beamed. "I didn't even have to run!"

"It seems you didn't." Peter pursed his lips and shrugged. "Of course, I don't either."

James raised an eyebrow, but ultimately ignored that rather silly addendum, too overcome with happiness at his newfound skill.

"Now, follow me!" Peter cried, bursting up through the branches.

James quickly, and rather gracelessly, followed him. He didn't need to be told that last part; he was terribly frightened of being left behind somewhere over the Atlantic or whatever magical oceans they probably crossed along the way, and following Peter was the only way to ensure that didn't happen.

James was a shadow trailing behind Peter's ankles. He smiled despite the fear, relishing the exhilarating feeling of the wind wrapping around his limbs and the weightlessness floating him up into the sky.

The flight seemed to take an eternity, and maybe it did. They flew like little birds over the top of London, and then over places James didn't recognize at all. Places filled with color and sparkling bursts of light, places that made him feel like he was tumbling, and then like he was slogging through wet sand. Peter seemed quite familiar with them, however. He darted in and out of clouds and mountains and who-knew-what like this was something he did all the time. Probably because it was.

Sometimes, James would find himself getting tired, but usually, just then, a cloud would envelop him or Peter would kick him in the chest, and that would wake him up. His lungs were burning and his arms and legs started to get very tired, though they weren't doing much flapping, when Peter stopped short in the sky and crowed.

James stopped short behind him, because it was his only real option, and stared down at the landscape below. His jaw dropped and his eyes flew open. There, hundreds of feet beneath him, was a vast jungle, twinkling with life, dotted with little oases here and there. There was a sparkling blue lagoon and a sea at its edge, occupied by a large and wicked-looking pirate ship, one that from this distance, he could barely make out—but it gave him a faint tickling in his chest.

"Is it—is this, is this it?"

"Yes, James. This is it. This is Neverland."

THREE

I<small>T OCCURRED TO</small> J<small>AMES THAT BRAKING MID-FLIGHT</small> was not yet something he'd mastered, so he clung to Peter during the descent. His arms and legs tingled as they floated down to the ground, that odd sense of vertigo making his stomach flip in terror and excitement all at once. After a minute, the boys landed easily on the ground of the giant, shimmering forest that was Neverland.

James tried to camouflage his wide eyes and frantic head-bobbing, but he found he wanted to look everywhere all at once. At the trees, whose leaves were all sorts of ever-changing shades of purple and pink and blue. At the sky, so deep and dark that the thousands of stars stood out like glitter. At the moons, of which he could currently make out three.

The air here was light, as though he would just float up off the ground if he wasn't paying attention, and he swore he could taste it on his tongue. The faintest hint of vanilla, a breath of gingersnaps. He smacked his lips curiously.

"I expect the Lost Boys should show up any minute now," said Peter.

James stood straight and brushed himself off, in a show of decorum that would've made his mother proud, pulling his attention from the air around him.

Peter eyed James strangely and cupped a hand to his mouth, letting out a crow that echoed among the trees. It was as though, in that moment, the whole of Neverland came to life. There were snaps and rumbles coming from the wood and little howls and chirps taking over the silence of the night. The leaves fluttered and flipped, changing manically from purple to gold to green to pink, as though they were so excited they couldn't decide what season they wanted to be, and the whole place around them lit up as fairies descended from the treetops to flit around Peter. James thought he had never seen anything more beautiful in his whole life.

One fairy in particular was bobbing around Peter's head and landing on him everywhere and chattering excitedly, which to James sounded like nothing but the frantic jingling of bells. He didn't speak fairy, but at that moment, he wished he did.

"James, this is my fairy."

It flitted toward him, paused in front of his face giving him a once-over, and James smiled brightly, wanting desperately to hold it. But it hastily returned to fretting over Peter, who seemed to be very much enjoying all the attention. He beamed, his delicate elfin features lighting up as James had never seen them do before.

Then, there came a crashing through the woods. James instinctively shrank back, not accustomed to dark, magical woods and things crashing around in them. Peter crowed again, and shot up into the air, right past his fairy, then came down again just as a troupe of boys came barreling before them.

"Peter!" they all cried simultaneously. "You're back!"

"I am indeed."

They were a bumbling lot, and they sort of just crashed around, each trying to reach Peter first. Peter grinned with one corner of his mouth, but very quickly turned deadly serious, taking on the air of a drill sergeant. "Boys! Tennnn-hut!"

The boys scrambled into a line in front of Peter, all standing perfectly still. James chewed on his cheek, standing there awkwardly, not entirely sure what to do with himself. Peter clasped his hands behind his back and sauntered back and forth in front of the line, inspecting each boy. For what, James had no idea. He suspected that neither Peter nor a single one of the boys knew either.

"Lost Boys, we have a new recruit. This is James Hook, a Lost Boy I found in Kensington."

A frown flitted across James's face at the title. He thought he'd made it quite clear that he was more a Boy on Holiday than a Lost one, but he chose not to remark on it.

"He's old!" cried out the tiniest boy.

Peter whirled around to him and glared into his face. That was enough to shut him up nearly instantly. "Now, sound off!"

The first in line was tall, little more than an inch shy of Peter. "Bibble!" he cried.

The next one, who could have been Bibble's twin, but was shorter because he hunched, shouted, "Bobble!"

The next, "Slightly!" James thought this boy's name ironic, for there was nothing slight about him.

The next, who had an excessive amount of freckles covering him all over, yelled, "Simpkins!"

And the last, the tiny one who had remarked about James's age, "Tootles!"

James stood there, blinking, having no clue as to what had just occurred. It sounded to him as though the boys had simply shouted out the first gibberish words that came into their heads.

"Well?" said Peter, turning to James, folding his arms across his chest.

"Well what?"

"What do you mean, *what*?" Peter narrowed his eyes.

James threw his hands into the air. "I mean, what?"

Peter shook his head and peered at the ground. "As I said, you Lost Boys. Not a brain in the lot of you. Get in line with the rest. When I say, 'Sound off,' you sound off."

James did as he was told, but it embarrassed him greatly, because he hadn't the foggiest idea as to what exactly he was supposed to say when he "sounded off." This embarrassment was compounded when he realized he would have to stand at the front of the line, for he was clearly the tallest of the Lost Boys (barely, and he guessed that Bibble was a bit older, but still.) He took his place, and Peter shouted, "Sound off!"

James squirmed and looked at the boys and then again at Peter and said the first nonsense syllables that came into his head. "Boofin!"

The whole company erupted into a fit of laughter, but stopped abruptly when they saw the look of anger on Peter's face. He got very close to James and screwed up his features so that he looked like a caricature of himself.

"What did you say, James Hook?" he hissed.

James blinked and recoiled. He'd never seen Peter like this, crimson-faced, eyes terrible little slits. He'd never seen Peter in any state other than happy.

Peter inched closer to him, and it made the hairs on the back of his neck stand up.

"I'm not entirely sure what I'm supposed to say." James looked at the ground, concentrating on breathing, and on disallowing his heart from stopping beating altogether.

Peter rolled his eyes. "Daft, all of you. When I say, 'Sound off,' you say your name. None of this 'Boofin' nonsense in my ranks."

James drew in a deep, vanilla-flavored breath, and tried very hard to appear taller and straighter as Peter turned away from him and paced back and forth. Then, he snapped his body toward the boys. "Sound off!"

"James!"

"Bibble!"

"Bobble!"

"Slightly!"

"Simpkins!"

"Tootles!"

Peter smiled. "Now, James, if you're to be a Lost Boy with the rest of us, there are some rules you'll have to follow."

James nodded, pushing away the voice in his head that thought it slightly concerning that Peter kept referring to him as a Lost Boy, in a more permanent sort of way than they had originally agreed.

"Number one, you're not allowed to know things that I don't know."

James frowned, unsure how exactly he was supposed to keep this rule. He was a pre-Eton man, and even pre-Eton men knew a great many things he was quite sure Peter didn't. He nodded anyway, wishing to seem agreeable.

"Number two," said Peter, pacing about and thrusting a finger into the air, "you're not allowed to be taller than me."

This seemed a fair rule. As he was only planning on staying a week, two at most, he didn't plan on growing any taller while he was there.

"And lastly, and most importantly," Peter lowered his voice and spoke very intensely, so that James had to listen quite closely to catch what he said, "absolutely no growing up."

There was a rumbled noise of enthusiastic agreement, coming from the Lost Boys. James nodded gravely, thinking that this rule shouldn't be too difficult to follow either, as growing up was not on the week's itinerary.

"Can you follow all of those rules, James Hook?"

"I can."

"Do you solemnly swear not to grow up at any cost?" Peter asked, coming within a hair's width of James's nose.

"I solemnly swear." James hoped Peter didn't recognize the trembling in his hands, or on every single part of him, honestly.

"Then," Peter said, smiling widely, "welcome to the ranks!"

James broke into a great smile, nearly matching Peter's, at this announcement. The others, he noticed, did no such thing, every one of them but Bibble showing him a sort of cool indifference, arms folded, staring down the tips of their noses at him, even the tinier ones. Bibble at least turned toward him and offered him his hand. James shook it and thought that this one had decent form.

"So," he asked brightly, determined to have every last drop of adventure he could before the week was up, "what do we do first?"

"The first order of business is—" Peter paused grandly. James thought that perhaps it was because Peter had no idea what the first order of business was, but kept quiet, not wanting to break the first rule already. "The first order of business is this. How many hooligans and sea dogs and pirates have you seen roaming about lately, boys?"

"Too many!" responded the boys in chorus.

"And what do we hate more than they?"

"Nothing!"

"Then, boys, tonight, we shall kill a pirate."

James swallowed hard, heart assuring him this was an exaggeration, gut whispering that his heart was a liar.

It was indescribably savage and disturbing, seeing boys as young as five painting themselves up, preparing for battle. James felt rather sick at the thought of it, at the little piece of doubt that this was only pretend, but allowed himself to be painted, nonetheless. They gave him a little dagger and smeared clay on his face in squiggly lines and designs. He could only imagine what his mother would say if she saw him.

"Come on, troops. It's time to pay a visit to the *Spanish Main*."

James felt a tiny jolt in his chest, a spark of recognition, but it was vague and quick, and it faded away before he could fully pay it any sort of attention.

They crept in a straight and silent line through the foliage, all except Bibble and Bobble, who crawled next to each other. Some of the boys held blades in their mouths and others had bows strapped to their backs.

James growled as now blood-red leaves tickled his back, and when he glimpsed their sudden color and sharpness, his hair stood on end. Little fairies bobbed around the company, darting this way and that, courteously lighting their path. The otherwise black air got denser and denser the closer they got to the sea, and it smelled strongly of saltwater, dissonant with the still-present flavor of vanilla. James coughed and shut his eyes, trying to clear his head of the feel of altogether too much sensation at once.

The whole line stopped slowly as they reached the massive ship, and James's jaw dropped. It was hulking and shining, carved of the most beautiful wood, swirls and sheen and rich brown coating it. There was a breathtaking, massive skull and crossbones carved into the ship's front, leering at him. James fought the urge to gasp.

He looked away from it and back to the boys when he felt them begin to move again. There was blood thirst in Pan's eyes when he turned around and motioned for them all to slip aboard. James felt a great disquiet at this, partially made up of guilt and partially of something he couldn't put a finger on. Something whispering to him that none of this was right, that this was, inexplicably, betrayal—or something closely related to it. He shimmied on the ground over to Peter, before the older boy could get a chance to climb aboard, and whispered in his ear, "Why are we killing a pirate tonight, Peter?"

Peter looked at him as though he was daft, as though he was terribly foolish for even thinking to ask the question. "Because he's a pirate, Hook."

James didn't understand and crouched there, not knowing what else to say. But when Peter made a move toward the ship, something desperate clawed at his insides, needing very much to stop the whole endeavor. He grasped at the first trivial question his mind gave him.

"Where does the captain sleep, Peter?"

The group of boys behind them began to wriggle and rustle, confused, impatient murmuring rising up in the air.

"Nowhere," said Peter through his teeth. "These pirates haven't got a captain."

James furrowed his brow. "No captain. That doesn't seem very sporting, killing pirates who haven't even got a captain when we have."

"Have you?"

"Why, yes, of course. You, Peter Pan."

Peter's entire face lit up at this. "Captain I am. Captain I am." Then he turned back to the ship as though the rest of the conversation hadn't taken place and he'd forgotten all about it.

"Peter, you promised I wouldn't have to kill—" James went to tug on Peter's shirt, and Peter thrust a hand out to stop him.

"Shh."

James shrank back, already having given up the fight for fairness. Slightly crawled past him up to Peter and whispered low, but loud enough for James to hear. "Look at that one there. Sleeping, right near the ship's edge. He'd be easy enough to pick off."

James's stomach flipped, eyes frantically darting between the grizzled old pirate and the Pan before him, and the dark, deep, gilded-around-the-edges wood of the ship—a slow, horrifying sense of recognition dawning on him.

Peter thought on this for a moment and beamed. "That one there. I'll slit his throat before any of them get a whiff of me. It'll be an ambush. Oh, the cleverness of me."

Peter scaled the ship's side as though there were footholds carved into it, and the rest of the Lost Boys followed suit. James miserably figured that he'd better come along, though with every forward movement, it was becoming harder and harder to ignore the dreadful foreboding; chain of command in this place didn't seem to be up for debate. He was the last one on the shining deck, and he arrived just in time to see a wicked grin come over Peter's face.

He'd heard the plan, of course, but seeing Peter do the deed was something different altogether. He was horrified as Peter silently drew a knife from somewhere in the folds of his clothes and flipped it in his hand, gripping it by its handle. The pirate was sleeping peacefully. Peter crept up behind him and tapped him on the shoulder. James was too panicked to do or say anything, part of him not believing that this was all really happening. But the gravity of it hit him full force when the pirate woke and scrambled for his sword. Peter quickly and quietly slipped the edge of the blade across his throat, blood flecking across the pirate's orange hair. His victim's eyes shot open wider then, but they didn't find Pan. They looked straight at James, bewildered, shocked, in pain. In that instant,

James knew why everything about this night had felt so wrong.

Somehow, he knew this man; he knew his eyes. He was certain he recognized his hair. This pirate, this scallywag, was one of the pirates he always dreamt about. He'd played elaborate roles in James's nighttime fantasies. This ship, these men, they were his. He knew it then just as surely as he knew that the sky was blue and the grass was green.

"*Oh yes. The Spanish Main,*" Peter had said back in Kensington. "*Full of bumbling, stupid, grown-up pirates. I've killed at least a dozen of them.*"

The *Spanish Main.* James's ship.

And here they were, and Peter was making good on his claim.

As the life ebbed quietly out of the pirate and the blood pulsed out of his throat, soaking the collar of his shirt, James knew that the pirate had recognized him, too.

It was silent on the ship, a sick, heavy stillness that pushed down on his shoulders and his heart and his fingertips. There was a mighty splash as James involuntarily let go of the ship and fell into the water. And high above him, Peter crowed.

FOUR

T HE WATER WAS COLD, BUT JAMES WAS NUMB ALREADY
so he didn't mind it much. Chaos was erupting on the ship
above him, pirates thundering out onto the deck, Lost
Boys and Peter Pan killing the brigands who wandered
too close to them. But that didn't matter much either,
because in the blanket of the glowing, nymph-infested
water, there was a sickly quiet, wherein James was only
bound to contemplate and to float.

It was the eyes. The pirate's, yes, but Peter's as well. In
the man's last look, James had seen pleading and confusion
and a general fading, and it was terrible. But in Peter's, he
had seen something he could never unsee. The innocent
boy who frolicked about and played Commandant and
longed for eternal youth had, in the moment his blade
slid across the pirate's throat, transformed into something
sinister. For the only look out of Peter's face in that instant
was pure, unadulterated glee. James shuddered, and he
wasn't sure if it was the chill from Peter or the water. But,
though his mind didn't seem to care about the liquid ice
around him, he knew his body eventually would. He felt
his limbs beginning to turn to slugs, and decided that
contemplating on land, further away from Peter and the
chance he'd be noticed, was preferable to doing so in the
water.

When he reached the shore, he looked upon the water at the little orbs of light that floated in the sea foam. Nymphs indeed, he figured, according to the mythological research he'd done in the last week. But he didn't care much for mythology at the moment. So he turned his focus to the pirate ship, quietly observing and considering his own situation. He wondered if he shouldn't try to swim to the *Main* again, throw himself in front of a pirate's (or Lost Boy's) sword. Perhaps if he was killed here, he would wake up in his bed, and he would never sneak into Kensington Park again. That was a happy thought.

The ship was nothing but chaos and insanity, roars and crows and clanging of steel slicing through the night. Peter and his Lost Boys were running, hopping, flying here and there, and the pirates were lost and bumbling, with no one to lead them and no idea how to fight back. James felt a very personal sorrow at this and needed to turn away from it.

It was at this moment that he noticed in the dimness a rogue pirate who had snuck away from the skirmish aboard the ship. He was coming right toward him. James didn't even have the energy to scamper off; the water had sucked it all away. When he tried to get up, it was as though the sand was holding him down. James grit his teeth, struggling against the white sand and the exhaustion, reconsidering his earlier suicidal musings, eyes trained on the pirate before him. He was running full speed at James, eyes like glowing marbles, teeth peppered with gold, facial hair wild and untamed.

James pulled himself from the sand and it sucked at his arms and chest as he rose to a wobbly standing position. He brushed his fingers over the little dagger Bibble had given him and squeezed its handle. He shook and struggled to maintain his balance, staring hard at the man, trying to look intimidating, to stand his ground, to be a man.

The pirate was roaring like some monster out of a book, which didn't scare James when he was far off. When he got close, still there was nothing. But, when he got really close, that was when the fear set in.

Then, something strange happened. The man stopped dead in his tracks and his roar was immediately quiet. He and James peered at one another, and the look on the rogue's face was so queer that James didn't have enough room in his small body to be afraid, only to wonder.

"Do I know you?" James finally let out.

"Captain," was the reply. The man dropped to a knee before him and put his hand over his heart.

James was struck with something—bewilderment, peace, fear, or some odd combination of all three. It wasn't possible. Not really. But he knew it in his bones, and besides, the pirate had said it, hadn't he?

Captain, said James's mind, chewing on the word, enjoying the feel of it. He was suspended there in silence for a moment until Peter and the rest of the Lost Boys shattered it, running back across the beach, whooping and bouncing as they came.

"Go, pirate," James hissed. "The Pan is coming."

The man obeyed without question. James stood, not wanting to appear mutinous, and followed the lively crew, very much lost in thought. When they reached a clearing in the center of the forest, the group slowed and one of the boys asked between gasps, "How many, Peter? How many?"

"I counted four," Pan replied, chest puffed out, hands on his hips.

James felt an extremely personal pain at this that he could not explain, as well as a low, bubbling rage that he could. Arrogance. Again. At the deaths of men.

The last thing he wanted was to be there, dripping, among a troupe of heartless children who were reveling in their unprovoked slaughter. Still, the infantile celebration continued.

Finally, when he could take no more, James shouted, "Peter!"

All at once, the merriment came to a grinding halt.

"Yes?" Peter said, turning slowly to face him. The trees rose, dark and tall behind him. James swore for a second that they actually grew.

"Peter, I've got to know something," he said, voice softening a bit.

"Ask it, then."

James shuffled back an inch, but tried to keep his chin lifted and strong. He ignored the warning looks from Bibble and Bobble beside him. "The man you killed—"

"Men," he corrected.

James could feel a bit of blood drain from his face, but he ignored that as well, or tried to. "One of the men you killed, I knew him. I swear I did."

The forest went very quiet then and Peter's face darkened as he slunk a step at a time toward James. "Are you a pirate, James?" Peter whispered, so close to James that he could feel Peter's breath on his face, see the small sprinkling of blood across his cheek.

"Of course not," James sputtered.

"Then what do you mean, you knew him?" Peter did not back away, did not raise his voice a decibel.

James could feel the sudden negative space in the area directly near him. The other boys had shrunk away. "I've seen him before," he stuttered. "Not here—in my dreams. Back home. In London."

James could feel sweat beading up all over his face, and he swallowed hard, wishing for something to soothe his raw throat. Peter backed away a little and stroked his chin. "In your Neverland."

James just looked at him, unable to decide what emotion to feel, caught between revulsion, terror, and curiosity.

"Your Neverland. That place just between waking and sleeping. You dreamt them there. That's how everything's built in Neverland—on dreams. The pirates are yours, then."

The trees began to slowly shrink back down to their regular tallness. "I—I suppose so," said James.

On the outside, James was very controlled, albeit trembling a bit. But inside, he was still quite frightened, and confused. He could hardly believe what Peter was saying. He'd created lives by *dreaming* them? It seemed impossible. But so did everything in this fantastical place.

Peter sheathed his dagger and laughed, somehow delighted. "I've been wondering who dreamt them up."

James let out a breath. Life re-entered the wood and the boys got back to their revelry.

"What do you mean, exactly?" said James, practically flitting with nervous energy as he followed Peter, who was pacing around in a circle.

Peter rolled his eyes and sighed, and Bibble stepped quickly between them. He grabbed James's arm and James frowned, but allowed himself to be led away, as Bibble's fingers seemed rather insistent on it.

"I say—" said James, but Bibble just shook his head, and Bobble appeared beside him in a wink.

"It's best not to ask Peter too many questions," said Bibble.

"He's awfully busy, after all," Bobble chimed in.

"Well I just wanted to know—"

"Why he picked you," said Bibble, flicking his sandy brown hair out of his eyes. "You're a *Dreamer*, James."

"We all are," said Bobble, flicking the same sandy brown hair out of the same bright green eyes.

"What do you mean? Everyone here? On the island?"

"Well, not everyone." Bibble's mouth turned in a smug little grin. "Peter dreamt up the Indians, and you did the pirates. At least, the ones on the *Spanish Main*."

"The Never Wastes are mine," Bibble's slouchier twin said brightly.

"Well, I came up with the nasty Graps who live there."

James raised an eyebrow. "Graps? What exactly are—"

Bobble laughed, ignoring James's question altogether. "Fat lot of good that did for poor Flobbins."

Bibble cast his eyes downward, and Slightly stopped whatever he was doing so that he and the twins could make a gesture James could only assume was a mimicry of crossing themselves, and spit.

"Flobbins," said Slightly, "may he rest in pieces."

Then Slightly went on about his doing-nothing, and James shook his head quickly, then returned his attention to the boys.

"So that's it, then? I'm a Dreamer?" He felt ridiculous even saying it, having no idea at all what it even meant.

"Yes," said Bobble, knocking on James's head. James shut his eyes and shrank back, a little more than irritated. "Pay attention. Peter liked what he saw and he took it to Neverland and kept it, and now you're here too. That's it."

Bibble spoke very slowly, over-enunciating, shadows from the fairies playing on his angular face. "You were selected. So you could come and go from Neverland as you pleased, and so did your dreams. Like little ghosts. But the ones Peter likes, they stay here forever. He likes your pirates, and apparently, he likes you. So here we all are. Got it?"

"But—"

But James was unable to finish his question, because at that moment, Simpkins made his way over to Peter and tugged on his shirt, and said, "Peter, I'm hungry."

Peter thought about this for a second and shouted, "Food!"

All the boys stopped mid-dance, mid-conversation, mid-everything, and sprinted over to Peter, huddling around him. At that, Peter's grin nearly overtook his face, it was so large. It was difficult to hate Peter when he smiled like that. Then, he motioned his hand in the air like he was grabbing some morsel and bit down on it, "it" being nothing. James was perplexed. (Not that that was new.) He noted minute looks of malcontent on all the boys' faces, but they disappeared as quickly as they came, and the entire party took up biting and tearing and scooping at the air.

James felt his countenance fall, for just then had he realized that he was starving, having not eaten a bite since he'd left London what seemed like ages ago. His hand was trembling when he raised it slowly in the air, and his stomach growled angrily when he curled his fingers like he'd curl them around a hunk of bread. He grabbed at nothing and brought it to his mouth over and over, teeth clacking hard, almost painfully, against one another. He did this until the motion was repetitive and almost frantic, as though if he consumed enough nothing, it would eventually sate the gnawing hunger in his gut.

At the end of this ritual, Peter lay back on the earth, his hands clasped behind his head, looking utterly satisfied. He stared up at the twinkling stars, which were swirling and swarming and chasing each other across the sky. James had only just now noticed this, having had no real time to focus on the celestial backdrop until now, and the sky held him in awe for a moment.

The others mimicked Peter, though the looks on their faces were significantly less convincing. He wagered they were all starved, like him, and that made him feel a bit better, for some wicked reason. James managed to pull himself toward the group, and lay beside Peter, clothes still slightly damp, moistening the mossy ground below him with seawater.

As the boys began to get drowsy, a thousand thoughts hit James at once, as though they'd all been waiting for days and were finally let out of the gate to overwhelm him at this exact moment. His mind was a whir of questions and misery and guilt and happiness and all sorts of strange mixtures thereof.

"Peter," he whispered, low enough that none of the boys woke, and Peter hadn't been asleep anyway.

"Yes?"

"Where does everyone sleep?" James asked, pulled in once again by the stars, which seemed all the brighter and more playful in the silence.

"Wherever we fall asleep. I've been scouting for a tree or something we could live in, but none's turned up yet, so we sleep wherever we are."

This was a bit disconcerting, as he'd pictured Neverland to have the most luxurious bedrooms, full of the forest and fairy magic. He wished Peter had taken *that* dream from him. The trees seemed large and disagreeable, and he swore the shadows on him were darker than on anyone else.

"You just sleep outside?" James said, trying very hard to swallow.

"If that's where we fall asleep." Peter's voice was flattening. James couldn't quite tell if it was from sleepiness or irritation, but something told him it was the latter.

"You don't worry about creatures and such chomping at you in the middle of the night?"

As he said this, a lonesome sort of whistle-howl rang out through the wilderness, and James shivered, even more concerned, if that were possible.

"No creatures wish to eat Pan. And very few would try to eat a Lost Boy under my watch."

"Very few" was not as comforting a statistic as he wagered Pan thought it was.

"What if you get cold?" James asked as a cool breeze ghosted over his skin.

"Just make-believe you aren't," said Peter with a sigh, which confirmed James's earlier assumption.

Make-believe he wasn't. Like he'd make-believed with the food. That was a colossal failure, or so his stomach thought. Thus, he did not have high hopes for make-believing he was comfortable. Nevertheless, he tried very hard to pretend that he wasn't chilly and that he wasn't frightened, but just when his eyelids would start to leaden, another crackle or jingle would wake him, or the leaves would start changing colors again. At one point, he swore he could feel a rumble in the earth—a low, hollow beating like a massive drum, as if Neverland itself had a heartbeat. He fidgeted and turned over and over, trying to unimagine that and to unhear the wind, which he knew could not have been softly whispering, "Peter" as it crept through the forest. But that worked about as well as the food debacle. He turned his head slightly to see if Peter was still awake. He was.

"Peter?" He felt a sharp elbow in his side and recoiled, shooting Bibble, who was beside him, a dirty look.

"Yes?"

"Are we meant just to fall asleep out here, by ourselves?"

"That's how we always do."

James bit his lip, searching the darkness for some sign of comfort, receiving none. "With no mothers to tuck us in?" he said.

James knew that this made him sound very childish, but at this moment, he didn't much care. He cared a bit, however, when Peter turned to him, lips pursed, a dark mood showing on his face.

"Don't say that word, James Hook. We don't speak of mothers here." There was raw pain and venom in his eyes when he said this, and James was taken aback.

"Don't speak of mothers?"

Bibble's elbow was digging into James's side again, and he wanted to elbow him back, or kick him at least. When Peter sat up and leaned toward him, though, James forgot Bibble and scooted back, wishing he could sink lower into the ground. "You've said it again. Once more and I'll wallop you, James, and don't think I won't."

James turned back to the stars and sighed deeply, beginning very much to regret his decision to spend his holiday here. He wondered if, perhaps, it was a nicer place in the day, and if the darkness of the sky brought out the darkness in Peter and in Neverland. He desperately hoped that this was true.

To make matters worse, the only image his mind could conjure when he closed his heavy eyes, when it wasn't bombarding him with pictures of hideous beasts and possessed islands, was that of the *Spanish Main*, beautiful, majestic, glorious. Then it was being overrun by little boys who wanted nothing more than to carve up as many pirates as they could before moving along to another adventure. Sometimes, that image was broken up by that of the pirate on the beach. When he'd got closer, James recalled that he'd had exceptionally friendly hazel eyes and little crow's feet around them, likely from smiling. A jolly pirate, then.

For whatever reason, this round of make-believe or memory or whatever you wanted to call it did warm the boy. He smiled lightly, envisioning that peculiar bow the pirate had given him, and drifted off to sleep with the word "Captain" on his lips.

FIVE

JAMES WOKE EARLY AND WAS QUITE CONFUSED, HAVING no idea where he was, part of him having surmised that the previous day's events were nothing more than a dream. But there was definitely a forest floor below him and a canopy above him, and no sign of a feather bed or breakfast or Mother. Then, his present situation came flooding back to him. He stood and yawned, wishing he had a toothbrush, for his mouth tasted foul.

Then, he heard music floating through the trees, and his ears perked up. Peter came prancing into the clearing, a pan flute at his lips, eyes sparkling. Over his shoulder was a makeshift bag of some sort. He put down the flute and said to the boys, "Breakfast!"

They all, James included, looked slightly suspicious until Peter let down the bag from his shoulder, and berries that were so bright they looked as though they were made of colored glass rolled out onto the dirt. James knew right away that this would be the farthest thing from a proper breakfast, so he let go of his dignity and scrambled to the food with the rest of the boys, fairly shoveling the stuff into his mouth. His favorite, he found, when he slowed down enough to focus on flavor, were the white, frosted ones that tasted like peppermint. They were followed very closely by the ones that blinked and changed color, mostly because they changed flavor too, while you ate them.

Pan looked pleased and just stood there watching them with his arms folded. The food quieted the roar of the monster in James's stomach until it was more of a whimper. James chose to be content with this.

After the odd food was all gone, James let his eyes wander, and they came to rest on the flute, which lay on the ground beside the feast. He reached for it, brushing it with his fingertips, curious, but the Lost Boys all gasped at once, and Peter's hand clamped like a trap around his wrist.

James yanked back, eyes wide, but Peter held all the more tightly, grip bruising.

"Don't you touch this," he spat. "Ever."

Wind swirled around Peter's ears, blowing his hair up in a way that would have been comical, were it not for the sudden greyness in the air and the horrible salted licorice flavor on James's tongue that rudely drove out the pleasant vanilla.

"I—I'm, ever so, ever so sorry, Peter. I only—"

"Touch it again and you'll lose a hand." Peter flung James's wrist away and snatched the flute back, turning his back to him.

James sat on his haunches and turned to the Lost Boys, searching for some sign that that reaction had indeed been as absurd as he'd thought. He got no real confirmation. Only a smug shrug from Slightly and somewhat sympathetic nods from Bibble and Bobble.

Suddenly, Peter's head perked up and he tilted it toward the east, or what James guessed was the east. He had no real way of knowing as there were many more suns and moons here than there were in London, and they all just sort of rotated about in the sky.

Peter held out a hand and the boys were instantly silent.

"Do you hear that?"

James didn't hear anything at all. But then, there was a small snap somewhere in the direction Peter was looking.

"Indians," Peter breathed. The boys were up in a heartbeat. James took another handful of berries and stuffed them into his pocket, then followed along, thankful that something else was the cause of the tension, for once. No matter his misgivings about the way this place was run, he wasn't just going to spend his entire holiday moping about it. He would have as many pleasant adventures as he could here this week, and that meant following Pan and the boys. So, he crept with them through the woods, rather excited to have another adventure so long as it didn't involve killing.

Bibble hung back with him, and when Peter was out of earshot, whispered, "It was a gift."

"What?" James furrowed his brow. He moved a smidge to the right, as Bibble's too-large proboscis of a nose was brushing uncomfortably against his cheek.

"The flute. It was a gift from his mother, from back when he was little and regular. No one's allowed to touch it."

James nodded and kept walking, having quite a difficult time imagining Peter as regular in any capacity.

"Bobble did it too, a long time ago. Peter forgot all about it right after; I wouldn't feel too bad."

James said, "Thanks," and walked on, keeping in step with Bibble and endeavoring to do so for the remainder of his time here, if at all possible.

The party came to an abrupt halt then. A flare of citrus in the air as Pan jumped in surprise. They, it seemed, were not the only ones who could be sneaky. For though they'd heard scarcely a thing, they found themselves very immediately face to face with the Indians. Their leader was a massive man; he looked like the incarnation of an oak tree. He stood erect, proud—every bit a chief.

"Friend or foe today, Chief?" Pan said.

The man scanned the lot of them slowly, letting his piercing, dark eyes meet each of the boys'. One by one, they let their gazes drop. But, though James was trembling fiercely when he met the other man's eyes, he refused to look away. Instead, he resolved not to blink. He stared at the serious man until a ghost of a smile began to play at the corners of the Chief's mouth.

"There is a new boy among you."

Pan drew his eyebrows together, almost as though he'd forgotten. Then, he met James's eyes. After a beat, in which James was very uncomfortable, something clicked in Peter's face. "Oh, yes. James Hook."

The Chief regarded him again, and James continued to stare back. The man was taller than James could have imagined, and not large in the way Slightly was large. Large in a way that dared anyone and anything to provoke him. James guessed that if any creature tried to push him, it would fall backward, fingers broken, and the Chief would still be standing there.

From behind his legs, a little person, a girl who looked to be around six years old, peeked out. Pan smiled at her, and she was entranced by him, eyes huge and shining and very dark, little perfectly bowed mouth set in a wide grin. James smiled as well, and she looked at him for a moment, then returned to her awe of Peter.

"Friends, today," the Chief boomed.

Pan nodded. James let out a great breath, drawing a suspicious look from the little girl, and beamed. No violence today, then. He'd already faced death the night before and wasn't keen on the idea of doing so again.

The Chief and the rest of his tribe turned around and made their way back to where they came from, and Peter and the Lost Boys stayed where they were. James had his eyes on the little girl, who looked back at him once and flashed him a toothy and innocent smile. One piece of real childhood in a world that had twisted it all around.

He blinked hard when Peter snapped in front of his face. "Come on, James. You don't want to be left here, do you? The Indians will come straight back across the river and shoot you in the heart."

James jumped to follow his companions away, unsure if this was exaggeration or the wicked truth, and unwilling to find out for himself.

WHEN THEY GOT WHERE THEY WERE HEADED, JAMES felt an elation rising up in his chest, and he smiled genuinely. There in front of them was a lagoon, of which the water was blue enough that James hardly believed he was seeing it right. It sparkled as the suns hit it, ebbing and flowing in lazy waves to the shore. James had to stand totally still for a moment and look without blinking in order to fully take it in. There was a massive cave that gaped at its back. Around it, trees James could only describe as weeping willows—though that wasn't quite right—bowed, ever-changing leaves caressing the shores and fluttering down into the water. What was even better than the lagoon's sparkling serenity and quiet beauty was its inhabitants. They were beings of pure grace and loveliness—mermaids.

They laughed at one another and dove in and out of the rich blue water, splashing and chattering. The bottoms of them were made of fish scales that caught the light in an indescribable way, and tails that flitted and flopped, spraying up water wherever they went. The tops of them were human and lovelier still than the scales. Every one of them had long flowing hair of all manner of bizarre colors that looked as though it was painted; it was too beautiful to be real. But, everything in Neverland seemed too *something* to be real. Too beautiful, too horrible, too fantastic, too savage.

Peter whooped and ran full speed at the lagoon, leaping into the water without hesitation. (James was coming to realize that his companion did everything without hesitation.) James and his fellows followed suit, ripping off their shirts and diving into the lagoon after him.

The water was cold enough to cool the boys down and warm enough not to feel like an ice bath. James noticed upon closer examination, then, that only the dry mermaids, the ones sun-bathing up on the rocks, had skin anywhere, and even then, only on the bone-dry parts of their bodies. The ones in the water were covered in thin, iridescent scales from their faces to their tails. The scales didn't detract from their beauty; rather, they added to the drama of the creatures. And another strange thing. The mermaids, whom he had so been looking forward to meeting since Peter had mentioned them back in Kensington, scattered away from him and the boys, and most were congregated around Peter. Peter lay up on a massive rock in the middle of the lagoon, grinning as they fawned over him, caressing his hair, cooing in his ear, laughing with him, whispering to him. But they gave the rest of the lagoon's temporary occupants looks that could freeze the water around them.

James focused on the boys and on splashing about and enjoying the day, deciding that for the better part of his holiday, he would focus only on Neverland's pleasantries and not on her faults. Eventually, though, the mermaids were not satisfied with paying Peter heed and freezing out the boys. One by one, they vacated the monstrous rock where Peter sat and splashed into the water in sprays of glitter, bodies colorfully scaling over as they drenched themselves. Part of James was happy at this, but the other part of him had a deep sense of foreboding.

The mermaids bobbed up and down in the pool, as mermaids do, and eventually came close enough to the boys to touch them. One was floating right within arm's reach of James, and she was smiling coyly at him. He thought that she was perhaps the loveliest creature he had ever beheld. But, then she dove into the water, splashing him in the face and bumping hard into him with her tail. He cried out, surprised and in a small bit of pain. He was quite sure that a bruise was forming already.

Then, several others followed suit, bumping and splashing around him until he was having trouble staying afloat. Several of the other boys had already got out of the pool, but James was unsure how to go about doing this. It was difficult to think with the water spraying into his face and the bodies bumping against him, and eventually he couldn't stay afloat any longer. He felt himself being pulled under the water and started to panic. A stab of fear coursed through him, for he found he had no idea which way was up. He was flipping and turning and rolling frantically, lungs burning, eyes stinging, thoughts blurring the longer he was under.

Then, there were several small hands on his back, yanking him to the shore. He felt himself being flung out of the water and lay there for a little while, coughing, sputtering, not eager to open his eyes. When he finally did, though, Tootles, Slightly, and the twins were staring, wide-eyed, at him.

"He lives!" shouted Bibble, and Slightly wiped at his pale brow, flinging a spray of sweat across the shore. Pan came skipping over to them. He looked perplexed. Not concerned, relieved, or alarmed. Just perplexed, as though he'd not realized anything out of the ordinary had occurred.

James shut his eyes, wondering how it was that, in Neverland, he was facing death daily, though, admittedly, he wasn't sure "day "was the right word. It seemed that they didn't keep time here. Maybe it didn't exist at all; James didn't know. Either way, there had been some sort of night, and today felt longer than yesterday, but it *was* marching forward as regular days tended to do. It was of little consequence. He'd only been here one night and two days, but there, lying on the grass, James felt a strange sense of urgency. Perhaps his little holiday had lasted long enough.

"Peter," he croaked, finally opening his eyes, "I'd like to go home."

SIX

PETER LAUGHED LOUDLY, AND JAMES STARED, unblinking, up at him. "Nobody wants to go home. Not from Neverland."

"I do."

Peter narrowed his eyes and James felt suddenly that lying on the ground was not the best position to be in for a negotiation. He sat slowly up and let his elbows rest on his knees, trying very hard to look casual. Every one of the Lost Boys backed off, until all he could see was Peter.

"You don't really want to leave. You'll have to go back to London. Grow up. Into a man." Peter shivered.

James flared his nostrils. "What, Peter, is so particularly awful about becoming a man anyway?" This elicited a collective gasp from the Lost Boys. James was secretly pleased at the reaction.

Peter opened his mouth to speak and then shut it quickly, tilting his head toward the lagoon.

"What is it, Pet—"

Peter cut Bobble off with a flick of his wrist.

Despite the seriousness of the conversation, James discovered that he, too, was quite curious as to what had Peter concentrating so hard a vein was nearly bursting from his head. Then, he heard it. *Tick-tock. Tick-tock. Tick-tock. Tick-tock.*

"I say," said James. "Is that a clock?"

It was as though he'd just asked, "Is that a bomb?" or, "Is that a soul-eating crypt keeper coming our way?" For all the boys were up in a flurry and panicking.

James frowned. "I did say 'clock,' didn't I?"

Pan hopped over to the group and pointed away from the lagoon, and they all began running as fast as James assumed physically possible into the woods. The wind blew quickly around his face and he squinted into it, frowning and confused, until he stole a glance back into the water. The mermaids were nowhere to be found, and gliding through the lagoon was a giant, scaled beast, monstrous and sickly green—one James had heard of, but never seen.

Its black eyes came out just above the water, shadow of a tail and torso large enough that James figured it must have been an illusion. The closer it swam to shore, the louder the sound of the clock became. James was frozen with fear, and absolutely unable to determine the correlation between the clock and the croc. But that was not his top priority. Filling that slot was the need to pick up his feet and convince them to carry him far away from there.

He was unable to do it, almost as though he was having a dream wherein he wanted to scream, but no sound would come out, wanted to run but found that his legs were made of sand. The crocodile edged closer and closer until its eyes met James's. They shared a cold, dreadful stare for a moment, before James's legs were finally jogged into motion. He hurled himself into the trees, running as far from the lagoon as he could manage.

After a somewhat significant amount of time, he caught up with the rest of the band and collapsed onto the ground into a pile of leaves. His breaths were ragged and heaving and hoarse, and he was sure his face resembled a plump tomato.

Peter raised an eyebrow at him. "You're here."

A surge of adrenaline coursed through him, blood rising to the surface of his skin, a sudden, thick jolt of rage making him shake. "Of course I'm here, you nitwit. But barely. That crocodile was coming straight for me! You didn't think to wait or come back for me?"

From the corner of his eyes, he could see Slightly's jaw drop, emphasizing the boy's crooked teeth and double chin.

"No," said Peter, voice hard, leaving no room for argument.

The rest of the boys looked at their feet, but Peter stared him straight in the eyes. It seemed he'd lost him at the word "nitwit."

"What if I'd been eaten?" James asked, quiet, menacing. The wind stilled until the air was so stagnant and quiet it felt heavy, as though it was almost sucking at him.

Peter didn't blink. "Then you'd have been eaten."

There was a hint of a challenge in Peter's words. James wasn't sure to what, but it was there nonetheless. "I want to go home, Peter."

Peter straightened, fists digging hard into his sides. "This is home."

"Not for me."

The boys stared at one another for a tense minute, James very badly wishing that at this moment he had broken Peter's second rule and had been just a bit taller. Being short gave him a disadvantage somehow, in the argument, which was rapidly turning into a battle over dominance rather than relocation.

"You're a Lost Boy now, James. There is no home for you but here."

"Stop saying that," James said, his voice low and dangerous. Rage was threatening to break through his carefully constructed façade of self-control.

"Why should I stop telling you the truth? It's what you are."

"I'm not a Lost Boy. I was never lost. You knew that the moment you met me." Fear was strangling him, words coming out all high and clipped and twisted. His hands had, quite without his permission, curled into fists at his sides.

"Nonsense. I only take Lost Boys back with me to Neverland. So, you must have been." Peter shrugged.

"You know I'm not and never was, and you told me I could come here on holiday. You said I could go back."

"So," said Peter, flicking a hand toward the trees, "go then."

James's lip began to tremble—not from sadness, from rage. Every muscle in his body was tightened. "You know I can't go back unless you show me the way."

"I never said I would."

Bibble shifted beside James, leaves crackling underneath his feet, and the rest of them all looked at one another and at the ground. Quiet. Charged energy in the air.

James could feel the darkest part of him expanding, taking him over. "Don't lie to me, Peter Pan. Good things do not happen to boys who lie."

A shadow fell over Peter's face, and he stepped dangerously close to James. "Is that a threat?"

The forest itself was darker, more menacing, the leaves all decidedly deep green, and the boys were utterly silent. It seemed that everyone had decided not to breathe. James was not sure what to do next. Peter grinned self-importantly and turned away from him, facing the rest of the boys.

"You're a liar, Peter Pan."

"Excuse me?" Peter turned his head slowly back around. The salted licorice flavor hung in the dense air again. James wanted to choke on it, but he bit it back.

"I said you're a liar."

Peter's eyes were barely larger than slits, and he shot a piercing black stare at James.

"Do not say such things to me, James Hook."

James was shaking everywhere; even his eyelashes quivered. Suddenly, the fury he'd been trying to control burst out of him, and he was barreling toward Peter Pan. White-hot rage coursed through his veins as he sprinted toward him. Peter caught him by the throat the instant he got close and squeezed. Then, he threw him to the ground. James swore he could feel every bone in his body crash against the dirt. The grass hardened and curled around him, scratching at him like long, spindly fingernails.

"Do not threaten me again, boy."

James said nothing. Who was this boy? The skipping, grinning boy from Kensington Gardens was gone, and in his place was *this*. Who had James trusted to take him so far from home?

He could feel the burning in his throat as he gasped for air. Had Peter really crushed his windpipe in one grab? After what seemed an age, Peter rolled his eyes and walked off. James jerked up as the grass softened again, and stood stiffly, breathing hard. His mind and heart were all awhirl with regrets and fear and desperate, stabbing, greedy hope. He looked blankly at the rest of the boys, blinked for a few seconds, and walked slowly away.

"Where are you going, James Hook?"

He jumped at Bibble behind him, when he was just inside the tree-line. "Leave me alone," James said, such pain in his voice even the wood could sense it.

"Don't walk too far that way. You'll wind up in the Never Wastes."

"I don't care."

Bibble looked hard at him. "You'll care when you step on the shimmering snow that's so sharp it shreds your feet, and when you come face to face with a Grap that's all white skin, because it's drained of blood. When he rips you to bleeding pieces on the ground, and the last thing you see isn't the stars, but a muted, empty sky that looks like day-old milk. You'll care then."

James stared blankly at him, his bright white skin, too-large ears, pale green eyes full of real concern, and allowed Bibble to turn him in the other direction. He nodded a half-hearted thanks, and took several steps in the way that did not lead to that horror, but probably to another.

"You'll be all right, James Hook. We all are."

James just kept on stepping.

Thankfully, the darkness lifted almost immediately, and here it was, afternoon. He'd forgotten it was daytime, in the heat of everything.

He stepped deeper and deeper into the woods, not looking at or feeling anything. He deliberately chose not to think anything, for the only thoughts, happy or sad, that popped into his brain evoked terrible pain. So, onward he walked into the depths of the forest, which was already shifting seasons again.

Finally, the adrenaline of the encounter wore off, and there was pain everywhere. He could feel tiny bruises forming where Peter had thrown him to the earth and where his fingers had dug into his throat. There was an ache in his bones, but he doubted that came from the fall.

Eventually, he stopped and eyed his surroundings. Trees to the right of him, to the left, all around. He sat heavily on a fallen stump and stared at nothing and tried very hard to think of nothing. But as the events of the day (days?) weighed on his mind and beat his spirit into exhaustion, he found that he did not have enough energy to keep the horrid thoughts at bay. Quite against his will, he gave in to them.

He was never going home. That was the thing that hit him hardest. Never going to meet his baby brother or sister—he didn't know which—never again going to harass Mother over her horrendous cooking, never going to greet his father at port and breathe in the salt smell of him, feel his strong arms around him. The image pounded the breath from his lungs, until he was left gasping and sweating and shaking like a madman.

Then, secure in the knowledge that he was utterly alone, he dropped his head into his hands and cried. The boy cried in a way he was sure he hadn't since he was a little child, all needing and disappointment and urgency and lack of any semblance of control. It was as though every bit of him was dying. But, part of it felt good, somehow, cathartic.

A leaf crunched behind the wailing boy and he sat up, wiping the tears from his cheeks, looking worriedly for whomever, or whatever, had made the sound. It was a good distraction, anyway.

"Hello?"

Nothing. Another crunch.

His limbs began to tremble. "Hello?"

More nothing.

James flung his head back and forth, beginning to panic, realizing that he was by himself in the middle of an enchanted wood and who knew what sort of creature would love to eat his bones for supper?

Another crunch. At this, he strongly considered leaving. As he was about to do so, the rogue noise-maker revealed herself. James let out a huge breath and his shoulders fell, relieved beyond words when he saw the little Indian girl walking shyly up to him.

"Hello," James said in a small voice.

"Hello."

Up this close, James guessed that he'd been mistaken. The girl was really just a bit older than six. Seven, perhaps. She had round cheeks and a long, straight nose, and brown eyes so dark, they looked nearly black. *A lovely thing, for being so small*, he thought.

"I heard you crying," she said, and she crossed her little arms.

"You're mistaken," he said, sniffing and sitting up straight. Despite the gravity of the situation, James was quite embarrassed at being caught weeping, and by a little girl, no less.

"I'm not. I know I heard someone crying, and I know it was you."

James stared at the little girl then patted the log beside him. She climbed up on it.

"You're perceptive."

"Not really," she said, shrugging. "Every animal in the woods heard you, I think."

They sat in silence for a little while, James getting over his embarrassment, the girl just sitting. James wished he had a way of knowing what she was thinking.

"What's your name?" she asked. Her skin was brown and pretty, and her voice was sweet, like he imagined a honeysuckle would sound, if a honeysuckle could speak.

"James. James Hook."

"James Hook." She giggled. "That's a funny name."

"It isn't!" he retorted, indignant. "What's yours?"

"Tiger Lily." Tiger Lily smiled with her teeth, quite proud, apparently, of the title.

James smirked. James Hook was certainly no sillier a name than *Tiger Lily*.

She held out her tiny hand and James shook it and smiled brightly, unreasonably thrilled at a familiar gesture.

"Why were you crying?"

"You're full of questions, aren't you?"

"Yes, I am."

He regarded her for a second, concluding she was trustworthy. Most children her age were. "It's just—it's hard to explain. Well, I, it seems I can't go home."

Tiger Lily nodded gravely, as though she really understood what he was saying.

He wondered, briefly, if somehow, she did.

He frowned. "How did I end up crossing paths with you anyway? I thought you lived across the river."

"I do."

"Well, I wonder how that happened." He stared away from her, eyes resting on the branches and the leaves and the grasses that swayed this way and that. The leaves were brighter now, back to usual, and James thought it very unfair that the foliage wasn't darker, for his sake. It seemed it should have been, all things considered. But he wasn't Peter. And the trees didn't care about him.

She shrugged and stared at the ground, kicking her little feet. He figured he must have crossed the river earlier, when he had no reasonable thoughts running through his head.

The silence was nicer, it turned out, in the company of the little girl. She sat, picking at the log and examining the wildlife peacefully, felt no need to chatter on, and he was grateful for it. He felt a flash of embarrassment when tears threatened to spring from his eyes again, but Tiger Lily just looked up at him and smiled too wise a smile for a girl of her age, and the flush in his cheeks went away. So, he cried quietly for what must have been several minutes at least, and Tiger Lily scooted closer to him, unabashed and trusting, in the way of small children, and laid her head on his shoulder.

When evening began to fall, the little Indian girl slid off the log, and James finally decided to get up. She pointed over his shoulder. "The river is that way." Then, she just turned and disappeared into the trees. James walked back, as best as he could remember, to the last place he recalled seeing the boys. After quite a bit of roaming, he managed to find the place, and he sat at the periphery. Peter noticed him and smiled, like there had been no argument, no fight, no unspeakable betrayal. Had he truly forgotten the incident? That didn't seem possible, as it had only occurred hours ago. But, Peter, he was learning, was rather adept at forgetting things, inconvenient things, impossible things. Perhaps he truly had forgotten.

James did not return the smile. He simply laid his head on the ground outside the clearing and closed his eyes. He'd no inkling of how to get to the *Spanish Main*, and he feared that once they'd realized he was part of Pan's crew, they'd turn on him even if he did know the way. Tiger Lily certainly hadn't invited him back to her camp. And he would rather stay with a threat he recognized than risk a Grap, whatever that was, swallowing him whole in the middle of the night.

Neverland was frightening enough during the day. Who knew what emerged from its heart in the dark?

No, he would stay with Pan and the Lost Boys, for, at the moment, he had no other choice. Though his heart denied it with every fiber of its being, his mind knew that home was no longer an option.

And he didn't cry. He didn't fret. He lay there on the earth, realizing and accepting and hardening. That was the night that James Hook began to grow up.

PART TWO

☠

SEVERAL YEARS (IF YOU COULD CALL THEM YEARS) LATER

SEVEN

THE WIND BIT INTO JAMES'S MUSCLES AS HE RAN, faster, faster, into the woods. He leapt the rapidly flowing river and crossed into Lost Boy territory, Indians hot on his heels. Despite the inherent danger in the situation, he was laughing. Loud, barrel laughs that reverberated off the trees. He could hear a war cry behind him and gave one of his own right back, stopping for an instant, only to be sure it was aimed in the Indians' direction.

"Come and get me, Chief! And give me my war!" he taunted, voice loud, confident, booming. Adrenaline coursed through him, fueling his powerful strides as he neared the Lost Boys' current encampment. The closer he got, the more distant the war cries became, until he was fairly certain that no one was trailing him anymore. He gradually slowed his pace to an easy trot and stepped into the barren clearing where Peter and the boys were waiting.

"Why are you alone?" Peter barked. "Where are the Indians?"

"Back across the river. They're not stupid, Pan. They won't fall for the same trick twice."

"Of course they won't. If you were half as clever as me, you would have got them here easily."

James set his jaw and raised an eyebrow. "If only I were half so clever."

Peter threw down his weapon in frustration, and the otherwise bright weather punctuated his tantrum with a single clap of thunder. James jumped. Peter flicked his hand out, signaling for the rest of the boys to come out of hiding. There would be no ambush today, and certainly no war with the Indians. James didn't mind. Peter, as always, minded terribly. It put him in a foul mood, which was not good for anyone in the vicinity. The boy stalked off, probably to cavort with the fairies. The fairies didn't endlessly disappoint him, it seemed.

"Bibble," James regarded, clapping the boy on the back as he passed. He noticed with a slight smile that he was significantly taller than Bibble now and looked a great deal older. How that had happened, he wasn't entirely certain, but he was definitely now the older of the two. Where Bibble had grown maybe a month and a quarter-inch in the last several years, James had grown by nearly five inches and at least that many years. He was sleek and tan, muscular and powerful, and regarded himself to be rather handsome, something no one could say for Bibble—or Bobble either, but that was something of a given. The twins were still all knees and elbows and too-large ears and noses.

James ran a hand through his black waves of hair, which reached nearly to his shoulders, and dunked his face into the water barrel nearest him, coming out and spraying the nearby area with water droplets. This elicited groans from all the boys nearby, but James just grinned. He walked through the camp and out of it, having nothing better to do with Peter gone. Several of the Lost Boys scampered up to him.

"Lagoon," he said, thereby creating a line of followers. The lagoon was teeming with life that day, mermaids frolicking, rainbow-colored birds whistling as they darted around in the skies above the water. He noticed the giant rock that jutted out of the middle of the lagoon, Marooner's Rock, was empty. Likely because Peter wasn't there to lounge around on it.

The mermaids shot James frosty looks as he removed his shirt and dove headfirst into the pool. He ignored them, which was typical. Tootles kept all his clothes on, and they about swallowed him, he was such a tiny thing. He dipped a toe into the water and slid slowly in, until the blue came all the way up to his little upturned nose. Fair-haired, freckled Simpkins dove in after him, attempting and yet again failing a perfect swan dive. Simpkins would claim, of course, that he'd executed it exactly as he'd intended. James snickered.

Most of the Lost Boys joined in, splashing one another, whooping and hollering, decidedly undisturbed by the lack of war between them and the Indians.

"Well done, James," taunted Bobble, swimming up to him, Bibble at his heels.

James rolled his eyes. "Please. The Indians were never going to fall for it."

"Well, no," said Bibble, "but you could have at least drawn Tiger Lily out and distracted him."

James swallowed and backed off just a bit. He'd been keeping his distance from Tiger Lily since she'd started to grow up into something undeniably more than a child. He hadn't even spoken to her or seen her up close for longer than he could remember. He kept it that way very intentionally.

Pan didn't like people touching his things.

Bibble narrowed his eyes, slightly more perceptive than his younger twin, and James felt his mouth go dry. Just then, Slightly, having reached the lagoon a bit later than the rest of them, leapt into the water, arms around his knees, and the splash he created was monstrous. It blanketed the twins as well as James in a wall of icy water, but James didn't mind so much. He'd never been so relieved to be soaked and freezing. If it stopped the twins from raising the questions he feared Bibble had been about to ask, the discomfort was entirely worth it.

While the twins, Simpkins, and Tootles exacted watery revenge upon Slightly, James swam quietly to the lagoon's edge and pulled himself out of the water, content to let his feet dangle in it, closing his eyes and letting the sun warm his torso. He forced his mind not to consider the blurry image of the Indian girl and to think on the suns and the sweet taste of the air. The numbing prickles in his toes. These last several years in Neverland hadn't been nearly as horrible as he'd once feared they would be. The lack of Father and Mother sometimes bothered him, but more often than not, it was a carefree sort of existence. There were moments of boredom, but generally, Neverland was quite an improvement over London.

James was disturbed when he felt a presence hovering over him. He opened his eyes to find Peter staring down at him, fists at his sides.

James smiled. "What? Still put off at the apparent peace I brought back from the Indians?"

"Come with me."

James furrowed his brow. He was generally a self-sufficient sort of person and quite happy to navigate Neverland on his own, but Peter held a sort of pull over him that he couldn't explain. It was the same sort of pull Peter held over the rest of the island; if Pan said it, James wanted to agree. If he was angry, James wanted to fix it. So, naturally, he followed Peter when he stalked off, away from the lagoon.

Peter had gone a good way into the forest, and James was struggling somewhat to find him in the bramble. But, find him he did, and Peter was floating a small way above the ground, chin on his fist, looking very lost in thought.

"Peter?" said James, sensing the taste of salt on his tongue, narrowing his eyes at the air.

"James."

There was no laughter in his eyes when he said the name. James had the distinct feeling of being sent to the headmaster's office at school, and of waiting to be scolded greatly.

"What do you need?" he offered.

"There's something I need to discuss with you," Pan said quietly.

The knot was back in James's throat. "So, discuss it," he said, willing himself to swallow.

Peter let his feet drop to the ground and stood. James slouched (though he hated to slouch), hoping to appear shorter than Peter and not doing a remarkable job at it.

"You've been breaking rules."

James's heart stabbed at his chest, freezing sweat springing up instantly on his back. "Have I?"

Peter gave him a look that said he was dense. "I haven't said a thing up until now, hoping you'd come to your senses. But you haven't, have you?"

James's jaw clenched; he was beginning to feel defensive. "I'd like to know what charges are being levied against me, exactly."

"Stand up straight," Peter said, folding his arms across his chest.

"I am."

"Don't lie to me, James," he said, voice low and cold. "Good things do not happen to boys who lie."

The sting of ancient words being thrown back into his face was not lost on James. The look on James's face darkened considerably and he rose to his full height. He was undeniably taller than Peter.

Peter took a step toward him, and James forced himself to remain steadfast, though he'd begun to tremble, and wanted to run off into the thicket behind him.

"Was I not clear on the rules the first day you showed up here?" Peter said, unblinking as he stared James down.

"Unmistakably."

"And yet…" Peter trailed off, no doubt trying to sound menacing. Then he resumed speaking. "And yet you've broken one of the first rules I gave you."

There was no denying that. "Is that all?"

"No. You and I both know it."

James straightened, glanced away from Peter for just a moment, long enough to gather his wits. "What is the second charge, then?" His voice came out weaker than he'd intended.

Peter looked away, focusing on some invisible point in the distance. Then, he turned back to face James. "I've noticed something disturbing in you, James. Something I thought I could trust you never to do."

"What is that?"

"You've been growing up." There was a strange light in Peter's eyes, one full of foreboding and poison.

The color drained from James's face. "I haven't been."

"Look at you. You're tall. You've got muscles. And you lost the face of a boy ages ago. You're turning into a man, James."

James shook his head, outwardly denying, inwardly knowing it was a lie. His nerves were whirring, on hyper-drive, and his pulse was erratic and spiking. "I do not wish to be a man, Peter. You know that. I'm a Lost Boy, same as you, same as Bibble and Slightly and Tootles. I swore to you that I'd never grow up. Don't you believe me?"

Pan shrugged. "I'd like to. But here you are, in front of me, more a man than a boy. What am I to believe?"

James felt a great panic welling in his gut.

"Believe me, Peter. Believe your friend. I'm not growing up; I swear it. And I'll—I'll get shorter. I'll figure a way to do it. You've got to believe in me, Peter."

Peter stepped back and assessed, flying around in the air, examining James from all angles. James didn't even really know why the whole thing was so unnerving, why he was becoming so unhinged, why the only emotion he was capable of feeling at the moment was cold, biting fear. He'd never heard of anyone breaking the rules, and for all he knew, the punishment could have been nothing at all. Tangible waves of panic washed over him relentlessly nonetheless.

Eventually, Pan sank back down to the ground and looked James deep in the eyes as he said, "I'll give you a chance, James. One." And he hopped away, chanting, "Oh, the goodness of me!"

James fell back against the tree nearest him and ran his hands over his face, cursing the small bit of stubble at his chin. He had no clue how to stop this whole "growing up" process when he'd already started it, and realistically, he wasn't going to be getting shorter any time soon. In all honesty, he was hoping that Peter would simply forget the whole thing, and they could go on pretending that he was still a Lost Boy, and not a shadow of a man.

That was less than likely.

He stayed there in the forest, mind turning so hard he was shocked no one could hear it, until night dripped down over him. He wasn't entirely sure which was safer at this point—staying there, risking a Neverbeast attack, or going back to the clearing and facing Peter, so he remained frozen.

A twig snapped to his left, and he bolted to his feet, fingers flying to the dagger he always carried at his side.

Bibble emerged, hands held up in front of him, and he looked—small. Had he always looked this small?

"You all right?" Bibble asked.

James deflated, body melting down onto the ground. Bibble sank down with him and picked up a twig.

"Where's Bobble?"

"At camp. They're trying to catch fireflies to keep as night lights."

James smirked, leaned his head back against the tree behind him. "How is it you're still so young, Bibble?"

"What?" Bibble cocked his head.

"Look at me," James said, stretching out his arms. "I'm bigger than all of you. Older too. You're the closest, and Bobble right behind you, but even you two are, what? Three years younger than I am? Two at the minimum."

Bobble pursed his lips, drawing with his twig on the forest floor. It lit up in a spray of colors wherever he scratched it, which was a slight comfort. Peter couldn't have been too terribly angry if the forest was acting regular. James remembered a time when the colorful lines on the forest floor would have delighted him. Was he too old now to enjoy such a thing?

"Is there a way to stop it?" James asked, rolling his head over toward Bibble.

"What?"

Bibble was avoiding looking at James's eyes. It was obvious he was dodging the question, stalling. James chose to humor him and repeated himself. "Is there a way to stop the aging, once it starts? Or to, I don't know, turn it back somehow?"

Bibble sighed and looked up at James, abandoning his twig. "I don't think so. It's your experiences, you know, that age you. After Flobbins died, I took it rather harder than anyone else; it was more or less my fault, creating that horrid Grap. It made me grow up quite a lot more than anyone else, and Bobble didn't like that I was older than him, so we tried to reverse it, spending all our time with the fairies and splashing the mermaids and doing silly things, like we did when we first got here. It didn't work."

James was silent. He shut his eyes, thinking that maybe if he didn't see Neverland, then for a moment it wouldn't be there, and neither would Peter, and neither would this whole problem.

"I'm sorry, James; I wish you could."

"So do I," James whispered, more to himself than to his friend.

"Come on, come back to camp. Food's on soon."

James took Bibble's hand when he offered it and tried not to notice Bibble struggling to help up his greater weight. They headed back to camp, and James didn't even eat the nothing that Peter had brought for supper.

FOR THE NEXT SEVERAL NEVERDAYS (WHICH WERE sometimes a month's worth of normal days, and sometimes only an hour's worth), they carried on as usual, provoking the Indians to battle, splashing around with the mermaids, killing the occasional pirate (though James usually found ways to conveniently disappear during those particular ventures), and dancing with the fairies.

One night, however, when Peter was in a dark mood, which was not unusual as of late—recently all his interactions with James had consisted of varying degrees of hostility—the forced gaiety and civility came to an abrupt halt.

The night was black, and the Lost Boys and hordes of fairies were playing near a roaring red fire that crackled and spat little bits of ash at them when they got close. It was casting strange, colorful hues and shadows on the ground and the timber, which James was enjoying, until he noticed the way they played on Peter's face. He was brooding, which he generally only did when he was alone with James, so easily distracted was he when in the presence of the other Lost Boys, of whom he was still quite fond. But not tonight. Tonight, James's presence— and he had no doubt that he was, indeed, the catalyst— was so offensive to Peter that toxin radiated out of him, even in the company of the others.

Peter's mood became blacker and blacker until every fairy had wisely disappeared from the party, and the air smelled vaguely like smoke and sulfur. James was becoming so uncomfortable that it was impossible for him to sit idly and enjoy the fire. He rose quietly from his seat.

"Where are you going?" Peter said, voice toneless.

"I'm not entirely sure."

"Sit, then," he said, baring his teeth in a poor mimicry of a smile.

"I'd rather not."

"Why not?"

James clenched his jaw, shaking from fear and anger. "Am I required to explain my every action to you now, Peter?"

Peter was silent, flipping his dagger over and over in his hand, staring at the licking flames. He looked up at the dancing boys, and the look alone was enough to stop the frolicking.

"We're going to have something special tonight, boys."

There was no answer, no sound, only the crackles from the fire and the gentle breathing of the wind. The silence dragged on until Tootles piped up. "What is it, Peter?"

"Tonight," he said, "we are going to have a Thinning."

EIGHT

J AMES RAISED AN EYEBROW. "A THINNING?"

"Yes."

The Lost Boys stood there, in varying states of confusion. Slightly scratched at his belly and Bibble pursed his lips, looking rather more worried than the rest of them.

Simpkins said, "Peter, what exactly is a Thinning?"

Slightly looked very important and he rolled his eyes at Simpkins. "I can't believe you don't know what a Thinning is." But he didn't elaborate.

James smirked. Slightly was of the opinion that he knew everything there was to know about everything, but generally that wasn't true.

Peter stared at his dagger. The firelight glinted off it in an eerie way, casting a ghostly glow on his face. Shadows danced across the bodies of the Lost Boys as they stood there, looking at Peter. Peter rose slowly from his seat on the log by the fire, flipping his knife in his hand again.

"James. We need to have words."

"But what about this 'Thinning?'" said James, muscles tensing.

"That's precisely what we need to speak about." Peter tilted his head toward the dark woods, leaves undulating and shifting slowly between deep green and silver and black. The air tasted metallic now. James shifted toward the wood, then leaned back, conflicted. One piece of him, the piece that couldn't help but wish for Peter's approval, wanted to follow him into the trees, but the other, larger piece of him deeply feared what would await him there. Pan was eyeing his blade a bit too fondly for James's taste.

"Then, speak," James said.

"Are you commanding me?"

James dug his fingernails into his palms, sure that if he pressed any harder, he would break the skin. "I'm not leaving."

Peter's brow shadowed his face and he sneered, the fairy part of him showing itself. "You defy me again."

"Peter, be reasonable."

Bibble cleared his throat behind James, and Tootles squeaked.

Peter started to hover above the dirt, a ball of rage. Lightning flashed across the sky. "I brought you here, James Hook. I rescued you from a dreary life in London and brought you to this place where you never have to grow up. You can be a boy forever, and what did you do? You spat it back in my face."

James's voice rose to meet Peter's. "Rescued me? From what, exactly?"

"From growing up, I thought. But look at you. You've gone and ruined it all, *man*." He said this last word with such venom that James felt the need to back away. "You betrayed me. You grew up."

James's breathing rapidly shallowed. "I didn't."

Peter shot higher into the air. "Fly up to meet me, James."

James stared up at him, pulse of the island thumping harder and faster in the ground. It had been quite some time since he'd had the need to fly.

"If you aren't a man, come meet me up here," he taunted.

Pan's fairy fluttered and bobbed beside Peter, giving James something bright to focus on for just a moment, before Peter flicked him away and sent him tumbling into the blackness. James was concerned, very briefly, for the little creature's life. But he didn't have much time for empathy.

The Lost Boys looked frantically between Peter and James, the face of Bibble the most void of color, the most strained. Bibble grabbed James's arm and urged him, "James, fly up to him. We can end all this."

Bobble echoed him. Soon, there wasn't a boy among them who wasn't chanting for James to fly. James swallowed, looking intently up at the boy floating in the sky who was daring him to join him. He thought the challenge was ridiculous, but if flying would convince Pan, then fly he would.

James thought of the happiest memory he could, one of those he'd pulled every time he'd needed to fly so long ago. It was a picture, slightly blurred at the edges, of his father and his pregnant mother, doing nothing important, just eating breakfast with him, back when he was a boy. He shook his head, denying then that his boyhood was in the past. He was a boy still, and the flying would prove it. He focused again on his happy thought, feeling it warm him from his core. And when he opened his eyes, he was deeply alarmed. For he was not in the air, but on the ground still.

Pan called to him. "Fly up to meet me, Hook."

James focused everything he had on floating from the ground, but flight would not come. A low rumbling panic set inside him and every muscle fiber, every pore, every hair began to tremble. He stared, wide-eyed, at Bibble, and Bibble's mouth fell open.

"What is it, Hook?" Peter called. "Can't fly?"

"I, well, I—" There was nothing left to say, but, "No."

It was in that moment that Peter had him. Boys could all fly in Neverland. No adults could. There was no more denying the evidence. James Hook was no longer a boy.

Peter shot toward the ground. "Tennnnnnn-hut!"

James instinctively ran to fall in line, but Pan shot his hand out at him. "No. Not you. This is for Lost Boys only."

James stepped back, looking crestfallen.

"Sound off!"

Bibble hesitated, flicking his gaze over to look at James, eyes dark and frightened. But then he said, "Bibble!"

"Bobble!"

"Slightly!"

"Simpkins!"

"Tootles!"

James felt a horrible emptiness at this, and Peter put a greater hole in him when he looked over James from his head to his toes. "And you, James. What shall we do with you?"

That soul-sucking quiet. The kind that pulled at his skin and set his ears to ringing.

"Shall I leave?" James said, his voice cracking.

"Not until after our Thinning." Peter smiled.

"What is this Thinning you keep going on about?" James fisted and loosened his fingers over and over again, until the movement was compulsory and frantic.

"Well, you see, James, I've recently realized that not every boy who is Lost can respect authority." He smiled wider, nostrils flared, the happy expression changing nothing in his eyes. "When Lost Boys start growing up, it is my job to keep Neverland pure, free, the way it was meant to be. The way I dreamt it to begin with. When Lost Boys start growing up, the responsibility falls to me to thin them out."

A trickle of panic ran down into James's stomach as his mind churned wildly, attempting to figure any other possible meaning for what Peter had just said. None of the other boys seemed to understand.

"You mean to—" James paused, drew in a deep breath, "—thin me out?"

Peter's eyes went feral then, and he went at James, dagger out. Panic assaulted James, but he was running on adrenaline. James sidestepped him and grabbed hold of Peter's back, thankful, for once, for his larger muscles, using the smaller boy's own momentum to fling him into the dirt. Peter rose, brandishing the blade, wild, aggressive, and looking like he wanted blood.

Bibble made an unintelligible, high-pitched sort of noise as the boy and the young man circled each other, each waiting for the other to slip. Peter flew into the air suddenly, then sped straight for James.

"Bad form, Peter!" he cried, frustrated that Peter would use his advantage against him. Peter kept coming nonetheless, and James jutted out his knee, catching Peter in the gut, but Peter's speed knocked James to the ground anyway.

The two grappled for a bit, filling the thick silence with thuds and grunts. James threw himself from the dirt, slamming into Peter, causing the smaller boy to wince and cry out. Peter wriggled around, slipping over him with such quickness James could hardly see him. And in that one move, it was over. Peter was on top of James, digging his knee into James's chest. It was nearly impossible to breathe. James wondered if any of his ribs were cracked, if a lung was punctured.

Peter pressed his dagger to James's throat. James could feel the life within him pounding fiercely against the blade, the scratchy leaves clawing his back, a large stick digging into his shoulder where he lay. He stared up at Peter, mind unwilling to accept what his body was saying to it—that, in minutes, he would be dead.

"Peter," he said, making one last desperate effort.

"Yes?"

"It seems bad form to kill me with that knife."

Peter hesitated. He was very concerned with matters of fairness, James knew.

"What makes you say that?"

James drew in a hoarse breath, struggling against the blade, air coming thin and precious. "You know as well as I that you could kill me with one arm tied 'round your back."

"Could I?" he asked, smirking.

From the corner of his eye, James could just make out the faces of the twins, mouths hanging open, eyes like the moons. "Of course," he said, gasping for air. "You don't need a weapon. You can fly circles around me, you're infinitely cleverer, and you could quite easily kill me with your bare hands. It doesn't seem fair to use a blade on me."

Peter lightened his suffocating touch, and James drew in a greedy, gulping breath. "That really *doesn't* seem fair, does it? I am quite clever and quite good."

"Of course you are."

Peter took his gaze away from James's face for an instant and looked off into the dark, lightening further the touch of the knife. James took what he knew was the only opportunity he would be getting tonight. He hurled all his body weight at Pan, and Peter was sent flying through the air. James jumped up from the ground and grabbed the stick that had been digging into his shoulder, and when Pan darted toward him, he swung it with all his might. There was hardly a contest in the area of brawn, so it connected with a sickening thump, and Pan fell.

Without looking back, James sprinted away. He had no idea where he was going or if Peter was behind him or if he was going to survive, but he ran on into the black. Trees smacked him in the arm, stinging him, cutting him, and the entire forest shrank in around him. The metallic air assaulted his tongue. The wind pounded darts into his skin. He could hear no Pan behind him, but continued to run. Then, he stopped. At his feet, the river ran, babbling as it did. Beyond this river lived the Indians. He stuck out his foot, and hesitated. It seemed to him that no good could come from crossing that river. None could come from staying behind, either. James was frozen in space, having no inkling as to what to do.

There was a distant crow behind him that sounded more like a boy's than an animal's, and that sound propelled him across the water. Ahead, a small fire glowed, sending up a pillar of smoke that was white against the darkness of the sky. He crept closer and closer to the camp until he could see silhouettes of the people milling around. Eventually, he could see the general features of their faces. He was unable to enter the camp, however, because a large man whom James recognized as the Chief came out of nowhere and blocked his path.

"James Hook."

He looked slowly up into the man's eyes. "Chief."

"We grow weary of your provocations."

The Chief was the same size as he'd always been, so James wondered for a moment if he himself had shrunk. He certainly felt small under the other man's hard scrutiny.

James took a step back. "I'm truly sorry for that, Chief. I beg no quarrel from you tonight."

"Then what do you beg?"

"Sanctuary."

The Chief looked at him for a while, dark eyes cunning and sharp. "Sanctuary from whom?"

"The Pan."

"Unexpected," he replied simply.

Stinging tears welled up in James's eyes, and he blinked to stave them off. "To both of us, sir."

James looked down at the ground, knowing full well that nothing he had done these past years warranted any sort of special favors from the Chief. Of course, they weren't always battling; sometimes they would have grand celebrations and hunting parties and dances. More often than not, however, James was attempting, under Pan's orders, to provoke them to war.

"Look me in the eyes, Hook."

James's gaze flickered upward.

"So, the Pan has turned on his boys?" The Chief crossed his arms, muscles like boulders, hard and bulging and bumping.

"Only on me. It seems I've been growing up."

The Chief looked him up and down, crow's feet around his eyes wrinkling. "It does indeed."

"He pursues me even now. I ask, though I know it is undeserved, that you allow me to join your ranks."

The Chief shook his head. "You are not one of us."

"I'm not one of anyone."

He set a large hand on James's shoulder and looked straight into his face. "You're a different sort of boy—a man, Hook. I wish to believe you. But I cannot risk the safety of my tribe. Were I to shelter you and find later that this was another of your tricks and you meant only to ambush us, I would have no one but myself to blame."

James closed his eyes slowly and opened them again. "Where am I to go?"

"You will find an answer."

The Chief patted him heavily on the back and left him there, walking back to camp. James slumped his shoulders and sighed, and it was a breath made of fear and anger and utter anguish. Then he started to walk away from the Indians and into nothingness.

"Wait," he heard a sweet voice say. He stopped.

"James Hook."

"Tiger Lily."

He could barely see her at first, in the darkening night. As the flavor of metal snaked its way deeper into his throat and the leaves turned a darker shade of silver, the sky darkened as though ink was dripping down into it from space.

When she stepped closer, his breath caught in his throat. The Indians and Lost Boys had met occasionally beyond the throes of battle, but, as he'd said to Bibble, he'd deliberately avoided Tiger Lily since he'd noticed her beginning to grow up by years, and looking it. She'd gone off from time to time with Peter and he'd seen a blurry figure of her here and there, but that was it. For his own sake, James hadn't really seen her up close since that night so many years ago, the one he preferred not to think about, the night he found out that he was never going home again. Whereas, since he'd seen her last, he had aged five years, Tiger Lily had aged nearly ten. She couldn't have been more than a year or two younger than him now.

Her hair was longer than he remembered and fell in black waves to her waist, which was gently curved and impossible to look away from. The rest of her was delicate but strong, like her namesake. She smelled like rain. She cleared her throat lightly, and James realized that he had forgotten himself.

"You know me," he said.

"Of course I do. I've seen you around with Peter. And I'd never forget that night, when I was just a little girl. I'd never seen a boy cry like that before."

James was glad, then, for the dark. It hid the deep red in his face. He coughed. "Yes. Well. Not my finest hour."

Tiger Lily stepped a bit closer, and James thought his windpipe might constrict until he couldn't breathe at all.

He decided, then, that avoiding her all those years had been a wise decision.

"You're bleeding."

"Am I?" Then James could feel the sting across his throat, where the blade had apparently sliced his skin.

"Wait here," she commanded, stretching her hand out. As if it were possible for him to do anything else. When she returned, she was holding something wet. She gestured toward the black earth, and James sank down next to her. Then she pressed to his throat something he determined must be a sort of cloth. He hissed at the prickling pain, and Tiger Lily rolled her eyes and touched his bare skin with her free hand. James swallowed hard, a buzz of excitement flooding him with her fingers touching his throat, her chest moving lightly up and down less than an inch from his.

"Where did you get this?" she asked.

"Courtesy of Peter Pan."

He saw something strange flicker in her eyes, and she looked away for an instant. Then, she regained composure of herself. "Is that—is he why you're running in the middle of the night?"

"Yes."

"I am sorry."

He didn't know why she should be apologizing, but didn't press her.

"I just—I wish I knew what to do."

Tiger Lily bit her lip. "I cannot offer you anything. Once my father has made a decision, it's final. I'm sorry." She hesitated for a moment, reconsidering, he hoped. But then she started up with the cloth at his neck again, swallowing what looked like guilt.

He caught her hand as she washed the blood away from his throat, and she looked up at him.

"Never apologize to me," he said, voice gravelly and tired. Older. "Thank you for your kindness. Now and years ago."

She stared intently at him, and he felt his heart quicken. Then, he let her go, hearing yet another crow somewhere off in the direction of the Lost Boy camp, but likely closer. Tiger Lily heard it too.

"Be safe, James Hook."

Tiger Lily disappeared then, and he was left alone again, mouth agape, foolishly sweaty, and not from running. But he pushed her face from his mind and made himself consider instead the very immediate threat that was likely heading toward him. He looked up at the stars and breathed deeply, dreading, fearing.

Anticipating.

With the Lost Boys and Pan turned against him and the Indians refusing to help, there was only one place he could go.

NINE

J AMES HEARD NOTHING AS HE CREPT ALONG, SAVE FOR his own footsteps and eventually the gentle sloshing of water against the shore. He questioned over in his mind if this was the decision of a wise man or an impetuous boy. Was there any wisdom to be found in seeking safety amongst a band of thieves? Thieves who would know he'd been part of the Lost Boys for years. Perhaps it was better for him to try to survive on his own. He chuckled darkly at that. Neverland was not a place for anyone desiring to live in solitude, with its dark corners and mirages of light. So, despite his misgivings, he soldiered on.

The salt smell of the ocean found its way into his nose, evoking horrible, painful memories of a moment years ago. It still haunted him, the face of that pirate before Pan slit his throat. The first kill he'd ever been a part of. And the face of that pirate was the reason he was here now, yards away from the *Spanish Main*.

It rose from the beach like a behemoth, moonlight casting the boat's large but elegant shadow on everything near it. The wood was beautiful and dark and solid, the lines carved by a master, and for whatever reason, James was so struck by it that he couldn't rip his gaze away. Deep in his soul, he knew that the master carver had been him, back when he was a boy and the world had still been simple. Back when he'd nothing to fear when he fell asleep, and had spent his nights dreaming of being the captain of the *Spanish Main*, swashbuckling and sailing the sea.

Faint notes of music rose up from the ship and spilled over the edges, getting louder and louder as James approached, until he was assaulted by it. It was not music in the typical sense, but noise, really. Raucous sounds and drunken men belting out notes he was sure were supposed to be following some sort of tune. Somehow, the hullaballoo was not intimidating; it was inviting.

Mirroring what he'd done years ago, he scaled the side of the ship, not as easily as he remembered Pan doing it, but effectively, and that was all that mattered. His muscles were burning by the time he reached the top, and he peeked his head over to eye what he would be walking into.

The air smelled strongly of whiskey and of men who hadn't bathed in far too long a time. It was filled with coarse merriment as well, making the otherwise offensive odor almost charming. There were at least thirty men on board, perhaps more, all in various states of debauchery, some dancing, some singing, some passed out, and some on the verge of passing out, but nursing their drinks anyway. It was a night for revelry across the island, it seemed.

James took several deep breaths and hoisted himself over the ship's edge, landing with a monstrous *thump* on the deck. All at once, everything stopped.

The pirates blinked at him for several tense moments in silence. The only sound was of the waves lapping against the ship's hull. James was frozen in a crouch, terrified, trying with everything he had to look proud. Then, the man he'd encountered on the beach years before stepped forward. His eyes crinkled in a smile as he walked up very close to James and bowed his head, then crossed his hat over his heart. "Captain," he said.

It was a scene that was very familiar to James, as he'd remembered it nearly every night before he fell asleep since it had happened. The part that followed, however, was new. The rest of the men looked to the one in the front and knelt in turn, each whispering the word, "Captain," as they did.

James was dumbstruck. Eventually, they all stood and looked at him.

"I'm, I'm—" he stuttered.

"Aye," said the leader, the one with smiling hazel eyes and a gold tooth. "Ye be Captain James Hook."

Captain. So, it *had* worked. He'd dreamt himself the captain, night after night in London. Sailed with this particular crew, commanded and pillaged and plundered with them, on this very ship. He'd fancied himself Captain James Hook, and here, that was who he was.

"I am," James said, though at that point he could barely form words. "And I know you. But, I'm sorry. I don't quite recall your name." He felt blood rushing to his cheeks at this, but it had been an awfully long time since he'd dreamt of them. It'd been an awfully long time since he'd dreamt at all, really. He hadn't dreamt a thing since leaving London. So the fellow's name was something buried in some dusty corner of his mind, and he was left standing there, rather embarrassed.

"Starkey, Captain," the pirate said, not blinking at the question. "And this be Bill Jukes." Jukes stepped forward and extended a muscled and heavily tattooed arm. James smiled widely, shaking his hand. It felt more real now than it ever had in his dreams, the massive man's hand flexing around James's like he could crush it if he wished, light of the moons glinting off his bald head. "And Smee." A portly little redheaded man with spectacles too small for his face stepped out from the crew and bowed grandly, flinging his hat out. He came up smiling, bright and warm. James was sure he would take a liking to this fellow.

Starkey introduced each pirate then, name by name. It struck James that somehow this crude band of pirates had many more marks of gentlemen than did the Lost Boys.

"We've been waiting for ye, Captain," said Starkey.

A tingling warmth spread over James from the crown of his head to the tips of his toes. A feeling he hadn't had since the last time he'd been home. "Have you?"

"Since before any one of us can remember."

A smile broke out on James's face. He took another moment to examine Starkey, seeing an unfamiliar deep scar that ran from his left ear down to the right side of his chin. But he also couldn't help but notice a familiar look in his eyes, in the way they creased at the corners, and in the way he held himself, all authority and knowledge. He couldn't place it yet, so he decided to pack the feeling away for another time and to play the role of captain for a moment. He puffed his chest out. "Where are the captain's quarters?"

He didn't know how true to his dreams the ship really was, but if it drew from them at all, his captain's quarters should have been something to behold. James followed Starkey from the quarterdeck back to a little room set off from everything else. When Starkey pushed open the door, James realized that the room was not little at all. It was massive, exactly as he'd dreamt it, down to the tapestries.

It was a grand cabin, filled with luxury, and several degrees warmer than the deck. There was a large bed in the corner of the room, draped in heavy crimson fabric, a blanket that looked like it could envelop you without a bit of effort, and an oak desk, upon which were the goblets—the golden ones he'd dreamt of what seemed like an eternity ago—filled with a beverage he could drink all he wanted now. A laugh bubbled out of him, despite himself. The room itself was swathed in reds and golds—large and perfectly gaudy curtains, rich dark wood on the floor, plush red rugs by the bed and under the window. He curled his toes in the soft rug, sighing at the feeling. It had been quite some time since he'd set his feet upon something that didn't wish to scratch at him or tickle him. In the corner hung a long red jacket and an extravagant wide-brimmed hat that matched it perfectly, a hat pulled straight from his childhood imagination.

James walked to the corner and pulled the jacket off its post, then draped it over his shoulders. He set the hat atop his head, quite unaware of anyone else around him. Then he made his way over to the floor-length mirror on the other side of the room and stared at himself.

His hair was long and wavy, much longer than his mother had ever let him keep it back home in London. And he was already taller than he'd been just hours before. He reached up to touch his face. There were small whiskers there, stubble really, where they had never been before. Despite only having been aboard the *Spanish Main* for a short time, he already smelled like the sea.

It struck him then that he was staring at a mirror image of his father. And that affected him deeply. He suddenly choked back a deep sob and turned away from it, breathless. James stood that way for a moment, chewing on his knuckle to ward off any threat of emotion, and then turned around to face the mirror once again.

He was his father. But he was also a captain, and he believed that to his very core.

"Starkey," he said.

"Aye, Captain?" Starkey peeked into the room, at the front of a crowd of pirates. He seemed inordinately delighted at the simple address.

"What is it that we do aboard the *Spanish Main*?"

"Plunder, sir. And pillage, and sail." He belched loudly, then, and raised a hand to cover his mouth. It seemed odd that he was embarrassed at all. "And drink, sir."

"What do you plunder and pillage?" James said, eyeing the mirror once again, adjusting his hat upon his head.

"I, er, I don't rightly know." Starkey's eyebrows knit together, leathery cheeks stained so little that no one but the boy who'd known him all his life would notice. "It seems to me that we've been planning to plunder or pillage something or other for quite some time. But, more often than not, we end up just waiting here."

From the corner of his eye, James saw Jukes start to laugh and Smee shift his weight nervously.

"That will have to be remedied," said James, chin in the air.

"Aye!" Starkey said, eyes lighting up once again, furrow disappearing.

The crew behind him echoed him with a thunderous, "Aye!"

Those with goblets raised them, and a good amount of alcohol was wasted in the general sloshing that followed. Slowly, the band of pirates dispersed back out onto the ship and resumed carousing, as though there was nothing out of the ordinary going on that night. Perhaps there wasn't. Perhaps James being there in his captain's quarters and in his pirate garb was the most perfectly natural and ordinary thing that had gone on since he'd got to Neverland.

James sat on his bed—he'd never been so happy to hear that word—and kicked off his ratty shoes. They were really more like hastily sewn together leaves than shoes, and they fell apart almost immediately upon contacting the ground. He lay back then, allowing himself to be enveloped by the bed's softness.

He hadn't realized until then just how exhausted he was. Adrenaline will do strange things to a boy's—man's—body. There was tiredness that seeped into the marrow of his bones, the kind of tiredness that does not come from a day's run, but from years of hardship.

He touched his face again, trying to get used to the strangeness of whiskers. Whiskers and a hard jaw line. He hadn't had those even that morning. He wondered, not for the first time that day, just how much older he'd gotten since the suns had come up. It was difficult to say. Perhaps as much as a year, perhaps a bit more. He swallowed down the grave fear that welled up inside him at that undeniable truth. He was getting older, and the acceptance didn't give him any sort of freedom or peace, only a heavy, terrifying knowledge. Back in England, everyone was moving slowly toward death together. But here in Neverland, it seemed he was hurtling toward it faster than anyone else, and there was something frightening, and strikingly lonely, about it. He shut his eyes.

His fingers trailed down to the angry, swollen stripe across his throat, and he opened his eyes once again. It was a clean line; the sharp stroke of the dagger had seen to that. And he doubted heavily that it would become infected; Tiger Lily had seen to that. But he could feel the depth of it and knew that it would be a scar he would always bear. On the outside and in his very soul, a stain that would never be lifted. It was another defining moment in his life, like the murder of the pirate. The face of a Pan staring at him, desiring his blood, affected him in a way that no other murderer's face ever would. For somehow, in the darkest depths of him, as Peter was trying to murder him, a piece of James wanted to give him whatever it was that he wanted.

His fingers left his neck, and he turned over on the soft bed. He'd liked the idea of the pillowy mattress at first, but just as it had been impossible to sleep without one the day he'd come to this wretched place, he found it infeasible to sleep in one now. No noises of wildlife, no shivering in the cold. It was a strange thing for him to have to get used to comfort. But, as time (if you could call it time) wore on, the pirates' singing became a coarse lullaby, and he drifted into sleep.

TEN

J AMES DID NOT AWAKEN TO SOUNDS OF THE WOODS
or to Peter barking orders at him to eat a breakfast that
wasn't there. He awoke to a gentle rocking and the sound
of the sea lapping against a boat. This boat. *His* boat.

He felt his face again, noting that it had hardened
further since he'd fallen asleep, and the stubble had grown
into a small beard. James rose from his bed and searched
for a blade somewhere in the room. He found one in the
top drawer of his desk, along with a container of cream
meant for shaving, and a brush. He thanked his younger
self for being so carefully detailed in his growing-up
fantasies, then dipped the brush into the cream, slathering
it on his face. As he slid the edge of the blade across his
cheeks and chin, down his neck, he jumped when he cut
too deeply, and a small bit of blood trickled out from him.
It drew his gaze to the swollen red gash at the base of
his throat. His eyes darkened, and he shaved the rest of
himself more slowly.

That wound. He desired not to look at it. The memories
it conjured were too ugly, too recent. James suspected that
no matter how much time passed, that would always be
true. So, he pulled on a shirt and quickly yanked the regal
red and gold jacket from its hanger. Then, he fastened it
across himself, buttoning it all the way to his chin. Now,

though his mind knew the gash was there, his eyes would not remind him every chance they got.

He reached over to his desk and took a sip from the already-filled goblet he'd dreamt up. It was early in the morning, but who would judge him for drinking here? He choked on the bitter liquid at first, then cleared his throat and set it down, eyes watering slightly.

He pulled a pair of oiled black leather boots over his pant legs and smiled. They were much more comfortable than those leaves he'd been wearing for the past several years.

With *his* hat, *his* jacket, *his* boots, today he was really and truly a pirate. No one who saw him could deny it. And not just a pirate—a captain. He smiled a little wistfully, then wiped the smile from his face before he opened the doors to the deck, wishing to appear menacing. In a band full of pirates, that was no easy task.

When he pushed open the doors, the men stopped what they were doing and looked up at him, one by one. He scowled.

"Captain," Starkey ventured, "what will ye have us do today?"

James hadn't yet thought of that. He was much more preoccupied with his status as captain than with the details of it. "I, um…" He knew that sounded less than captainly.

"Captain?" stammered a small voice from the midst of the group.

"Speak."

"If you have no objection, of course, we were thinking on starting the day with a spot of breakfast."

The rest of the men behind this portly, nervous fellow nodded heartily, and grumbled their approval. James had no semblance of an objection to this; what his stomach was doing couldn't truthfully be called growling. It was roaring.

"I will allow it," he said, feeling very adult. "What is your name, sailor?"

"Smee, Captain sir."

Smee. He remembered him from the previous night, as well as many more London nights before that. A gentle fellow, for a pirate.

"Well, Smee, what have we to eat?"

Smee smiled broadly and tottered away, beckoning James to follow. He did, with reservation. He was halfway looking forward to a meal and halfway afraid that these pirates couldn't tell the difference between fact and fiction either, and he would wind up with an empty stomach yet again. He grinned broadly when he discovered that such was not the case.

Smee led him to a splintered wooden table spread with breads, cheeses, fruits, meats, and bottles and bottles of rum. James could feel himself salivating and wanted to dive onto the table and shovel the stuff into his mouth. After that, he thought he would like to bathe in a vat of rum. Instead, he sauntered easily to the table and pinched a small piece of chicken between his thumb and forefinger. Then, he nibbled at it and nodded. The rest of the crew took this as permission to dive in, and dive they did. James tried to maintain decorum for a moment longer before his stomach won out, and he joined the rest of his fellows in the scarfing.

After he filled his stomach until it bulged, James sat at the ship's hull, crossing his feet over one another. The black leather of his boots was supple and shiny, flexing with his feet. Then, all at once, he uncrossed his boots and leapt up.

"Starkey?"

Starkey charged toward him. "Aye."

"Is this vessel seaworthy?"

"Aye. Should be, Captain."

James set his jaw and observed his surroundings, scanning the glittering sea and the cotton-candy horizon, and tried to think of the most piratey words he could say.

"Avast, ye scurvy dogs! Hoist the mainsail; pull in the anchor! We're leaving port."

Then, there was a flurry of activity, men pulling ropes and turning wheels and running about, wherein James assumed they were avasting and hoisting the mainsail. James returned to lean over the edge of the ship and stared at the endless blue. It made him feel idiotic. How could he not have seen this before? Of course he didn't have to fly out of Neverland. He could sail out of it.

"Captain," Starkey said.

"Yes?"

"Where do ye be planning on sailing this day?"

James gripped the railing until he could feel every grain of the wood on his palms and fingertips. Breathed in the salt air that for once, tasted nothing like vanilla or blasted gingersnaps. The taste of the sea was overpowering. He smiled, still gazing out over the open water, heart twisting around and filling to the brim. "London."

Starkey frowned and scratched at his head. "I'm unfamiliar with a London."

"I'm not." James returned to staring out at the sea, imagining the look on his mother's face when he returned home, the strong shake of his father's hand when he came back a man. He grinned when he felt the ship moving under him. Though he had no idea as to the direction they were heading, he expected it wouldn't much matter. As long as they could get away from Neverland, he would find a way to walk on England's foggy shores again.

It was a trick to be sure, as he was fairly certain they weren't even on the earth, or perhaps they were, but it was a different version than the one he'd been born on. A little piece hidden, tucked away, that no one in London or across the Atlantic would ever be able to see. But he and Peter *had* flown here. He had to believe that he could sail back.

The crew looked both in and out of place, somehow. Like this was what they should be doing, but they had no idea how to do it. A pirate ship that never pirated. Strange, like everything else in this place.

James clacked along the ship's wooden planks, playing with his hand, pacing nervously, anxious to be out on the open sea, to disappear from view of Neverland's shores forever. Eventually, the chaos of the ship quieted as each crewmember fell into his assigned role. The ride was smooth, like sailing on glass. James found that he could hear nothing, and he wasn't sure if it was because everyone was silent or because his mind could only see and hear and touch the thought of England. Finally, a bellowed cry broke into his consciousness.

"Land, ho!" called Bill Jukes from the crow's nest.

Everyone was running this way and that, pulling on this rope and moving that sail. James felt a great excitement stirring in his gut. Every muscle quivered with anticipation as the ship moved closer. He was quite sure the shore was not England's—they hadn't been sailing long enough—but that didn't matter in the slightest. What mattered was that it was land, and that perhaps that land had no allegiance to Peter.

The amount of water between the ship and the landmass started to shrink considerably, and the ship slowed as James's heartbeat quickened. Closer and closer, until James could see every tree outlined, and eventually every blade of grass. The twinkling lights darting in and out of the forest, and the dock at the water's edge. The faint taste of vanilla and gingersnaps. The dock. James furrowed his brow and leaned harder over the ship's frame.

"Starkey, where are we?"

Starkey shrugged. "Captain, I'd say we be in Neverland."

James shook his head quickly, like he was trying to empty it of something pesky. "That cannot be right." Then he turned on his crew and scowled. "You incompetent mongrels. What have you done, turning us right back 'round? Get your heads on straight and steer this ship away from Neverland!"

The pirates moved with great urgency, quickly leaving Neverland's dock once again. After what couldn't have been more than an hour at sea, Jukes once again called, "Land, ho!" And James once again looked on with tightly wound muscles and wide eyes as they once again approached the dreadful shores of Neverland. James was overcome with a black rage, and his muscles began to quiver. This was impossible. These impotent men were turning the ship around. He would fix it and be back home within a fortnight, drinking tea and milk, and laughing with Mother and Father about all his adventures in Neverland.

Despite the happy thought, a great panic was quickly welling up in him. He rumbled toward the man who was steering the boat and threw him forcefully out of the way, denying to himself that he'd picked up this particular habit from Peter.

"Fool," he muttered and took hold of the wheel himself. It was to no avail. On and on throughout the day, he commanded the ship's tenants to steer it away from Neverland. And on and on throughout the day, he ended up exactly where he'd started—resting on the very shores he wished he'd never laid eyes on in the first place.

James grew more and more panicked with each glimpse of Neverland, denying with everything in him that the place was refusing to let him go. No. He was a man. A pirate captain, no less. He could steer a bloody ship. He could do this. He could.

Night fell, and the stars spun and leapt around the moons in the sky. The crew was dragging along, exhausted. All but James, who was in a frenzy. His eyes were wild and frantic, bloodshot, and he was rapidly losing control of himself. Cursing up at the stars, who were moving too quickly for his liking, swearing at every person who came near enough to him, James grumbled again and again, wrenching the wheel this way and that, every thought, every emotion swiftly replaced with desperation. He ran a hand through his hair, nails scratching his scalp, coming away with little red flecks beneath them. James cared very little about that. His muscles abuzz, his nerves electric, he jumped when he felt a small hand on his shoulder.

"Captain," said a gentle voice.

James did not wish to answer.

"Captain, if I may."

James closed his eyes heavily, and his shoulders slumped. "What is it, Smee?"

Smee set his rounded fingers upon James's shoulder. "It doesn't seem that we will be leaving the dock tonight, sir."

"Is that so?"

"Perhaps you should be getting some rest in you," Smee said, speaking gently, like a mother coaxing her child into naptime.

"Perhaps."

James Hook did not have enough wits about him to concoct original words, and as such, was relegated to simply repeating Smee's, so defeated a man was he.

"Why don't you let go of the wheel, Captain?" Smee said, glancing around at the ship, which, James barely had the awareness to note, was populated by tired, unmoving men.

"Why don't I?" he said, sighing, and he did as the portly, genial pirate suggested.

"And go have a rest."

He didn't answer. He just stalked off to his quarters. Without thinking much, he removed his jacket and hat and boots and shirt and lay in his soft bed. It didn't seem all that soft now. Though he couldn't see it, the blasted scar was there, breathing right along with him, and eventually it was just he and his scar, alone in the dark. No hope or dreams of plunder or longing for England's shore. Just he and the silence and the beating scar, left to spend the wretched night together.

ELEVEN

BY MORNING, JAMES HAD COME TO HIS SENSES. He was pacing rapidly, crossing his room and crossing it again. Now that daylight had broken and he had his wits about him, James had the good sense to be embarrassed. Yesterday, he had shown terrible form, especially for a captain. And he hadn't really been a captain, had he? He'd been a lunatic. He half-expected that the whole crew would mutiny when he showed his face, and they would maroon him somewhere in the darkest part of Neverland. Then, in the middle of the night, some horrible child's conjured Neverbeast would gobble him up.

But, when he finally plucked up the courage to exit his room, he found no such mutiny waiting for him. Rather, the entire crew was at the worn table on the deck, gorging itself on breakfast again, just as it had the morning before. When the first pirate noticed James, the man simply opened his mouth in a cavernous, gap-toothed smile and tipped his tattered hat at him. The rest mimicked him, when they realized their captain had emerged.

"Morning, Captain," said Jukes, smiling widely, crinkling the little skull and crossbones tattoo on his cheek.

"Good morning," said James.

Jukes nodded politely, and James nearly laughed. The huge man's sincere etiquette felt so at odds with his appearance, not to mention his profession.

James smiled to himself and approached the table, inhaling the warm smell of fresh bread and roasted meat. The others had left a place for him at the head, so he sat heavily, booted toe scratching at one of the thousand stains on the floor below it. His mouth moistened with hunger, and he grabbed a giant turkey leg and ripped off a piece of it between his teeth. Years ago, he would have found it odd to eat a turkey for breakfast. Lately, however, there wasn't much he would call "odd." He had, however, retained a large bit of decorum, so when a bit of juice dribbled down his chin, he dabbed it away as quickly as possible.

"Captain," Starkey said, voice raised above the din of the crew.

"Starkey."

"Will we be sailing again today, sir?"

The crew's voices lowered until they were silent, and they all looked toward him, eyebrows raised. There was no skepticism in a single pirate as he looked from man to man. No, the sincere depth was there in Starkey's face and the innocent willingness to follow in Smee's. Jukes's eyes were surprisingly warm and creased at the corners. They were all ready to do whatever their captain wished.

James was struck by this and sat back, staring openly, as it seemed that, despite yesterday's insanity, the whole crew was willing to listen to him—and excited to do it. He felt a large responsibility then. Though a hefty piece of him wanted to try again to sail for London, the other piece knew it was pointless. He pondered for a moment.

"Yes, Starkey. We will sail today."

Starkey nodded. "Shall we hoist the mainsail, then?"

James was still unsure as to what exactly that meant, but told Starkey that, yes, hoisting the mainsail was in order. "We will set a different course today, men."

The gap-toothed fellow who had greeted him earlier sighed in what looked like relief.

"Where will we go?" Jukes asked in his large, baritone voice.

"To the Mermaid's Lagoon."

The men in the vicinity murmured among themselves, most of them looking somewhere between excited and terrified. James didn't blame them, but he also didn't change his mind.

After the initial light panic, the crewmembers leapt to their positions, several stocky men thundering over to the black sails, a gangly one with dark skin sprinting across the deck, another James didn't yet know, a peg-legged fellow, grabbing at the wheel.

James took his place at the ship's helm and closed his eyes as the sea sprayed his face and the chilly wind whipped at his hair.

"Captain," the ever-amiable Smee started.

"Speak, Smee," said James, opening his eyes.

Smee averted his gaze. "What shall we do once we've reached the lagoon?"

"We do as pirates do, of course."

"And how is that?" Smee grabbed at the frayed edges of his coat and twisted them around.

James shrugged. "We plunder. And pillage."

"From the mermaids, sir?"

"Of course from the mermaids."

In truth, James hadn't been entirely sure who exactly he'd planned to pillage, as he'd spent most of his time on Neverland far inland. He figured there had to have been other pirates somewhere, sailing in and out of the place as they were dreamed up, but he'd no inkling as to where to find them. And perhaps there was some ghostly population in the Never Wastes to battle, but he hadn't been keen on going there. So the mermaids it was.

Smee looked at him, admiration shining in his bright blue eyes. Then he scampered off, stopping all along the way to whisper in the ears of any nearby pirates. James grinned as their faces all brightened in turn. Every man aboard the ship approached his task with more vigor by the minute.

Finally, the dock was long gone, and the ship circumnavigated the island slowly, silently, like an eel slithering in the water. The air on the ship danced with excitement when the crew could make out the distant beginnings of a cave. This was the lagoon's entrance if you approached it by sea.

James's eyes sparkled as they turned toward the little strip of water. Silence fell over the ship as the cave approached. Then they were there, at its mouth, the giant opening lined with little diamonds, like a massive geode. The clean scent of water permeated the air, and James breathed it in deeply.

He could just begin to hear a quiet splashing and a spray of high-pitched giggles as the mermaids frolicked in the lagoon at the cave's other end. He held up a hand to ensure that no errant sound would escape the lips of any wanton crewmember, and the ship snuck easily into the hollowed stone.

The temperature dropped by degrees when they entered the cave, gentle sloshing and lapping against the cave's walls drowning out the mermaids' background noise. They were enveloped in darkness, the ship and her crew, and James could only just begin to make out his fingers in front of his face. It was chilly in there, and damp, and in all the nothing, James began to wonder if their little voyage would yield anything at all. Now that he considered it, he wasn't entirely sure that mermaids *did* keep treasure. But, then, something glimmered in the cave wall. James hurried up to the man at the wheel with the peg leg and too-large nose and instructed him to stop. The man listened, and the ship glided to a slow halt, and the rest of the men looked out in the water, tense and quiet. It was a little lighter now, closer to the open lagoon, so James motioned for his crew to stay put, knowing they could likely see him. He quickly removed his jacket and shoes and hoisted himself over the edge.

He climbed fluidly down, long fingers caressing the wood of the boat, then let himself drop into the water. James winced at the splash, but, after a beat, decided that no mermaids had heard him. The water was a bit warmer than he'd expected. That made the task of swimming toward the glistening object decidedly more pleasant.

He swam to the wall of the cave and pulled himself up, slithering silently over the jagged rocks. Then, after several precisely placed footsteps, James's fingers found what they were looking for—a goblet, made of pure gold, adorned with all colors of sparkling jewels.

He held it up so his crew would see, proud of himself for his find. But he noticed that the eyes of the pirates were not trained upon him. They were staring off into the distance. James whipped his head around, and his pulse immediately began to race. Up ahead was the mother lode—the walls glittered with treasure, to his right, his left, the ceiling above him. Everywhere, reds and blues and emerald greens sparkled down at him.

He jerked his head toward the plunder and about half his crew splashed into the water below, the rest drawing weapons, remaining on deck for loading purposes as well as, James assumed, defense. The pirates were clumsy and careless; they ripped treasure from the walls and laughed loudly, stirring up the water and flinging delicate things up toward the deck. Not a soul was as elegant as James, but he expected as much. So, when the splashing and laughing from outside the cave came to an abrupt halt, James was not surprised. Nor was he worried when a group of very angry mermaids came barreling toward them.

"My sword!" he called. "Fetch me my sword!"

The pirate at the wheel hurtled into James's cabin and came back out with a very ornate sword, its golden handle glistening. He threw it out over the water, straight at James. James was not concerned that it was headed for his heart. He simply made a small but dexterous maneuver and turned his body out of its way, catching it by its exquisite handle as it tried to fly past him.

He tossed his goblet to the pirate nearest him and slogged forward, water clinging to his clothes, dripping from his hair. The mermaid at the head of the pack—group? school? He wasn't quite sure what to call them—charged toward him, face red and scowling, giant fin flapping dangerously about. Scales were splashed across her face, shimmering and colorful, freckled across the bits of her that looked like skin. That was something that never failed to distract James; he'd never quite gotten used to it.

In his peripheral vision, he could see several of his men backing up, the pirates on the *Main* aiming their weapons.

"Drop those things," the woman commanded, purple eyes flashing.

Inwardly, James flinched. Every Lost Boy on the island had been injected with a healthy fear of the mermaids. But this wasn't nighttime, and she had no weapon, and less than half his manpower. He clenched his jaw. "I will not."

She raised her eyebrows. "You can't have them, James Hook. They're ours."

Something in his greater sensibilities stung at this. But how many bruises, over the years, had he endured at the hands and fins of these women? How many times had his lungs burned for lack of oxygen, and how many times had he nearly drowned?

He'd spent a great deal of time at the lagoon growing up and always tried to keep a safe distance from the mermaids. But by the end of a swim, they had always found some reason to harass him, particularly at night, when the harassment had a much more deadly end goal. Everything around here went more vicious at night, it seemed.

He'd never been able to reason exactly why the women hated him so, but likely it was simply because he wasn't Peter Pan. The sting of guilt left almost as quickly as it came, and he met her gaze with a new resolve.

The rest of the mermaids crowded in around the one in front, stopping in a haphazard, brightly colored group when James looked over the lot of them, eyes steely and cold. Silence fell in the cave and he glared again at the leader. She wavered, her gaze flickering from James to the pool below her. James took this opportunity and lunged, gripping the back of her neck with his left and raising the blade slowly from his hip, the point at the mermaid's throat. "I will take your leave to relieve you of some of these possessions," he said, sneering.

The several mermaids who flanked her made moves toward him at this, but all froze in one motion, mouths set in angry lines, eyes burning. James glanced back over his shoulder. At the ship's helm was Starkey, staring down at the brood, gun in hand, cocked and pointed at the maid to James's right.

The mermaid in his hands jerked half-heartedly. But when James hardened his grip on her neck and his fingers caught in her cherry-red hair, she stilled and said nothing.

She simply trembled and clenched her fists and breathed, scales on her face disappearing as her face dried.

The pirates stood frozen for a moment until James whirled around and shouted, "Well, what are you waiting for, fools? Load the ship!"

And load they did.

With all their wealth disappearing before their eyes, cornered and powerless, one of the mermaids beside the leader sprang forward, baring her teeth, kelp hair flying behind her, and that was when Jukes let a bullet fly. It grazed her arm and lavender blood rose in little bubbles to the surface of her skin. James whirled around and every mermaid shrank back, the kelp-haired one's face draining of color.

After that, with at least fifteen weapons trained upon them and that many more large, dirty bodies in the water carting away all they had, the mermaids gave them no more trouble. All the while, James oversaw and tried to ignore the stricken looks on the mermaids' faces. As the cave lost its sparkle and the ship gained it, James made his way aboard.

"Many thanks, lady," he said with a tip of his hat, ignoring the guilt in the back of his mind, and the *Spanish Main* faded out of the tunnel.

THAT NIGHT, JAMES SAT IN HIS CAPTAIN'S QUARTERS, idly flipping a doubloon over and over across his fingers. He was staring quietly into the mirror, not really seeing himself, just staring, so as to avoid the raucous merriment of his crew outside. He was willing himself not to feel the guilt boiling beneath his façade of poise.

A soft knock interrupted his musings.

"Come in."

"Captain, sir, Captain, sir," Smee interrupted, "I thought you might want to have a look at this."

When he saw what it was, James's mouth fell open. "Smee, where did you get this?"

"In the plunder, sir. There's quite a pile of it if you'd like to see."

James waved him into quiet and grabbed the thing from Smee's hand. It was a pan flute. And not an ordinary pan flute; James recognized it instantly as Pan's flute. He turned it several times, examining it, wanting to be sure. Caressing its distinctly grained wood and focusing on every little scar it had gotten over the years, he was quite certain. It was an item of great value to Peter, one of the few things the boy truly treasured. He knew that Peter was sharp enough to guess as to its whereabouts when the mermaids undoubtedly tattled to him of James's pillaging.

James stared at the flute thoughtfully and dismissed Smee with a single flick of his hand. He followed the man out minutes later and leaned against the dark outer wall of his cabin, staring at the flute.

"Captain," said the fellow with the comically large nose who'd steered earlier. His voice wobbled and cracked when he spoke.

James fought the urge to snicker. "You did well today," he said instead, and it was true. "What's your name, pirate?"

"Flintwise, sir." He kept his eyes fixed on the ground.

James clapped his hand down on the man's shoulder and Flintwise looked up, a little smile on his lips when James said, "Yes, you did well, Flintwise."

Flintwise nodded and headed back to the pile of treasure, *clop-clop-clopping* as his leg banged against the wood of the ship.

James's attention turned quickly back to the flute, since the rest of his men were quite distracted. The noise of celebration and drunkenness provided an odd background to his considerations. He should take the flute back. He knew that this was the sensible thing. Or he could keep it for himself and provoke Peter to come and get it. Perhaps, if he was well enough prepared, he could defeat the boy. And if he could do that, he could guarantee his passage back home. The easier choice was clear. But the nastier, more violent one was decidedly more enticing. He was, after all, a pirate.

TWELVE

THE *SPANISH MAIN* WAITED QUIETLY IN PORT AS SEVERAL Neverdays passed. James spent them pacing on the ship's deck and brooding in his quarters and occasionally staring at the flute that he hoped would be his ticket home.

One night, as he was staring out over the darkening sea, he noticed a chill shift in the air. It was not a usual sort of chill or a usual sort of darkening. It was the kind that came only from Peter Pan. When the boy was in a foul or sinister mood, the island often mirrored him, something James had always found overwhelmingly annoying. Tonight, however, James was grateful for the sorcery. He twisted his lips into a smile and spun around to face his crew, the eerie darkness creating a foreboding backdrop for the captain.

"Men!" he shouted over the rumble of the distant thunder. The crewmembers all stopped what they were doing, mid-drink, mid-clean, mid-breath.

"Aye, Captain," shouted Starkey.

"Make preparations. Tonight, the Pan is coming aboard."

The pirates did not hop to action, for none of them had any inkling as to what those preparations would be. James rolled his eyes, secretly pleased that the crew needed him so greatly. He motioned for Starkey to come near him.

"Do we have any oil aboard the ship?"

Starkey raised a bushy eyebrow. "Aye."

"How much of it?" James demanded.

Starkey frowned and hesitated before saying, "A large amount, I believe. Meant for lighting lamps, Captain."

James nodded. "Ask the men to bring it out."

"Aye, Captain."

Starkey bowed his head and left, bringing several crewmembers with him below deck. Then, James crooked a finger at Bill Jukes, who descended promptly from his crow's nest, clambering down unevenly. He practically fell from rung to rung, and James wondered how one didn't snap beneath him. Perhaps a smaller fellow ought to hold such a position.

"Captain?"

James put his knuckle to his mouth and rested it there, pondering. "I need you and the rest of yours to rig something for me."

Several pirates filled the space behind Jukes, cocking their ears.

"What's that?" Jukes said.

"A net."

Jukes frowned.

"Pan will try to scale the ship. He'll do it there." James strode to the side of the ship and leaned over it, stretching his arm past the gold border. He pointed to one particular spot, where the wood was just slightly discolored and worn, varnish peeling.

He remembered climbing in that exact spot, every time he couldn't convince Peter to let him stay behind. Children, after all, were creatures of habit. And Pan was nothing more than a "children."

James sneered. "We're going to douse it in oil. Even Peter won't be able to grab hold. He'll fall. And then he'll fly. When he does that, I want him to fly straight into our trap. Can you do that, Jukes?"

"I think so, sir."

"Do it, then."

Jukes nodded and walked heavily away, trailed by four men in brown rags who only looked so skinny because they were standing next to that kraken of a man.

James surveyed his ship, proudly noting the hurried actions of each member of his crew.

After he was satisfied that every man was working, he retreated to his quarters, the warmth of his cabin prickling his skin. James pulled the pan flute from a drawer and set it atop his desk's shiny surface. Then, he retrieved a tarnished pair of scissors and sat before the mirror. He grabbed a lock of his too-long, coal-black hair and slowly snipped it away, strand by strand, until it hung in waves to just below his jaw. His face was already shaven and clean—captainly. And he noticed, for the first time, curls of chest hair peeking out above his shirt, which was unlaced and hanging low. He was getting older and older all the time. Nineteen or twenty now, he suspected.

James paused thoughtfully and wondered if his parents would even recognize him if—*when*—he got home. Then he shrugged his red coat over his shoulders, fastened each button, and set his hat atop his head. Even if he was preparing to fight a war, it was not uncalled for to preserve a bit of etiquette and good form.

He creaked open the door to the outside, cold and warmth mingling strangely in the air, and noted, with satisfaction, the ever more tumultuous sky, the peals of thunder cracking like whips through the air, and the lightning illuminating the angry clouds. The stars racing and nearly crashing into one another. Peter was getting furious.

James walked across the deck, happy with the bright sheen of oil on the ship's side, and the net, which, in any other weather, would have been visible, if not obvious. But, in the dark, Pan might miss it. James stood at the ship's helm and smiled in a way he hadn't smiled since he'd come there. It was a smile of sinister darkness, curdled with hope. His hair blew behind him as he faced the storm, features lighting up with the sky. It was enough to give noticeable chills even to the pirates on his crew.

Then, there was a silence, one that fell and hung for a moment between the thunderclaps. In that thick quiet, James heard it—a snap of a twig. Then another. The Lost Boys were at the ship now, and Peter was with them.

James looked out into the trees. They were slate-grey, leaves quivering.

He held a finger to his lips and the pirate crew receded into the shadows. It would seem to Pan and his boys that the ship was empty. At least, that was what James hoped. There was a tap on the boat's side, and several more followed.

Tap, tap, tap, and a sliding.

Tap, tap, tap, slide.

James smiled secretly. Starkey and Jukes each moved quietly to their posts on either side of the net.

James pulled out Pan's flute, leaning against his cabin, and waited for another silent moment to come. When one did, James brought the flute to his lips and blew out. Long, slow breaths that the flute amplified with its low, mournful whistling. Flintwise, who stood beside him, shuddered.

Then, the thunder crashed, much louder than before, and Peter shot up over the deck, knife already drawn. It sliced easily through the net and Peter sprang through it, walking on air on the other side. James was stricken, knowing in the depths of him that if it came down to hand-to-hand combat, Peter would best him every time. The color drained from his face when Peter stopped above him, put his fists on his hips, knuckles buried in the familiar makeshift outfit—drapings of hide and moss—and looked down and smiled.

"Well, pirate, it seems you have something of mine." He smiled with his teeth.

"Yes, fairy, it certainly does."

Peter frowned. "Do not call me 'fairy,' for you know my name is Peter Pan."

"Then do not call me 'pirate,' for you know my name as well."

"Why would I ever learn your name, pirate?" he said, eyes bright, spinning briefly in the air.

James's face darkened. "You know me, boy."

Peter crossed his legs and set his face on his hand for a minute, lines in his forehead deeply creased. "No, pirate. I don't believe I do."

James's nostrils flared, a dark hate blooming in his chest. "Lies."

"Never."

James laughed, but it was completely devoid of humor. "You lied to me once, Peter Pan. Of course you would do it again."

"I did no such thing," Peter said, thin eyebrows arched. "I've never even met you."

"James Hook. You know me."

Peter looked genuinely confused. James furrowed his brow, and a deep pain, one that tore at him harder, even, than when Peter had tried to kill him, spiraled in his gut. "Is it possible that you really don't remember?"

"Yes. Because we have never met. Why would I recall you if I've never seen you?"

James was overcome with rage and confusion. Was it truly possible that the boy somehow didn't know him?

After all that time together in the Neverwoods? It hadn't been so long since he'd left, had it? He had a compulsion, only for a moment, to race to the edge of the ship, to stare down at the Lost Boys waiting there and be sure that Bibble hadn't forgotten him. Or Bobble or Slightly.

But no, they hadn't. Surely they hadn't. Peter was nothing if not egocentric. In the past, if anything hadn't related directly to him, or he'd found it irritating or useless, he'd forgotten it, sometimes instantly. Peter had always been prone to forgetting unforgettable things. James had just never reckoned that he would be counted among them. Rage bubbled up inside him.

"Take me back home, Peter, or I swear to you, I will—"

"You'll what? Catch me in a net? Did you truly think you could catch Peter Pan in a net? Did you think I wouldn't see it in the storm?"

Starkey and Jukes grumbled and shifted uneasily, and James's mouth fell open, for that was indeed what he had thought.

Peter laughed a loud, taunting laugh and stretched out his arms, the little dagger he always had balancing on those dexterous fingers. James recoiled automatically, knife flashing in his mind, hurtling him back into an unwelcome memory of that very blade digging into his neck, those long, thin fingers crushing his arms, his windpipe.

"Foolish man!" called Peter, gripping the knife again, drawing James out of his reverie. "I saw it when the sky flashed. Even the lightning loves me!"

James shook his head for he knew what the Pan said was true, but he regained his composure quickly and shouted up at the boy, "Fine, then. Come and claim what's yours."

Peter grinned devilishly and James outstretched his sword, thinking it bad form to spring it upon the boy.

Peter brandished his own dagger. But, when he shot downward, he did not come at James. Instead, he went after a pirate James did not yet know the name of.

The other pirate was as stunned as James, and he fumbled for his sword. Several men started toward him, blades outstretched. James saw the dread in the man's face and dropped the flute, running as quickly as he could to defend his crewman. There was a great fear in the depths of him, welling quickly up, devouring him. He could not have another innocent man's face in his head, dead at the hands of Peter Pan. It was this fear that drove the generally elegant man into fumbling, and he knew before Peter struck that he would not get there in time. Nor would Starkey or Jukes, who were both barreling toward him, both knowing as well as James that their guns would do nothing against Pan; he was too quick. But getting within sword-fighting distance was impossible.

Peter drove his dagger to the hilt into the pirate's chest. Blood spilled over the blade from the wound. And James was left, once again, with an image that would haunt his dreams forever.

James's face went through a myriad of changes in a moment. From terrified to stricken to denying, and finally resting on malicious. Malice, James could do.

"Peter, yet again you provoke me," he said, voice barely audible over the fierce wind.

"What will you do about it, old man?"

James thought for a moment, seriously contemplating his answer. Then, he turned his face up to the boy and gave him the most honest reply he could. "Kill you, Peter. I will kill you."

Peter laughed at this, a shaking, loud belly-laugh. "You can never kill me."

"Can't I?"

"Of course not." His mouthed quirked up and crossed his arms. "I'm Peter Pan. No one wishes to kill me."

In this answer, James had to turn his face away, for he refused to let Peter see the raw emotion he had stirred up. "I do. You killed me first."

Peter frowned, then shrugged, as though his statement was of no value whatsoever. "Nonsense. Why do men always speak such nonsense?"

James turned again to face him, face lit by the periodic flashes of lightning in the inky sky. "What I say now is not nonsense. I will kill you, or I will die trying. You can consider that a promise."

Peter clapped his hands together. "What fun."

"Come and fight me."

He crossed his legs in the sky and leaned his cheek against his knuckles. "I'm bored of this adventure."

"But you can't leave yet. Not without—"

James was silenced by Pan's shrill, merry whistling on his flute.

"How did you—"

"I nicked it. While you were staring at something or other. I can't remember."

James's jaw clenched and he stared up at Peter, brow shadowing his features. "The pirate. I was staring at the dead pirate." A gruff cry went up from his crewmen, and his own voice was shaking with his body, trembling with dark, dangerous rage. "The man lying in his own blood on my deck, Peter. The same blood on your knife. The one you just murdered minutes ago."

Another angry shout from the men.

"Oh, yes. Some fellow or other. I always forget them after I kill them." Peter dismissed the point with a wave of his hand. Then, he stood and bounced off nothing, rocketing into the sky, taking the storm with him.

"Off to the tree house, boys!" he called.

James stalked over to the ship's edge and peered over. The Lost Boys were traipsing off across the beach, frantically following their leader. James laughed angrily. Peter hadn't even allowed the boys to battle. Arrogance. He'd wanted them to come see him do something grand, but no one was allowed to fly into a war with him. So if they couldn't climb, he figured they'd all simply wish to risk their lives in order to watch. A muscle twitched in his jaw, and he stayed the hands of the pirates who were aiming various nasty things at their backs. James had no desire for killing children, his friends. Not ever, really, but certainly not tonight.

After the adrenaline of battle had disappeared, he turned away from Pan and his boys to the pirate lying on the deck. He walked over to him and knelt beside him, then brushed the man's straw-colored hair out of his face, wishing to see it.

"What is this fellow's name?" he called.

No one answered.

"His name, men, his name!"

Bill Jukes stepped forward, eyes downcast, wringing his hat in his hands. "Larsen, Sir. Larsen Griggs."

Larsen Griggs. James burned the name into his mind. This man deserved to be remembered; he certainly wouldn't be by his killer. But he would by his captain.

James choked, looking at him, and breathed shakily in and out for a while. Then, he left without a word, leaving the pirates to clean up the dead man, resolved to dwell on something other than Larsen Griggs's blood on his hands.

In his cabin, he sat on his bed and pondered darkly, twirling his sword by its hilt. "Tree house," Pan had said. So, they had a tree house now, did they? Perhaps he would look for it tomorrow. Perhaps he would find it. And perhaps Pan would be inside. And, perhaps, no, for certain—for certain, James would kill him.

THIRTEEN

IT WAS A CHALKY SORT OF DAY AS JAMES STOOD ON THE dock. The clouds were pastels, like swaths of cotton candy, and the light chill rose a trail of goose bumps on his skin.

He'd left the ship several minutes earlier, snuck away silently. This mission was not the sort one asks his entire crew to carry out. No, this was the sort a man waits his entire life for, and then he tells his friends to let him do it alone. As it was, James didn't have any friends. So, he simply left.

But now, standing on the mooring and surveying the island, he found he did not know where to start. Neverland was such a vast place, and treacherous, and filled with all sorts of nooks and crannies. Where was one supposed to find the den of a part-fairy and his band of children? He knew for certain that they resided in a tree, but that was no real help at all. He might as well have said that they lived above ground or that they lived somewhere surrounded by air. The trees were innumerable. But, James forced himself not to think such thoughts, and instead, decided to consider the vague clue a real advantage.

James raked a hand through his hair and felt the slight stubble on his defined chin, the new wire in his biceps. Yes, somewhere early in his twenties now for sure. He could be no younger than twenty, by any stretch of the imagination. The words "old man," as crowed by Peter, echoed in his head as he stared out at the vast forest.

A sharp pain stabbed through his stomach at that, a needle of worry. He had always wanted to become a man anyway, so the sentiment shouldn't have affected him so. But affect him it did, and as he stood there doing nothing much but getting older bit by bit, he found that he was afraid.

When that fear settled in so snugly that James knew it was to be a stubborn, welcome-overstaying houseguest, he figured there was nothing to do but distract himself from it, and that was when he took his first step onto the beach. After that first step, it was not so difficult to take another, and another. Thus, he made his way across the Spanish Beach (that was what he called it now, in honor of his ship) and entered into the looming forest.

The bramble bit at his calves and the branches on the trees scratched his forearms as he passed them. He wondered, first, if this was somehow intentional, if the island knew what he was after. And second, he greatly regretted his choice of wardrobe—a sort of threadbare, very piratey-looking shirt that rolled up at the elbows, and some thin pants that rolled up at the knees and— goodness—he hadn't even thought to put on shoes. He shook his head and decided that this sort of foolishness proved conclusively that he wasn't full grown yet. And, through the spiteful forest, he pressed on.

Deeper and deeper into the humid wood he moved, until there was a sort of cadence to the trek. Then, he was no longer thinking, no longer the scheming, conniving pirate; he was a predator. He moved lithely, operating only on feeling and instinct and whatever else it is that propels a hunter. He found that, without intending to, he was running, waiting to happen upon the tree he knew he would recognize instantly; he could feel it. But, the running came to a very abrupt halt when, all of a sudden, he felt an arrow whizz past his nose and stick into the tree to his left.

James stepped back, a surge of adrenaline coursing through his veins, and jerked his head to his right, fiercely searching for whomever had just tried to shoot him. There was a snap of a twig and a flash of color in his peripheral vision, and James was the hunter once again. Abandoning his quest for Peter, he shot off toward the flash, powerful legs carrying him faster, faster. He could feel that someone was near, someone who wanted him dead. Then, he could hear him breathing, and finally, when James's lungs and muscles were on fire, he was right there, upon him.

With all the force he could muster, James rocketed himself at his assailant and careened into him, knocking him to the ground with such force that both of them bounced a little. James snarled and sat on top of the assailant, sweat pouring down his face into his eyes. The person beneath him was refusing to look at him and was covering his face with his hands. The stinging sweat made it difficult enough to see without the cover, and James was not amused. He jerked the boy's arm away from his face, snarling, surprised at how easily he was able to do it, how little resistance with which he was met, and pinned it to the ground.

His eyes cleared, and he sucked in a quick breath and blinked rapidly, immediately befuddled. "I—Tiger Lily?"

She was furious; that much was clear. Her mouth was set in a hard line, hands clenched into fists. The look out of her eyes was made of pure venom and a bit of fear.

"James Hook," she spat.

James remembered himself then and scrambled to get off her, trying not to focus on the smooth, dark skin of her bare arms, the feel of the soft curves of her body beneath his. He looked away from her for a second, hoping against hope that his face was not nearly as red as it felt. Then, because he could not ignore her for long at a time, he looked back at her face. She was proud, staring at him unabashedly, looking somehow regal despite the twigs tangled in her long, black hair and the dirt streaked across her cheekbones. She was older, still, than she'd been last he saw her, somewhere between his mother and cousin back in London. Sixteen, he thought. And it showed. Her face was lovelier, eyes large and deep and dark, the lines of her waist and hips and chest more defined; she had quite literally stolen his breath.

"You tried to kill me," he mustered, having a hard time speaking at all.

"I tried to kill *you*? Excuse me, but I wasn't the one on top of you just now."

A grin flashed across his face, but he subdued it quickly and made himself focus on the conversation at hand. "You think I just came after you for nothing? You shot an arrow at me."

She looked away, and James was pleased with himself. He had her there.

"Well, you shouldn't be running through the woods this early in the morning. You should know that's when we hunt. You looked like an animal." She sniffed, her long angled nose wrinkled, and she looked down at him from the bottoms of her eyelids. "And you smell like one, too."

James narrowed his eyes. He opened his mouth to protest, but a small breeze made its way to his nostrils and he shut it again. Spending any significant amount of time on a pirate ship, it turned out, did not do good things for a man's scent. He made a mental note to have a bath when he got back onto the *Main*.

He straightened and nodded curtly. "Well, I apologize for manhandling you earlier."

Tiger Lily stopped picking leaves out of her hair and bristled. "I hardly think you manhandled me."

The corner of James's mouth turned up. "Really? What would you call it, then?"

"I'd say you surprised a poor girl out of nowhere and tackled her before she had a chance to respond. And I held my own, anyway."

James could not stop himself from laughing. "Yes. You had me fearing for my life there with your remarkable self-defense."

She harrumphed and returned to cleaning things out of her hair and brushing several purple and gold leaves off the tawny leather wrapped around her. "I could level you in an instant with my arrows, you know."

"Oh, I've no doubt of that." Then, under his breath and leaning just slightly toward her, he said, "You could level me easily without an arrow, I think."

"What?"

"Nothing." He stared at her, drawn in by her. This was why he'd stayed away from her for so many years—this thrumming of his heart, the heat at his skin, the wickedly delicious thoughts swirling around in his head.

She frowned and looked him over, from head to toe. "So, you've become a pirate, have you?"

He jumped at the sound of her voice. "I have."

"I never figured you for a pirate."

"How do you mean that?" James asked, face hovering between a smirk and a frown.

"I didn't think you'd turn into a brute is all."

Now, it was James's turn to take offense. "I'm no brute. I'm captain of the fiercest ship in the sea."

Tiger Lily shrugged. "All the same."

James sat up straight. "Who's told you I'm a brute? Only because I'm a pirate?"

"I saw what you did to the mermaids' lagoon," she said, leaning in toward him and raising an eyebrow.

The hairs on the back of his neck stood up at the closeness of her. "That's it? And you don't believe the mermaids deserved every bit of it?" he managed.

Tiger Lily tilted her head in a sort of affirmation of that. "Well, Peter, of course, hates pirates dreadfully."

James had to concentrate on breathing and on not making himself menacing at the mention of that name. He forced his face into a careful blank, muscles in his arms tightening. "Yes, Peter does."

Tiger Lily raised her eyebrows then, as though she had just recalled that Peter Pan might be an offensive reference to the pirate before her. James was quite sure that his face confirmed that notion.

"I'm sorry. I suppose you don't much care what Peter thinks, do you?"

His mouth flattened into a disappointed line, recalling the time she'd spent with Peter over the years, secret hours away from the rest of the Lost Boys. He suspected that, for Peter, it had never been anything more than play, but for Tiger Lily, well, he'd always figured it was something else. "I suppose you care very much."

Tiger Lily's brown face flushed brightly. She reached out to his neck, and the touch of her fingertips erased thoughts of anything else. "Your scar's healed well."

James couldn't form a response. He could barely swallow with her so close. She leaned in to examine the scar, and James realized that she smelled very much like her namesake. Every muscle in his body was tensed, tightly coiled, and he was afraid one of them might actually snap. When she was satisfied, she leaned back, and James relaxed again, glad that she was farther away, but also wishing she wasn't.

"What were you doing in the woods this morning, anyway?" Tiger Lily asked, crumbling a pink leaf between her fingers.

"Looking for something."

She raised her head. "Did you find it?"

"No. I was too busy getting shot at."

He made his face very grave then, overly serious, taunting her. Tiger Lily smirked and picked up a handful of dirt, then threw it at him. It coated him in a cloud. He choked.

"Now, now, Princess," James coughed. "It's not wise to incur the wrath of a pirate."

"Is that so?"

"Absolutely. We're all scoundrels. There's no telling what I might do if you provoke me." He smiled wryly and raised an eyebrow.

Tiger Lily stood and brushed herself off. "Well then, I shall have to steer clear of you, won't I?"

He looked sadly at the ground. "I hate to tell you, but that won't work either, I'm afraid."

Tiger Lily raised her eyebrows. "And why not?"

"That would only make my attentions worse."

"How so?"

He leaned back easily against the nearest tree, stretching his arms out behind his head, and stared up at her. He thought for a moment that he saw her pupils darken, expand just a little, and he held back a smirk.

"Well, you see, that's the way of pirates. We always want what we cannot have."

She met his gaze and clenched her arms across her chest. The laughter in both their eyes dissipated.

"Is that so?" she said, and her words sounded as if they came from a dry throat.

"Aye," said James, staring at her.

"Well, what if I'm not yours for the wanting?"

They both knew to whom she was referring. James didn't look away, didn't let his gaze flicker for a moment. "That makes it worse, Princess."

They looked at each other for a silent minute until Tiger Lily broke the stare.

"I need to go, James."

"Can I see you again?" he asked, standing slowly.

She looked off into the trees. "I don't know that that's a good idea."

"Well then, it's a good thing I'm a scoundrel. We don't require all our ideas to be good ones."

Tiger Lily tried to hide her smile, but James saw it anyway.

"Perhaps I'll see you again. I don't know."

"Well, you see, I've been planning to plunder your village anyway—"

She hit him in the arm and smiled.

"So, I'll likely be up and around there for a while. Scouting, you know."

Tiger Lily smiled and stepped backward. "Well then, see each other we may."

She picked up her bow and left, looking once back over her shoulder. James smiled to himself and stood when she'd disappeared, and spent the better part of a Neverday meandering around the forest, pace slower than he'd intended, caught somewhere between searching for Peter's tree and reliving every little touch Tiger Lily had given him.

When he finally walked back toward his ship, he was not as disappointed as he expected he'd be to have found nothing of a hideaway. Rather, he was in quite a good mood, and determined to have that bath, and to be back to Tiger Lily's village as soon as possible.

FOURTEEN

WHEN JAMES GOT BACK TO HIS BOAT, IT WAS SITTING peacefully at the dock, as James knew it would be. But its inhabitants were not nearly so serene. They were scrambling back and forth and yelling at one another, looking like a collection of bugs running from a bird. James wondered for a moment how exactly they'd gotten on at all before he'd shown up.

"Captain," Starkey said, thundering up to him, out of breath.

"Don't bother me now, Starkey. I've got things to attend to."

He knew in his inmost self that the odds of taking that bath and returning to Tiger Lily with any sort of haste were not high in light of this mysterious chaos, but he pressed on toward his cabin nonetheless.

"But, Captain, it be of the utmost importance."

"Later."

Starkey stepped in front of him, and he was hulking and no easy man to step through. James stopped and flared his nostrils, frustrated but largely unsurprised.

"Please, just take a look."

Starkey handed him a spyglass, which he took with exaggerated reluctance. What he saw snapped him quickly out of his apathy. He strode quickly across the deck and leaned over the edge, as if that would give him a clearer view.

"A ship."

"Aye."

He narrowed his eyes. "Pirates?"

"I doubt Pan would allow a regular sailor dream into Neverland," said Starkey, and James nodded.

He pursed his lips and tossed the spyglass aside. "Take in the anchor! We're heading out to sea!" he hollered, hand cupped over his mouth, voice booming and echoing. And, in the few minutes it took his crew to ready the vessel, he prepared himself. He put on the hat and coat and boots which, by now, were like pieces of him, then took a deep breath.

The ship freed itself of the shore and began to sail slowly toward the other boat. There was a tense hush that fell over the crew as they came closer and the distant ship became larger and larger, and, consequently, more and more real. The closer it came, the more details James could make out about it. It was made of a similar wood to his own ship, dark and polished, swirls and knots everywhere in the grain, and it was only slightly smaller than the *Main*. The fellow who captained it wore a scabbard at his side, a dark, scraggled beard, and a wicked grin on his face.

"That man is certainly no merchant," James muttered, and Starkey simply shrugged.

There were men of several shapes and sizes—tall, short, skinny, large, all in various states of filth, blackness in the air around them. They wore eye patches, peg legs, and all. He could almost smell the rum sweat radiating off them from here. Swords glinted on the deck, lying around or hanging off the pockets of men who carried them so casually; there was no explanation but that they used them often.

He wondered, then, having had little to no real exposure to pirates other than his own, if there was some sort of code amongst these ruffians. Would they pass peacefully by one another, nodding to their shared love of criminality? Or were they supposed to stop and board each ship together and have a grand lecherous celebration and drink rum and sing and dance until morning? Or, were they expected to fire upon one another and plunder and pillage, business as usual? His musings were answered with the sound of a cannon.

James jumped and immediately fell to his stomach as a cannonball blasted over him, landing on the other side of the ship into the water with a thunderous splash.

There was sudden pandemonium aboard the *Spanish Main* as men who were not accustomed to sea battles were forced to evolve into war strategists rather instantly. Smee tottered about, scrambling as quickly as his round little body would allow him, accomplishing less than nothing, but that was unsurprising. Jukes grabbed at a weapon and hurtled toward the cannon, another pirate with missing teeth beside him. And Flintwise jerked on the wheel so hard that the ship threatened to topple.

Only Starkey stood solid and resolute, hand on his blade, tense and ready for battle.

James pretended that the rattling he felt was not the shaking permeating him to his bones, but the vibration of cannon fire.

"Take them, men!" James snarled, forcing himself to be brave. "Aboard the ship! No mercy!"

A mighty cry went up from the pirates, and they drew their blades and clambered on board the other pirates' ship. James steadied himself, steeling his wicked nerves, and took a running start. Then, drawing his sword above his head and looking magnificent, he leapt from his deck to the other, landing with a less-than-graceful thump into terrifying, bloody chaos.

James had little time to regret his decision, for the fellow with the terrible cry and rancid breath bearing down on him with an axe was worth much more immediate attention than his roiling emotions. James had no time to think, only to react, and react he did, plunging his sword into the soft belly of his attacker. He forced himself not to get sick when the blade came out, slick with another pirate's bright blood.

James's stomach knotted up, blood draining from his face as the blood of the pirate drained from his body. Until this moment, murder was something he had managed to avoid. He'd been proud of it. Running with Peter's crew, even Bibble had had to kill a pirate or Indian or two. But not James. Not until now.

He was a thread away from throwing up onto the deck.

He shut his eyes for a painful instant, and then opened them, telling himself that this was all make-believe. It had to be. He had to get past the killing if he was to survive this venture. So he pretended, and he killed.

Pirates were falling left and right, and the scent of blood was in the air. James carved his way through the slithering mass of bodies, as though he was clearing an overgrown forest and not a thicket of men.

Finally, he found himself face to face with the captain of the vessel. Their captain was the most horrible-looking of them all. He was short and squat with a shadow over his face from his unshaved whiskers. And several of his teeth were missing. When James felt his black gaze upon him, a chill invaded his blood.

Adrenaline coursed through James as the man smiled an ugly smile and drew his sword, laughing a sinister and drunken laugh. James pointed his sword at him and hoped against hope that his opponent did not notice the shaking.

The man's battle strategy matched his look. It, too, was unrestrained, out-of-control, ugly. But, despite his lack of finesse, the force of the first blow resonated through James's blade, shaking his innards. This man could split him in two if he landed one.

James backed away, instantly terrified at the reality of it. The man struck and struck again. James blocked every blow, fairly cowering. But, something in him changed when the other man opened his pit of a mouth, flexed his muscles like a strutting peacock, and laughed, clearly and loudly, at him. In that moment, he resolved to give the captain nothing more to laugh at.

When the other captain struck again, James struck back. His foe's eyes widened and James drove him back, back to the ship's edge. Strike and counter-strike and parry and dodge. James could feel that the larger man was getting exhausted, and he knew that that exhaustion would eventually make itself apparent in a mistake. And it did. For, precisely when he shouldn't have, the captain raised his sword above his head with both hands. Seeing his opening, and knowing full well that in this instant he was to kill or be killed, James barreled into him, and drove his sword into the man's sternum, burying it to its hilt.

The captain dropped his sword. James slid his blade out and let the man fall to his knees himself, with dignity.

"I'm—I'm sorry," he couldn't stop himself from saying.

The other captain sputtered, spraying out small specks of blood as he coughed and grabbed at his chest. James looked away for a second, trying desperately not to lose the contents of his stomach on the polished wood. Then, because he believed it good form, he swallowed down the horrified disgust inside him. And he removed his hat and nodded solemnly, looking straight into the man's eyes as he died.

As man by man realized what had happened, the chaos came to a close, and James paced around the ship, surveying the damage. Most from his crew yet lived, while most from the other lay dead on the deck. There were several left, seven or eight. A few were cowering, sniveling, and James couldn't see them clearly. But standing tall before him were a large man with muscles that threatened to rip right out of his dark skin, a tan man with curls of shiny black hair whose stature nearly matched the black man's, and a pale one with several missing teeth and both hands fixed on backward. It was an odd sort of child who'd dreamed this crew up.

"You. You're all that live of your crew."

The large, dark-skinned man stepped forward. "Yes, sir. We will happily go to the crocodiles waiting for us below."

Honor, then. These men had honor. That was a rare trait, amongst thieves.

"Would you, truly?"

The man looked over the edge at the crocs that had recently appeared, waiting for a meal, and all three in the front stood still, eyes hard and bold.

"We will not die like cowards, sniveling and begging for our lives. We walk the plank ourselves," said the one who'd taken charge of the exchange.

"Do it, then," said James. The tan one and the one with the backward hands followed the large man solemnly to the ship's plank. The four who'd shrunk back simply trembled and stared. As the leader of their little group of survivors took his first step bravely onto the plank, James held out his hand.

"Wait."

The other man stopped.

"Do you truly desire to die?"

There was a silence, one that was only interrupted by the quiet and strange tick-tocking that accompanied one of the crocodiles in the water. Then: "No. But I accept it."

James peered at him, and then at the rest of them, locking eyes with them one by one, evaluating. "Then, you will not die. Join me."

He frowned and stepped back onto the ship, eyeing James suspiciously.

"Men as brave as you are rare, in my experience. And I've lost a good many today. Sail under my flag, the lot of you."

The men looked surprised, relieved, confused. James stepped back and folded his arms across his chest. "Do it now, or go to the crocs. The choice is yours."

The large man stepped forward and knelt before James.

"I give you my sword. Daniel Thatcher."

And the tan one. "Cecco."

And the one with the odd hands. "Noodler."

James held his hand out as the four terrified pirates approached him, eyeing a knock-kneed one who'd only just slunk out from behind the wheel.

"Not you. You four cowards will not sail with me. You will take this broken vessel and sail across the rest of the Never Sea and tell all you meet of the terrible and wonderful crew of the *Spanish Main*. And of their brave and horrible Captain, James Hook."

The knock-kneed man stepped back quietly to the wheel, shaking with the other three, and James nodded to his crew to board their own ship again. So they, with three new pirates aboard, released themselves from the ill-fated ship and sailed back to shore. James stared expressionlessly ahead, wishing he could push away the haunting thought that today, when he had killed those pirates, he had killed the dreams of a child, just as Peter had killed his so long ago.

When they were docked again, James chose to ignore the celebrations of his companions. Instead, he looked at the sweat and dirt and blood on his chest and hands and blinked slowly. He quietly made his way out onto the beach and stared over the ocean, wondering if he was imagining the little stripes of blood coming in with the tide. He was almost certain that he was. Nonetheless, he privately, and as quietly as he could, fell to his hands and knees and lost the contents of his stomach in the water.

FIFTEEN

IT WAS SOME TIME BEFORE JAMES DECIDED TO VACATE his room. It was unreasonable, James knew, for death to affect him so when his chosen vocation was captain of a pirate ship. But staring a man in the eyes as he dies, particularly when you are the one causing the dying, is not something one gets over quickly.

He sat on his bed, occasionally relocating to his floor or his closet in the rare moments he decided to change clothes, and he ran his fingers darkly over his sword. Jukes and Starkey came in from time to time attempting to rouse him, Smee delivered him food, and once Cecco came in, offering to clean the blood from his sword. James had refused, rather viciously. He wanted to see it. Wanted to feel it. Wanted to remember the look on that first man's face and on that of the captain. He pondered the strangeness of taking a man's life, not a man's gold or his ship, his *life*, and what were the implications of that when the man was invented anyway? Did a figment of imagination have a soul? Was it worse for him to murder someone if he did or didn't have one?

James didn't know, and neither did the wine. Nothing made him feel better. So, he allowed himself to wallow for a while.

But one evening, when the hurt had finally let up and the boredom set in, he lowered himself into the tub for the bath he'd needed for several Neverdays, ran a comb through his hair, pulled on his trousers and linen shirt, and slung a pack over his shoulder. And, to the open jaws and wide eyes of every man on the *Spanish Main*, he opened the door and stepped off the ship.

The night was crisp, without the coldness of winter or the warmth of the summer. Generally though, nights in Neverland were always crisp. In fact, when James had first become a resident of the island, he'd wondered often if it had any sort of seasons at all. He concluded eventually that it did not.

But the crispness of the night mattered little to James at the moment. He didn't have room in his head for much consideration of the weather. No, with his mind cleared of murderous distractions, he was focusing only on the destination ahead. And that destination consisted of a fire and food, and, he hoped, a beautiful Indian princess.

The forest in Neverland was always darker than he thought it would be. Always darker and always scarier, as though it would eat him up if he forgot, for a moment, where he was. But, James ignored the lick of fear that trailed up his spine and ventured further into the darkness, toward the Indian encampment. He began to doubt himself as he came closer to it, and when he was so close that he could smell the smoke from the fires in the camp, he stopped, intending on doubling back. Surely Tiger Lily would think him a fool for coming out here. She hadn't really invited him, had she? If anything, she'd discouraged him from coming. He sighed forcefully and resolved to head back to the *Main*.

"Leaving so soon?"

James started. "Ah."

"Indeed." Tiger Lily raised an eyebrow and chuckled at him.

He raked a hand through his hair and looked back over his shoulder, toward the beach, and then at Tiger Lily. He chewed the inside of his cheek, corner of his mouth turned up.

Tiger Lily sighed and shook her head. "Really, James. There's no sense in coming all the way out here and then leaving all on my account."

"Your account?" he asked, smirking.

"I doubt you've walked here to see my father." A playful glint sparked in her eye, and James quickly forgot how embarrassed he was supposed to have been.

"No, you're right. I told you; I'm scouting."

He grinned at her and she rolled her eyes, then started to walk in the opposite direction, heading deeper into the forest. The leaves were slow and quiet tonight, silver and blue, and James could not decide if that was ominous or relaxing.

"Where are you going?"

She looked back at him, over her shoulder, and raised an eyebrow. "What do you mean, 'Where am I going?' Follow me, you fool pirate."

James snorted, but followed her anyway, more relieved than his masculine pride wished to admit that he had a guide through the black wood. Eventually, they came upon a large clearing, and Tiger Lily sat right in the middle of it. James walked slowly up to her and sat as well, inexplicably uneasy. There was something off about this place, something he could not put his finger on. He peered at their surroundings, but they were so cloaked in shadow, he could barely see anything.

"What are you looking at?" she asked, burying her hands in the cool grass.

"Nothing, I suppose."

"Well, have you brought anything to make a fire? It's freezing out here."

James opened his pack and pulled out a small piece of flint, which Tiger Lily took from him immediately.

"Excuse me," he said.

"What?"

James frowned. "How am I supposed to build a fire if you've taken my things?"

She just looked at him for a moment, where he, unexplainably, felt very foolish.

"Come now, James. How many fires have you built the entire time you've lived here?"

It was a fair question. The answer was, as Tiger Lily had clearly surmised, none.

James scowled. Tiger Lily just laughed and collected a small pile of kindling from the area where they were seated.

"Have you got any steel with you?"

James shrugged and tossed her his sword.

"Are you serious?"

"Why?" James frowned, glancing at his sword, back to her eyes, lingering there. "What do you need it for?"

She shook her head. "I sincerely hope you never find yourself in the Never Wastes. You'd die in a breath."

James narrowed his eyes.

"This will not do good things to your sword if it takes me long, pirate."

"Well, then don't take long."

Tiger Lily shook her head, clearly trying to disguise the little smile playing on her lips, and took a small box from the folds of her clothes, in which was some sort of black material. She struck the flint against the sword several times, during which James flinched over and over. She succeeded in drawing a few sparks, and they set fire to the black cloth in the box. Before long, there was a small fire glowing in front of them. James's sword, however, was a bit worse for the wear.

James snatched his sword back from her and a jolt of heat traveled up his arms at the little brush of her fingers against his. Tiger Lily warmed her hands, sleeve falling back, exposing her delicate wrist. James looked away. He'd never thought a wrist could be so alluring. Tiger Lily, thankfully, chose this moment to speak and distracted him from the observation.

"Do you always carry that thing with you?" she asked.

James cocked his head. "Generally."

"Why?"

James sat up, quite intentionally looking away from her, focusing on the orange flames waving and jumping into the air. "A pirate's got to have his weapon always, and he's got to be prepared, lest some ruffian catches him unaware."

While he was saying this and staring into the fire, Tiger Lily had gotten up and snuck behind him. He realized this only when he felt the cold of a small blade against his throat and a feminine voice whispering, "Someone like me, you mean?"

His breath caught and his pulse pounded wildly; he could feel her lips against his ear as she spoke, and he prayed she'd do it again. "Perhaps," he mustered, swallowing hard.

"I'd like to see what use your sword would be to you now."

The longer she spoke, mouth touching his skin, the hotter his skin became. "Yes, well, I believe we've established that I'm quite powerless against you."

The blade softened against his throat and he could feel Tiger Lily's smile on his ear, the pulse in her neck jumping against his. She released him, and he leaned over, elbows on his knees, trying to make up for the breath Tiger Lily had stolen when she'd been so close.

It was so strange, after so long avoiding her entirely, to be there with her, letting himself feel the buzzing in his veins and the crackling on his skin when she breathed near him. To wish to kiss her and not be concerned what Peter would think about it.

Tiger Lily cocked her head toward him. "And what would you do if I'd caught you and decided to kill you? Or tortured you for information? If your blade failed you, what would you do then, pirate?"

"I keep this on me as well."

He tossed her a small vial, filled with green liquid. It was a poison he'd dreamed up as a boy, figuring that all good captains must have something deadly on their person, something to drink lest they were caught. It was all very dramatic, but James kept it anyway. An homage to the child who'd died there some time ago.

"Poison?"

"Aye."

Tiger Lily scowled. "That doesn't seem very heroic."

"It isn't. It's a last resort." He held out his hand, not liking the idea of something so deadly being so close to her. She gave it back without protest, and he curled his long, slim fingers around hers momentarily. When he let go, he swore he saw her blush.

Desiring to change the topic from death, he asked her, "Why aren't you back at your camp tonight?"

Tiger Lily sighed. "Apart from the fact that a rogue pirate stole me away?"

"Apart from that." James grinned.

"They're having a celebration tonight, in my honor. Again."

"That doesn't seem so horrible."

Tiger Lily shifted, focused on the leaves upon the ground, picked at them. "Not by itself. But they have these little parties all the time. Whenever Father believes he's found someone suitable for me."

James felt a hot flash of jealousy, and bit down on his tongue.

"Of course, every gathering is wasted. I hate them, and then the wedding is cancelled and life goes on as usual 'til the next one."

He glanced up at her. "You don't wish to get married?"

"No. Never, not to anyone," she said, looking out at the darkness over James's shoulder.

"Why not?"

Her eyes flicked to the scar on James's neck and away again. And then he realized what it was.

"Because of Peter," James said.

Tiger Lily bristled. "Peter? Absolutely not. What would make you say that?"

"You love Peter." A muscle twitched in his jaw, but his voice was soft. "It's all right. Everything on this island does."

He looked away from her darkly, not wanting her to see the expression on his face. Then, without knowing why he asked it, he said, "Has he ever kissed you?"

"Excuse me?" Tiger Lily said, taken aback.

"I've seen him killing Neverbeasts with you, and battling and racing with you and swimming with you. But has he kissed you?"

"No. Of course not."

James felt his pulse spike at that, and he noticed, then, that they were sitting a good deal closer than they'd been at the beginning of the evening.

Tiger Lily narrowed her eyes. "I suppose you've kissed hundreds of women."

James smirked. "Not hundreds."

Tiger Lily pursed her lips.

"Only one," James said. He rather enjoyed the small smile that played at her lips. "Susan Weaver. I was twelve years old, and she was my girlfriend. It was all very romantic and serious." He smiled. "We didn't much know what we were supposed to do, being together, so more often than not, we just held each other's hands or said nice things to each other. But once, she kissed me." He couldn't help but notice the spark of jealousy in Tiger Lily's eyes, and he tried to camouflage the grin in his own. "We kissed quite a bit after that, but I suppose we weren't very good at it. Anyway, eventually, I caught her in the schoolyard holding Edwin Booker's hand, and our committed love affair came to a very explosive end. Tragic, tragic."

He chuckled, remembering how he'd thought it the end of the world. But, the chuckle faded off quickly, for he realized then that he hadn't kissed anyone since. It wasn't the lack of kissing, really, that bothered him. It was the reason for it. There wasn't much opportunity in Neverland, was there?

"Where is this 'Susan' now?"

"Back home."

He said "home" with such longing in his voice, such pain, that it surprised even him.

Tiger Lily bit her lip and moved closer to him. "Where is home?"

"Not here," was all he said. He feared that if he said the word "London," he would start to cry, right there, in front of Tiger Lily. That sort of thing was hardly acceptable when one was a little boy. But it was certainly disallowed when one was a grown man.

"I'm sorry," Tiger Lily said simply, and she laid her head on his chest. He could smell the sweet perfume of her hair as it spread out over his shirt, and her cheek was touching his skin where his shirt laced open. He was not entirely sure what to do, but decided to lay his arm over her shoulder and hold her as long as she allowed, breathing in the scent of her.

"James?" she asked, and his heart jumped at the movement of her lips against his chest.

"Hmmm?"

"Why did you never battle with me? Or swim or play? All that time, I sometimes wondered if you hated me."

James's breath hitched, and he ran his fingers over her arms, then back over the goose bumps he was quite certain he'd put there. "I don't know that I can answer that for you. Or that I should."

She shifted, then, and mumbled something into his shirt.

"I'm sorry?"

"Nothing," she said. "I only said I'd never been kissed before."

James moved back, and Tiger Lily sat up.

"Never? Not even by one of your droves of suitors?"

She hit him in the arm. "No, not even by one of them."

They were both quiet for a minute, each very obviously looking away from the other's face. He slid his fingers over to thread them between hers, over her knuckles on the ground. Then, James looked straight at her and said, in a low voice, "Do you wish to be?"

Tiger Lily's mouth fell open, and she blushed. James held his breath and wondered if he'd been too bold. Perhaps he had. Fool. What was he doing chasing Peter's girl, anyway? He was a dolt, clearly.

"Tiger Lily!" a baritone voice echoed in the clearing.

Tiger Lily leapt up. "Put that fire out. It's my father. I've got to go."

James tightened his grip on her hand. "Don't go."

"I have to, James. What are you doing? Put it out."

He pursed his lips and dropped her hand, then grabbed a handful of dirt and threw it on the barely flickering fire, though it was really more embers than anything at this point.

"Can you find your way back?" she whispered.

"I'm not an idiot. Of course I can."

She turned to leave, then looked back at him. "Are you still sticking to that 'plundering my village' story?"

"Absolutely."

She pinched her chin between her thumb and forefinger and considered him, then smiled mischievously. "Well, then, as Princess, it's my solemn duty to stop you."

"And how do you plan on doing that?"

She grinned. "I suppose I shall have to sneak aboard your ship in the night and kill you. There's no other way."

James stared at her. "Well, then, I shall be waiting for you."

And Tiger Lily disappeared into the dark.

SIXTEEN

<hr>

THE SMOKE DISSIPATED INTO THIN RIBBONS THAT slithered up into the air, little bits clinging to James's clothes and skin. The smell was almost enough to overcome the faint aroma that Tiger Lily had left behind on his shirt, but not quite. For that, he was glad.

A tiny light bounced and bobbed beside him, and he smiled at the sounds of tinkling bells as the fairy passed him. Soon, more followed, and he found that the vague irritation he usually harbored toward the fairies wasn't there tonight. They hated him, generally, because Peter hated him, and more often than not, when they saw him, they would take turns doing frustrating little things like pinching him or kicking him or biting him before fluttering off. But, for whatever reason, they let him be tonight, and he was able to simply enjoy the music of their laughter and the beauty of their glow as they flew and swirled and darted and bobbed about, looking an awful lot like the stars overhead.

He allowed himself to watch the little parade for a few moments, then turned to head out of the clearing. But just as he was a step from the edge, he heard a voice. A voice he was loath to hear at this moment, or at any moment.

"Oh, the cleverness of me!" it shouted.

The blood in James's veins turned to ice. No matter how many times he faced the boy, the thought of him would always make him go cold. He shrunk back behind a tree, fingering his sword, holding his breath, waiting for Peter to pass by. But, he did not appear until after the fairies had left. And then came the boy, prancing into the clearing, hopping and flying and tiptoeing in turn, a single fairy fluttering beside him.

James shrunk closer to the tree that was camouflaging him, suddenly conflicted. A piece of him, inexplicably, found the boy endearing and wanted to smile and to ask him what it was that had him so merry. But, the other part of him was filled with a molten hate. The fury was so consuming he could nearly taste it. It overtook the better-natured part of him, and finally, all he could feel was rage. Rage and a desire for blood. Before he knew it, he was creeping out from behind his tree. And there was Peter, laughing and prancing and unsuspecting.

James drew his sword to his waist and clenched his fingers tightly around it, every muscle in his body shaking with anticipation and terror and the feeling of being wound as tightly as a muscle could be. He took a step forward and a leaf crunched beneath his foot. He froze. Peter dropped immediately to the ground and cocked his head in James's direction. James tried not to breathe.

After a tense minute, Peter returned to his bouncing and bobbing, and James crept out again from his hiding spot, trying to channel Tiger Lily's ghostly quiet. He followed Peter silently until the boy was almost at the edge of the clearing. Before Peter made his way into the wood, James leapt out and charged into him, knocking him into the dirt.

The breath fled Peter's body, citrus flavor flaring into the air, and James drove his shoulder into his back. Peter flung his small body weight back up against James and wriggled out from under him. James tumbled backward, leaves and sticks cracking beneath him. But, everything in him needed Peter's blood. So, with impossible quickness, James leapt back up and forced his head into Peter's stomach. The boy cried out, and James only pushed harder. He barely had to exert force, he found. Peter was so much smaller than he, so much skinnier now. So a breath of extra energy sent Peter tumbling through the air. Peter frantically grabbed at James's long hair as he flew, yanking at it, bringing tears to James's eyes.

James called out in a mixture of fury and pain and threw his arm around Peter's little waist. The boy was light as a fairy. He mustered all the strength in himself and jerked backward, a snap coming from somewhere on Peter he couldn't pinpoint. Peter yelled and once again took a handful of James's hair and flew back, then looked, shocked, at James. There was utter confusion in his eyes as James reached out and grabbed his neck with one hand and his sword with the other. Allowing cold wrath to decide every move for him, he tightened his grip on Peter's neck, fingers almost able to touch in a perfect circle.

He wanted to crush it, wanted, with everything in him, to see Peter writhing on the ground, gasping for breath, and then lying dead still. But somehow he was unable to. Instead, when his mind commanded him to squeeze, he threw the boy down onto the ground. Peter landed with a thud and a strangled string of grunts. Then, James brought out his sword, pupils darkening and growing as the moonlight glistened off the steel. He dropped to the ground, knees on either side of Peter's chest. Peter just gaped up at him, that horrible confusion and denial staring at James, threatening to evoke pity in him. It would not work; it would not, he swore to himself. His heart pounded furiously, his skin flashing hot, heart warring with his mind over what he wished to feel versus what he actually, truly, in the darkest depths of him, *did*.

As his adrenaline wore slightly down, he began to notice little fairies biting at him and pinching at him. He shook his head, grit his teeth, trying his best to ignore them altogether.

James dragged the tip of his sword to Peter's throat, almost feeling the boy's pulse beat against the blade's edge. The sword shook violently with James. And he let out a cry of pure anguish. It was a sob and a growl and a scream all rolled into one. He was still trembling everywhere as he bellowed, "You took everything from me!"

Peter blinked and stared up at him, wondering, perplexed. Then, he frowned. "James Hook?"

"Yes, Pan. James Hook."

"You promised to kill me once," said Peter.

So, *that* he remembered.

Peter looked suddenly, terribly afraid, and the air tasted abruptly of coal and ash. His lower lip began to tremble, and he started to thrash beneath James's greater weight. Pieces of him threatened to float up from the earth, but James was older and much larger and forced him to remain on the ground.

"I will kill you, Pan. I've no choice."

The fairies strengthened their assault, and James could feel little bubbles of blood popping up on his arms, his neck, his thighs.

The blade pressed a little further into Pan's throat. Pan swallowed, Adam's apple bobbing against the metal.

The trees shriveled into themselves, and the sticks on the ground clawed at James's legs.

"Strike, then," Pan said. "Kill me now, and put an end to this adventure. I do not like it anyhow."

The look on his face tore into James's heart. It was the confusion that hurt him so. That, and the profound misunderstanding Pan had regarding death, as though it was nothing, temporary. Hate him though he might, James knew that he was readying himself to kill a child. A child who deserved nothing less than death, but a child nonetheless. Like Peter had killed the child in him so long ago.

That, in truth, was all Peter was—a wicked, selfish boy who thrived on play and imagination and youth and understood nothing of the real world. James's arm shook more and more violently, as did the blade, and he felt a helplessness welling up in him. Though everything in his heart told him to gut the boy and be done with it, he could not. He could not kill Peter Pan.

With his free hand, he reached up and felt the scar on his neck and moved the sword a bit lower. Without letting himself think much on it, he drove the sword's edge past Pan's flesh and flicked, drawing blood and leaving a line across Peter's collarbone that was dripping with blood.

Peter screamed out and arched his back. Then, all the coldness was back in James, and he clapped a hand over Pan's mouth and came close to his face, close enough that he could feel the moisture from the cold sweat on Peter's cheek.

He leaned down until his breath was brushing Peter's ear, and whispered, "I could kill you now, Peter Pan. I could kill you now and not a soul would hear you. You stole my life from me. I could do it."

He pulled back and looked away, into the night sky. Then, back at Peter's wide eyes. And then, more to himself than anyone, "But I won't. I am no brute. I will spare you."

He leaned back, weight off the boy, and Peter scrambled to get up, shooting into the air in a cloud of sticks and leaves and dust. He touched his collarbone and brought his hand away. Bright blood stuck to his fingers.

He looked at James, fear and anger darkening his features. "You cut me."

"I could have killed you," James spat.

Peter smirked. "You didn't. No one wishes to kill the Pan."

"I do," James said, mercy gone again, filled with trembling, pulsating hate.

"Well then, why didn't you? Are you a coward? Yes? None can kill me!"

And Peter spiraled into the air, fairies spiraling below him, and crowed, as though this was a victory for him somehow. James clenched his hand into a fist. He wished he *had* killed him, then. When Peter came back down, he flitted behind and in front of and beside James.

"The pirate captain cannot kill Peter Pan, can he? He couldn't if he tried."

When he came too close, James reached out and grabbed his collar. He drew Peter so close that he could feel the child's breathing on his face.

"I could have easily gutted you tonight, boy. If I'd cut you a centimeter higher, you'd be bleeding out on the leaves."

Peter started to laugh, and that black anger fell again over James. He drew the arm that was not holding Peter across his body and released it like a spring, slamming it into Peter's face, knocking him to the ground in a black cloud of dirt. When Peter floated back up, his features were darkened with rage, fists trembling at his side. Salted licorice flooded in around James's tongue.

"Do not touch me again, pirate," he hissed.

James said nothing.

Peter floated higher into the air. "You will regret this night, James Hook. Mark my words." And he sprung off the air and flew away over the treetops.

James stood there in the clearing, shaking for a while. He dropped his sword, feeling the fullness of the cold in his bone marrow. The darkness curled around him like a blanket, willing him to stay a while, whispering things to him that were at once comforting and terrible. When he could stand no longer, he covered his face with his hands. Then, he dropped to his knees in the dirt and wept.

SEVENTEEN

THE WATER WAS BARELY WARMER THAN ICE, AND THAT suited James just fine. It had been four or five particularly long Neverdays since the incident in the clearing, and James was still reeling from the aftereffects. He'd been doing very little since, apart from contemplating—trying and failing to work up the nerve to go find Tiger Lily, singing quietly to himself when he thought the crew wouldn't hear. Mostly, he was sullen and isolated from the men, though that wasn't particularly out of the ordinary, still kicking himself for not carving the boy up when he'd had the chance, still unable to imagine actually killing him. It was an unfortunate place to be.

James floated in the salt water, the ship's shadow still quite visible. Part of that was because he didn't have the energy for swimming a great distance, and part of it was because, deep in his mind, he heard constantly the taunting voice of Peter, saying, "You will regret this night." And he believed, with every bit of him, that Peter would fulfill the threat. So, he didn't desire to find himself too far from the *Main*. But, he did feel that he needed to get out of his cabin. Swimming in the sea seemed a good decision, in light of this.

He flapped his arms slowly through the glittering nymphs, moving centimeters at a time, relishing the numbing feeling of the water as it prickled against his bare chest and drenched his hair. The only sound in his ears was the sea as it moved in gentle waves to the shore.

That peace was interrupted by a soft splash near the beach.

James sent his feet shooting down into the water, scattering the nymphs, and he peered over the surface. Scrutinizing, searching. There was a dark shadow beneath the water swimming toward him, and he was filled with an overwhelming dread. He knew that it could only be Peter. Heart pounding, anger and fear running together in his veins, he dove under the waves and propelled himself toward the figure, determined that, this time, he would kill Peter if he caught him.

Salt water poured off his muscles and shone in the red-gold light of the setting suns as he came up for breath. He dove beneath the water again, seeing that the shadow was moving closer, determined to reach it before it reached him. Finally, his legs bumped into a body, and he grabbed it with his powerful arms, pulling it up, breaking the surface of the sea.

His eyebrows shot up when he saw that it was not Peter, but Tiger Lily. She coughed and shook her head fiercely, spraying water everywhere.

"Is there a time you're not going to assault me upon meeting me?" she yelled.

James's mouth fell open. Perhaps it was time he stop assuming that everyone in the vicinity was looking to murder him. In all fairness, that was hard to do when he was the only sworn enemy of Peter Pan in a world that loved the boy.

"I'm sorry; I thought you were..." He paused. "... someone else."

Tiger Lily pursed her lips and lowered her voice. "Are you going to let me go, then?"

James realized then that Tiger Lily was pressed very tightly against him—and, being that he was wearing no shirt and very thin pants and she was soaked and every piece of her clothing was clinging to her, he could feel all of her on his skin. He pushed her away with much more force than he intended.

Tiger Lily frowned.

"What are you doing out here, anyway?" he asked her.

She pursed her lips. "Well, I was going to sneak into your quarters and kill you like I promised, but then I saw your boots and shirt on the shore, and there you were, splashing about. I figured heading into your room wasn't a good mode of assassination if you weren't there."

James smirked.

"Don't worry," she said. "I'll get you yet." And she smiled wickedly back at him.

They floated in the water for a bit before Tiger Lily shivered.

"It's frigid out here, you know. It wasn't nice of you to entice me into the ocean and fool me into thinking it warm."

James scoffed. "I don't remember inviting you in."

"Even so."

"So you're angry with me because *you* stalked *me* all the way out here and jumped in the sea in the middle of the cold?"

She folded her arms across her chest. "Yes."

James swam a bit closer to her until he was much nearer than he'd ever been to her face. The sky lit it up in such a way that she was even more breathtaking than he remembered, streaks of glittering gold and bright pink and deep crimson playing on her eyelashes, her high cheekbones. Without thinking, he slid his arms around her through the water and pressed her close to him again. The chattering of her teeth came to an abrupt halt.

"And now?"

Her breathing was ragged, and he could feel her pulse racing at his touch, which sent his heart pounding even faster than it had been.

"I…" She looked away, and he could see the conflict written plainly across her face. He let go of her then, not wishing to be a part of her inner turmoil, and started to swim back to shore.

"Where are you going?"

"To my ship."

"And what am I supposed to do?"

He hesitated. Then: "Come with me. The men are below deck now anyway. No one will see you."

Tiger Lily treaded water for a moment, then followed him back to shore. James deliberately did not look back as she followed him, fearing he would do something stupid if he saw her as he imagined she looked—dripping, fabric sticking to her everywhere, lit up by the sunsets.

They both slogged across the sand in silence, James unable to banter wittily, too focused on not looking back at her. Tiger Lily was mimicking the silence, so the walk was uneventful. When they got to the ship, James held his hand out behind him, still focused on looking straight ahead, and Tiger Lily took it. Her hand was cold and delicate, and James found himself wanting to grasp it and pull her closer to him, but at the same time not wanting to break it.

They climbed on board with no real incident, and, upon reaching his cabin, James gently pulled her in front of him, so as to retain gentleman status and allow the lady to pass through the door ahead of him. He pushed open the door and she walked past him, and it was at this point that he lost the battle with his eyes altogether.

He had been right; that dress clung to her in a way that accentuated everything, silhouetting her in the most distracting way. His mouth went dry as he took in the soft shape of her breasts, her stomach, her legs. She brushed against him as she passed, and that sent a flare of heat up his body and a chill down his back. He looked away, focusing very intently on his dresser.

"Do you want something dry?" he asked, voice rough as he pulled the door closed.

"Please."

James rummaged through his drawers and pulled out a long white shirt. Everything in his wardrobe looked the same, so it matched the one he chose for himself. Credit that to the creativity of a twelve-year-old. He held it out to her and she took it from him, touch lingering on his fingertips. He turned away from her and walked to the other end of the cabin.

James pulled a clean shirt over his torso, deciding to keep his wet pants on. It seemed indecent to strip in front of her. So, half-dry, half-soaked, he stood in the corner of the room. James stared, unblinking, at the wooden walls as he heard her wet clothes drop to the floor and his bed creak lightly. He brought his fist to his mouth and tried to think of anything but the fact that Tiger Lily was sitting naked on his bed.

"You're quite the gentleman," Tiger Lily said.

James took this as an invitation to turn around. He wished immediately that he'd let her stay in the wet clothes. Watching her sit there in his oversized and threadbare shirt, big enough to make her look small, small enough that it barely covered her thighs, was infinitely worse.

"Sit with me," Tiger Lily prompted.

"I'd rather not, I think."

She furrowed her brow and looked away from him, at everything in his room. Within seconds, his resolve weakened. His feet were stubbornly pulling him toward her, despite his protests, and he found himself sitting on the bed then, much closer than he wanted to be. Heat radiated off her, pricking his skin. His gaze was pulled to her bare collarbone, exposed from beneath the undone laces of his shirt. And then, it trailed lower.

"James?"

James jumped. "Yes?"

"You haven't heard a word I've said."

"I'm sorry."

"You're distracted."

He swallowed hard. "Somewhat."

She bit her lip. "Perhaps I should go."

Tiger Lily stood from the bed. James grabbed her wrist.

"Please. Don't."

She pursed her lips and looked down at him. Eventually, she consented and sat.

"What's got you so distracted?"

He paused. He couldn't very well say it was the transparent spot her wet hair was forming in the shirt, or the fact that, inexplicably, despite just having had a swim in the ocean, she still managed to smell like flowers. So, he said something else inappropriate.

"Peter."

He regretted the word as it left his lips.

Tiger Lily raised her eyebrows. "Peter?"

James sighed and his shoulders slumped. "Always Peter. Have you seen him lately?"

She was quiet when she said, "Yes. You have as well?"

"Oh yes. I have."

Tiger Lily furrowed her brow.

"You needn't worry," James said, lips twisting. "I didn't hurt him. Much."

Tiger Lily glared at him and shrunk back. "What does that mean?"

"It means I chose not to kill him, which is rather a large thing for me."

"What did you do?" She jumped up from the bed, anger emanating from her, wet hair sticking to her face. James rose with her.

"I encountered him. In the woods. I could have killed him in an instant. But I chose not to, and that's the end of it."

She set her jaw. "You're lying."

James looked away from her eyes, voice still hard and cold. "I may have sliced him up a bit."

Tears sprung to Tiger Lily's eyes, and James wished deeply that he hadn't said anything.

"You hurt him? How could you?"

James's mouth fell open. "How could I? What I did to him will barely leave a scar, Tiger Lily. What he did to me, what he took…"

Tiger Lily shook her head and bent to gather up her sopping mess of clothes from the floor. James reached for her arms. "You don't understand."

Tiger Lily jerked her arms away and met his eyes with defiance. "Then explain to me, James Hook."

"You were *there*, woman. Don't you remember the night we met? The night you found me crying in the forest?"

Tiger Lily's eyes flicked to the ground. "Yes."

"Did you suppose that was for nothing? It was him. That wretched boy. He took me away from London—" when he said "London," his voice cracked horribly, "—and promised me he would take me home. He swore it to me. He swore." With that, he broke down. The emotion was too raw and overpowering for him to feel anything else; he was unable even to feel self-conscious for losing control in front of this woman.

Tiger Lily softened and sat back on the bed, and James fell into her, sobs wracking his body. He clung to her like a lifeline, fingers digging into her shoulders, inhaling that lily-sweet smell that was thrilling and soothing all at once. Tiger Lily ran her fingers through his hair and down his back, whispering over and over small sounds that meant nothing to him, a language he did not understand. But her touch was comforting, and eventually, the anguish inside him cooled and he laid his head in her lap.

She didn't recoil; she only kept her fingers playing at his scalp and the nape of his neck. A peace he hadn't known since he'd been spirited away to Neverland fell over him, and every muscle in his body relaxed. His mind cleared and he could only feel the calming warmth of her legs against his cheek, the softness of her fingertips. And Pan, for once, meant little.

He lay there with her like that for a while, and he did not know how long it had been when she moved just slightly under the weight of him.

"I have to go," she said softly.

He did not argue, for he knew she could not stay.

"Thank you," he whispered, throat raw from crying.

"You need not thank me," she said, and she bent over and kissed him on the cheek, her lips feather-light and soft and sweet. He sat up from her lap and stared at her for a moment. Then he grabbed her hand as she made a move to leave.

"Come find me again," he whispered.

"I told you I would."

Wearing his shirt and holding her clothes, Tiger Lily left the ship. James lay back on the mattress, utterly exhausted, sleep refusing to acquiesce him. And so, for quite a while, or it seemed that way, he lay there and thought of Tiger Lily, until slumber finally made its bed with him. When he woke, for the first time, it was not to the ghost of Peter Pan. For once, when he woke, he was completely alone.

EIGHTEEN

T HE SHIP WAS QUIET, AND, UNUSUALLY, JAMES WAS not in a foul mood. He lay in his bed, hands clasped beneath his head, and stared up at the ceiling. Though Pan was a constant somewhere in the recesses of his mind, on this morning, the boy was buried very deep. Consuming James's thoughts was a woman.

He wondered what she was doing at this moment, if she was spearing a deer or swimming in the lagoon or fending off a barrage of suitors. He wondered when she would choose to come see him again. Most of all, he wondered if she was thinking about him as well.

There was a soft knock at his door, and James was so content, he didn't even conjure a glower.

"Come in."

Smee tottered in, smiling and apologetic. Smee was always at least one or the other, James found. He was not a usual sort of pirate. For whatever reason, that pleased James.

"Captain?" he asked in a quiet voice.

"Aye."

Smee's eyes were darting around the room and he was clasping his hands tightly and rubbing them together.

"Speak, Smee."

"Oh, it's nothing, sir. Nothing at all. Forget I said a thing."

James rolled his eyes. "Out with it, man."

Smee chuckled nervously and busied himself in James's cabin, arranging crooked things and closing drawers all the way and picking up a cloth to polish things. James thought that this was more uncomfortable than whatever it was Smee could have had to say.

The anxious pirate bent to pick up something on the floor and stopped for a moment, then sighed. His face was beet red when he held out a thin, beaded necklace to the captain.

"Someone dropped this, it seems."

Ah. Tiger Lily. That's what this was about.

"Give it here," James said, sitting up. He took the piece of jewelry from Smee's slightly shaking hand. "Are you truly that afraid of me?"

Smee laughed. "I fear I'm just about this afraid of everyone."

He looked down bashfully and James found that he was unable to be annoyed with the man for his timidity. "Say what you came to say, Smee."

Smee let out a breath and crisscrossed his fingers, then sat on the chair by James's desk. His bottom was too large for the chair and it puffed over the edges a bit. He crossed his plump legs as well, looking more and more awkward by the second.

"Well, Captain, it's just that, I wondered if—I was wondering if the lady princess was going to be staying here often."

James raised an eyebrow. "Lady princess?"

"The princess, sir, yes. Tiger Lily," Smee said, fiddling with his fingers.

"What leads you to believe she's been here at all?"

Smee refused to meet his gaze, concentrating instead on every item that was not James in the room.

"Smee," James said, hitting his bed frame. Smee twitched. "Answer me."

He bit his lips and puffed out his cheeks. "Well, it's only that I saw her leaving your quarters last night, Captain, and I just assumed…"

"Assumed what?" James barked.

Smee jumped, and the timbre of his voice rose instantly. "Captain, don't think I'm undermining you or challenging you or saying anything about your captainship."

"Go on," James said, voice lowered, eyes narrowed.

"It's just, I wonder at the risk. We've already made enemies of the mermaids, and Peter hates us even more than he already did, if that's possible. I only hope we don't provoke the Indians, too."

James knew that what Smee was saying was not in challenge to his authority and that Smee was shaking in his boots being there at all, but still, he found himself getting defensive.

"So, you believe it your job to enter my quarters in the middle of the morning and control whom I do and do not see?"

"No, Captain," he said, alarm written all over him.

"And you've enough foolish gumption to come and tell me that I'm getting us into too many skirmishes for your taste?"

Smee was nearly bouncing in his chair at this point. "Captain, I'd never—"

"And you presume to ascertain the nature of my relationship with Tiger Lily when you know *nothing* of it, other than a memory of someone you thought you saw vacating my quarters in the middle of the night?"

James had stood from his bed and towered over the blustering Smee.

"I don't mean to overstep, sir. Please, don't take it that way."

"Well, you have."

Smee looked downward and folded his hands in his lap. He looked so glum that James couldn't help but feel sorry for him. He would have to banish this empathy from himself, whenever he figured out how. As of yet, he hadn't, and so his voice softened, quite without his permission. Smee reminded him so of his mother that he was unable to maintain any sort of anger at the man for a decent length of time.

"Smee," he said, voice low, drumming his fingers on his desk, "my relationship with Tiger Lily is something you needn't concern yourself over. Do you understand?"

Smee nodded.

"Nor is the amount of enemies we've made on the island. That's a captain's consideration, and a captain's job. Not a cook's."

Smee nodded and folded his hands, looking miserable.

James sighed and rolled his eyes. "Get up, man."

James reached for his boots, and sat, pulling them over his calves one at a time, and Smee nearly knocked his little chair over in an effort to obey.

"Since you did ask, Mr. Smee, Tiger Lily will likely be spending a somewhat significant amount of time aboard the *Main* in the coming days."

"As you wish, sir."

James smiled to himself and fixed his hat atop his head. A captain was only really half a captain without his hat, after all. After Smee waddled out of his chair and onto the deck, James followed suit, boots *clack-clacking* on the hard floor.

The suns were shining brightly, and the men were up and working. James beamed, and beaming was an action he rarely took. The sea was a bright blue, and active, all manner of sea-creatures swimming around in it. Little blue dolphins jumping and splashing, glowing nymphs dotted here and there, a large purple sea turtle. Even the usually foreboding forest looked merry, and the ocean begged to be sailed upon. The various trinkets they'd stolen on their voyages glistened in the bright morning air. Today was a good day to be a pirate.

James breathed in the humid ocean air, looking over the vast and endless sea, and smiled. But something at the edge of the horizon caught his eye. There was a strange shape in the clouds, and an odd color. It looked as though someone had been working on a bright blue patchwork quilt and a foolish friend had sewn in just one patch that was the wrong color. There, at the odd-looking cloud, the sky was a dark, purplish grey.

The sky in the distance started to swirl, as though it was preparing for something truly horrid. James furrowed his brow and peered in its direction. The longer he stared, the stranger and larger and darker it became, until his entire crew had stopped working and they were all looking at the sky. It spun and mixed and wound around itself, looking strange and beautiful and horrifying at once. And the air tasted a bit like pepper.

James nodded slowly to himself. The weather was behaving in a way it only did when it was linked to a very specific island native. James knew without a doubt that it was he. Peter Pan was coming. Coming to make good on his promise. Yes, James knew with absolute certainty for whom the weather was twisting, before he felt the shift in the wind or saw the sea rumble or heard the distant crow echoing amongst the trees.

He readied himself, as he always did when he expected a battle with Peter, and stood on the eerily quiet hull of the *Spanish Main*. Another crow, haunting and soft, and James steeled his nerves, preparing his mind to murder a child.

NINETEEN

J AMES'S COAT BILLOWED, A FLURRY OF RED AND GOLD
behind him, and he stood overlooking the vast, darkly
churning landscape of Neverland. Any minute now, the boy
he hated would come flitting through the trees, searching
for an adventure. That adventure, James was quite certain,
would involve the Pan attempting to kill him. And what
choice had he then but to slay the boy?

It set him all aquiver, the thought of robbing the boy
of his breath, of slitting his throat, of stopping his heart.
The quivering, however, came only partly from eager
anticipation. The other piece of it came from dread. He
hated to acknowledge that, for it seemed terribly unmanly,
or at least unpirately—and certainly uncaptainly. But it
was the truth. He knew that, despite his intentions, he
was affected by Pan's spell just as was the rest of the
cursed island. Perhaps that was why it was so impossible
to imagine doing the deed.

Not only that, but there was something that felt foul
in the idea of killing a person so young. Although in truth,
Peter was only a few years younger than him—fourteenish
to James's somewhere-around-twenty—those few years,
between people so young, felt like a lifetime. So his spirit
recoiled, as if, the instant he did it, he would lose the last
shred of innocence his soul so desperately clung to. That,

in that moment, he would be stealing another's childhood, and his heart would become like that of the Pan's.

Truthfully, that was the thing he feared most.

There came a whispering through the leaves on the trees. One that spoke of the boys who were on their way, the side for whom all of Neverland would be rooting, and the tense nature of a place in the seconds before battle. And then, there came a deadly quiet.

"Where is the captain, captain, Captain Hook?" sang a loud voice, faceless behind the trees. But all knew to whom it belonged.

"Off to find the captain, captain, Captain Hook."

James shuddered despite himself and drew out his sword along with the rest of his crew, trying not to imagine that the voice was coming from a spirit who could best him at every turn. Starkey took a step toward him, shielding him.

"Ah, and there's the captain, captain, Captain Hook."

Peter emerged from the forest, hovering just a bit above the ground and grinning from ear to ear. The air that flooded in around James was sickly sweet, almost nauseating. And the green grass swayed in time to Peter's song.

"Going to bleed the captain, captain, Captain Hook."

James's hand faltered a bit; the metal of his sword was suddenly extremely heavy. Bill Jukes drew closer to him as well, elbow propping the sword up, so no one saw that James was weak. Peter shot closer to the *Spanish Main* until he was upon it, his fingertips resting lightly on the edge of the boat. Only half his face was visible; James could just see his red hair, laced with sparkling tendrils of gold, and his excited eyebrows and squinting eyes, which gave the final verse of Pan's song a strange quality.

"Going to kill the captain, captain, Captain Hook."

Peter leapt easily up and stood, bare feet on the ship's ledge, hands on his hips. The hide and moss he wore was falling off his shoulder, but he didn't seem to mind. James could see in Peter's eyes, the boy was thinking only of blood. No one made a sound, save for Pan's Lost Boys, who were dutifully scaling the side of the *Main*.

"Why don't you let them fly with you, Peter?" James asked, though he knew it was an inappropriate time.

Peter cocked his head. Then, he grinned. "I'm the only one allowed to fly into battle, James Hook. It's the rules."

"Ah, we've added another to our list, have we?"

Peter shrugged.

"Are you quite certain you want to take part in this little adventure?" James said.

James was being very obviously overly polite. It seemed to give the boy pause, and he didn't reply for a moment. But then: "I am."

"Foolish boy."

Peter lowered his brow and stared at James from the tops of his bright eyes, strands of hair blowing around with the wind. It made him look especially wicked. "Do not say such things to me, pirate."

"I'm only attempting fairness," James said, voice calm and even. "I think it unsporting to invite you into a battle you believe you can win."

Peter threw back his head and laughed, floating up into the grey air, and then came back down. "Everyone knows I'll beat you."

James's pirates snarled and sneered, and James raised an eyebrow. "Do they?"

The Lost Boys hopped over the ship's edge one by one.

"Of course they do," said Pan. "This is Neverland. I cannot lose."

James's face took on a sinister quality and he lowered it and glared at the Pan. Then, he held out a single finger and beckoned him.

After that, the *Spanish Main* became an instant flurry of activity. Several Lost Boys, boys he recognized— Tootles, Bibble and Bobble, Simpkins—all drew their tiny swords and sprinted into the fray, children's battle cries accompanying them. It twisted a tight knot in James's stomach, which he resolutely ignored.

His band of pirates charged back. There was general clanging and sliding and scratching and gruff yelling as the battle began, but James could hardly afford to pay attention to the boys, Lost or otherwise, whether or not his heart was urgently pointing him toward his old friends. He had a much more immediate concern.

The bloodthirsty child leapt here and there, flitting from gangplank to crow's nest to the side of the boat in impossibly quick jumps. James struggled to keep up, pupils darting this way and that.

"Up here, old man!" Peter laughed.

James turned to see where the noise had come from.

"Oh, too slow. And here I am again."

James spun in a full circle, looking a fool. Laughter bubbled out of Peter, and James let out a harsh cry of exasperation.

"Come and fight me like a man, boy!"

Peter stopped mid-air, long enough for James to fix his eyes upon him.

"Stupid pirate," he spat. "I do nothing like a man!"

James realized then that he was quite close to his cabin, and he backed up against it, splinters digging against his back, not because he was frightened, but because he knew it would force Peter to come to him. And force him it did, for the child could not go long without a violent activity. Patience, Peter Pan did not possess.

Peter flew down at him, dagger out, and James broke his lean and stood erect. He swung his strong arm and clanged his sword against the boy's, much harder than Peter could ever hope to do. The sheer momentum of it sent Peter tumbling in a somersault to the ground, but he simply rolled into a standing position, deftly, as though he'd meant to do it.

"Here I am, *Captain* James Hook," he called, voice taunting, words themselves nearly sneering.

"So you are."

Peter set his fists at his sides. "Come and try to gut me again."

"I assure you, that is not in your best interest," James said, an arrogant smile quirking his lips.

"Ha! Last I knew, you were too much of a codfish to do anything to me at all."

James's gaze brushed Peter's collarbone. Not even a scar.

This boy, this wretched boy.

"I promise you, Pan, your fate will not be the same should I catch you again."

Peter's eyes sparkled as they circled each other. The hullabaloo was going on around them, but James could hear nothing of it. He nearly forgot that anyone else was there, so focused was he on the child and his blade. James took a step toward Peter and Peter shot into the air, then landed on the deck with a *thump*. Peter made a move to fly at him, and James pointed his sword at the boy's heart.

"Improved at swordplay, I see, old man."

"Indeed."

"But still afraid of me." Pan opened his mouth in a twisted grin.

"What gives you that impression?" James's heart crashed against his rib cage, in time with the thunder, acknowledging that what Peter said was true. But his face gave away none of the terror he felt.

"Because every time I look at you wrong, you flinch! Ugly old pirate. A braver man would have swung his sword at me by now."

James's fingers twitched against his sword. "And a smarter child would know enough to keep his mouth shut and not taunt his elders so."

The proud look on Peter's face was what baited the captain, and he could not stop himself from lunging at him. Peter's wild eyebrows raised and he smiled brightly and met James's sword with his smaller blade. James pressed on, throwing his body weight behind the sword, and breathed into Peter's face.

"I could kill you now, Pan."

"Do it, then," Peter hissed, and he pushed James off him. Then, the duo was back to circling one another.

"I could do this for ages," Pan boasted.

"I already have."

Peter lunged at James, who easily parried the strike, and again, with the same result. Then, he darted upward, knife in his mouth, and plunged to the deck behind him, kicking him in the back. James tumbled over, slipping on a pool of blood, he didn't know whose, and landed on his hands and knees on the worn wood. He flipped around quickly, brandishing his sword, unhappy to be on the ground but decidedly more comfortable facing Peter than having him at his back.

Peter was above him then, knocking into him, pushing the breath from him. He was strong, for a boy. They grappled for a minute on the ground. It was all very undignified, kicking him in the groin, being bitten in the shoulder, grabbing him by the throat.

And then, with his right hand clasped around Peter's windpipe, James stopped. His ears perked up as he heard a strange *tick-tock, tick-tock, tick-tock,* the one that had accompanied that crocodile a short time earlier. Without intending to remove himself from the fight, he turned his head instinctively to find the direction from whence the phantom sound was coming.

Without warning, there was a searing pain just above his wrist, as though someone had taken a sledgehammer to it. *Tick-tocking* forgotten entirely, he turned and cried out. Where he'd once had a hand, there was nothing but mutilated flesh. Bone, muscle, vein, everything splintered.

Pan smiled devilishly and floated up and away from him, holding James's severed hand in his own. James paled and gasped for breath, yelling out with every bit of oxygen he had left. He was certain that the real pain hadn't yet set in, and nor had the realization. He could not truly believe, even if he'd wanted to, that the hand in the child's fingers was his own.

James sat, dumbstruck, clutching his stump of an arm, as crimson blood soaked his jacket and dripped onto the floor. He looked up, somehow both horrified and numb, as Peter flung the hand over the ship's edge. Despite his handicap, James scrambled, crawling, one-armed, to the end of the boat, and stared, wide-eyed, as his hand landed in the open jaws of the crocodile.

The croc's eyes looked the same as Peter's—heartless, cold, and indecently, unusually satisfied with the taste of his blood. Pan spun into the air, twirling over and over, and crowed as he always did. The Lost Boys and pirates stopped their fighting, and every person on the boat turned to look at James.

James met, for only an instant, Bibble's eyes. They were large and dark and sad and horrified, and James's chest was a playground for all sorts of terrible emotions. The chief one was stabbing and aching all at once—betrayal.

He turned his face away from Bibble, his *friend*, struggling to breathe, and knelt on the floor, blood soaking the knees of his pants. He turned his attention to the nothing at the end of his arm, still in shock.

When the battling was over and there was only silence and Peter's whooping in the air, that was when the pain set in. James breathed in and out shortly for several seconds, then let out a scream that was different than any sound he'd ever heard or made. It was pure anguish and rage. He screamed for several breaths until he was lying on the floor, and the corners of his eyes started to go dim, and everyone was gone but he and his pirate crew.

There was a great deal of chatter then, and a furious amount of activity around him, but James barely paid heed to any of it. He was nearly delirious from pain and loss of blood. He made out a few words here and there.

"He be bleedin' out, lads. He'll be dead in a moment."

"His entire hand. His hand! And did you see the crocodile?"

"Wait, I've got it. The coals! Pick him up; bring him to my cooking pit."

James's head lolled around as they picked him up from the deck, and he felt himself fading in and out of consciousness. Then, they thumped him down. He could feel heat rising like soft wool around him and smiled.

"Someone, grab his arm. No, the other one, idiot. The right one, with the blood all over it."

"Sit him up straight."

James was dizzy. He wished they would all shut up for a moment so he could go to sleep. Couldn't they see he was sleepy?

"I'm terribly sorry, Captain," said Smee's gentle voice.

There was a horrible sizzling and burning at the edge of his arm, and then there was nothing.

TWENTY

GONE. MISSING. SEVERED. DETACHED. DEPARTED. There were lots of ways to describe James's conspicuously absent hand, but none he could wrap his mind around. He could not really convince himself that not only had a rather important piece of him vacated his wrist, but it was likely that it no longer existed at all. It wasn't waiting somewhere, eager to reattach itself to him; it was somewhere in the belly of a crocodile, being digested.

He sat in the warm sand at the shore of the Never Sea, nymphs and other small sea creatures flowing in with the tide and back out again, but he paid no attention to them. He flexed his left hand over and over again, marveling at the complexity of the muscles and the veins, checking occasionally to see if somehow the one on his right had reappeared. It felt sometimes as though it had; strangely, he could still feel it doing hand-like things from time to time. But, each time his nerves deceived him, his eyes reminded him of the truth.

"Captain?" said Starkey, approaching his right side.

James did not answer.

"There's something I'd like you to see."

James continued staring at his hand. Starkey sighed. Likely the entire crew was used, by now, to James's melancholy. Ever since the incident, he hadn't interacted much with anyone, except to occasionally eat or drink.

He cocked his head. "Why do you suppose it ticks, Starkey?"

Starkey jumped at James's voice. "Beggin' yer pardon?"

"Why does it tick? The crocodile?"

Starkey cleared his throat and furrowed his brow. "Eh, well, I imagine it's because some time ago, it swallowed a clock. Been tickin' ever since."

"Hm."

James's mind went blank again, and he returned to flexing and stretching his remaining hand.

"Captain, I hate to force you up from the beach, but I've got somethin' for you. Somethin' I've made. I think it'll brighten you up," Starkey said, staring straight into James's vacant eyes.

James pursed his lips and rolled his eyes up to Starkey. Starkey was something of a persistent man. He felt a vague current of irritation but rose from the sand anyway and stood on the shore for a moment before finally deciding to walk toward the *Main*. They boarded the vessel together, and James turned to his crewman, arms folded expectantly.

"A moment, Captain," Starkey said, and he walked off down the beach, disappearing into a tiny cave near the shore.

James stood there, ignoring the open stares of his crewmen, trying not to look at the awful stump at the end of his arm. It had healed nicely and was no longer painful to the touch, but it was peppered with little spots and burn scars, reminders of the terrible coals. After what felt like several minutes, Starkey clopped up onto the ship, cleared his throat, and James turned.

In Starkey's hand was a shiny cuff, delicately filigreed with leaves and vines and several other markings James couldn't quite make out from where he stood. Attached to the top of the silvery cuff was a hook. It was perfectly crafted, thick and with a wicked curve, bright and gleaming, and deadly sharp. James's mouth fell open, and something foreign, murky, but decidedly positive, bloomed in his chest. Something like gratitude.

"Where did you get this?"

Starkey looked almost embarrassed. "Made it."

James almost smiled. "Made it? How?"

"Blacksmithin's somethin' I've always done. I've got a little makeshift smithy over there in that cave." He cocked his head down the beach. "Just seemed right to give ye somethin' that matched your name. Should fit." Starkey nodded once, not looking directly at James's face.

James took the hook and tested it in his hand. It was heavy and solid. A finely crafted piece, and quite pirately. Then, he looked at Starkey, with something that wasn't quite a smile, but wasn't a scowl either. James stared at the contraption for a beat and tossed it up lightly and caught it. Then, he bent his right arm until he was looking straight at the horrible stump, and he fastened the cuff upon it, tightening the little leather straps that hung from it and tucking them beneath the silver. It was a perfect fit.

He swung his arm in the air several times, enjoying the feeling of something weighty where his hand used to be. It turned out that he rather liked it, more than he let on. He acknowledged Starkey with the grimmest of looks and headed over to his cabin, nodding without humor to the men who smiled at the cruel arm piece as he walked by. Jukes seemed particularly impressed, frowning at the hook and back to his own arm. James wondered for a moment if the man wasn't considering lopping his own hand off. He chuckled and slipped into his room.

James stared at himself in his floor-length mirror, as he was wont to do, and swished the hook in front of himself several more times. Then, he brought it across himself, noting with satisfaction just how threatening he looked now with the weapon fixed to him. He was scowling menacingly when he heard a creak behind him. He whirled to find his door cracked just slightly open.

James frowned, and his gaze darted around the room. "Who's there?"

There was no answer.

He paced to his bed, and again, "Who is there?"

He grabbed for his sword, rubbing his fingers over the hilt, and his gaze moved to his closet, full of linen shirts and boots and pants that all looked the same. But, one little thing was out of place. There was a small brown ankle peering out at him from beneath the clothes.

"An assassin then," he said, forgetting about his hook and his sword. He grinned as he pushed back his clothes and found Tiger Lily standing there, hair cascading down her shoulders in lightly tangled waterfalls.

"I wanted you to find me," she said, proud nonchalance in her expression. She stepped out of his closet, little strands of hair still clinging to James's clothes.

"Did you?" James raised a brow.

"Yes, because—"

She stopped, eyes fixated on something. James followed her stare and was shocked, once again, by the absence of his hand, but only for a moment.

"Your hand!" Tiger Lily shouted, cupping her hands over her mouth.

"You don't prefer the hook?" James asked darkly. "I rather think it suits me."

"What happened?" Her face was a mask of concern, and her fingers reached for the metal.

James shrank back.

"What happened, James?" Her voice was high and terribly sincere, unusual. She took a step toward him and something fluttered in his chest.

James took a step back and scowled. He was loath to admit that her boy had bested him in a fight; it was humiliating that the child had not only taken his hand, but he'd fed it as a snack to a crocodile.

"It doesn't matter. I'm a pirate; we put ourselves and our hands in constant danger."

Tiger Lily bit her lower lip and said, in a voice that barely registered above a whisper, "It was him, wasn't it?"

James spun around, face vicious. "Why would you assume it was him? You believe he'd beat me, too?"

She did not back away from his ferocity, but instead straightened taller. "No, James, and don't behave like a child. I say it because there's a look you get only when you're talking about Peter, and it's all over your face."

James faltered, softening immediately. "I'm sorry."

Tiger Lily hesitated. Then, "He cut off your hand?"

"Yes. And *fed it* to a crocodile."

"Why?"

A muscle jerked in James's jaw. "Because the Pan will never fight fair."

Tiger Lily looked downward and sat on his bed. James sat with her, allowing himself to get a bit closer than he normally would. She moved just a mite closer to him as well, and James wondered if he'd imagined it. He couldn't trust his perception of reality; her mere presence intoxicated him.

But, he looked down at the small space between them and was met with the sight of that wretched hook, a hook that would never hold her or touch her the way a man was meant to touch a woman. Who, after all, would choose the feel of cold metal against her skin when she could have the fingertips of any man she wanted?

"How long has it been this way?" she asked him.

"Not long. It happened just after you left. Several Neverdays, I suppose. And I was only just given the hook."

"It makes you look ever the pirate," she said, a slight hoarseness in her soft voice.

James stared down at the hook. "It does, doesn't it?"

Her hair touched his face when she bent a bit to look at it, and he closed his eyes and breathed deeply, air shaking in his lungs. It always hurt him when she did things like that, but unmet longing was a sweet sort of pain.

"Does it hurt?"

"Not so much. Not anymore. I can't feel anything, really."

She touched the iron of his hook, then, and he noticed that her hand was trembling.

"You can't feel this?"

"No." He shook his head.

"And this?" Tiger Lily moved her hand up to his wrist.

A frown crossed James's face for a moment but left quickly. He could feel her pulse pounding in her wrist, hammering in time with his own.

"Yes," he said. A rush of nervous energy as her nails brushed over his arm.

"And here. Can you feel me here?"

James's breath started to come quickly and raggedly as Tiger Lily trailed her fingers up to his collarbone. She was breathing strangely too, and he noticed a light flush in her cheeks and the hard pounding of her pulse.

"Yes," James whispered.

"And here?" Tiger Lily stopped when her face was a breath away from his.

James stared at her eyes. They were large and questioning, and, he knew, terrified.

Of him? Terrified, somehow, that *he* would not reciprocate?

There was total stillness in the room as Tiger Lily froze and James wondered. And then, because he'd been waiting to do it forever, and he could hold himself back no longer, he reached out his hand to grasp the back of her head and pulled her toward him, meeting her mouth in a fiery outpouring of longing and desire.

She tasted like nectar, and he kissed her so deeply that he could feel it everywhere, in every part of him. Tiger Lily wove her small hand in the curls at the base of his neck and he lost himself in the smell of her hair, the taste of her mouth, the feel of her skin.

Before he wished it to be over, Tiger Lily suddenly jerked back. He furrowed his brow, desperate to find a way to get her into his arms again. But Tiger Lily cried out and jerked harder.

"Tiger Lily—"

James shrank back in horror, then, for he saw a piece of his hook embedded in her shoulder, and blood dripping from the wound. James removed it as quickly as he could and leapt up, tearing a strip from one of his shirts to bandage it. She grabbed at her shoulder, fat red drops falling between her fingers and trickling down over her knuckles, her hand, landing on his bedspread. He felt it like a punch to the gut when he saw her taking small gasping breaths and trying like the devil not to cry.

When he pushed the fabric to her shoulder, she winced, and there was another stabbing pain in him. "I'm so sorry, Tiger Lily; I didn't mean it."

"I—I know," she said in a strangled whisper, teeth clenched.

"I forgot myself. I'm so sorry. I'm so sorry."

He was beside himself, frantically wiping up the blood from her arm and the floor, wishing furiously, not for the first time, that he'd never had his hand robbed from him. He touched her cheek with his left hand, desperately searching her eyes for a hint of forgiveness. He saw none, only pain, moisture in her eyes and a grimace as she focused on breathing.

"I didn't mean it; I swear it."

She shook her head, in control of the tears now. "I know."

"I'm sorry, Tiger Lily."

"James," she said, putting her hand on his shoulder. He looked up at her, eyes pained and revolted. "I know."

She stood up from his bed.

A stab of panic rushed through him. "You're going, then?"

Her voice still shook when she spoke, and the fabric on her arm began to redden. "I need to get this tended to."

"Wait. I'll have Smee take a look at it. Please."

"No," she said with a swift, hard jerk of her head. "I'm going back home. You have no doctor here."

"Let me go with you," he said, reaching for her good arm.

She jerked back. "I'm *fine*, James. Just let me go."

James dropped his hand to his side. "Yes. All right. Go," he stammered, his mind a whir of guilt and passion and sorrow.

Tiger Lily stole out of his room, and James sat brooding on his mattress. She'd kissed him. He'd touched her and tasted her and held her, and he'd fouled it all up. Probably she hated him now. Who wouldn't hate a man who'd stabbed them for nothing? James jumped up from his bed and pulled at his hair, yelling gruffly. Then, he composed himself, and everything in him ran icy cold.

This hook, this blasted hook. It was Pan's fault, all of this. Tiger Lily might never come back to see him, and it was the doing of the Pan. So, for the captain, waiting and baiting the boy was no longer enough. He would feed the wickedest part of him and become wholly the captain of the pirate vessel. And he would seek Pan out for himself and slice him open with this hook, and then who would be the cursed one?

James stepped out into the cold twilight and glowered at any who passed. Finally, Smee stopped in front of him and questioned, "Captain?"

James thrust out his hook, moonlight glinting off the steel. "No, Smee. Not just 'Captain.' Not anymore. Call me Captain Hook."

PART THREE

☠

WHEREIN WE ARE INTRODUCED TO CAPTAIN HOOK

TWENTY-ONE

CAPTAIN HOOK STRODE ACROSS THE DECK, EACH step taken with terrible purpose.

"Hoist the mainsail," he growled, aware now exactly what it meant.

Noodler and Daniel Thatcher set to tugging on the rope, raising the sail, and Bill Jukes raised his eyebrows and stopped beside the captain.

"Now, sir?" Jukes said, staring up at the inky color dripping down from the sky into the water. Night was falling, and fast.

Hook flared his nostrils and stepped up very close to Jukes, breathing in his face and pressing his hook hard against the man's chest.

"Do not question me," he snarled, and Jukes narrowed his eyes, but did as the captain said, slowly lumbering toward the others.

Hook leaned out over the ship, glaring at the open sea, and Starkey leaned next to him. But where Starkey looked cool and collected, Hook looked as though he was ready to skewer any who dared come too close to him.

"Where are we headed, Captain?"

Hook pointed out across the ocean at a tiny vessel that, from their vantage point, looked like a speck.

"Do ye remember what happened last time we encountered a boat?" Starkey said, setting his mouth into a hard line.

"Absolutely," he replied, a menacing glint in his eye.

Starkey looked at him and shook his head in a small, but noticeable, motion.

"You have an objection?" Hook asked, voice low and dangerous.

Starkey hesitated, then stepped back away from the captain. "No, sir. Sail away."

Hook sneered. "Thank you for your permission."

Starkey bit his cheek, looking somewhat sour, and his nose twitched in irritation before he joined the rest of the crew in their preparations.

Hook frowned at that, keeping his gaze trained on Starkey as his first mate moved quickly, fuming, across the deck. That little twitch was a familiar gesture to the captain. He'd seen it a hundred times before, when he was young, and his father was frustrated at him.

But he forced his face away from the pirate ghost of someone long gone and focused his attention instead on the dark and angry sea. The *Spanish Main* moved faster than any aboard had ever seen it move, fairly flying across the water. Hook paced powerfully back and forth, eyeing the horizon with a restrained rabidity in his eyes.

"Bring out Long Tom," he said, and sneered.

Smee, who was busying himself with inane little things around the ship, stopped and dropped open his jaw. "Truly, Captain?"

Hook whirled toward him, fire in his eyes, telling himself again and again that this decision was the right one, that it was not driven by insanity, that this was the role he was born to fill. "Why does everyone feel the need to question me tonight?"

Smee shrank back and scuttled off toward the ship's intimidating, but little-used, cannon.

They closed quickly in on the distant, unfamiliar ship, and Hook curled his lips cruelly. Pan had brought yet another pirate ship to the Never Sea, one that looked nearly the same as all the others he'd ever seen on the horizon. Only the color of its flag, bright red, differentiated it at all. For being a powerful enough dreamer to imagine the whole of Neverland into existence, Peter was sorely lacking in creativity in regards to the dreams of others he allowed into this place.

Before the other vessel had a chance to fire, Hook sent the order. A giant blast perforated the silence, and Hook drew his sword. The wood in the enemy ship cracked as a giant hole appeared in its side.

"Draw your swords and bring out the guns, boys!"

His crew did as he commanded and armed themselves. Then, with a ferocity none of the crewman had ever seen, he sprang to action, hurtling himself onto the other boat. The rest of his pirates followed suit, and aboard the vessel, there was a terrible flurry of activity. Shots rang out and blades clanged against one another, little droplets of blood spattering here and there on the old wood, creating chaos in the air.

All the while, Hook plunged forward, smiling conspiratorially at his new fellow, Daniel Thatcher, who was quite skilled with a weapon. His hat and jacket and hair were marvelously in place, and when he reached the captain, who was quite an unsavory sort of man, even for a pirate, Hook paused in front of him. The man was large and smelled like spoiled meat—and he was covered in a layer of grime it would take several baths to scrape off. Between them, there was a strained silence in the midst of the cacophony. The other fellow flared his cavernous nostrils, bared his black and yellow teeth, and simply stared at Hook and his horrible claw.

"Do you wish to surrender the contents of your vessel?"

Hook chose to ask him thus, because he deemed it good form.

"I do not," the other captain hissed.

"That's unfortunate for you, because I wish to have them."

Something rumbled from deep within his opponent's chest, and the man rushed toward Hook, flashing his mammoth blade. Hook smiled and stepped forward to meet him. Hook clashed swords with the man, glad that he was capable with his left. The blades clanged against each other over and over, and Hook lashed out with his shining claw. It was not as easy to use as he had hoped, and the sheer weight of it propelled him forward. It stuck into the wood of the ship, and Hook yanked back, eyes large, pulse racing, pulling at it once, twice, a third time. A sweat broke out on his face and he yanked harder, fresh desperation washing over him in a heavy wave. The other captain ran at him, and Hook finally freed himself an instant before he was met with a blade.

Quite on accident, when he pulled it out, it flew farther than Hook intended it, and it connected with the other unfortunate captain's throat. Blood sprayed everywhere from his jugular, little droplets clinging to Hook's face. He winced and stepped backward once, then wiped it from himself. He did not bat an eye and pretended that the stroke had been intentional.

He was pure steel, unaffected by the brutal death, or so he told himself. There was, in reality, a deep and instant remorse rolling slowly around in him, the kind that manifested itself in a queasy terrible feeling in the pit of his stomach. But, on the outside, he looked only the cold captain. And he stood above his felled foe and yelled out over the ship: "Men!"

The activity came to a grinding halt. "The vessel is won!"

The few bedraggled men who were left from his opponent's crew stood, blinking, or sat with their heads bowed and tired and bleeding. Hook's men cheered and set about plundering the ship, loading their arms with gold and weaponry and all the colors of gemstones that could be imagined.

"You!" he called to the other ship's survivors. "You will sail across the sea in this pile of wooden excrement, and you will tell all my name."

"What is your name?" one small man said, shaking violently now, skin covered in blood and nearly drained of color.

"My name is Captain Hook."

Hook cocked his head, then, hearing a strange sound, that *tick-tock, tick-tock, tick-tock*. It was a sound he hadn't heard since Pan had thrown his hand to the crocodile. He turned toward the edge of the ship, heart *thump-thumping*, pulse in his ears, until he wasn't entirely sure which rhythm was his heart and which was the clock. Hook shrank bank immediately after reaching the edge, scrambling to the middle of the deck, hand fisted and shaking and digging into the folds of his coat. Waiting below, he saw nothing but a shadow beneath the water and a pair of eyes sticking out from it. Those eyes, those cold, hungry eyes that somehow seemed to be staring straight into him, asking him for another bite. He swallowed, though he swore dust coated his mouth. And, trembling, he whipped around and vacated the ship, running to the safety of the *Spanish Main*, shutting his eyes when he reached the door of his cabin and leaning against it, trying to displace the terrible face from his mind. His crew followed him, arms full of treasure and the like, back to the ship.

One of the crewmen, Hook did not know who, backed the ship slowly away from the enemy vessel, and Hook pulled on the handle to his door, needing desperately to be in his room, in his bed, beneath the covers.

But, when he reached his bed, no sooner had he sat and removed his boots, than he heard a powerful knocking. He ignored it and removed his hat and jacket. And then again. Darkness flooded his face.

"Come in," he said in a low voice.

Starkey walked into the room, and Hook frowned.

"Captain."

"Starkey," Hook said, making no effort to conceal his displeasure at the other man's presence.

Starkey did not look afraid or even awkward. Hook felt himself get a bit smaller under the man's glare. But, he puffed up his chest.

"Why have you come to my quarters? Why are you not joining the revelry with the others?"

"Why do you not join?" Starkey's voice was even, his eyes appraising. There was hard disapproval in his eyes.

Hook clenched his jaw, instantly young again, as he often seemed to be under Starkey's scrutiny. He shook his head, ground his teeth against one another. He was taken aback, and hoped immediately that none of that was showing.

"Who are you to challenge me?" he said, recoiling, shrinking, furrowing his brow.

"My station matters not, Captain Hook."

Hook shook his head once more, tersely, as though that would rid him of his regression into childhood. He hardened his face and stared at Starkey, nostrils flared. "Is that so?"

"I mean no disrespect and I mean no mutiny. But, I do mean to be telling ye that, should ye keep on like this, the *Spanish Main* is done for."

"How do you mean?" Hook struggled to keep command of the conversation, but he was frustratingly engaged in whatever Starkey had to say.

Starkey rose taller, lines on his forehead deepening. "Captain, since you've taken this vessel, you've spent a great deal of time holed away, isolated from the crew. Just when ye get me believin' you're taking real charge, ye come back here again while we be celebratin'."

"What business is it of yours how I choose to celebrate?"

"Because, I sense the change in you, sir, and I know ye be planning to plunder and pillage every vessel in the sea. We can't be making enemies all over Neverland if we haven't a captain to lead us."

Hook rose from the bed and closed the distance between himself and the other man, distress and rage in his voice absolutely evident. "You presume to tell me how to run my own vessel? And you insinuate that I behave in a manner unfit for a captain?"

"No insinuatin', sir. Tellin'." And there again, a nose twitch, and a flash of his father. Hook paled, just slightly. Then, overcome with hot fury, he brandished the hook in Starkey's face.

"How dare you. I ought to rip you up here and now."

Starkey did not step back, did not deflate or shrink at all. He stood, unblinking, a mite taller, even, than Hook, and quite a bit broader, and looked over him.

Hook was shaking with anger, and, if he admitted the truth to himself, fear. "I will not stand for my men speaking to their captain this way."

"Then be a captain, sir."

Starkey turned away from him, exposing his back to the potential wrath of the hook, and made for the door. Hook did not even consider plunging the steel into the man, but pretended thus nonetheless. He did consider stopping Starkey and threatening him with all sorts of dreadful things, but ultimately decided against it. Instead, he sat back on his bed, and said quietly, coldly, "Starkey?"

Starkey stopped before opening the door, and turned. "Captain?"

"Do not ever speak to me in such a way again."

Starkey nodded and vacated the cabin.

Hook sat, blinking silently for a while, considering. Starkey was wrong. He was. Hook insisted this to himself in the same way he'd insisted it to himself when he was a child and he'd been scolded for something, whether just or unjust. He hated feeling like this around his own first mate—small, childish, vulnerable. But he'd made Starkey this way, hadn't he?

As much as he hated to admit it, perhaps Starkey was right. Perhaps to truly become Hook, to truly be worthy of captaining the *Spanish Main*, he needed to be more than a plunderer and pillager and murderer. And, though he hated to admit this even more, somewhere in the deep, dark, hidden parts of him, he wanted Starkey to be right, and to be pleased.

He swung his hook around in the air, feeling the weight of it, and took a long look at the iron, noting the dried blood encrusted upon it. It was the intermingled blood of several men. He was overcome with disgusting guilt, not only for murdering a score of men, but for refusing to commit to the captainship that was his responsibility. He let that wash over him for a while, until the silence was heavier than the revelry outside. He pulled on his boots again, and put on his jacket and hat. Then, he took out a napkin, and cleaned his hook until it shone.

He opened the door of his cabin and stepped out onto the deck. Alcohol was flowing, and the men were laughing and carousing and literally throwing pieces of treasure into the air. A hush fell over them at the sight of the captain.

He waited for a beat before addressing them.

"Men," he said, stopping once more, out of eloquent words to speak. Then, he smiled, a rare thing. "Toss me the rum."

The crew cheered and he joined them, earning a subtle nod and smile from Starkey. Daniel Thatcher stumbled into him, massively drunk already, and Bill Jukes hit him from the other side. Hook chuckled, drowned out by their thunderous, slurring laughter.

"Congratulations, Captain Hook, on your victory today," said Daniel.

"On *ours*, Thatcher." He took an entire bottle of the spiced alcohol and ran his hook across the top, slicing the glass. He tipped it back and let it slide down his throat, relishing the heat, as the men cheered again—all but Smee, who just sort of giggled and sipped on his quarter-glass. And the music and the dancing and the rum filled, for a moment, the painful emptiness in his gut.

As the night wore on, Hook celebrated the victory with the rest of the crew and kept up even with Jukes and Starkey, matching them drink for drink. He danced and stumbled and slammed alcohol, losing himself in celebration, until Neverland began to quiet with the night, and that midnight stillness crept into the air.

Then, there was no one awake but he and Jukes and Flintwise. They were sitting on the ship's forecastle, Hook leaning back in an old chair, booted feet crossed on another chair in front of him. Flintwise sat to his right, at the wheel, and Jukes in the middle of them, forming the last point of a very drunken triangle.

"You love that Indian girl, Captain?" Flintwise asked, sloppily turning his skinny neck, raising an eyebrow at Hook.

Hook took another swig of the alcohol in his hand. At this point, he could hardly taste the difference between wine and rum, but he was fairly certain this was the former. "You've seen her?"

He should've been more surprised. Had he been sober, he reckoned he would've been.

"'Course I have, Cap'n. We all have. Not such a secret," Flintwise said, belching. Jukes laughed.

"Perhaps," said Hook, finishing off the bottle, reaching for another.

"I was in love once." Flintwise's voice cracked, and he leaned back against the wheel, shifting to the left, then overcorrecting to the right and nearly falling to the floor.

Jukes boomed out a good-natured laugh. "You? When?"

"Some time ago. With one of them mermaids."

Jukes laughed harder at that, and Hook simply cocked his head.

"A mermaid?" Jukes spat between peals of laughter and enthusiastic gulps of rum. "If that's love, we've all been smitten!"

He looked at the captain conspiratorially, and Hook laughed a little.

Flintwise stood, then thought better of it, sitting heavily back down. "I have been. I was in love with her."

"No," said Jukes. "You were just thinkin' with your flint."

Hook did laugh at that, and Flintwise grabbed himself, which only made them both laugh harder. Jukes toppled over, barely able to breathe, and crashed hard onto the deck.

Flintwise joined and stumbled over to him, and Hook somehow pushed himself up from his chair and made it over to help him, reaching out his right. Jukes eyed him and took Flintwise's hand instead, and it was then that the captain realized that he'd offered the man a hook, and not a hand.

He fell backward into his chair and stared at the deck.

"We're heading under, Captain," said Jukes, and he and Flintwise tripped below deck with the rest of the men, leaving Hook alone with the black night.

Hook found that he was rather sad to be alone.

He drank a little more, then stood, feeling his legs give way beneath him, and caught himself on the ship's edge. His hook stuck in the wood, and he grimaced, feeling the sudden urge to cry. He let out an angry growl instead, yanking it from the wood, and threw the half-full bottle overboard. The rest of the wine bled out into the water. Another thing he'd torn open and wasted, like Tiger Lily.

He shut his eyes and unfastened his hook, feeling the weight of it in his hand. Then he stared out over the dark, glassy surface of the sea. More than anything, at this very moment, he wanted to toss it away, let it sink to the bottom.

Maybe if he did, he would wake up with a hand, and the world would be normal again.

He laughed darkly and reattached the hook. The world would never be normal again.

Hook gathered several half-empty bottles in his arms and lay down on the deck, right where he stood. If he stayed out there, he was less alone. If he stayed there, he was simply the latest remnant of a party. And if he stayed drunk and awake, then he didn't have to sleep and not dream.

Sometimes, he wished he could dream.

TWENTY-TWO

T HE NEXT DAY WAS STILL YOUNG, AND JAMES HOOK was quite drunk. He stumbled about the ship in a rum-induced semi-stupor. None of his crew seemed to mind, as he was decidedly more pleasant under the influence of the stuff, smiling and singing rather than brooding and barking orders.

No one else was still drunk, but then again, no one else had stayed up all night, drinking through painful reveries until that very moment.

Hook felt strange and fuzzy, but found that he was enjoying it, though he assumed he wouldn't enjoy it so much later. He lurched into Smee, who chuckled pleasantly, and raised his eyebrows.

"Smee, the cook!"

"Yes, Captain."

"Captain Hook, Smee. Captain Hook!"

He tried to sound menacing when he said this, but it just came out blurry, and he devolved into a fit of laughter, because the inadvertent rhyming of "cook" and "Hook" struck him as funny.

Smee nodded and averted his eyes, and Hook threw his arm around the man.

"Careful there, sir. Don't want any injuries from that hook you're throwing around."

Hook laughed then, but it was humorless. "Any *more* injuries, you mean?"

Smee scratched at his cheek. "More, sir?"

"I've killed a hundred men with this thing. And I've skewered more." Hook knew in the part of him that had any sobriety left that this was a gross overstatement, but the larger, drunker part of him did not care for facts. "I killed a captain and stabbed a Tiger Lily."

Smee's eyes shot wide open. "Tiger Lily, Sir? The Indian Princess?"

"Aye, one and the same." Hook gazed down then, looking like a shamed child.

"Captain Hook, you mean to tell me that you stuck your hook in the princess?"

Hook shut his mouth and puffed out his cheeks, then, trying very hard, and very unsuccessfully, to hold in a cackle. Quite quickly, the cackle won out. "Hardly," he laughed, blustering. Generally, he was not inclined to laugh at such bawdy things, but alcohol did strange things to a man. "But, I did stick her with this."

Smee rolled his eyes. "Why would you do such a thing?"

His face fell. "It was an accident, Smee. A terrible accident."

"Is she all right?"

"Of course. But she hates me now. Hates, hates, hates me."

Smee put his arm around the captain's shoulders and smiled consolingly. "Now, now, Captain, I'm sure it's not as bad as all that. Why don't you just go lie down?"

He crossed his arms. "I won't. I won't lie down."

"Even a pirate captain needs rest sometimes."

Hook was following along with Smee even while he was vocally protesting, so inebriated was he. Smee opened the door and Hook fell into his room. Smee then crossed the floor to his bed and turned down the covers, patting the mattress, as though Hook was a boy and Smee was a mother, trying to coax him into having a nap.

"That's where it all happened, Smee," Hook said, sitting in the middle of the floor, playing his fingers on the soft rug, staring up at the bed.

Smee pursed his lips. "Oh dear."

"I'm in love with her, you know."

"I didn't."

As Smee was making conversation with the captain, he was tidying things up and gesturing toward the bed. He looked a fool, Hook thought. A silly, busy fool.

"I'm in love with her and she's all I can think about, and that blasted Pan took my hand. It's his fault I stabbed her, Smee," Hook said, standing and rubbing his head.

"Of course it is."

Smee pushed him toward the bed, and Hook frowned. "It *is* his fault," he said, shaking Smee off. "Of course it is. Why am I here, then? Why aren't I out there getting rid of him?"

"You're in no shape to be killing Peter Pan, Captain."

The captain stood straight up and thrust out his hook, then smoothed his hair down with his hand. "Fetch me my sword, Smee! Fetch it for me."

Smee frowned. "I don't think you should be handling a sword in this state."

Hook pushed past him and threw his hand around the handle of his sword, yanking it up, brandishing the blade. Smee held up his hands and backed toward the door. Hook barely noticed the fellow in his stupor, and pressed through to the deck.

"Men!" he bellowed.

Starkey sprinted up to him and stopped, "Captain?" He wrinkled his nose and eyed the captain's disheveled clothes and hair. "Been hitting the rum?"

Hook ignored him and stared, glassy-eyed, at his crew. They looked somewhat bedraggled, red-eyed and moving slowly. The effects of a hangover were unpleasant, even in a place as magical as Neverland.

"We're leaving the ship," he said, and raised his sword into the air.

Starkey was the only one among them who didn't look as though he'd already been through a battle. Well, Starkey and Smee, who was avoiding the whole situation by scurrying off to the cook's cabin.

Starkey stepped in a little closer to Hook and lowered his voice. "Captain, I don't believe it wise to be headin' off the ship with you in this state."

Hook glared at Starkey, and Starkey stepped back with the rest of them, shaking his head, nose twitching in that familiar way.

"We, fellows, are going to kill ourselves a Pan," Hook said, enthusiasm lighting up his eyes.

The group did not raise a grand hurrah or react, really, at all. Hook glowered at them.

"I said, 'We are going to kill the Pan!'"

The pirates looked at one another and then threw their arms in the air and shouted. Several of them winced at the loud noise, but Hook smiled with his teeth and staggered off the ship, falling off the side of the walkway a step too early and cackling as he plunged into the waterlogged sand. He pushed himself up and tripped onto the beach, his band of miscreants, Starkey included, following loyally behind him.

At the mouth of the forest, he stopped and looked to his left and right, then reached out his hook to steady himself. He didn't remember the forest ever spinning before. After a beat, he followed his feet into the trees, having absolutely no clue as to where he was headed, but fueled by the confidence that only vast amounts of alcohol can provide. He barreled through the trees, clumsy and brash and wholly un-Hook-like. Then, he stopped and his ears perked up.

There was a soft whistle heading toward him, a note from the pan flute Peter played so often. He grinned wickedly and headed in the direction of the noise. The land gently sloped up and down, hills rolling beneath him, trees on every side. He stopped and pushed his hook out at the men behind him. There was Pan, in the valley below, hopping and skipping in such a way that he blurred. The Lost Boys were all present. Hook thought he recognized several of them—the twins, Simpkins, Tootles, Slightly, but one or two were completely unfamiliar to him.

On a regular sort of day, he would not have approached the situation as he did. He would not have ventured into the woods without a plan. He would not have compelled his entire blundering crew to accompany him. He certainly wouldn't have called out Pan's name and given away his position. But, Hook's blood was fairly running with alcohol, and so this was no normal day.

"Peter Pan," he cried, voice reverberating in the clear, green valley beneath him.

Pan looked up toward him and smiled, flying up to meet him.

"Captain Hook," he said, forgetting the flute. "Come all the way out here just to see me?"

"Indeed."

Peter screwed up his face. "You stink, Hook."

The crew beside him shifted, grumbling with one another quietly. Hook furrowed his brow. Peter laughed, injecting instant rage into his blood. Hook thrust out his sword, wavered, and dropped the blade, then bent uneasily to retrieve it.

Pan laughed even more loudly in Hook's face. "In rare form today, aren't we? Catch me if you can, old man."

That was all it took to bait the captain. Pan flew down toward the boys, and Hook sprinted, falling down the hill after him. The men went along, brandishing their swords and guns and yelling in a very controlled, post-night-of-revelry sort of way.

When they reached the boys, Hook's eyes darted this way and that, searching frantically for Pan. Peter, of course, was flitting about above the battle, calling out various taunts and jeers that Hook could not presently make out. A jumbled sort of frustration seeped into his head, and he cried out gruffly, some harsh rumble that no one knew quite how to interpret.

He spun to his left and then to his right, hook and blade flashing brightly each time he spun. Peter darted down beside him and grabbed his hook. "Well, this is nice, isn't it? Is it new?"

Then, he flew back up above Hook, snickering loudly, and swiped off his hat with one hand. Hook was seeing all of this through a red haze. At one point, he was completely convinced that Peter had somehow duplicated himself, for there was no other sensible explanation for the two Pans flying around his head. Eventually, they fused back into a single boy, and Hook swung his sword around clumsily. Peter hopped to the ground, and as he jumped back up, the captain swiped with his hook. He froze, however, blood running instantly cold, when he felt it connect with something. Pan? But, no. Pan was darting around somewhere in the periphery. He slowly turned to look at whoever or whatever was stuck at the end of his hook, and the blood drained from his face.

Only just now had he realized that he was fighting against the Lost Boys. It was not only Pan he'd brought his men down upon. As the alcoholic rage sharply and painfully receded, he could see the faces of his friends in the foreground, as more than just an afterthought.

Especially the face of this one. His favorite one. Acid boiled in his stomach, threatening sickness.

Bibble. He was sure of it. Tall and awkward and sweet. Bibble, there was no mistaking. Anyone. Anyone but him.

The blur was gone, as was the cloudiness in his mind, and the clarity was sudden and startling and horrifying.

Bibble blinked several times and looked down at his stomach, then dropped his little sword. Blood soaked his shirt, spreading across the fabric. With disbelief in his eyes, he stared up at Hook. Then, he frowned.

"James Hook?"

When Bibble said the words, little droplets of blood leaked out of his mouth. Hook's throat constricted, and his windpipe closed. He stared back at the child and gently pulled his hook out of his stomach, feeling the sickening give when it came free.

"Aye, it's me," he said, voice gravelly, choked.

Bibble blinked slowly again, and Hook grabbed his arm, fingers shaking, helping him lower himself to the ground. Bibble choked up a little more blood and furrowed his brow, not saying much, just sitting there, staring.

"Bibble?" Hook said, staring into the boy's eyes, his own stinging, everything sharp and aching. "Does it hurt much, Bibble?"

"Does what hurt?"

"Your belly, child."

Bibble looked down and then back up at Hook, eyes glazing over. "What happened there?"

Hook's face crinkled and a cry escaped his lips. "I'm so sorry."

"You look old, James." His words were becoming less and less clear.

Hook let out a heavy breath, blinking past the tears stinging his eyes. "That's because I am old."

"James?"

"Yes?"

Bibble breathed in raggedly. "The sky looks funny."

"Does it?" He choked back another sob, not wishing to alert the child to the fact that he was dying.

"It doesn't look like Neverland anymore, James."

"What does it look like?"

Bibble smiled softly. "Home."

And his body relaxed onto the ground. Hook stared at him, guilt and disbelief overcoming him, and dug into his arms—fingers, hook, and all. Crimson blood trickled out over the steel and Hook recoiled, pulling the hook away, as though this shell could still feel him.

He'd killed him. There Bibble was, lying there, his friend—his best friend really—heavy and bloody and still. Hook fought the urge to retch into the leaves outside the clearing.

Pan flitted down beside him, and Hook recoiled. He was afraid if he allowed himself to look into Peter's face, he would see himself reflected there. He'd murdered a child now, hadn't he? How were they different? Pale, heavy sickness snaked into his stomach.

"What's this?" said Pan.

Hook hopped up, hand steady on his sword.

"What did you do, Hook?"

Hook took several steps backward. By now, no one was fighting.

"Did you kill him?" Peter cried.

Just then, Hook felt a presence race past him. Bobble stumbled over to his brother and collapsed onto the ground beside him. "Bibble? Bibble? We're having a war, Bibble. You need to wake up," he said, frantically, shaking the dead boy.

"I—I didn't mean it," Hook stuttered.

"You killed him!" Bobble shrieked, and Simpkins rushed to his side. Bobble was shaking and red, hysterical and out of control.

"I'm sorry," Hook said, barely able to speak, certain that he was going to be crushed under the weight of his own sadness and disgust.

Simpkins was solemn and angry. He picked up Bibble's ankles and dragged him along the ground, leaving a little trail of blood as he walked.

Hook wondered, briefly, if Simpkins had replaced him as the twins' friend after he'd left. Then he shook his head. None of that mattered. What mattered were the boys he'd known, mourning or frantic or dead.

All the boys turned to Pan, who had utter confusion all over him. Peter hovered just an inch above the ground, face turning from Bibble to pale, bleeding Bobble. "What did you *do*?"

"He didn't, Peter," said Bobble. "He's fine, he's fine, he's all right—"

Peter grabbed Bobble by the shoulders and shook him. "He *isn't fine*, Bobble." Bobble froze, and Peter glared darkly at Hook, then back at Bobble. "He's dead."

Peter grabbed his little dagger and pointed it dangerously at Hook who, at that moment, would not have protested being murdered. Peter's face was awash with bewilderment, and he kept pointing the blade, dropping it, staring at everyone, and picking it up and pointing it again. He looked so young. They all did. Hook wondered if this was the first time Peter had ever been at a loss as to what to do.

Bobble sat, paralyzed, on the ground, and the rest of the boys gathered around him, and Peter looked over his boys. "Let's go," he said, voice unusually quiet.

The group followed him, and not a pirate tried to stop them. When he passed, Bobble looked at Hook in such a way that Hook felt it in his soul.

Hook watched the group leave, and he swore that both Bobble and Simpkins grew several inches in front of him. Peter hovered just beside them, and there was no denying that he was the shortest of the three. He looked away from the boys, wishing he hadn't seen that, more pain needling into his insides. They were growing up, now. There would be a Thinning soon.

The rest of the pirates shared Hook's daze. He suspected they had never actually killed a Lost Boy. He wished that was still true. Peter, he would destroy gladly now, without a second thought. But the boys. Never the boys. Never his friends.

The walk back to the *Main* was slow and quiet and sober, and no one spoke when they boarded. And Starkey did not invade his quarters this time when he holed himself away, replaying in his head over and over Bibble's final word—Home.

He wondered, as he lay there blanketed in guilt, if Bibble really had gone back to London, if perhaps, he'd freed the boy when he'd murdered him. For a moment, he considered breaking a wine bottle on his desk and slashing his own wrists.

But he was too tired and heavy and muddled, and concerned that perhaps he was making more of it than it was. If death was the key to going home, then Peter was constantly trying to send him back to London—and that couldn't be true, could it?

No. He was exhausted and reading into the confused thoughts of a dying child, and that wasn't something to kill oneself over.

He thought and lay there and wished for wine and to turn back time and in the middle of all that, he fell asleep.

He wasn't sure when. But it was quite a while before he woke, trying not to think of home.

TWENTY-THREE

IT WAS TWO OR THREE NEVERDAYS AFTER THE INCIDENt with the Lost Boys when the island began to darken and grow cold. There was no storm, no mayhem to rock the skies, but it was one of those grey-green days that felt as though the suns had been stuck below the horizon. The light was bright but sterile and cold, and the leaves themselves were dull orange and brown and shades of grey.

Neverland, it appeared, had simply shrunk inside itself, shriveling and inviting the snow that swirled in the air and frosted the earth. Hook paced back and forth on the beach, noting the strangeness inherent in the frozen sand and slushy water, the lack of nymphs in the sea, and the paleness of the sky.

"Starkey!" he called, breath showing itself in a puff.

Starkey came running off the ship and stood at attention in front of the captain.

"What is this? What's going on?" he demanded.

"With the weather, do ye mean?"

Hook gave him a single, curt nod, and hugged his coat around himself.

"Aye, Captain. This weather be strange. It only goes like this when Peter's gone."

Hook looked up at the sky again, slowly tracking the rolling green clouds as they inched along in the air. "Gone?"

"Aye."

A shadow fell over Hook's face, and he spat on the deck. Peter was gone. And here he was, stuck in the cold, in a world full of things that wished him dead. A shudder of hatred coursed through his body, along with a note of terrible sadness, and he turned away from Starkey for a moment. Peter was home. *His* home. Probably traipsing around in Kensington, ignoring the fairies. He wondered briefly if Peter could see his house from where he was. He would have given anything at all to be there with him. Or preferably, without him. No, with him, killing him, sticking a hook in his heart before he headed back to his house and dined with his mother and father.

Hook breathed in, shaking a bit, trying to rid himself of the poison that had just exploded into his veins, his heart.

He shut his eyes. "Replenishing his stock of Lost Boys, no doubt," he said, refocusing the conversation.

"Most likely."

"How long do you expect him gone? A week, two?"

"How long, sir?"

Hook made a frustrated sound and looked away from Starkey. This fool place. Whenever he mentioned time, the most competent men turned to idiots; no one had any notion as to what it was.

"Never mind, Starkey. Leave me."

Starkey tipped his hat and headed back onto the ship. Hook paced even more feverishly now. Pan was gone. Of course he was. He could feel the island's wickedness soaking into his innards. It made it all the easier to give into that very same wicked streak in himself. He smiled and strode up to the ship. Upon arriving at his cabin, he reached inside and took up his sword, then closed the door and walked around the deck, twirling it absentmindedly. When Smee saw him, he held up his hands and gave him an appraising look.

The ice had actually warmed Hook up, and he laughed out loud at this. "Not to worry. I've not had a drop of rum."

The fact that he could once again form coherent words seemed to satisfy Smee, so he tottered off. Hook set his elbows on the ship's edge and continued smiling, looking almost dreamily out over the water and the deep turquoise ice floating in shards atop it. He breathed deeply. The air, for once, tasted like air. Not like vanilla, or the ash of Pan's fear, or the metal he'd tasted the night he'd killed Bibble. He'd known then that Pan was slaughtering his too-tall Lost Boys. Blood and iron in the air. But not today. Today, it tasted, simply, like water and salt and the wind above the sea.

A time without Pan. A time without provocation and flying and arrogance. That ever-present feeling of irritation that was always tickling him under the collar disappeared, and he was free to simply sit and taste the nothingness.

As he gazed out over the ocean, he suddenly stepped back and tilted his head. He squinted and looked again, then knit his eyebrows together and called for Starkey.

"Aye, Captain?"

"Do you see that, over there?"

He pointed out just across the sea at a small island off the coast of the mainland, one he'd somehow never seen. There was something off about it, as though it wasn't fully real. But the longer he stared at it, the harder the lines became, the more vibrant the colors, until within minutes the dream-like peculiarity had worn off.

"Aye," said Starkey, a wistful smile turning his lips. "Keelhaul Isle."

Hook tilted his head. "Why have I never seen it before?"

"It only shows up when Pan's gone, Captain, when the darker parts of Neverland show their faces. It's a place built on drunkenness and lechery."

Hook smiled then, eyes alight. "Drunkenness and lechery? Sounds the ideal place for a pirate ship to make bed."

"It does indeed, Captain."

"Well, what are we waiting for? To Keelhaul!"

A hearty cheer rose up from the men, and Hook looked eagerly toward the island. He was more than ready to lose himself in a bit of debauchery.

It did not take long to reach Keelhaul, which was surprising, given the amount of ice floating in the sea. But Peter's absence seemed to give Hook new life, new power, and perhaps it gifted the *Main* as well. It was faster—larger, almost. The dark wood gleamed like he'd never seen it do. Everything else in Neverland was chalky and dulled and pastel, but the *Spanish Main* was vibrant. Without Pan to keep him and his dream in check, Hook could feel it in his bones, as though the muscles in his arms were harder, the blood itself rushing through his veins with more enthusiasm.

When they docked, he stepped off the boat into the darkness. It was night there, though he could look out on the rest of the Never Sea and see that it was bright everywhere else. Perhaps it was always dark on Keelhaul Isle. This suited him just fine.

What wasn't black as night was cast in a glow that was almost red, like an ember, and the place smelled like smoke and heavy perfume. Men laughed loudly, bawdily, and women joined them. It wasn't quiet, like the *Main* often was. But the grimy ruckus gave Hook an odd peace that the mainland never had.

He stood there for a moment, cracking his long fingers with his hook. This place, it seemed, had not fallen under the murky spell that had overtaken the rest of Neverland. It was teeming with raw, dirty color and life. There were women and men alike running along the dimly lit cobblestone streets, some plundering storefronts, some playing raucous instruments (and not very well), some drowning themselves in alcohol.

Hook's crew joined him on the dock, and he smiled widely.

"What will ye have us do, Captain?"

He shrugged. "Whatever you wish."

The pirates scattered, but Thatcher, Smee, and Cecco remained with Hook. He ignored them, largely, strutting through the black streets, tall and imposing and dreadfully elegant. When he passed, women and men bent and whispered urgently to one another, and stared, wide-eyed, at him. This gave him pause, but he walked on as though he didn't notice.

"Captain?" Thatcher inquired.

"Indeed."

"That storefront over there, it seems unoccupied."

Hook looked in the direction Thatcher was speaking of. It was dark, and the door was closed. Through the dimness, however, he could make out the jewelry glimmering gaudily in the windows. He raised an eyebrow at Thatcher. "Observant."

"It's a jewelry store, Captain," the man continued. "Full of gold."

"Get to it, man."

Smee and Cecco and Thatcher bounded off for it, and Hook stopped in the middle of the street, arms folded across his chest, grinning smugly as his boys slammed down the door and raided the place. Within minutes, they were heading toward him, arms full of treasure.

True delight warmed him and he laughed. Keelhaul was a pirate's paradise. He wished for a moment that Peter was dead (which was not a new sentiment) or stuck in London (which *was* new) so that they could make port here instead of the child's island.

Hook walked on across Keelhaul, casually taking note of the landscape and inhabitants thereof, seeing more and more awed onlookers. The stars here were clouded by the smoke and dirt that lifted into the air, and the scent of alcohol and unwashed bodies lingered in the darker, dirtier corners of the place. The taste of spice melted on his tongue when he breathed in, and every now and then, he caught the distinct aroma of heavy incense.

There was a definite spring in his step as he and his followers made their way through the dark streets, candlelit lamps flickering and casting shadows on their faces.

Hook stopped when he reached a particularly dilapidated and wholly unimpressive little wooden building. It was glowing from the inside, and a little light just barely illuminated a crooked, rotting sign that hung over the doorway. It read "The Crow's Nest."

Hook pushed the door open with a slow creak and walked inside, enjoying the hushed silence that fell over the occupants when he did. There was an old piano in the corner that no one was playing, and a barkeep with a salt-and-pepper beard who was sloshing alcohol over the mugs he handled. Hook first wandered to the bar.

"What'll you have?" said the barkeep in a voice that suggested that he'd sampled more rum that night than he should've.

The captain brought his hook to his face, considering, a force of habit from when it had been a hand. The barkeep's eyebrows shot up and his jaw dropped.

"Hook? Are you—Captain Hook?"

"I am."

The barkeep leaned just slightly backward, but Hook did not miss it.

"Drink's on me, Captain," he said, and he handed him a glass of rum.

Hook brought it to his lips and leaned back against the bar, eyeing the room. The only men from his crew there were Jukes and Flintwise, so the tavern was comprised largely of strangers. Strangers who stared at him and whispered.

It was strange, he thought. He hadn't done much in the way of sea exploits, but, perhaps he had by Neverland terms. Or perhaps it was only that he'd always imagined himself to be the fiercest pirate in the sea, and so here, now, that was reality. Either way, he did not complain, for it stroked his ego vigorously.

He tipped his head back and drained the glass of every drop, then stood from the bar, noting that several of his crewmates were now seated in the tavern. He walked quietly over to the piano, touching a single ivory key with his hook, and it made a hollow sound. The instrument had the sort of tinny timbre one expected from a tavern's piano. He slid his hook gently down several more keys, and sat at the bench.

He'd played the piano a long, long time ago. He'd always hated it, he remembered. Mother forced him to play the thing, day in, day out. And, once upon a time, he could make it sing. He wasn't entirely sure if he could anymore, what with his hook replacing his hand. Hands, it turned out, were particularly important things when it came to playing instruments.

When he played the first bar, it was slow and awkward. Strange playing with just six fingers (or fingerlike things.) But he played another quiet, hesitant measure. And he kept playing, until the music was neither stilted nor awkward. It was beautiful, at least in his mind. James and Chopin had not always gotten along, but he and *Nocturne in C# Minor* played well together. So, the pirate allowed the haunting melody to sweep him away.

It was not a piece that was fitting for the place, but Hook did not care. He was far away; sweaty, sour bar smell replaced with the smell of home and London— sweet and clean and damp. He was small, sitting in a tiny living room, fingers melting across the old piano keys as the church bells rang out in the night, a strange harmony. His mother sat beside him on the bench, soft and smelling like flowers, pretty pale wrists laid over the edge of the keys, not playing, just listening and smiling softly.

Finally, the memory died out, and he reached a point in the song he'd not yet mastered. And he never would. He opened his eyes and stared around the room at the dirty men who were drunk and mesmerized.

There was not a sound in the place. But then, one of the men began to clap, and several others joined in, and the place was filled with noise, all directed at him.

"Hook!" someone chanted. And another, and another, until the entire patronage was chanting his name and clapping and whistling. Hook stood, trying to camouflage the smile that was popping up on his lips. He made his way back to a secluded table, grabbing more rum on the way.

The corner was dark, and Hook found himself enjoying the solitude and simply observing.

"Captain Hook?" a sultry voice intoned.

"Aye."

He stared at the woman over his stein. She was lovely, tempting, all curves and softness. Long red hair and bright green eyes and a full mouth that said his name beautifully.

"Your reputation precedes you."

"Does it?"

He gently kicked a chair out and she sat in it, crossing one leg boldly and slowly over the other.

She leaned over the table. "It does. I've heard your name whispered in many dark corners on the island."

"I've not had the pleasure of hearing yours," he said over the mug.

"Malena."

He took her hand and brought his lips to it. She did not blush.

"What brings you to my table, Malena?"

"I wondered if you'd buy a drink for me."

Hook considered for a moment, and she leaned over closer to him. Her scent was sweet, and she was boldly perfumed. She smelled nothing like Tiger Lily. And perhaps that was the precise reason that he gave in to her.

She was pleasant enough in conversation and certainly a pleasure to look at, and, to his surprise, he preferred her company to the dark solitude he'd been craving.

"Having a drink with the famous Captain Hook." She laughed a girlish, sultry little laugh. "None of my friends will believe it."

"And none of my crew will believe that I've had the pleasure of the company of someone as lovely as you." He grinned at her and stole a glance over her shoulder, at Jukes and Flintwise, who were cackling and looking in their direction. His grin deepened and turned a bit wicked.

She smiled at him coyly, and then yawned. "I'm quite tired, Captain." She ran her dark red fingernail along the rim of her glass in slow circles.

"I hate to see you go."

He didn't feel much of what he was saying, as though someone had scripted the lines for him. But, he did feel a very noticeable jolt of heat when she whispered, "There are some awful rogues about. I wonder if you'd walk me to my room."

He set down his glass and let her take his hand and lead him upstairs. When they reached the door to her room, she leaned back against it.

"This is you?"

"Yes." Her bold gaze did not leave his for a moment when she asked, "Would you like to come in?"

Hook was uneasy, and he shifted his weight from one foot to the other.

"I'm no harlot," she said. "I live above the tavern."

"Is that so?"

"I swear it." She leaned harder against the door and opened it, and Hook was drawn inside with her. Her room smelled like her perfume—strong, sweet, and sensual. She closed the door again and stood there, waiting for him in the candlelight. His pulse began to race, and he reached out and touched her collarbone. He couldn't decide if the heat in his torso, in his face, his throat, was from desire or guilt.

Probably it was an extremely potent mix of both.

His fingertips burned where they met her skin, and he breathed in shakily. She took a step closer to him and put her hand on his torso, then let it fall downward, until it rested low on him, much too low. Hook ground his teeth against each other, and she grinned up at him. Tiger Lily's face flashed across hers, and he blinked and stumbled backward. None of this was right.

"I can't do this," he managed, voice rough and conflicted.

"Don't worry about her."

He frowned and looked at her again. "Who?"

"The girl. Whoever's got you looking so guilty."

He looked off into the corner of the room. Tiger Lily's dark, smooth skin, her smoke-and-flowers scent, her laughing voice. Those things mattered. They *mattered.*

But Malena pulled him back to this place, this room, with her fingertips and silky voice, when she said, "She's not here with you. I am. Think about me."

Malena took off her overcoat, exposing her shoulders and the swell of her breasts. Hook clenched his jaw, torn. She was not, and would never be, Tiger Lily. But she was beautiful, and she was soft, and she was standing there, inviting him into her bed. He drew in a ragged breath, and despite Tiger Lily's face in the back of his mind, he reached out his hook and flicked it across the top button of her shirt, sending it falling open. Then he jerked the hook back, terrified of touching her skin with the thing after the disaster with Tiger Lily.

His pupils darkened as her chest rose and fell, and his heart pounded through his ribcage, and she wet her lips. One look at her body was enough, and Hook gave over to her. She tore off every piece of his clothing and he let her, trying to ignore the fact that her skin was too pale, and her smell was too sweet, her voice too smooth. When she kissed him, he growled low and kissed her back with fervor. If he could drown in the taste of her, he could black out the memory of Tiger Lily's lips.

She was eager and sensual and clawed at his back and shoulders as he buried his face in her neck and used her as an escape. It was bare, meaningless feeling. And, hollow though it was, it felt good. But no matter what he did, no matter how hard he tried to focus on the feeling and the body of the woman beneath him, he could not push Tiger Lily's face from his mind. When it was over, and she was sleeping, naked, against him, he found that he was emptier than he'd been before. And Tiger Lily haunted his thoughts.

TWENTY-FOUR

Pan was absent from the mainland for quite some time, and as Hook was something of a celebrity on Keelhaul, and with no Peter or Tiger Lily to motivate him to leave, the *Spanish Main* stayed docked there for the length of the captain's sabbatical. The pirates busied themselves with rum and looting and the occasional woman. Hook did not behave entirely differently.

He found that being known to every citizen of Keelhaul did not work against him in any capacity. Every tavern he entered had a free drink waiting and a host of women more than willing to throw themselves at him. At first, he found it difficult to ignore the guilt, unable to force Tiger Lily from his mind. But as this grown-up paradise in the midst of Neverland grew colder, so did he. Consequently, his bed grew decidedly warmer.

One morning, after a heavy snow had fallen the night before, Hook woke and looked out the window. There was a woman lying next to him, one whose name he could not recall, and he did not care to. The sunlight streaming happily in and warming his pillow had him somewhat preoccupied.

The woman stirred and turned over, eyes heavy, hair mussed. Hook did not turn; he simply stared out the window.

"Captain?" she asked, voice still having that dreamy, scratchy quality it has when one wakes.

"Hm," he replied.

The woman sat up, not regarding the soft sheet when it fell from her chest. She ran her fingers up and down Hook's bare back. He did not react.

"Distracted?"

"It's warmer today," he said, uneasy energy building in his limbs and gut.

She frowned. "Seems that way."

Hook stood and wrapped a blanket around his waist, then walked over to the window, leaning halfway out of it. The sun warmed his torso. The snow that had buried this place the night before was reduced to a couple small piles of slush, puddles melting and running in brown rivulets down the streets.

He ran his tongue along his lips and squinted up at the sky. That familiar flavor back on his tongue. The sky that impossible blue.

"He's back," he snarled, throwing the blanket to the ground and whirling away from the window.

"Peter Pan?"

Hook pulled on his clothes and boots and strode out the door purposefully, without giving so much as an acknowledgement to the woman. Starkey and several members of his crew were already gathered outside.

"Captain—"

"I'm well aware, Starkey. Time to cast off."

Starkey nodded.

"Gather the rest of the crew. Meet me at the *Main*. And hurry." If the island faded into nothing as quickly as it had appeared, they didn't have long.

"Of course, sir."

Hook walked powerfully toward his ship, compelled to return, knowing that if he stayed on Keelhaul a second longer, he was risking disappearing with the island, and he wouldn't have the opportunity to return to Neverland until Peter left again. He boarded and stood, and ran a hand through his tangled hair. It was longer than it had been when they'd first come here. And there were whiskers on his face, lining his jaw and popping up over his upper lip. They weren't more than a shadow, but they pointed to the time he'd aged since he'd been here.

He perked up when he heard the familiar sound of a clock in the vicinity. The crocodile. The blasted crocodile. What was it doing all the way out on Keelhaul?

Following you, whispered a voice. He backed up instinctively, shrinking into the middle of the deck toward his quarters, blood cold in his veins, and reached for his sword, starting to shake. "Pick up your feet, dogs!" he cried, muscles seizing up. "Or I'll skewer the lot of you."

This seemed to quicken the pace, and Hook smiled coldly, masking the panic that frayed his nerves. *Tick-tock. Tick-tock. Tick-tock.* The men boarded one by one, and Hook backed away from the wheel.

"To the mainland!" he cried, voice uneven.

The pirates responded with a collective shout. And they set to work. Hook stared back at his own little piece of Neverland, quivering from his head to his feet when he caught a glimpse of the massive reptile splashing into the sea and smiling coldly at him.

Hook stumbled back into his cabin, slamming the door shut and scrambling over to his bed. He crawled in and rolled over to his side, pulling the covers up over his shoulders. Focused on the warmth. Pretended, for just a moment, that he was six years old again and his father was going to come in at any moment and dispel his nightmares of nasty creatures in the shadows.

He shut his eyes until the cold had mostly gone away, and the thought that the massive beast was lurking just feet beneath him had mostly retreated into the inaccessible recesses of his mind. Then he sat up, one corner of the comforter still hanging from his shoulder, running his hand over his face.

As he gazed around his empty quarters, he was immediately regretful that he hadn't convinced a woman, any woman, to come back with him. Without a body next to him, he was reminded why he'd avoided this place for the last several Neverdays. This cabin was nothing but painful. He clutched the blanket, knuckles whitening and disappearing into the folds. Here was where he had kissed Tiger Lily. And where he'd fouled it all up when he'd gored her.

The scene played out in front of him, hazy and just as painful as when it happened. About this time was when he would usually go in search of a distraction. But here, on the sea, there was none to be had. He slammed his hook down onto the frame of the bed. She was gone, and she would continue to be gone, and that was all there was.

So he was left with nothing but a loneliness that gnawed through his bones.

But crashing through the silence came a loud thumping on the deck, and then a thundering, as if every pirate aboard had suddenly taken up running and had chosen to train around him, in all directions. Hook shook his head, snapping out of his sorrow, and stood quickly, brushing his fingers over his coat.

When he left his cabin, he was met with Starkey in his face, urgent and panicking. He reached out without a word and took the spyglass from Starkey's hand, then brought it to his eye.

Filling the circle was a flag, flapping and waving in the air. The emblems sent a shot of fear straight into Hook's heart. He knew them as well as any good English boy obsessed with pirates. The only history lesson he'd ever paid attention to. There was a skeleton brandishing a spear in one hand, directing the tip toward a blood-red heart. And in the other hand, he held a goblet. According to legend, the undead fellow on the flag was toasting the devil.

He brought the spyglass down from his eyes and looked at Starkey. Both of them said in the same breath, "Blackbeard."

He remembered drawing pictures of the sail, tacking it up in his room. Sometimes, he'd even pretended that that was where his father went, all those days on the sea, even if it didn't exactly fit within the time frame. It wasn't possible, really, that it was Blackbeard in this vessel, either. The fellow had died nearly two centuries ago. But, in Neverland, stranger things had happened.

"Some fool child's conjuration, no doubt," Hook grumbled under his breath.

Starkey quirked a brow. "Come again, Captain?"

"Never mind, Starkey. Ready the cannons."

As he said this, a blast rang out, and the ship jolted and trembled. Bits of wood splintered off the ship's side and flew into the air. Hook jumped, slack-jawed for the moment, and tried to convince himself that it was one of his men, an unusually prepared crew member already firing upon the enemy ship. But he could not lie even to himself. They'd wounded the *Spanish Main*. Bested him. This brought out the fear in him as well as the malice. For Hook, the two generally went hand in hand.

He whirled around and glared, fiery-eyed, at his crew. "Fire on them, you fools! Don't just stand there, or I'll kill you myself," he cried.

The men hopped to organized action in the presence of their captain. Several of them were at the cannons, and several more were grabbing the guns. Hook and another few went for the swords. He would always prefer the sword, despite its lack of power. He enjoyed its elegance.

The cannons fired again and again, from both sides, but he did not flinch, did not even slow down. He simply pressed forward, looking ever more the devil, wondering if perhaps the skeleton on the flag was toasting him.

The ships careened toward each other, and the men braced themselves as they crashed. Jukes winced as a shudder rippled through the *Spanish Main*, and the ships scraped against one another. Hook ground his teeth, hoping the damage to the *Main* wasn't too great.

Though he had easy access to the other ship and her captain now, Hook hung back, cool and unaffected—and not just on the outside. Let the braggart come to him, for Hook was made of more than a menacing flag and a bloated reputation. He was Captain Hook.

It was not long before Blackbeard and his band of reprobates boarded the *Spanish Main*. They were aggressive and loud, roaring as they jumped onto the ship. Large, with tattoos on several faces. One fellow even had a mouth full of gold and thick piercings in his nose and eyebrows. Another was short and fat and dirty, and the one beside him had to have been nine feet tall.

Hook, however, was focused on an altogether different quarry. He took one look at Blackbeard and tugged his jacket sleeve over his hook, hiding the iron. Then, as the opposing captain noticed him, he raised an eyebrow, turned on his heel and walked easily over to the starboard deck.

Blackbeard bellowed. Hook clenched his jaw and smiled wickedly, shrinking his hook farther into his sleeve. The beast of a man thundered toward him, but Hook remained with his back facing the ruffian, and he twirled his sword round and round. At the last minute, when Blackbeard's breath was nearly upon his neck, he turned, blocking the man's cutlass with his sword.

They were total opposites, the captains. Where Blackbeard was hulking and terrible, Hook was thin and elegant. Where the brute had a thick and scraggly but extravagant beard, Hook had a shadowy spray of whiskers that spoke of easy nonchalance. Though Blackbeard's cutlass was monstrous and heavy, Hook's was light, almost lovely.

Hook noticed the difference in the blades, and with Blackbeard's weight on him, shaving bits of metal off his sword, Hook grinned wryly.

"What?" Blackbeard growled.

"Oh, nothing. It's just that your reputation suggested something entirely different than what you are."

The men separated and Blackbeard came at him. Hook easily parried the slow and hurtling blows.

"How so?"

"Well," said Hook, blocking and blocking again, and thrusting for good measure, "you're large, that's for certain."

"I've cracked skulls with one hand behind my back," the other man grunted, movements becoming labored.

Hook struck then, powerfully, a loud clang in the midst of the roar of battle around them. He leaned against the blade, and his face was no more than a few centimeters from his enemy's. "That, I believe. But you don't frighten me in the slightest. You're strong, you've got a sword the size of Neverland itself, but you'll never land a blow. There's as much brain in you as there is in that skeleton on your flag."

Blackbeard fairly roared at that and slowed even more. Hook, however, was only gaining momentum. "Tired?" he taunted.

The other man's nostrils flared. "Never."

Hook smiled and came at the man, feet nearly dancing with the swordplay.

"A man as small as you would dare challenge me?" the pirate rumbled. "I'll split you in two in a blow."

"I'd pay to see that. And a man as stupid as you would challenge me? Have you never heard my name?"

Hook mustered all the power in him and drew his sword across his chest. He released it into the other pirate's blade with impossible force, feral scowl practically radiating from him, and his hair blew around with the blade, making his face even more menacing, if that were possible. His hook crept out from beneath his sleeve, gleaming in the sunlight. The ruffian stepped back suddenly, eyes bulging. Hook smiled, kicking the man's sword away with his boot. Then, he held up the hook and stared down at the man.

"I didn't—You're, you're—"

"Captain Hook? Aye. Perhaps you've heard of me."

He pulled his hook back, vicious light in his eyes, and began the slash intended for the ill-fated pirate's chest. But he was stopped mid-swing by a small voice.

"Wait! He's not the captain! I am."

Hook turned to find a small boy staring back at him, and he raised an eyebrow, an uncomfortable sort of recognition in the depths of his heart. The little boy had freckles sprinkled across his face, cropped medium-dark hair, a mischievous look in his eye. He couldn't have been more than eight years old, and he looked almost comical in a captain's garb, brandishing a much-too-large-for-his-body cutlass. He pointed the cutlass at Hook, tip bobbing this way and that, as his skinny arms tried to hold it up.

Hook ignored the odd feeling in his gut and asked, laughing, "Is that so?"

"Yes. Now, unhand the knave," the boy said, voice bright and loud for his size, blue eyes narrowed.

"You dare challenge the authority of Captain Hook?"

The child laughed brashly, in the way of little boys, then stared into Hook's face and faltered, mouth falling open, tip of the sword crashing to the ground.

"Father?" said the boy.

Hook was silenced rather immediately. The boy staring back at him, he realized, was no miniature pirate. Hook was staring at a near mirror image of himself.

TWENTY-FIVE

WHAT DID YOU SAY?" HOOK SAID, VOICE UNSTEADY.
"Only that you look just like…"

"Spit it out, boy. Or my hook will persuade you." He thrust out his hook at the boy, and the child shrank back. The threat was empty, but to an eight-year-old it was effective.

"You look just like my father."

Hook breathed in and out, barely noticing when the clanging and the gunshots quieted. Daniel Thatcher behind him jerked his knife across a man's throat. After the fellow thudded to the floor and soaked the wood with blood, he simply stood, eyes trained on Hook and the boy. Starkey and the man he'd been grappling with both stilled together. Blackbeard hadn't yet risen from the floor, and one by one, the rest of the pirates, his and the boy's both, had slowed to nothing.

There was a charge in the air, one that no one could ignore. It made the hairs on Hook's neck stand on end.

Hook clenched his jaw, staring the boy down, peering into his eyes, which were the exact same shade of blue as his, and the little half-smirk he kept waiting at the corner of his mouth, the lips that were thin and expressive, like his. But it wasn't him, not really. His hair was much darker than the boy's, and the child had a prominent spray of freckles over his nose and slightly rounder cheeks. But the straight nose, the high cheekbones, the cornflower-blue eyes—everything else was the same.

What's your name, pirate?" the captain asked, slowly letting his hook fall to his side.

"I am Captain Bloodheart," the boy boasted, puffing out his tiny chest.

Bloodheart. A name that could only be conceived in the mind of a child.

Hook rolled his eyes. "No. Your real name."

He lowered his gaze a smidge, then glowered back up at Hook. Then, he heaved a great sigh. "My real name's Timothy. Timothy Hook."

All the air left Hook's lungs, and he bit down on his tongue. He blinked several times, too quickly, and noticed that all the members of each crew were gathered around them.

"Starkey!" he shouted.

"Aye, Captain?"

"Send the rest of these men back to their ship. The boy comes with me." He grabbed Timothy's upper arm.

Timothy blustered, but furrowed his brow until he looked quite brave and quite menacing. "Don't leave without me, ye scurvy lads! Or I'll have you all clapped in irons."

Starkey snickered, but none from the other crew reacted. They simply obeyed, walking heavily and slowly back to their ship. Timothy stumbled along beside Hook, who was forcing himself not to look at him. Hook opened the door to his quarters and gestured for Timothy to enter.

Timothy kept his face carefully expressionless. He truly did look like a tiny pirate captain, Hook mused. But gruffer than him, apparel-wise. His garb was deep brown and weathered, layer upon ratty layer sticking to his little chest. He had worn leather straps that crisscrossed in front of him, a gun fastened in them. The boots were scuffed, his hat wide-brimmed, but not elegant, not garish. Simple. Like the rest of his outfit, deep brown.

"Timothy Hook?"

"Aye."

"Do you know my name?" he asked, voice low and imploring, fiddling with his hook.

Timothy smiled proudly and puffed his tiny chest out, and Hook realized that his front tooth was missing. "Of course I do. You're the scourge of the seas. Captain Hook."

"Captain James Hook."

Timothy frowned. "James Hook?"

"Indeed."

"Strange," he said, looking at the ground and then back up, peering into Hook's eyes. Did he see his own there, Hook wondered, when he looked?

"You're familiar with the name?"

Timothy screwed up his mouth and looked at his shoes for a moment. "It's odd. I've heard Mother whisper it in her sleep. And Father too. I'd a brother once. Name the same as yours. I never met him, of course. Died before I was born."

Hook was staring at the boy, not even blinking. His voice cracked when he said, "She still does that?"

"What?" Timothy said.

"Talks in her sleep?"

Timothy took a step backward, stubby little fingers brushing against the wall behind him. "What do you mean?"

Hook breathed in shakily and sat on his bed. "I'm not your father, Timothy."

"Of course not," Timothy said, rolling his eyes and crossing his arms tightly in front of him. "I'm not an idiot."

"I'm your brother."

Timothy regarded him with shock and grave suspicion. "You're—you're not my brother. You're Captain Hook."

"I am both."

"You're dead."

Hook sank down further into the bed and crossed one leg over the other, resting an ankle on his knee. He regarded his brother, gaze intense and focused, and set his chin in his fingers. "That's a truer statement than my presence would suggest."

The boy backed up until he reached a heavily gilded and crimson-padded chair. Then he sat, the gigantic seat making him look even smaller than he was. "How do I know you're telling me the truth?"

"I never tell a lie." Hook looked up at the polished, wooden ceiling of his room then, and allowed himself, for the first time since he'd come here, really, to *remember*. "Your father," he said, "he's a sailor. When he comes home, he looks just like me, but with hazel eyes, and without all the getup. He smells like the ocean. And your mother, she loves music, sometimes more than you, you think. But it's all right because when she sings you can feel it in your soul. And when she cooks, you can feel it in your stomach, but it isn't anticipation. It's dread. She's always been a horrid cook."

Timothy's little face was white; his mouth was hanging open and he was clenching and unclenching his hands over and over again. "How could you know that?"

"I'm your brother, Timothy. I swear on the *Spanish Main* herself."

"You're a figment of my imagination."

"I resent that." Hook sat up straight and raised an eyebrow.

Timothy got a rather haughty look on his face. "No, that's what you are. I'm only dreaming anyway. It's where I always come at night. Well, not dreaming exactly. In that in-between place. And here you are. You know all these things because I know them, so of course you would if I dreamed you up. Just like I dreamed up Blackbeard and my pirates and my ship."

"You're a quick one," Hook said, smiling. It was strange to see himself in the face of a child. "But, while you're here anyway, you might as well indulge me. It's not often a boy gets to have a chat with the infamous Captain Hook."

Timothy seemed to give this some consideration, and he scooted back a bit further on the chair, crossing his tiny legs and settling in. "Fine then, figment. What questions have you?"

Hook paused thoughtfully.

"Don't take too long, pirate. I'm liable to wake up at any time."

Hook stifled a laugh at the boy's demeanor. Then, "Mother and Father, how are they?"

"Quite well," he said, picking at his nails, casual, as though this was all terribly normal. "Mother doesn't sleep much, but she never has. And Father's always off on his adventures at sea, you know. Rose is little and annoying."

"Rose?"

"My sister. She's more of a pain than anything else."

"I've got a sister…" Hook trailed off, looking out at nothing, trying to suppress the jealousy burning in him. It wasn't fair to be angry at his parents for replacing him. Of course they had. They'd thought him dead, and what were they to do? But, use whatever logic he might, he could not get rid of the dull pain. His family had built a new family. And he had never replaced them. "Do they talk of me?" he asked, ashamed at the hoarse crack in his voice.

Timothy shrugged. "Sometimes. Not usually. It makes Mother too sad, and Father just gets angry. They talk about you a lot when Mother sits at the piano. She says you were a thousand times better than she ever was."

Hook smiled. She was speaking the truth. "And you, boy. What of you?"

"What about me?"

"What are you like? What sorts of things do you do?"

He considered this for quite some time, and his face was very thoughtful. He was giving this a great deal more concern than any of Hook's other questions. Of course he was.

"Well, I'm a dreadful student. Father thinks I've got no chance at all of getting into Eton."

Hook bit his cheek. Eton. He hadn't thought of that place in a while.

"But it doesn't matter anyway," Timothy said, shaking his head. "I don't want to grow up and be an Eton man."

"What do you wish to be?"

"A pirate."

Hook felt a grave melancholy at this, a hard knot in his stomach, and he looked away from the child in his cabin.

"I'd like to be a pirate who's just as fearsome as you, Captain James Hook." Admiration and innocent excitement laced his voice, and his eyes brightened when Hook looked back toward him.

"You're doing a fine job of it already," Hook said, giving him a little nod. "Your men respect you a great deal."

Timothy jumped off the chair and stuck out his chin, inspecting all of Hook's things from the bottoms of his eyes.

"They do, don't they? They fear me."

"It seems so."

"I'm the second-fiercest pirate in the sea, you know," he said, crossing his arms. Then he turned to look at Hook. "Second only to you."

The edge of Hook's mouth ticked up. "I don't doubt it."

Despite only having known him for a short time, Hook felt a great kinship with this child; the bonds of brotherhood were able to overcome any difference in lifestyle or reality. So, he was betraying his fierce reputation with uncharacteristic kindness.

"Someday," the boy said, pulling his little sword from its sheath, "I'll be even more fearsome than you."

"I don't know about all that. I'm rather a tough figure to best." Hook stood and straightened his hat.

"Have you ever plundered a place?" asked Timothy, cheeks raised and rosy, eyes alight.

"Many."

"Kissed a wench?"

Hook was taken aback for a moment by the boy's language, but answered him nonetheless. "More still."

Timothy paused. "Killed a man?"

Something clenched in his gut, but he answered, "Hundreds." This may well have been an exaggeration, but the boy would not know the difference.

"How about a boy? Have you ever killed a boy?"

Hook looked away from Timothy then, ignoring the sharp twist of pain in his belly, and stared off into nothingness. "One."

Timothy shrank back just slightly from Hook. "And what of the one boy? The forever boy?"

Hook darkened and stared intently into Timothy's face. "Peter Pan?"

"Yes."

"I prefer not to speak of Peter Pan."

Timothy continued anyway, words running into and over one another. "They say he's your mortal enemy, the only one you can never beat."

Hook slammed his hand onto his desk. "I prefer *not to speak* of Peter Pan."

Timothy flinched a bit and nodded, and then he approached the captain.

"Can I see it?"

"What?"

"Your hook."

Hook unfastened the cuff from his arm and handed it to Timothy. His brother was at first distracted by Hook's mangled wrist. It was a sight to behold, and undeniably fascinating if one was an eight-year-old and was drawn to violence. Hook did not try to hide it; he allowed the boy to look.

Hook peered at Timothy, struck by his youth. Had he only been here for eight years? He chewed on his cheek. It felt like a great deal longer than that. And his face suggested that he'd aged more than eight years. Ten, perhaps. Eleven? He blinked rapidly, trying to bury the sudden, intense feeling that he'd been robbed. Of his brother, his sister, of years of his life.

When he tired of the gore, Timothy held out his hand and took the cuff and hook, and Hook jumped, drawn from his introspection by the touch of the boy's fingers.

Timothy beamed, and set the hook atop his hand. Then, he leapt and danced around the room, yelling out various pirate-like phrases and jabbing at the air with his little sword and the captain's massive hook.

Hook leaned back against the wall and watched him, filled with pain and peace intertwined. How long ago had that been him? Bouncing and laughing and dreaming of piracy? Forever. It had been forever.

Timothy wound down eventually, and he walked up to the captain and held out the hook. He took it from the boy and put it back on immediately; it was uncomfortable now to be without it.

"I think I'll be going home soon," Timothy said, unafraid to look Hook directly in the eyes.

"Yes, you're looking a bit dim around the edges."

"Well, I've got to wake up for school, you know."

"Of course." Hook nodded and wondered if Timothy could see the sadness he felt in every part of him.

"This was a good dream." Timothy smiled.

"Agreed."

"Captain?"

"Yes?"

Timothy hesitated. "Are you really and truly my brother?"

He regarded his brother rather mournfully, mouth drawn downward at the corners. "I told you, boy, I do not lie."

Timothy took several steps closer to him. Then, he looked up into Hook's tired face and bit his little lip. "I'm awfully glad to have met you. You're even better than I imagined."

Hook smiled. "The sentiment is mutual."

Timothy yawned. "I'm going now."

Hook stepped past him and pushed open the door, and Timothy walked beside him. At the doorway, Timothy stopped.

"What's wrong?" asked Hook, cocking his head.

"If you're really my brother..."

And he threw his small arms around Hook's middle, wrapping him in an innocent and unabashed hug. Hook laid his hand on the boy's head, choking back a cry. But, he felt him beginning to fade.

"Go to your ship, Captain," he said.

Timothy smiled widely at him and tossed his hair out of his face, then made his way across the ship.

Starkey approached the captain.

"He won't be walkin' the plank, sir?"

Hook sighed, watching his brother walk away. "No, Starkey. I'm not in the business of killing children."

Timothy Hook and his ship of dreams slowly faded into nothingness, and Timothy returned to London, and the *Spanish Main* returned to the shore.

TWENTY-SIX

JAMES HOOK PACED BACK AND FORTH ACROSS THE deck of the *Spanish Main*, mumbling to himself under his breath. Lately, he spent a large fraction of his time pacing, as, since he'd returned to the shores of Neverland, his life had consisted of one distressing thing after another. Most of these stresses revolved, unsurprisingly, around Peter Pan.

In the couple of weeks since they'd left Keelhaul, Hook had lost a score of pirates to the boy. Peter's preoccupation with pirates and dreamers thereof had helped him in this matter, replenishing his crew as new pirates appeared every now and then, but it was distressing nonetheless. Peter had taken to sneaking aboard Hook's ship in the middle of the night, and in the morning another crewman would be always lying somewhere, dead. It was endlessly frustrating, and generally resulted in Hook losing hours and hours of sleep. This was all besides the endless onslaught of thoughts of his brother—staying up nights just hoping to see him again, wondering if he would bring Rose. Wondering if, since Timothy was obviously a Dreamer, Pan was going after Timothy next. Hook never did see his brother. He just lost sleep.

His hair was long and disheveled, and he had dark circles under his eyes. Thankfully, those things did something to draw attention away from the shadow of whiskers across his chin and above his lip. He needed sleep desperately, but that was one luxury he was unlikely to get any time soon. So he paced back and forth, rabid, in the cage that was the *Spanish Main*. After that had accomplished a significant amount of nothing, he decided to settle for a short leave of the prison.

He stopped at the ship's forecastle and called, "Starkey!"

"Aye, Captain." Starkey was beside him in a blink.

"I'm thinking of heading off the *Main* for a bit."

Starkey's face drained a bit of its color, but he made no vocal protest. "Aye, Sir."

Hook leaned over the bow and stared out over the sea, tapping his hook against the wood. Starkey had hesitated; of course he had. Leaving the ship for any amount of time at this juncture was terribly irresponsible.

"You think it unwise?" Hook said, looking over at Starkey.

Starkey sighed. "Captain, we're losing men right and left. If Pan were to come aboard and ye weren't here, well, I shudder to think what'd happen."

Hook chewed on this thought for a while, staring back over the deep and churning sea. It was the one he'd been wrestling with for days. How could he, the captain of this vessel, take any sort of leave while they were essentially under constant attack? It was foolish and selfish, but his nerves were fraying rapidly. He'd barely eaten the last several days, or run a comb through his hair.

He tapped the ship's railing with his hook, clenching his jaw, considering.

"Pan doesn't generally attack at twilight."

"That's true, sir. He waits until the middle of the night, and then he kills the man on watch."

Hook cocked his head and peered at Starkey. "Would it be such an uncaptainly thing of me to leave for just a short while, then?"

Hook knew, of course, what Starkey would say before he said it, and that it would be in conflict with what he *wanted* to say. But he asked anyway, wanting fervently for someone to give him blessing to go, however false that blessing would be.

Starkey opened his mouth and closed it again, biting off his words. Then he said simply, "Of course not, sir."

Hook looked back out over the shadowy blue waves then, and he bowed his head, resting it in the crook of his elbow. His shoulders slumped and he leaned there for quite some time, quiet, utterly exhausted.

"Don't humor me," he said, voice muffled by his arms. "I'd be a fool of a captain if I left. You know it as well as I."

"Well, just look at ye, though. Ye look like half a ghost, pacin' around here at all hours of the night. What kind of a captain are you in this state, anyway?"

Hook straightened, clinging to Starkey's words, however patronizing was the root of them. In an instant, his eyes looked just a tad less hollow, and the color of his skin less pale.

"I'm not sure about it." As he said this, though, he was already making his way slowly to the ship's exit.

"Go, Captain. I'll hold things down around here."

"I won't be gone long."

Starkey hesitated, unconsciously reached for his gun and brushed his fingers over it. "You'll be back before nightfall?"

"Of course."

Without allowing himself to reconsider, Hook left the boat, pausing for a moment to feel the sand against his boots. The gentle wind whispered through the space between his back and his jacket, but it wasn't chilly; it was comforting. The forest was green and lovely and, for once, wholly inviting. And the little nymphs were back to lighting up the sea, one of the few advantages to having Peter back in Neverland—the weather and the island itself.

He let his feet lead him where they would and paid no heed to the destination before him.

He walked for quite some time, a great deal farther than he'd intended. When he stopped, just before him was the river, ribbons of red and orange and blue gurgling and spilling over the rocks. This was the river that signified the border of the Indian lands. *Tiger Lily.*

"James Hook?" came a sweet voice from across the river.

He choked. "Tiger Lily?"

She hopped easily across the stream and stood in front of him. She looked harder than he remembered, her long, angular face a bit older, but that could very well have been the shadows on her face and the daggers her eyes were shooting at him. Her fists were clenched at her sides, and she was practically vibrating everywhere. Hook was compelled to take a step backward.

"Where have you been?"

He frowned. "I—Why? Have you been looking for me?"

Her eyebrows shot up, and she made a noise that sounded like a laugh, but almost certainly wasn't. "Of course I have."

Hook scraped his teeth across his lip. "I don't understand."

"Well, you're in good company."

Tiger Lily crossed her arms, and Hook stepped forward and threw his hand and hook into the air. "Tiger Lily, last time we saw each other, I gored you. You left. What more could you possibly want to say to me?"

She coughed out an irritated breath, and Hook was torn between wanting to back away for his safety, and wanting to get closer for his sanity.

"Of course I left, James, you dolt," she spat. "You *stabbed me.* I needed medical attention. Would you have preferred I'd stayed and bled out on your floor?"

Hook fumbled for something to say. Unfortunately, though he'd rehearsed his piece in this conversation many times, at no point had he prepared a response for this reaction.

"I—I had no idea. I thought…" His general eloquence was reduced to inelegant sentence fragments. It was impossible to think clearly around the woman.

"Thought what, exactly?" Tiger Lily uncrossed her arms and let them dangle at her sides.

He fiddled with his hook, staring down at it, then back up at her, forgetting to breathe just for a second when her beautiful, angry eyes flashed at him. "I thought you were through with me."

She shook her head and looked up at the sky. Then, she turned away from him, digging her heels into the ground. "You're a fool, James Hook."

Hook reached his hand out to her, this close to touching her, then drew it back. He was at an absolute loss, and found that he was in something of a panic.

"Tiger Lily, I am truly sorry," he said, the deepest kind of fear washing over him.

She did not turn, and he stood, breaths shallow, staring at her back in the clearing. He could feel the space between them like it was solid. Electric, tempting him to cross it, terrifying him into staying put. This was ridiculous. Managing a crew of pirates, he did with ease. But managing a woman was something else entirely.

"Where have you been?" she said quietly, back still turned to him.

Hook blew out a breath. He would not lie to her. "Keelhaul."

Tiger Lily spun around and jealousy flashed across her face. She took several long steps toward him, nostrils flaring. "Keelhaul?"

"Indeed."

Her voice lowered, and she stared up at him, inches from his face, eyes wide and unblinking and pensive. "You've finally done it, then."

"Done what?" Hook's pulse jumped, skin hot with the nearness of her. He stepped just an inch closer to her, and she stood her ground.

"Become a pirate."

He paused, then said, voice rough, "I have always been a pirate."

Tiger Lily shifted so that her chest was almost touching his and looked into his eyes, lips parting. He was overcome with the need to taste them. But suddenly, she turned away from him and cocked her head. She was staring at something through the trees, something that Hook could not see. Hook let out a breath, shoulders relaxing when she moved away.

"Do you hear that?" she whispered.

"Hear what?"

She did not answer. She simply walked toward the sound that Hook couldn't hear, and he could do nothing but follow her. It wasn't long before Hook picked it up as well. The sound was haunting and beautiful, like nothing else he'd ever heard. He knew in a beat that it was the mermaids.

The lagoon was quite a ways away, too far away for their voices to reasonably carry, but mermaids had a way of doing impossible things, Hook had found. Their voices were ethereal and smooth, like they came from the spirits of bells.

Tiger Lily walked slowly and sat in the silvery blue leaves, wrapping her arms around her knees. Then, she closed her eyes and tilted her face toward the sky, entranced and smiling softly. His breath caught when he saw her that way, and he stopped walking.

The moons had just risen, bringing a soft glow to her face, silhouetting her body. Hook couldn't help but hold his hand out to her. It trembled just slightly as he waited for her.

She opened her eyes and stared up into his. The coldness was gone, replaced with a sort of enchantment. And she gave him her small hand. He pulled her up and drew her to him, heart racing as he pressed her body to his. He slid his hand down to her waist and to the small of her back. Then, gaze never breaking hers, he drew her arm gently out, raising a trail of goose bumps he knew were not from the cold, and encircled her hand with his hook. She did not shrink away from the metal; she just wrapped her fingers around it.

Hook stared into her eyes and stepped. She stumbled a bit, and he smiled. Then, he stepped again, and she followed. They spun in slow circles around the clearing, moons illuminating everything. He lifted his hook and spun her once, then brought her to his chest, pulling her much harder and closer than she'd been before. He could feel the little catch of her breath, the pounding thrum of her heart against his, and he was at once petrified and at peace.

It was a dark waltz, made of haunting voices and forbidden touches and hidden desire. Hook pressed his fingers into her back and led her in the dance. Then, he brought his face against her cheek, intoxicated by her nearness, relishing the sweet scent of her. His long hair fell into hers, and they tangled together. Hook did not know why this pleased him so.

"Your hair is longer," Tiger Lily said, and her voice was hoarse.

"Long hair is the mark of a pirate and a fiend," he whispered low into her ear, lips brushing against it. "Both of which I am."

She shivered, and he grinned. He continued to spin her slowly, thoughts of her pounding heart and flushed cheeks rushing through his mind, and the sirens' music began to fade. He drew back. His heart skipped when he saw that her eyes were closed and her lips were just barely parted. He reached out his fingers and ran them along her jaw. She leaned into his hand, and heat flooded over him. Tiger Lily opened her eyes and looked into his, then, and unveiled something that he'd only hoped was hidden there before. In her eyes was wanting, and then it turned to a need.

Hook could barely think, barely breathe, not with her looking at him that way. He glided his fingers up to her cheek and rested them there. Without giving himself time enough to reconsider, he bent until their faces were a breath away from each other. Electricity jumped back and forth in that little agonizing space between them. And then, he touched his lips to hers. When her mouth yielded to his, a flare went through him, and he knit his fingers in her hair and kissed her deeply, slowly, in a way that he'd never kissed any of the nameless women on Keelhaul, or Malena, or Susan Weaver.

It was a kiss made of longing, and passion, and hunger, and it sent shivers all over him. When she clasped her hands around his neck, he drew her even closer to him, wanting to be a part of her, and she gasped at that, in the midst of the kiss, breathing him in. The thing that hypnotized him was the craving he felt in her lips; she wanted him too. He ran his hand down to her collarbone, and his hook down her arm, and she shuddered lightly.

He was drunk off the feel of her, the sweet floral taste of her, so much so that it was minutes before he realized the mermaids' music had ceased. When he forced himself to back away from her, his voice was husky, his throat dry.

"I have to go," he said, only then realizing that the sky around them was inky black.

She was trembling everywhere, but managed, "As do I."

She turned to leave, and he caught her by the hand.

"I'll be there, this time, when you come to see me."

She grinned at him wryly, kiss still there, hidden at the corner of her lips. "Of course you will."

Tiger Lily disappeared, and Hook started to make his way back to the *Spanish Main*. The sense of urgency he should have felt was masked by the wine of the woman, and for the breadth of the trip back, Hook found himself thinking of her. He wished to be consumed by her, feel her in every piece of his soul. She was worth every second of his captivity in Neverland. She was worth everything.

Starkey, however, disagreed. For by the time Hook reached the *Main*, Peter had already struck.

TWENTY-SEVEN

<hr>

THE CAPTAIN CLENCHED HIS JAW AND DUG HIS HOOK into the soft wood of his desk. Little pieces spiraled out and fell to the floor. He dragged the hook until he reached the end of the desk, and then he strode over to his window. There was a light coat of frost upon it. Hook narrowed his eyes.

"Starkey!" he yelled, a rumble in his voice.

Starkey appeared at the door seconds after he called him. "Aye, Captain."

The look on his first mate's face was grim, with a note of accusation. Hook ignored it for the moment.

"There's frost on this window."

"And?" Starkey clenched his jaw and turned toward the door, and Hook's nostrils flared. He took two monstrous steps and caught Starkey's shoulder with his hook.

"Do not be so brazen as to take your leave from me."

"Sorry, sir," Starkey said, voice low and insincere.

Hook pressed the metal into Starkey's shoulder and turned the man to face him. "I am your captain. Not the other way 'round. Don't take to forgetting yourself."

Starkey stared back into his face, eyes hard and angry. "Of course, *Captain*." Starkey's nose twitched, and Hook refused to be intimidated by his father's familiar, angry gesture.

"Excuse me?" Hook said, eyes burning with anger.

"A man died last night, sir. Again. And yer concerned with the frost on the windows?"

Starkey's voice had risen a decibel.

"You believe this is my fault?"

"I do."

Hook's eyebrows shot up. In truth, he was almost impressed with Starkey's boldness. But, he was leaning decidedly toward enraged. His voice lowered dangerously, and he pointed his hook at the other man. "You, Starkey, are the first mate. And I am Captain Hook. Before I took charge of this vessel, you were *nothing*. You spent all your time drinking and getting slaughtered by that boy. Do not forget that."

"Forgive me, Captain," Starkey said, face reddening, "but what exactly has changed?"

Hook struck the man across the face with his right (which was, unfortunately for Starkey, no longer a hand), etching a clean line of blood into his cheek and breathing hard. Starkey blinked and stood straight, staring back at the captain. His eyes were carefully absent of fury and sarcasm.

Hook neared Starkey's face and said, "Next time, I will not hesitate to kill you."

A muscle twitched in Starkey's jaw, but he gave his captain a single nod.

Hook backed away a step and drew in a deep breath, calming himself. "Now, Starkey, as I said before, there is frost on my window. The Pan is gone. Again."

"Aye," said Starkey, standing rigid, face carefully devoid of expression.

"How can he be gone again already?" Hook said, brow deeply furrowed. "He only just returned."

Hook's face was burning, tinted a deep shade of crimson. Pan had left again. And there had never been a time when he'd wanted to kill the boy more. It was absolutely infuriating.

"I don't rightly know, sir."

Hook jerked his hook to point toward the door. "Leave me, Starkey."

Starkey did not need to be told this twice. He closed Hook's door behind him a tad harder than was necessary, and Hook rolled his eyes. He picked up a handkerchief and folded it around his hook, wiping it clean of the small coating of Starkey's blood. Starkey's tendency to always be right was infinitely frustrating. It was his own fault that another man died last night, and one man, at this point, was no small thing. Their numbers were shrinking dramatically. He had less than thirty pirates on his vessel now.

Of course Pan was gone. Again. It was inconsiderate of the boy, given the captain's strong desire, at this very moment, to plunge his hook into him. But there was not much that he could do to rectify the situation. So, he chose to take it as a gift.

He exited his cabin, head held high, past Smee, who was fumbling with his fingers and looking at the ground, and Cecco and Noodler and Thatcher, who were mumbling low to one another, daring to have a glimpse at him one at a time. Jukes stopped in front of him at one point, and Hook narrowed his eyes. "What?" he growled.

Jukes blinked and leaned backward. "Nothing, sir," he said, and he lumbered away to join the rest of the men.

Though Starkey gave him a look that could have melted the skin off anyone caught in its wake, he ignored him as well, hugged his coat tightly around him, and strutted off the *Spanish Main*.

Who he was looking for was obvious. Where exactly to find her was not. He walked through the woods, however, unfazed. It seemed he had a knack for finding her, even when he'd no idea where she would be. So, he simply followed his instincts, which took him to the Indians' river. Lightly colored mist rose off it, blanketing the nearby grass in cold fog.

When he reached the riverbed, where Tiger Lily was not, he took a risk and headed to the clearing where they had danced the night before. He did not really expect her to be there; he doubted that the waltz and the kiss had meant as much to her as they had to him. But, there was no harm in looking, was there?

When he made it to the meadow, he stopped short. The venom that had been running through his blood since the encounter with Starkey dissipated instantly. Hook was unable to stop himself from smiling, too large a smile; he was sure he looked rather foolish. There was Tiger Lily standing in the midst of the yellow-green grasses, back turned to him. Hook was silent as he headed toward her, stopping behind her. She jumped when he slid his arms around her waist and brought his lips to the spot just behind her ear.

"James! I didn't hear you."

He turned her around to face him, unreasonably thrilled when she did not pull away from his arms. She opened her mouth to say something to him, and he covered it with his. She jumped lightly at that, but her hands pulled him closer, and he smiled against her lips.

"So it wasn't just the sirens?" he said, grinning.

"What?"

He backed up, still close enough that their lips were nearly touching. "I was rather concerned that you only kissed me last night because you were under the spell of the mermaids. I shall let you take it back, if you wish."

A playful spark lit up his eyes, which was certainly a rarity for the captain. His arms were still tight around her, and he ran his thumb up and down the small of her back, touching her so low, nervous prickles ran up his arm. Her skin was chilled, along with every other piece of life in the clearing, apart from Hook. She turned up one corner of her mouth and kissed him on his cheek.

"What the mermaids sang had very little to do with what we did last night."

"Ah. So you admit they influenced you a bit."

She bit her lip and grinned. "A bit."

"I suppose I shall take it."

He swept his gaze down her figure, and back up. He'd been right, when he'd seen the age on her face. She couldn't have been younger than eighteen.

Tiger Lily pulled back from him, but he kept his hand at the small of her back, starved for any touch she would allow him. She sat in the middle of the clearing, and he reluctantly broke the hold and sat across from her.

"I've missed you," he said. No matter how desperate that sounded, it was true.

Tiger Lily rolled her eyes. "We haven't been apart for more than a Neverday."

"Yes, but that could mean any amount of time in Neverland."

Tiger Lily smiled and looked distantly over his shoulder. Hook turned and found nothing there, nothing but the still, grey trees, and the glittering frost covering the leaves. He frowned for an instant, but chose to ignore it. Women did strange things frequently, he was learning. He scooted a fraction closer to her.

"Tell me, what brings you out to this particular meadow today?" His voice itself grinned; he was looking for a very specific answer, one that revolved around him.

Tiger Lily said nothing. She simply continued staring off over his shoulder.

"Tiger Lily?" he said, frowning.

She blinked and turned to face him. "Hmm?"

"Did you hear me?"

"I'm sorry, James. I'm not feeling very well." He could see it then—the distinct pallor in her skin, the dullness in her eyes.

He scooted even closer to her, coming to sit beside her. Their hips were touching, a fact that Hook was overwhelmingly aware of. He inched his face closer to hers, lips just behind her ear, and said, "Anything I can do to help?"

She laughed, in a strange way. "I doubt that."

Then, Hook understood. He stiffened. "It's Peter, isn't it?" he said, pulling back.

"No," she said, but she wouldn't look at him.

He bit down on the side of his tongue, hard. Voicing his opinion on the matter would be a mistake. But, he was somewhat well-versed in making mistakes. "Of course it is, Tiger Lily. It's always Peter Pan."

"You have no idea what you're talking about."

She stood. He stood with her.

"I have more of an idea than you believe." His nostrils were flared and he was shaking, instantly so furious he could barely see straight.

Tiger Lily turned her back on him and crossed her arms.

"What is wrong with this place?" Hook shouted. Rarely did he ever lose control, but with her, he was on the edge of panic every second, so raising his voice was barely optional.

"James, you don't understand."

"You're absolutely right," he hissed, low and clipped. "I don't understand."

He took a step, standing in front of her now, staring into her eyes, compelling her not to look away. He kept his voice harsh and low so that no passing Peter-loving inhabitants of Neverland would hear the exchange.

"I don't understand how everything on this cursed island revolves around the presence of that boy. And I don't understand how anyone can look in his smirking, arrogant face and not wish to smash it. And what I really do not understand is how you can kiss me and dance with me and hate me for taking a leave to Keelhaul, and yet you cannot look at me when I mention his name."

"I should go," she said.

"Don't," he said, somewhere between livid and desperate. "Not yet."

She shot a deadly glare at him. "You cannot blame me for my nature, James Hook. I did not ask to be bound to Peter."

"Finally, she admits it!" He threw his hand and hook in the air and took several steps away from her. "How, Tiger Lily? How can you 'be bound' to a child? That's all he is."

"He's not a child. He's not much younger than I am; you know that." Hook laughed harshly at that. She was every bit a woman, and Pan was every bit a boy. She ignored him and continued. "And I cannot help what I feel. I'm his dream, James. I'm *his*. Without Peter, I don't even *exist*; can't you understand that?"

Hook's jaw went slack, and he was breathing hard, as though he'd just run the length of the island. He'd known that, somewhere in the dark, inaccessible crevices of his soul. But he'd never acknowledged it. Had never heard it put so cleanly. The thought that she really, truly was Pan's robbed the breath from his lungs.

"Tell me, pirate," she said after he'd been silent for a while, "how am I to change what Neverland has willed me to be? You clearly couldn't."

Hook recoiled, ripped from his musings, struck by her words. "What did you say?"

Tiger Lily shook her head, and shifted from one foot to the other. "I'm saying that you were not a scoundrel when you came here. You were not a pirate. But it was your destiny, wasn't it? So you ran off to Keelhaul Isle and you drank and pillaged and made a name for yourself, and you probably bedded a thousand women—"

Hook took a step toward her, voice rising with every word. "Oh, is that what this is about? My 'thousand women?' I only ever had any woman other than you because you made me believe you were done with me."

Tiger Lily drew in a sharp breath and dropped her gaze to the cold forest floor. The pain that came over her face was sudden and unexpected, and it cut Hook to the core. The silence that followed as they looked at one another twisted the knife inside him.

But then Tiger Lily said, voice quiet, pained, a little dangerous, "So, it's true?"

Hook inched backward. "What?"

He knew exactly what she was asking but wished to put off the pain just a moment more.

"You did bed all those women. I'd heard it, but I didn't believe it."

There was a note of desperation in his voice when he said, "Tiger Lily, I told you. I thought—"

She curled her lip inward. "It doesn't matter what you thought."

He reached out toward her, and she leaned backward. Just a hair's width, nearly nothing. But enough.

"That isn't fair. All the time I've been fall—" Hook stopped himself before he made a confession he couldn't take back.

"Go on," she said, but her voice was cold.

His heart pounded painfully in him, palms slick with sweat. "All the time I've been—desiring you, I've known you truly wanted someone else. Someone I hate with

259

every fiber of my being. It's always been a struggle with you. So, when I do something terrible and you walk out the door, what else am I supposed to believe?"

Tiger Lily looked away from him. He was smug; she could not answer that question, not truthfully.

"Anyway," he said, clawing at any chance to change the subject, "we are not talking about my conquests. You know I only did those things to try to forget about you. And I never would have done if I'd believed, for a moment, that you weren't in love with Peter Pan."

Another silence as Tiger Lily stood there, arms dangling like weights at her sides, mouth falling open.

"I'm not in love with him," she said, crossing her arms tightly over her chest.

"You are. You're standing here in front of a man who would do anything to be with you, and you're fouling it all up for a boy." His voice rose with the frantic panic inside of him.

"I'm going, James." Tiger Lily took several steps toward the frozen trees, and Hook caught her by the arm.

"No," he shouted, breath coming out in a hazy puff. "You don't get to just leave like this. You can't walk away from me because it's too hard to give me an honest answer." He feared, for a moment, that he didn't want her honesty. He did not want to hear again that she was Peter's, that she'd always been, that the choice he'd made as a boy to stay away from her had been the right one. He did not want to hear it, but he needed to. So he searched her eyes, his own dark and desperate.

Tiger Lily looked up at the sky, which was dark and angry and rumbling.

"It's going to rain," she said, eyes suddenly red and wet. He could hear the hoarse breathiness in her voice, certain she was on the raw edge of crying.

"Toss the rain." Hook drew her gently in to him, fingers ghosting over her palm. She leaned into him, and his heart beat feverishly against her cheek.

Her assessment, it turned out, was correct, and the rain started to fall, cold, almost snow. It came down slowly at first, coating them lightly.

"Do you love him?" he whispered, staring down at her, not bothering to camouflage the pain etched into his face. She stepped back and looked up at him.

The rain fell harder, until fat wet drops were pounding all around them.

"Do you love him?" he asked again, louder against the downpour.

The water was soaking both of them now, and his hair stuck to his shirt. Her dress clung to her body.

"Yes," she said so quietly that he could scarcely hear it.

"What?"

"Yes," she screamed. "I wish I didn't, but I do."

Hook looked away for a moment, then he grabbed her in a fit of passion.

"How? How can you love a boy? Does he kiss you?"

He brought her to him and slanted his mouth hard over hers, desperately, angrily. And he pressed her against his chest. He poured all of his frustration, passion, into her in that kiss, wishing he never had to end it. But when she grabbed at his shirt and tried to bring him closer to her, he pulled back.

"Can he touch you, Tiger Lily?"

The rain was falling in sheets now, and he could see nearly every bit of her beneath the fabric of her dress. He trailed the tip of his hook softly down the back of her neck, and slowly slid his hand down to her collarbone, stopping there, looking at her eyes. Her dark, haunted brown eyes. She made no protest, and so he let it fall farther down, until it was cupping her breast. Touching her there was the sweetest sort of agony, and his fingertips trembled, fire lighting up his legs, his stomach, his chest, almost driving away the reminder of the Pan between them.

Her face held a mixture of pain and pleasure, and he dropped to the ground.

"Can he ever do these things to you?"

He clutched the back of her leg and brought his lips to her thigh. She drew in a sharp breath, and he could feel her shaking beneath his jaw. He kissed her again and again, until his mouth was around her hipbone. She shook harder, and he stopped. If he kissed her again, he would not be able to stop himself, would not be able to remind himself that she wasn't his. That this could not last, would maybe never go on beyond one forgotten moment of passion in the woods. Not if she still loved Peter Pan. Not if she only chose to be with him because *he* wasn't here.

So, he lingered there for a second longer, memorized the smoky-sweet taste of her skin, and then ripped himself away.

"He will never love you like I can."

He left her standing there, quivering in the rain, and he walked back to his ship.

TWENTY-EIGHT

It was twilight in Neverland when Hook was roused from his cabin. He had a sinister disposition from the earlier encounter with Tiger Lily and was scowling from the moment he opened his door. What exactly had brought him onto the deck, he was unsure, but he'd felt a humming beneath his skin, a buzzing in the air. And he had been compelled to step out onto his ship.

Upon first glance, nothing seemed to be out of the ordinary. It was slightly chilly and grey and quiet. No one aboard the *Main* was doing anything of note. A look of grave suspicion came over his face as he surveyed the ship. And then when he looked up into the sky, his heart jumped. Distant, a speck in the clouds, there flew Peter Pan. He thought he saw several other specks with him as well. He grinned wickedly and jabbed his hook into Smee's sleeve, catching him as he passed.

Smee toddled backward, nearly falling, which would have been unfortunate, as he likely would have been rather maimed had he slipped.

"Smee," Hook said, voice low and brimming with excitement, "get Long Tom."

Smee raised an eyebrow. "Long Tom, Captain? But there's no vessels about."

Hook was thrilled enough by Peter's reemergence that he did not even berate Smee for questioning him.

Instead, he simply held out his gleaming hook toward the sky, which was darkening by the second. Smee rubbed his spectacles, then peered up into the clouds.

"Pan," he breathed. Without another word, he ran off and gathered several of his crewmen with him to bring out the giant cannon.

"Captain!" called Daniel Thatcher after the men had spent too long with the monstrous weapon, "Long Tom is ready."

Captain Hook marched across the deck and slid his hook down the length of the cannon. It screeched loudly, and the majority of the crewmen covered their ears with an enthusiasm they rarely displayed elsewhere.

It was dreadfully dark already, which seemed impossible. But most things in Neverland, when they had to do with Peter, seemed impossible.

"Where is he?" Hook yelled, voice muted in the strange quiet of the air.

Smee twisted his hat around in his hands and looked up at the clouds. The rest of the crew followed suit. They looked like a particularly foolish lot, all standing still, mouths gaping and staring at the sky. Then, Hook perked up. A tiny, bright yellow glow appeared in the black, bobbing and flitting about. "Look, there."

The pirates turned a collective head.

"Pan's fairy?" Starkey asked.

Hook glowered and gave a terse nod. "They're all with her, no doubt," Hook said.

"No doubt, sir. No doubt at all."

"Gentlemen," Hook said, puffing out his chest and straightening his hat and jacket, "fire."

The crew bustled around in a chaotic moment, and the light suddenly disappeared. Hook felt a panic well up in him, and he grabbed Thatcher's shoulder.

"Do it now, Thatcher. Now. We'll lose them!"

The pirate lit the fuse on Long Tom. There was utter silence everywhere for a moment. Even the wind was tense and hushed; not a sound came from a Neverbeast on the island. Then, a thunderous boomed ripped its way through the quiet, tearing through the clouds.

The crew of the *Spanish Main* waited with bated breath, each member staring up at nothing, for nothing was precisely what they could make out in the sky. After a beat, Hook left the cannon and made his way to the gunwale, then leaned heavily over it. He was so intently focused that he could hear nothing going on around him. He shut his eyes, searching for some feeling, some indication that the Pan was dead. And yet, he found none. If anything, the air was warming slightly.

"Long Tom has failed us," he growled, whirling around, waves of black hair flying. "Peter Pan lives."

Smee was standing next to Hook, though he didn't even realize it until he said, "Indeed, Captain. But, what shall we do?"

"Find him, Smee. We will find the boy, and we will kill him."

Smee nodded solemnly and Hook made his way throughout the rest of the ship, readying his men. Not a single man was left aboard; every pirate was requisitioned for the plot. So, into the black forest they went.

The woods looked particularly uninviting that night as the dark branches loomed over them. The leaves were frantic and dark-colored, fretting, crimson, black, silver, and then crimson again, and the air chilled Hook's skin. For once, however, this struck no beginnings of fear into the captain's heart. It was too filled with hatred to allow an ounce of anxiety to settle in.

There were faded, burning pictures, flashing in his head of all the things Peter had destroyed or taken from him. Tiger Lily. His parents. Timothy. Rose, whom he'd never meet at all. Hook sped his steps, half-running.

All at once, he detected to his right a pistol being drawn. He shot his hook out and grasped Starkey by the shoulder.

"Captain, let go of me shoulder. Yer diggin' into the bone!" he gasped.

"Put back that pistol."

"It's a boy, Captain. A Lost Boy, runnin' through the woods. Did ye not see him?"

Hook's voice was low. "We shall not slay any Lost Boys tonight. I do not wish to kill another child. And you will not either. Understand?"

Starkey winced in pain as the captain withdrew his hook from his shoulder, and he nodded and put back his pistol.

"Spread out, men," Hook commanded. "Tonight, we *will* find Peter Pan and his Lost Boys. They cannot be far off now, not with the one running about in the woods. Should you come upon them, you return to me immediately, and do not touch Peter under any circumstances. You leave the boy to me. Understand?"

The men responded with a loud "Aye!" and, brandishing their torches and guns and swords, they rambled off into the night.

Hook commissioned Smee to accompany him and left the rest to Starkey.

Smee crackled along the leaves behind him and panted loudly.

Hook slowed a bit. "What is it, Smee?"

"Would you mind slowing down?"

At that, Hook heaved a great sigh, the night's exertion weighing down on him suddenly. "I'd stop altogether, Smee. But this boy—he compels me to move forward."

Smee set his hand upon the captain's shoulder, a gesture so reminiscent of his mother he choked for a moment. Hook stopped.

"Is it your hand, Captain?"

"Aye. That's among them. And the crocodile. And the boy and the girl. And the woman. There's a host of things, Smee. A host." Hook rested his head in his hand, massaging his temple.

Smee smiled at him, and though there was a thread of pity laced throughout the smile, it was not offensive or patronizing. Something about the way of Smee soothed the rage running hot in Hook's veins.

The seat he'd chosen warmed slightly underneath him, which brought him out of his thoughts. He frowned at it, as though that would prompt his strange little chair to explain itself. And then, it grew warmer and warmer, until it was alarmingly hot. He jumped up from it and stared at it accusingly.

"Smee!" he said. "This—this—"

"Mushroom."

Indeed, it was a mushroom. But even after all these years in Neverland, Hook still felt foolish saying something so fantastical. It was simply too large and too vibrantly colored and glittering to be a piece of fungus. Nevertheless. "This, er, mushroom—it's hot. Curiously hot. Come touch it."

Smee cocked his head in the manner of a dog and rested his fingers on it. He snatched them away fairly quickly.

"That's odd," Smee said.

"It is, isn't it?"

Hook stretched his long fingers out to the thing, which was, even by Neverland standards, unusually large. He grasped it by its top, then, and pulled. Rather than resist, it popped directly out of the ground. Smoke began to pour out from the stem, billowing into the air, eliciting a cough from Hook's lungs.

"A chimney," Hook whispered. After the puff of smoke disappeared, he and Smee leaned over it. There was a soft glow coming from inside it, and the murmured sounds of children's voices.

"Where is Peter? How is it he's not back yet?" said one of them.

"He's coming. Of course he is."

"I'm hungry."

"You're always hungry."

"Am not."

"Are so."

The conversation devolved into a scuffle. Hook set the mushroom gently back atop the chimney and stood. Then, he looked around him. There were trees encircling the place that would have looked perfectly ordinary had a passerby not known that there was a house below his feet. But, when one was privy to this information, the strange holes in the trees became obvious.

"Doors," said Hook. He laughed. It was not a cackle or any wicked thing; it was a laugh of genuine amusement. "Look, Smee. They've each carved a separate entrance for themselves. Each boy with his own door. How like children."

The laugh was tinged with pain, for he could not help himself thinking that it could have been him picking a tree. And he couldn't think past the sadness that he'd only recognized the voices of two Lost Boys, Tootles and Slightly. He shook his head quickly and stood taller.

Smee laughed as well, but Hook was not sure if Smee understood fully what he was laughing about.

A *tick-tock tick-tock tick-tock*, cut the laughter off.

"Do you hear that, Smee?"

Cold fear washed over Hook, and the blood drained out of his face. He'd never seen the croc this far inland.

"It sounds like a ticking, Captain."

Hook was in an instant panic, seeing in his mind the croc's terrible jaws and dead eyes and hungry smile looking at him, thirsting for him.

"Back to the ship," he said, and his voice was low and urgent.

"But Captain, how can we leave now? We've finally found—"

"Quiet," he said, voice loud and metallic, despite his attempting a whisper. "Run, Smee!"

Smee ran, and the tick-tocking grew louder and louder, and Hook's heart crashed harder against his chest. There was nowhere to hide there, he knew. Nowhere that crocodile would not smell him out. Hook drew in a breath, coughing, feeling that the air was made of glass, and sprinted.

Tick-tock tick-tock tick-tock.

He quickly overtook Smee, unable to worry for his crewman's safety, and when the men reached the *Spanish Main*, Hook fled to his quarters and slammed the door behind him, the sound of the clock still fresh in his head. Though he'd found Pan's hideaway, his nerves were decidedly unsoothed. The captain lay wide-eyed in his cabin, and he knew he would not sleep. The horrible sound and picture of the crocodile accompanied him to bed and remained his companion throughout the night, and he could not sleep for the terrible thoughts of clocks and scales and horrible eyes and sharp, smiling, hungry teeth.

TWENTY-NINE

DREAMING WAS ONE OF THE THINGS HOOK MISSED most about London. He wished that, rather than feeling the dead eyes of the crocodile filling his stomach with cold, leaden fear, he was asleep, and touching Tiger Lily. But, he supposed, it seemed odd to dream when you were living in one. So there was nothing for him but an endless cycle of reality, and sleeping, and reality again.

That did not stop him wishing and imagining the taste of Tiger Lily's lips, the feel of her skin, remembering what it felt like to have his mouth at her hip.

Inevitably, every thought of her turned to a crocodile. Her smile became a row of sharp, hungry crocodile teeth. Her footsteps became the slow, steady ticking of a clock.

He tried to remember London, to remember his mother and father and brother, but his pictures of them were so blurry that they did nothing to stave off his horrible imagination. So nothing would lull him to sleep, and he tossed and turned violently, wondering just how long this Nevernight would last.

Eventually, when his body had reached such a state of exhaustion that his eyelids forced their way closed and he had just begun to drift off, there was a loud rapping at the door. He jumped up to a seated position and gripped his sheets, ready to shred them. Hook scowled and rose from his bed, pulling a cover around his waist. He flung the door open with vigor and said, "What sort of fool—"

He stopped short when he realized who was standing in his doorway, suddenly very conscious of his bare chest and lack of any clothing beneath the blanket.

"Tiger Lily," he said, suddenly entirely out of breath.

"I'm sorry; I shouldn't have come so late." Her gaze flicked from the top of his head to his feet and back up again, and she blushed.

He scratched his head with his hook and tried to gather his wits about him. This was no easy task, it turned out, being that he'd just been roused from sleep. "No, no," he said, still in that half-daze of near slumber. "Come in."

Tiger Lily accepted his invitation and walked into his room. He closed the door quietly behind her and turned to face her, heart rate rising rapidly. She stood there for an awkward moment, wringing her hands and looking at anything but him. He gave her what he deemed a reasonable time to begin talking. She did not take it. Finally, after what seemed an eternity of silence, he was compelled to speak.

"What—" he started, unsure whether to draw close to her or back away. He chose to stay backed against the door. "What are you doing here?" His words were clumsy, he knew, but eloquence had fled his head completely. Tiger Lily was there, in the middle of the night, with him.

Tiger Lily looked directly at him, and he thought what he saw in her eyes was guilt. Panic overtook him. This was it. She had come to end it for good. His throat constricted.

"James, I—"

"Don't say it," he said hoarsely, unwilling to hear what he knew she would tell him in moments. "Please, don't." He took a step into the room.

A better man could have handled it. A stronger man would have heard her out and sent her away and slept off the pain, or drunk it off. Clearly, he was neither better nor stronger. With the woman in the room, he was nothing but vulnerable and raw. He hated it at that moment, more than ever.

"James," she said, taking a step toward him.

Hook turned away from her, swallowed hard. He was fully aware that his actions were those of a child. But the pulse pounding dangerously in his throat and the sweat breaking out all over him made it impossible for him to react in any other way.

"Please, James, just—"

"No," he pleaded. "Please, don't even tell me. I cannot hear it from you. "

Tiger Lily made a sound of exasperation and forced her way in front of him.

"You fool pirate," she said, and she grabbed his head and kissed him. The feel of her mouth took his breath away, and at first he didn't even kiss her back, he was in such shock. But he quickly came to his senses and kissed her, deep and hard, with everything in him.

Tiger Lily pulled away for a moment. "What did you think I'd come to say?"

His voice was husky. "I thought you'd come to tell me you were leaving me."

She rested her fingers lightly on his bare chest, and his breath hitched. "I've made my choice, James Hook."

"Have you?"

She swallowed hard and drew closer to him, fingers spread over his collarbone. He shivered.

"I cannot spend my life loving a boy."

Hook's pulse quickened. "And can you spend it loving a pirate?"

Tiger Lily stared up at him. Both of them were frozen, it seemed, heavy breath the only sound in the room. Tiger Lily broke the spell. She brought his mouth to hers, and Hook encircled her body with his powerful arms, forgetting about the blanket, letting it fall to the floor. He breathed into her, a low, guttural groan that came from the depths of him, and he let go of all the passion he'd been restraining for so long.

He pressed his chest hard against her and pushed her into the cabin wall, and she gasped. Hook tangled his fingers in her hair and kissed her over and over, deeper and with more longing than he ever had. The touch of her was exquisite, overwhelming. He was reluctant to pull back from her lips, but he had a greater need to explore the rest of her.

His fingers glided down to her shoulder and he stopped when they reached the edge of the fabric of her dress. He looked into her eyes, hoping, questioning, next to pleading.

She looked straight into him, and a corner of her mouth turned up.

"Are you sure?" he whispered, voice cracking.

She clasped her fingers around his and slid the sleeve of her dress down until it bared the top of her arm. Hook breathed in shakily and did the same to the other. The curve of her neck, the smooth lines of her shoulders, they were unreasonably enticing. He slid his fingers up, behind her neck, gentle, barely touching her. Then he leaned against the wall, hook digging into the wood, and brought his lips to the hollow of her throat, feeling the rapid pulse beneath his lips. He drank in the taste of her skin, sweet honeysuckle and smoke and earth; it was intoxicating.

He moved lower, teeth brushing against her collarbone, stopping when his mouth reached the curve of her breasts and kissing her slowly. Then he backed away once again and slid his hand up the length of her leg. She was trembling. He clenched his fist around the fabric of her dress and slipped it off her.

Hook stood there, still, unable to move, unable to breathe, staring at her. Her body was smooth and curved and heady; he couldn't even blink. Then, Tiger Lily pressed up against him and kissed him, and he lost all capacity for rational thought. There was nothing in his mind, save for her soft body against his and the feel of his fingertips across her. He laid her on the bed, completely vulnerable to her, letting his hand and hook glide softly over every surface of her body. He lowered his face and kissed her throat, up to her jaw, stopping at her ear.

"Tiger Lily," he whispered, barely able to form words at that point, "I love you."

He waited, skin burning atop hers, breath catching in his throat, terrified that he would not hear it back from her. Then, in a voice so low he could barely hear it, she said, "I love you, James Hook."

Her body melted against his, yielding to him, and he gave himself completely over to her. He was totally consumed by her, enraptured by the feel, the taste, the beauty of her. And when she let out a small sound of pain, he brought his lips to her ear and kissed her gently until she relaxed against him and they moved together.

Afterward, Hook lay beside her in the darkness, running his fingers up and down her back, hardly believing that the woman he'd loved since he'd been able to love was lying next to him, skin against his, breathing rhythmically in and out as she slept. He wondered, briefly, if tomorrow he would wake up and find that this had all been a dream. But that wasn't possible here, was it? For the first time, he was thankful for that. He smiled, thoughts clouded and fuzzy.

It was difficult to think clearly with her so close, even though she was asleep. As Hook lay, spent and peaceful in the night, stroking her skin softly, he found that there was nothing more on this island that he wanted. Nothing more than her.

The thought of slitting Peter's throat did not sound so thrilling then, not with Tiger Lily there, wanting to be with him. It was as though all his life, he'd been searching for breadcrumbs, desperately needing breadcrumbs, but laid before him was a spread of pastries and fruits and fine wines. And were that the case, who in his right mind would long for the breadcrumbs?

Perhaps the killing of Pan was not a worthwhile venture. Perhaps, if Tiger Lily loved him, Pan was not what he needed at all. Perhaps he could brave all of Neverland if this woman agreed to be with him.

"Tiger Lily," he whispered.

The rhythm of her breathing hitched, but then resumed.

"Tiger Lily," he said again, brushing her raven hair away from her back with his hook.

"Hmmm?" she answered, half in the throes of sleep.

"Run away with me."

Tiger Lily gave him an answer that was clearly influenced by grogginess. "Not tonight, James. It's late out."

"No. I don't mean now. I mean ever. Run away with me."

Tiger Lily was quiet for several seconds, then she rolled over to face him. Hook tried to ignore the feeling of her bare skin moving against his.

"What did you say?"

"I asked you to come away with me."

She grazed her fingers up the length of him, playing with the soft curls of his hair that lay over his shoulders.

"What do you mean, come away with you?"

He kissed her between her jaw and her ear. "I mean, leave all this."

"It isn't possible."

"I know we can't leave Neverland. I know. But we could leave this all behind, go somewhere without Peter and the crocodile and your father forcing a barrage of suitors on you." He smiled into her throat.

"Where? The Never Wastes?"

"Yes. Perhaps. Or some part of the island we've never seen. Or a little place off the coast I haven't sailed to yet."

She frowned up at him. "The Never Wastes—that place is nothing but nightmares. You'd regret it the moment you set foot in it."

"Not if you were with me. And we don't have to go there. We'll sail off." He kissed her, unable to keep from feeling, tasting her lips.

She smiled and moved her fingers to his chest, absentmindedly running them through his chest hair.

"You're a pirate. Would you have me live aboard the *Spanish Main*?"

"If you wished it."

"I'm not a pirate, James."

"Then I'll leave it," he said, shrugging.

"Leave it?" She scoffed. "You are Captain James Hook, the fiercest pirate in the sea. You'd leave it all behind for a woman? I hardly think so."

He brought his hand to her face, staring into her eyes with utter sincerity. "I'm not lying to you, Tiger Lily."

She closed her eyes and smiled as he ran his thumb over her cheek. "What about Peter?"

His thumb froze.

"What about Peter?" he asked, voice immediately dark.

"Could you give up your quest for revenge on the boy? Could you really stop caring about him?"

He relaxed and stared over her out the window, considering.

"Yes. I haven't known peace since I was a boy. Now I know it with you, and no thirst for revenge can rob it from me. I'd forget about him."

Tiger Lily bit her lip. "You don't know what you're saying. Give up piracy, give up your ship, give up your Pan. It's sleep talking."

"It isn't."

"We will talk about this in the morning, when the woman beside you isn't naked and you've your wits about you."

Hook grinned, and she rolled over. His heart beat quietly against her back, and he closed his eyes and breathed deeply. And he wrapped his arms around her and fell asleep kissing her neck.

THIRTY

When Hook awoke, Tiger Lily was not in his bed. He wondered, for a moment, if perhaps last night really had been, impossibly, a dream. He sat slowly up and flung his legs over the edge of the bed, morning confusion muddying his thoughts. Hook stood and pulled on his pants, letting his chest stay bare; Peter was back in Neverland, which meant he could walk outside not fully clothed without freezing.

He walked out of his cabin and onto the deck, telling himself that he hadn't invented the night with Tiger Lily but doubting it somewhat. His bed was empty, after all. He shook his head, trying to clear the haze from his mind, and furrowed his brow when Bill Jukes plodded past and snickered, Flintwise at his heels, very conspicuously avoiding the captain's eyes.

He swiveled his head to glance at his crewmembers, and no one, save for Starkey, would look him in the eye.

"Starkey," he said, making his way over to his first mate.

"Captain."

Hook leaned over the ship's bow, not pressing, simply waiting. Starkey was unable to keep his opinions to himself, Hook had found. He didn't have to wait long.

"It's a bold move, Captain."

"What?" he said, turning his head, elbows on the edge of the ship.

"The Princess?" Starkey said, raising an eyebrow.

Hook sighed. "You all know, then?"

"It'd be hard not to, her leavin' your cabin this mornin' and walkin' right through the middle of everyone."

Hook chewed on his cheek. He was not required to defend his actions to his crewmen. Nonetheless, he felt like he needed to. Heat rose to the surface of his skin.

"She's Pan's, isn't she?" said Starkey quietly, looking out over the glass sea.

Hook whipped his head around with a snap and growled, "What would give you such an impression?"

Starkey looked into Hook's snarling faced and calmly replied, "I meant no insult, Captain. But she's been runnin' round with Peter since she was little. We've all seen 'em here and there. I'm only sayin' it's bold, is all."

James breathed slowly in and out, inwardly recoiling, expecting a lecture. He felt extremely young, preparing to be berated for pursuing a girl he shouldn't have, as though Starkey could punish him, level him with a word. Something about Starkey often made him feel this way.

The other man simply narrowed his eyes, compelled Hook to meet his gaze, studied him hard. Then Starkey jerked his head toward the starboard side of the ship and said, "She's down there. On the beach."

Starkey turned and left him, heading toward the breakfast table, where most of the men had gathered by then. Hook stood there, blinking. What had caused Starkey to simply let him off without a word?

Perhaps he approved? Or perhaps, after all this time, Starkey had finally accepted him as Captain, finally agreed to let him make his decisions and to follow them, whatever his own opinion on the matter. He stole a glance back at his first mate, and Starkey did not look up from his food. Hook straightened, running his fingers through his long, black hair, and left the ship, bare feet sinking into the warm sand. Then, he saw her.

She was standing on the shore, long hair whipping in the breeze. The suns were just rising, sky pastel and lovely, nymphs lighting up the sea. He breathed a sigh of relief. Tiger Lily did not turn; she was completely still, water bubbling around her ankles, sand creeping up her legs. She was exquisite, stealing the breath from him. He almost hated to disturb her, but he wanted to touch her more than he wanted to let her alone. So, he walked quietly over to the woman and stopped behind her. Somehow, she still couldn't hear him, so he slid his arms around her shoulders and kissed her lightly behind her ear. She jumped.

"You weren't there when I woke up. I feared last night wasn't real," he said, voice still low and gravelly from the early morning,

"Quite the opposite," she said, smiling.

"Are you well this morning?"

"Very," she said. Her voice was somewhat dreamy.

"I slept better than I have in ages." He slid his fingers down to hers, then, and she curled her fingers around his hand. He started walking down the beach toward the little coves scattered here and there, and she walked slowly with him.

She laughed. "I think you may have been at least half sleeping even when you were awake, from the things you said to me last night."

"Is that so?"

"You said you'd give up the *Spanish Main* for me. So, you tell me."

She was teasing him, he knew. He thought for a moment as they walked, and the low murmur of the men on the *Main* faded into near silence, the only sound the gentle whip of the waves, the occasional bird singing out. They stopped at the mouth of a tiny cave.

"I don't know. Part of me wants to tell you that your feminine wiles influenced me into saying crazy things." He nudged her just inside the cave's opening and kissed her again, this time at the spot just where her neck met her shoulder. It was difficult, he was learning, to keep his lips from touching her.

She grinned.

"The other part wants me to tell you that I'm irreversibly in love with you, and that there isn't anything I wouldn't give up to be with you."

Tiger Lily turned around, eyebrows furrowed. She wrapped her arms around his neck and leaned up against the cold cave wall. It was so small and close in there, barely room for them to stand. He leaned into her warm skin.

"The *Main*, James? You'd leave your ship? Give up being a pirate?"

Hook brushed a tendril of hair behind her ear and unwrapped his arms from around her. Then he heaved a sigh and sat on the soft floor of the cave. He played with the sand, grabbing a handful, sifting it through his fingers.

"Truthfully? I'll always be a pirate, Tiger Lily." He looked at her out of the corner of his eye. "Take off that dress again and perhaps you'll hear me saying something entirely different."

Tiger Lily laughed and sat beside him, shadows playing on her face. She slid her hand between his shirt and his skin. He felt a chill go up his back.

"Ah, so it was babble in the throes of passion then," she said, smiling and running her fingers up and down his spine.

"I can't forget who I am. And I won't." He arched his back lightly under her fingertips and shuddered. "But that does not mean I don't wish to run away with you."

Her hand froze. "Think about what you're saying."

"I have."

Tiger Lily snatched her hand from his back and grabbed her arms, frowning.

"What?" Hook asked, turning to look at her. "Is that so insane?"

"It's just, I've never been anywhere but home. I can't simply leave everything."

"Fine," he said, leaning closer to her. "Then I'll go to the Chief and I'll tell him to leave your suitors well enough alone. I'll tell him you've chosen Captain Hook."

She laughed aloud. "Would you? Would you, really?" Sarcasm dripped from every word. "My father would have every man in the camp on you in a second. You'd be dead before you could turn around."

"I don't know about that. I like to think the Chief and I have something of a rapport."

"James," she said, smiling without humor, "you're a pirate. He will never allow me to be with a pirate."

"Then, that brings us to our former argument." He turned toward her and cupped her face with one hand, eyes burning and intense. "I won't abandon piracy forever, and I won't give up my ship entirely. But I'll leave with you. We can go anywhere. Someone else can take my place until we return, whenever that may be. I'll not worry about the *Main* for as long you wish it. I'll think of nothing but you." He slid his fingers down her arm, drawing goose bumps where he touched her, and kissed her palm. "And see nothing but you." He kissed her again, on her arm. "And feel nothing but you." He brought his lips to her shoulder, heat between them all the more striking in the cool, dark closeness of the cave.

Tiger Lily rolled her eyes and batted him away, shivering. "I can't think when you're kissing me like that, pirate."

He chuckled mischievously and sat back, folding his arms across his chest. "Fine. I shall fight fair. Know that that's an honor I rarely afford people."

She shook her head, smiling, then sighed heavily. "Where would we go, truthfully? I'll not live in the Never Wastes. You'd certainly not survive there."

Hook narrowed his eyes and smirked. She was right; he was somewhat inept at wilderness survival. Then, he turned out toward the ocean. "Keelhaul. We could go to Keelhaul."

A shadow fell over Tiger Lily's face. "Yes, James. Let's go to Keelhaul, where you've been kinder to all the women than anyone who's ever visited its shores."

Hook bit his cheek and conceded the point.

He stood and peered out over the island. There were little peninsulas and tiny pieces of land that could hardly qualify as islands, all of them dotting the landscape. "Not Keelhaul, then. But look around. There are a thousand places we could go, little Never Isles off the coast that neither of us has ever seen." He knelt again, fingers playing in the soft pieces of hair at the base of her neck. "I'll give you a life you've only dreamt of, Tiger Lily. We can be together anywhere. Then, when we've tired of some perfect little paradise, you can sail away with me on the *Main*."

"What of Peter?" she asked, staring at some dark spot on the cave wall.

"What of him?" said Hook, voice instantly low and angry.

"You would forget him so quickly?"

"Yes," he said, words just this side of a growl. "Why is that so important to you anyway? Would *you*?"

"James—"

Hook stood, crossed his arms. "I tire of this."

Tiger Lily rolled her eyes. "Of what?"

"This," he said, waving his arm at her. "Even after last night, he's still here. He's always *here*."

"Stop it, James," she spat. "I haven't even laid eyes on Peter for a week—"

"A week?"

"—and last we spoke, he wanted little to do with me anyway."

Hook frowned. "What?"

Tiger Lily drew her arms tighter around herself and pulled her knees into her chest. "He says I'm growing up."

"You are," said Hook, reaching out to touch her, kneeling in the sand, trying very hard not to think of the day he'd heard those very words from Peter.

"For you," she said, looking over her shoulder at him. "I grew up for you."

Hook drew in a breath.

"I can't decide whether I love you or hate you for it, James Hook, but I did, and now here I am."

His pulse spiked and he laid his hand on her shoulder, running his thumb in little circles on her skin. "You grew up to be with me?"

"Yes," she whispered.

"That can't be," he said quietly. "You'd been growing up long before you knew me."

"Yes," she said. "Consequences of being the Chief's daughter. You grow up quickly, experiences and all that." She bit her lip. "But I'd stalled, you know. I was quite happy to stay where I was, young, a girl, and then I met you again. And everything changed."

"Is that—" His voice cracked, and he drew in a deep breath. "Did you come to my room last night because—because you're too old? Because Peter no longer wishes to be with you?" Vocalizing it at all made him sick to his stomach.

"No," she said, spinning around to face him, hands at the base of his jaw. "I came to your room last night because I love you."

His gaze dropped to the floor and then rose to hers. "Then why mention his name the moment I ask you to leave?"

"Because if I'm to leave with you, I need to know that you love me more than you hate him. He dreamt me. If he dies, I'm not—I'm not entirely sure…"

Hook nodded. He knew what she was wondering, for it had crossed his mind as well. If Peter died, would Tiger Lily still live? He reached out and touched her face, pulling it to his.

"I love you more than I long for London, more than I love the *Spanish Main*, more than I hate Peter Pan." He kissed her slowly, deeply, and she tangled her fingers in his hair. "Come away with me," he breathed.

She bit her bottom lip. "I don't know about it, James."

"Are you afraid?"

"A bit."

He paused for a moment, skin buzzing from brushing hers. "Of what? Leaving, or me?"

She let out a breath. "Not you. It's no small thing you're asking of me, James. You're asking me to leave everything I've ever known, to abandon my family, my people. I can't decide it in a night."

"Then don't," Hook said. He twitched his hand toward her and played with her thin fingers absent-mindedly.

"Perhaps you could persuade me," she said and leaned into him, sliding her arms under his shirt, around his waist. Fingers playing under the waistband of his pants against his bare skin. He breathed in sharply, and his eyes darkened, instantly hungry.

"How so?" he said, sliding his hips toward her, slightly beneath her.

"Well, if you told me how beautiful and wonderful I was and all the things you'd love to give up for me again, all the things you love less than me, I could see myself leaning toward it."

He smiled deviously and rolled over on top of her, pressing her wrists into the sand.

"Devil woman. Trying to get me to babble unintelligibly and make false promises once again?"

She bit her lip, eyes alight.

"Well, that can be arranged," he said, and he pressed his hips into her and let his mouth go where it wished and forgot, for a little while, about anything coherent.

THE NEXT SEVERAL DAYS WERE CONSPICUOUSLY ABSENT of Peter Pan. Hook barely even found himself thinking of the boy, so consumed was he by Tiger Lily. He was shirking his duties as captain, if he was being completely honest with himself. But Starkey was managing things fairly effectively, and he figured that if he and Tiger Lily did leave, Starkey would have to learn to do these things anyway, at least for a while.

He lay in his bed, where he'd been spending a significant amount of time as of late, and ran his fingers through Tiger Lily's hair, scratching her back lightly with his hook.

"James?" Tiger Lily said.

"Aye."

"I'll do it."

His hook froze. "You'll what?"

"I'll do it. I'll go with you."

He sat up and Tiger Lily did the same, pulling the blanket around her breasts.

"Not to Keelhaul," she said.

"No. Of course not to Keelhaul."

"And not to the Never Wastes."

"No, not there." Hook felt a great excitement welling up within him, and his smile covered half his face. "We'll go to an outlier, some place neither of us has ever been."

She looked pensive for a moment, then smiled, staring up at him from under her eyelashes. Hook grabbed her face and kissed her, then sprang up from the bed.

Tiger Lily slid out of the bed as well and got dressed. "How are we to do this, James?"

"What do you mean?"

Her eyes were bright, and she lifted her shoulders in a shrug. "I mean, how are we to get past my father? He'd slit you if he found out we were leaving."

Hook scoffed. "He would try."

Tiger Lily rolled her eyes and walked around the bed. "It does not matter. There's no way for us to cross Neverland without my father finding out about it."

Hook furrowed his brow, quiet for a short while, and leaned against his desk, considering. "We won't go through Neverland."

"What are you proposing, then?"

"We'll go around it." His eyes lit up. "Tonight, go back to your camp. Get whatever you need. Tomorrow, at twilight, sneak away to the clearing, the one—"

"I know the one."

He grinned. "I shall send a couple of my men to get you. Smee and Starkey, I think. They'll take you to Marooner's Rock. I will meet you there. And I'll take you away."

Tiger Lily pursed her lips and considered. Then, she walked up to Hook and slid her arms up to his neck. "I'll meet you there. Tomorrow."

He dropped his hand and hook down to her waist, letting them linger there, enjoying the feel of her hips against him, trying halfheartedly to ignore the heat that flared in his chest.

"Do you have to leave yet?" He closed his lips around her jaw and earlobe and smiled when she sighed. But she pushed him away.

"I have to go, James. My father—I need to give him a proper goodbye."

"I don't know that I can wait a full night to see you again. Let me give *you* a proper goodbye." He kissed her again, lower, letting his hand trail down across her back.

"Pirate."

His eyes glittered. "Indeed."

Tiger Lily ripped herself away from him and pressed her palm against his chest. "I have to leave. I'll see you at Marooner's Rock. Tomorrow night."

Hook grabbed her hand, holding it and feigning sadness until Tiger Lily turned and breezed out the door laughing, leaving him somewhat unsatisfied, but ultimately thrilled. He left his cabin soon after, considering the course he would chart. Starkey nodded at him as he strode past on the deck.

"Captain."

"Starkey…" Hook stopped beside his first mate. "I need to speak with you."

Starkey cocked his head and drew closer, and Hook gestured for him to follow him off the ship.

"What is it, Captain?"

"I've a responsibility for you."

"What is that?"

Hook chewed on his cheek. Then, "I've made a decision which I believe will cause…something of a stir. It's of the utmost importance that you listen to me, for yourself and for the *Spanish Main*."

A look of concern flitted over Starkey's face.

Captain Hook tapped nervously on his leg. "I'm leaving."

Starkey's eyebrows shot up. "For how long?"

"I'm not sure."

Starkey lowered his voice and grabbed Hook by the arm. "Captain, could you try to explain to me what exactly yer sayin'?"

"Tiger Lily," he said, pulling free of his crewman. "I'm leaving with her. Tomorrow."

Starkey blinked at him.

"We're going away. Not forever, but, for a while."

"This is mad, sir. Do ye know what'll happen to the men if ye leave? We did nothing without you. *Nothing.* And you've riled up every pirate in the Never Sea against the *Main*, not even countin' Peter Pan. If ye leave…"

"Starkey, do not attempt to convince me to stay. It will not be effective. I'm going, and you and Smee are going to assist me."

Starkey shook his head, hands curling into fists at his sides. "Yer Captain Hook, sir. Ye can't abandon yer own ship."

"Do not question me," Hook warned, flattening his mouth into something grim and edged with a threat. "Until tomorrow, I am still your captain."

Starkey turned away from him.

"While I'm on my leave, I bequeath the *Main* to you."

Starkey turned back toward him, questioning.

"You were charged with running the *Spanish Main* before I came to Neverland, and you will do an adequate job of it once I'm gone."

"Sir, I don't—"

"I'm uninterested in protests. Go back to the ship."

Starkey closed his mouth into an expressionless line and walked heavily toward the *Spanish Main*.

Hook stared out at the waves. The sea was all salt and foam and possibilities. He pushed away the slight guilt that accosted him as he stood there. It wasn't forever. The men would survive for a little while without him.

Nonetheless, when he boarded the ship, several of his men glowered at him, while others just looked on, jaws hanging open. He felt a heavy queasiness in his gut. The faces of Jukes and Smee, particularly, needled at him. And so Hook looked straight ahead, trying to black out the stunned faces of his men, and focused only on getting to his cabin. He opened the door and slammed it behind him.

THIRTY-ONE

THE SHIP WAS QUIET AS HOOK LAY BACK ON HIS BED, staring at the ceiling. There was a creak at the door and it opened slowly, letting in a sliver of bright light. Hook jumped, sitting up.

"Captain?" came a little voice, one that pierced Hook's heart.

"Yes, Smee?"

Starkey followed behind Smee, looking at the floor. Hook could feel the man's anger and hurt. That, he knew, was what was rendering Smee incapable of speech. That didn't matter. It didn't.

Smee sighed. "We were, eh, just leaving. To go get the princess."

Hook nodded, coughed. "Yes. Good. Well."

Smee looked back up at him and opened his mouth, like perhaps he was going to say something. But the words were lost in his throat and he snapped it shut again, then waddled out of the cabin as quickly as he could. Hook swore his kind, warm eyes were shining when he left.

Starkey, for his part, twitched his nose and locked his jaw, turned stoically on his heel, and shut the door behind him, without so much as a second look or word.

Hook stared at the closed door for a while, utterly torn. He gazed at his cabin, touching every piece of furniture there one last time, fingertips lingering too long on everything. His golden wine goblet, the smooth dark wood of his desk, the walls even. He was thrilled at the prospect of sailing away with Tiger Lily, but the thought that this was the last time he would see the *Spanish Main* in who knew how long left him with a profound sense of sadness, as though he was leaving one of his children and did not know when he would return.

He sat there, inhaling the sweet smell of cedar, for some time. But as the suns began to sink and the room became cloaked in shadow, he stood, gave the cabin one final appraising look, tipped his hat to it, and left.

Hook boarded the small boat he would take to the lagoon, slowly bobbing toward it on the waves. He felt nearly naked in the tiny dinghy, as though he was floating along with nothing around him.

The waves carried him gently to the lagoon, and as he neared the place, his pulse quickened. He drew in a deep breath and stared into the darkness as his boat drifted into the mermaids' cave. It was dark and cold and moisture hung in the air, clinging to his skin.

The cave ended soon enough, and Hook's boat emerged on the other side. It was not a great deal lighter outside the cave, but he was able to see out there, which was quite an improvement. What he saw, however, was not what alarmed him. It was what he did not see. What was conspicuously absent from the lagoon, and from the giant rock in its center, was Tiger Lily.

When his boat reached Starkey and Smee's dinghy, he searched quickly for any possibility that she may have been hiding there. But it was clear that she was nowhere.

"Where is she?" His voice echoed over the water. Smee and Starkey both stared at him as though he'd gone insane.

"Where is Tiger Lily?" he asked again, trembling in his voice.

"Captain?" Smee said, shaking as well, but for a wholly different reason than Hook.

"Where is she?" he roared, his face a disturbing shade of crimson.

"We let her go, of course."

Hook had no reaction stored away for this particular statement. He stood there stupidly for a moment. Then: "Let her go? What do you mean, you let her go?"

A terrible fear seeped into his stomach, leaking out to every part of his body. She'd not come? She had truly changed her mind. This was not happening. He refused to believe it.

"It was you, sir," Smee said, brow furrowed, voiced pitched high. "You told us."

"I told you *what*?" Hook's voice, on the other hand, was terribly low, and full of menace.

"You said for us to release the woman."

The statement hung there between them for a moment, accompanied by the low sloshing of the water against the boats, and Hook's mouth hung open.

"Release her? She was not a captive, you fools. What would have possessed me to say such a thing?" His eyes darted around and he threw his hook up in the air. "I will not hesitate to strike you here and now, Smee. Where is the woman?"

Starkey moved forward. "She's not here, Captain. I swear on Davy Jones we heard you say to let her go. She swam off."

"You're both mad."

He ran his hand through his hair, hard, nearly yanking some of it out. He was shaking everywhere. Why had he allowed them to escort her at all? He was a coward. He should have taken her himself and braved the idea of an Indian assault on the trek. What had she thought? That he'd changed his mind? Fear overcame him completely;

he found he could not breathe at the thought of losing her.

Then, he heard a voice cut through the terrible stillness.

"No madness in your men, sir. Only in you. You truly believe that you are the mighty Captain Hook?"

Hook's head shot up. The voice was a remarkable replica of his.

"Who do you say you are, stranger?"

"I am Hook, Captain of the *Spanish Main*, and the fiercest pirate to ever sail the seas!"

There was something off in the particular timbre of the voice, something that made Hook's hair stand on end. But he could not place it.

"If you are Hook," the captain said, voice even, "pray tell, who am I?"

The voice laughed, full of wickedness and spite and youth. "You, sir, are a codfish!"

Hook's eyes narrowed, and he scowled deeply. The title was an all too familiar one.

"And you." His voice lowered until it was dark and horribly cordial. "Do you masquerade as another?"

"Sometimes."

Hook felt a sinister sort of satisfaction in his gut. How long ago was it that he had been a child, throat crushed beneath the heel of Pan's hand? He'd fooled Peter then into believing he was *special* and *brilliant*, and that he, Hook, was nothing but a naïve child.

Just as he would fool him now.

The issue with arrogance, it seemed, was that sometimes, someone *was* cleverer than you.

"Are you animal?"

"No."

Hook spun slowly around the lagoon, searching for the place the voice had come from.

"Vegetable?" He tried not to breathe, needing to hear every decibel of the response.

"No, no."

"Mineral?"

"You're not a whiz at this game, are you?"

Smee shifted uncomfortably in the other dinghy, and Hook closed his eyes, trying to shut out the sloshing from the little boat behind him.

Ah. There was the direction from whence it came.

Hook turned his head, fear and satisfaction and adrenaline twisting together in him, just as it had when he was a child at Peter's spectacular failure of a Thinning. The feeling was almost delicious.

"Are you a man?"

The voice lost a bit of its camouflage, and cried out, "No!"

Hook grinned. The location was narrowing. "Boy?"

"Yes. Wonderful, marvelous, clever boy!"

"Ah."

"You'll never guess, pirate."

"Alas, you're likely right." Hook was staring at the spot he'd picked for the boy, and his eyes were cold and black, like marbles.

"Then, I will tell you. I am Peter Pan!"

Peter shot up, whirling around, from behind the rock where Hook had pinpointed him. There was a thrill in his veins as Hook dove headfirst into the water, swimming powerfully for Marooner's Rock. The hateful energy buzzed around him, so much so that none of the mermaids lurking in the deep even bothered to come after him.

When he came up for air, there was a great deal of splashing and commotion. A horde of Lost Boys (and one girl, whose presence momentarily befuddled the captain) had appeared from nowhere, and had set upon Starkey and Smee while he was under the water.

But when he saw Pan on the rock, the commotion faded around the captain. He slid up onto Marooner's Rock; everything there was amplified. The grit against his fingers, the cold spray of the water against his torso, and the breath of the Pan, assaulting his ears, echoing, taunting, pounding as he climbed.

The rock was slippery, and he put out his hand to steady himself as he stood, waiting for the boy to come out from behind it. He was consumed with hatred, and so felt no guilt or fear or anything that usually accompanied his plots to murder the child. He brandished his shining hook and grinned, lying in wait.

Pan leapt up, standing at the top of the rock, and, before Hook could think to react, Peter darted out and grabbed Hook's knife from his belt. The color drained from Hook's face. Peter smiled, toothy and gleeful.

Pan raised the dagger, and Hook was assaulted with a memory of long ago, when he'd witnessed that first murder, Peter killing the pirate. The look out of Peter's eyes was the same now, and it set him to trembling. Hook shook so hard that he lost his balance, and fell to the edge of the rock.

The boy had the marked advantage; there was no denying that. Peter dove through the air, Hook's own dagger in his outstretched hand. Hook shut his eyes, fear freezing his limbs, and waited for the kill. But the hot slice of the blade did not come. Instead, he was met with Peter's hand clasped around his, helping him up.

Hook paused for a moment in utter confusion. Guilt flooded through him, and rage, and hate, and several other things he could not put a finger on. Peter had a sense of fairness that was endlessly frustrating when it came to the business of hating him.

No. Hook hardened. Peter had already robbed him of too many things. The boy would not rob the pleasure of revenge from him as well. He drew his hook back and plunged it into the boy's hand, flinching slightly when the blood oozed out around the metal. Peter cried out, and his eyes widened. Hook pushed past the guilt and focused on the rage, and he cried out in anguish and anger mixed, barely sounding human. He slashed out at Peter, landing his hook in a leg, catching it on a rib when he thrust it upward. The rip when he pulled it out of Peter's side nauseated him. Curse Neverland's wicked hold on everyone there. Stabbing Pan felt as though he was plunging the hook into himself.

Peter fell to the rock and stared up at the sky, bleeding in several places, saying nothing. Hook tried to ignore the ache that shuddered through him at the prospect of Peter's death.

Tick-tock tick-tock tick-tock.

Hook froze and tore his gaze way from Peter. He whipped his head around, panicked, searching frantically for the crocodile. When there was nothing there but the awful sound of the clock, he dove instantly into the freezing water, forgetting Smee, Starkey, Peter, the Lost Boys. None of that mattered now.

Hook's breath fled him as the water prickled around him, and he swam furiously for the shore of the lagoon, but he felt as though he was moving through slush, skin burning, every stroke too weak, too slow. The sound of the clock shuddered through him, from his ears down to the tips of his toes. The mermaids were cold and laughing at him, taunting him, cruel voices echoing off the cavern walls, bouncing off Marooner's Rock. They giggled and splashed, hoping to see the croc turn the lagoon red with his blood.

He scrambled up to the shore and stumbled, then ran, soaking and freezing and terrified, hair flapping in damp ringlets behind him. Black leaves scratched and stung him as he ran past, but he could barely feel the barbs.

His lungs and muscles burned agonizingly, begging for him to stop. He realized, then, that he could no longer hear the *tick-tocking* of the clock. So, in the middle of the meadow that he had shared with Tiger Lily, he collapsed. The croc wouldn't come there, to their place. He could feel it in his bones. It was too far inland. He fell to his knees, gasping for breath, and clawed at the earth, face down in the dirt. And he tried not to think of Tiger Lily, or of the crocodile, or of dying, bleeding Peter Pan.

THIRTY-TWO

WHEN HOOK AWOKE, HE WONDERED BRIEFLY IF HE was a boy again, and he looked around, influenced by the haze of sleep, for Peter. He hadn't woken on the leaves since a morning long, long ago. And so, he was back in time for an instant, the sweet vanilla taste on the air still a wonder, searching for Pan and the Lost Boys and pondering if the breakfast he would receive would be real or imaginary.

Dead leaves stuck in his hair, and they made his scalp itch as he sat slowly up. He froze when he saw the woman sitting a few feet away from him, staring off into the trees. Reality came flooding back to him, and he was a man and the captain once again.

Tiger Lily was crying, and her hair was tangled, and there were dark circles under her eyes. Had she been there all night? He stood up from the ground and shivered, then walked over to her and knelt on the ground. He reached his hand out and cupped her face, then turned it up toward his.

"How long have you been here?" he asked, voice rough with sleep, and the lack thereof.

"Since early this morning."

He ran his thumb along her cheek, and she closed her eyes, turned her face away, and stood. He frowned but chose to ignore the odd gesture.

"Are you all right?" he whispered, standing with her.

"Not entirely."

"I know yesterday did not exactly go according to plan…"

"Not exactly." She laughed, but it was hollow, tired.

It was too warm outside, and Hook rubbed at his arm nervously, trying to focus on the weather and not on the unsettling strain in Tiger Lily's face. "It wasn't me who gave that order, Tiger Lily. I swear it," he said, the first note of pleading already in his voice. "If he told the men to release you, whatever it was he said that made you go, it wasn't me. I wasn't turning my back on you. You know I'd never—"

"I know, James," she said, raising her gaze to meet his and running her hands under her eyes, drawing tear stains across her cheeks. "Peter can fool a great many inhabitants of this island, but not me. I know him too well."

James frowned and shifted backward, crunching against the newly dying leaves on the ground, a hard discomfort in his throat. Why had she said it was Pan's voice she knew so well, and not his? He closed the distance with a breath of desperation and rubbed a strand of her hair between his fingers.

"And you know me. You know I would never leave you. I never want to let you go."

She stared up at him, and her eyes said that she agreed. So, he breathed out heavily, relieved, dropped his shoulders, and brought his fingers to her jaw. Then he pulled her face in to kiss her. Before their lips met, she pulled back.

"I cannot do this."

"What?" A breath of panic whispered through him.

"I—I cannot do this, James. Run away. With you."

Hook shook his head quickly. "I don't—Why?"

Tiger Lily looked away from him, into the shadows of the trees. They were black and grey and brown, and she was fixated on them. It was a gesture that frustrated him endlessly. She refused to ever look into his eyes when she did not want to say a thing. But, she turned back to him, and then he wished he hadn't seen her eyes at all. They were dark and pained, and they grew that panic in him greatly.

Her voice was very quiet when she asked, "Did you come after me when you saw that I was gone?"

Hook was silent. Fear. Cold fear was all there was.

"Come, James. You want me to answer your questions? Then you answer mine. Did you come after me?"

"I—I was attacked, Tiger Lily."

She narrowed her eyes and cocked her head. "That is not entirely true."

"It is; I swear it." He reached for her hand, and she snatched it back.

"I saw you in the lagoon. When you sailed in and saw that I was missing, how long did you spend just waiting there before Peter sprang out at you?" The warm wind blew strands of her hair up and around her face, making her simultaneously beautiful and threatening.

Hook choked. "I didn't know it was him. I had to know who gave that order."

"I don't believe that for a moment. The things he shouted at you. *Wonderful, marvelous, clever boy*—anyone would have guessed it was him. I know you. And one thing you are not is stupid."

Hook opened his mouth to protest, then shut it, backing several steps away from her.

"You heard us?" he said, frowning. "And saw it all. Where were you, Tiger Lily?"

She raised an eyebrow and folded her arms, as she always did when she was feeling defensive. "Just outside the lagoon, hiding in the grasses."

"You were that close and you said nothing?" His voice rose. "You allowed me to believe you'd vanished? *Why?*"

"I—" She choked, and strode toward him, face red and slick with sweat. "Do not change the subject, James Hook. Perhaps I was hiding, but you were attacking Peter rather than looking for me."

The panic and the anger and the puzzles were overwhelming now, making it impossible to think. He had no decent response, for however unreasonable were her actions, what she was saying of him was true. The entire time in the lagoon he had spent worrying about Pan, thinking about how best he could kill him, infuriated that the boy would throw a hitch in his plan. Not once had he thought of the woman he loved.

"You do not care about me," she said in a low voice. "Not as much as you care about Pan."

"That isn't fair," he said, pleading with her, muscles in his neck straining.

"It's the truth."

Hook struggled to breathe, to think clearly. "I love you, Tiger Lily." He took a step toward her. "More than I hate Pan. More than the *Spanish Main*. More than breathing. I've always loved you. You must know that."

"I question it."

She walked several paces away from him, near the edge of their clearing. The distance was suffocating.

"Tiger Lily, please…"

"And I saw you yesterday, fighting with Peter on the rock. You stabbed him and you slashed at him. A *boy*, James." Her voice was high and clipped, and she gestured wildly when she spoke.

Hook slammed his hook against the nearest tree. Then he pointed at her, hand trembling. "Do not toss that in my face. After everything he's done? To me? To my family? To the Lost Boys—to you, even. He is a cruel, wicked thing. You've always known I'd slice that boy up if given the chance."

Tiger Lily shook her head. "I didn't know you would truly do it."

"I'm a *pirate*, Tiger Lily. Of course I would do it."

Her nostrils flared, and she clenched her hands into fists. Something clicked in Hook's head, then.

"That isn't what it is, is it?" And he took several long strides toward her.

"What?"

"You're not leaving me because I didn't prioritize you or because you doubt that I love you. You're leaving because of Pan."

Tiger Lily's face darkened. "How dare you."

A muscle twitched in Hook's jaw. "How dare I what? Accuse you of somehow *still* being in love with Peter? You and I both know it is true."

"Do not make this about me," she said, her voice low, on the verge of growling.

"How can I not? It's the truth, isn't it? Where were *you* when I was battling with that boy up on the rock?"

"I told you. Watching from the grasses."

"Why?" he said, hand gripping her shoulder in fear, hook pressed flat against the other. He pulled her in to him, heat from her radiating onto his skin. His pulse quickened.

"No, James. This is not about me." She shook, and Hook's nostrils flared at the evasion. "The truth is that you are so consumed with hatred for Peter Pan that you can never truly value anything else," she spat.

Hook's voice raised by several decibels. "And you, Tiger Lily, are so enchanted by him that you cannot love the man who would bring you happiness."

"That is not true."

"It absolutely is." He let go of her and took a step back. They stared at each other for a tense moment, the air between them hot with fury.

"You cannot stand the thought of me spilling his blood because, in the depths of your soul, no matter what I say, or what I do, or what I make you feel…" He touched her, just below her throat, and let his fingertips slide up to the back of her neck, delicately twisting them in her hair. Tiger Lily shivered slightly. He closed his eyes and took his fingers back. "None of that matters, does it? Not when you're under Peter Pan's spell."

Tiger Lily said nothing; she just stared boldly into his eyes. Of that small thing, he was appreciative.

"Why now?" he said, something breaking deep in his soul. "Why not before you kissed me? Before you gave yourself to me? Before you told me you loved me?"

Tiger Lily drew in a shaky breath. "Because, yesterday, in the lagoon…" she paused, eyes shining with pain. Hook almost did not want to hear what she would say. "Yesterday, he came for me."

Hook's jaw dropped open. "He *came for you*? He rescued you? You were never captive to me!"

"I know that. I know. But Peter didn't. He risked his life for me. That's why—that's why I left."

Hook could barely draw in enough breath to speak. "And what? You believe he loves you now? You truly think that he came and 'rescued' you from my ruffian hands because he wants to be with you?" He could feel blood rushing to his cheeks, to his ears, in fury.

Tiger Lily bit her cheek and looked at the trees.

"Do not turn away from me again, Tiger Lily." She clenched her jaw, stared down at his mouth. "Look at me. Listen to these next words, for they are the words you will hear over and over again for the rest of your life if you walk away from me now. You will be haunted forever by them because you've chosen to surrender your heart to a heartless thing."

She waited for a beat, then looked up into his eyes.

"He will *never* love you."

"You don't know that," she whispered.

"Pan is incapable of love. He fought for you in the lagoon because he fancied a war with a pirate. You will never be with him, Tiger Lily. That I can promise you." His words were as rough as his voice, and they dripped with the sort of venom that can only come from terrible pain.

She let out a defeated breath. "I'm sorry, James."

"If you would just leave this place with me, if you would go off onto the sea, you would be free of him."

A small tear slid down Tiger Lily's face. "I will never be free of him."

"Do not act as though you have no choice in this. You could leave all of it behind; you know it as well as I. If you would just go with me, I swear to you his hold over you would break. If you would just come away from this cursed island."

He was desperate now, saying anything that popped into his head, true or not, to get her to stay. He was quivering with anger and hurt and deep, biting fear. He grabbed her hand and pulled it to his chest. He could still feel the electricity between them, the want deep in her, making her fingers shake against him.

"I could make you happier than you've ever been, Tiger Lily." His voice was low and gravelly. He drew her closer and brought his lips to her ear. "I would love you forever."

She did not speak for some time, and Hook's pulse was racing, erratic and hard. Then, she pulled away from him.

"You lied to me," he whispered, his face a mask of pain.

She stared at him, eyes welling up, red and wet.

"You swore to me that you didn't come to me that night because of Pan, that you wished to be with me regardless of him. That you loved me. But now that you believe he cares about you, what we have means nothing."

"And you didn't lie to me?" she said softly, staring up at him.

"What?"

"You promised you wouldn't touch him. Because of me. Because we don't know what would happen to his dreams if he died. You risked my *life*, James. For him."

His mouth went dry. He had nothing to say.

"I'm sorry," she whispered, shutting her eyes, and she walked slowly into the shadows, swallowed up by the still, colorless trees.

Hook stood in the empty clearing, head just slightly bowed, waves of hair hanging into his face. He stood there like that in the void for a while, blinking, in disbelief. Perhaps this was all another dream. Perhaps in a while, he would wake, and Tiger Lily would be lying warm against him in his bed, dreaming of forever. This was, he knew, more than unlikely. Here, in Neverland, it was impossible.

Hook was paralyzed, not knowing where to go, if he should stay in the clearing, if he should go after her. But, after his racing thoughts calmed, he made the decision to head to the *Spanish Main*. There, he could drink a glass of dry red wine and sit at his desk and think.

He was numb as he made his way back to his ship. *His ship.* The *Main* was still his, despite his foolish promise to Starkey. It rose before him, smooth and powerful and more beautiful than any woman. He stalked aboard, eyes furiously alight.

Smee said, "Capta—" but Hook slammed the door to his cabin before the man could finish. Then, he sat at the desk and took a bottle from one of its drawers. It was crimson liquid, seductive and lovely. He stuck his hook in the cork and removed it, then watched as the wine slowly drained from the bottle into his glass.

Face carefully expressionless, he lifted the glass and inhaled, letting the sweet, pungent smell overwhelm his senses. He brought it to his lips and let the velvet slide down his throat. When he closed his eyes, savoring the feel of the alcohol as it warmed him, he could see nothing but her. And he snapped.

He grabbed the wine bottle and hurled it across the room, and it shattered, sending shards of glass and cerise liquid spraying everywhere. He stood and let out a harsh cry, agony and malice combined, and as he did so, thrust his hook down upon his bedspread. Feathers coated the room as he shredded the blanket, sticking to the wine. And he jammed the hook into the wood of his desk, splintering it in several places, then flipped it over.

When there was nothing left to break, Hook collapsed on the floor, and the yelling dissolved into weeping. He buried his face in his arms and let the last piece of him that was left unbroken shatter into oblivion.

THIRTY-THREE

THE CAPTAIN SAT IN HIS CABIN, STARING DARKLY AT HIS sword, running the point of his hook up and down the blade. It screeched terribly, but it did not hurt his ears. Or, if it did, he didn't notice. He was numb everywhere. It had finally sunk in that Tiger Lily was not coming back, and it was all because of Peter Pan. The boy's very existence was offensive to him, making his hook twitch in the night.

His blanket was still shredded and the pieces of glass had mostly been cleaned up, with some exceptions. The cabin still smelled strongly of wine, which did not bother Hook so much. Smelling it somehow calmed him enough that he did not need to drink it, at least, not as often as he would have otherwise.

The cabin was silent, in a muted sort of way. In the choking quiet, Pan's hideaway called out to him, beckoning him, tempting him. He stood, seeking a distraction. In this state, raiding Pan's tree house would not be wise. There was a dark flash in his mind of the last time he'd gone drunkenly after the boy. He locked his jaw, sinking into his chair.

He wished, not for the first time, for Keelhaul. He wanted nothing more than to drown himself in wine, or rum perhaps, and women and music. Perhaps if he journeyed there this time, he would choose never to come back. But that was not a possibility. None but the wine was a prospect here on the *Main*. Blast his twelve-year-old self for not dreaming up a piano to put on the ship. If only he hadn't had such a hatred for practice then.

He clenched his jaw and reached into his jacket, and his fingers came away with a little vial, the one filled with death. It nearly glowed green, and he could practically feel the poison buzzing into his palm. One touch of his lips to the rim, and all this would be over. One touch.

He rolled it around, examining the contents, considering. What had he left to live for, really? Tiger Lily was gone, his family had forgotten him, and he had ascended to the highest level he could on these seas. What was left? Nothing.

Nothing, whispered the darkness creeping into his spirit. *Nothing but killing Peter Pan.*

He took one longing look at the vial and slipped it back into his jacket, honing in on the lone thought. Nothing but killing Peter Pan. Then, he rose from his chair with terrible purpose.

He ran a blade across his chin and throat, clearing away any stray facial hair, trimming it until he looked like the captain once again. His hair was falling over his shoulders now, in shiny curls. The mark of a pirate and a fiend, he had once claimed. And it had been the truth.

"Starkey," he called, voice steady, exiting his cabin for the first time in a while. "Ready the men."

"Captain?"

"After the suns fall, we are paying a visit to Pan and his Lost Boys."

It was to Starkey's credit, Hook thought, that he did not protest in the slightest, but consented immediately. Hook had wondered, upon first returning to the vessel, if he would be met with resistance from his first mate. He had declared the fellow temporary captain, after all.

But Starkey greeted him immediately as his captain, as though they'd never had the conversation at all.

Starkey went off and spread the message to the rest of the crew while Hook waited, veins buzzing with terrible anticipation. He stared off into the trees, wondering what exactly Pan was doing now, if he was attacking the Indians or playing with the mermaids or sleeping in his hideout beneath the ground. Whatever it was, he was quite certain the boy would not be doing it come nightfall.

Starkey returned and looked out over the island with him, solemn, calculating. In his eyes, Hook could see that he was always calculating something or other.

"You mean to really kill him this time, do ye, Captain?"

"Aye."

Starkey narrowed his eyes, staring into Hook's. "Can ye truly kill him tonight? He is only a boy, after all." Starkey was not challenging him; he could feel it. Starkey's tone of voice said that he was partly curious and partly meaning to prepare Hook for the task ahead. The one he'd, as of yet, been unable to complete. That was why Hook felt no need to lash out at the man. He was quiet for a little while, contemplating his answer. Starkey did not pressure him to speak.

"I feel it in my bones," he said, rolling his fingers over the handle of his sword. "Tonight is the night that I will slay him. And I feel no remorse about it. He may be but a boy, but he is a fully wicked sort of boy."

Starkey did not nod or say a word; he simply stood beside the captain, looking over the rolling ocean, letting him finish the soliloquy.

"He took everything from me, Starkey. My family, my home, my childhood, the only woman I ever loved. He took it all, and he feels not an ounce of guilt over it. A child, a heartless child." Hook heaved a great sigh, leaning heavily over the edge of the boat. "No. I will do what needs be done tonight. I will not feel guilty for it." And then, more darkly, "The deepest circle of Hell is kept for Brutus, Judas, and Peter Pan."

NONE IN THE HISTORY OF THE ISLAND HAD EVER TRULY set out to kill Pan, at least not with the sincerity that the captain possessed. Any who had ever battled him (including Hook himself, in the past) had always had a piece of his heart that desired to let the boy win. But not Hook, not tonight.

So puzzled was Neverland at this unexpected and impossible turn of events that the weather itself was a paradox. Stars churned and stopped, the sea nymphs unable to decide whether to glow or stay hidden. Hook and his men vacated the boat with furious speed as the night fell. As Hook and his band of men crashed through the trees, he found that he was at once warm and chilled to the bone. He felt both soaked and parched, blind in the darkness and clear-sighted, following a sort of light that none could see. It was an odd set of feelings, to be sure. But the emotion that overtook him, beating all the confusion that Neverland could throw his way, was hate. Deep, black, festering, necrotic hate.

There were several varieties of hatred, he had learned in the past several days. There was the kind that sent a man spiraling into himself and kept him chained to his bed, unable to do anything but sleep and wallow. And there was the kind that possessed a person and drove him to distraction. The kind that forced him to seek escape in wine and women and inane adventures.

Those sorts of hate were certainly terrible and had profound effects on a person. But the third kind, that was the most lethal. The third was the kind of hate that infected a man, and it replicated and ran through his veins, replacing his blood. And it drove him to do terrible, vile, murderous things. That was the sort that propelled Hook forward into the trees that night.

His troupe of men followed behind him, black-hearted and happy to carry out the raid, but they were all compelled to do so by loyalty, and some by a mite of fear. Hook was driven by a dark, urgent need. He replayed the image of Pan in his head, writhing, dying, bleeding beneath him. The more he thought it, the less the guilt and disgust elbowed into his heart, until he felt nothing in the imagining. Nothing, save for a grim satisfaction and prickling numbness.

So intent was he on the end goal, so focused, so bloodthirsty, that he did not at first realize that he had run into a body. But when it spoke, he was snapped out of his dreadful musing.

"James Hook," said the body.

When Hook looked up to see who it was, he recoiled.

"Chief." Hook's voice was not smooth or confident, not in the presence of the Chief. Hook had always been tall, but the Chief was quite a bit taller and twice as wide. His presence was solemn and hulking and infinitely wise, like his eyes themselves held all the quiet knowledge in the world. It made Hook feel inferior, like a boy.

"What brings you out into the forest so late at night, Hook?"

It bothered him somewhat that the other man refused to call him by his title, but he could not address it, he found. Hook tapped his fingers against his upper leg. "Nothing of any importance, sir."

"Do not lie to me," the Chief said, and Hook shuddered, shrinking, for in the Chief's face and in his words, Hook was reminded of a conversation not so long ago, one he'd had with the Chief's daughter. It brought a crippling pain to him, and his knees buckled for a moment in surprise. But he regained his composure quickly, unwilling to look weak in front of the man before him.

Hook then straightened and puffed his chest out. "Chief, I beg no resistance from you and no special favors. But this is not your land; I am not trespassing. I ask only that you let me pass."

As Hook's eyes adjusted to the darkness and to the world outside his mind, he saw that behind the Chief was a score of people. It seemed that the entire tribe was gathered behind him. He wondered for a moment if Tiger Lily was among them, and his eyes darted from man to man. That sent his pulse pounding.

"James Hook."

Hook blinked. "Aye."

"Do your ears trouble you?"

"No, sir."

The Chief crossed his arms and looked down at him hard, shallow wrinkles at the corners of his eyes making themselves known. "I wonder, then, why it seems you cannot hear the words I speak to you."

Hook stuttered. "I apologize, Chief. If you wouldn't mind…"

"I feel a sinister wind in the air tonight, boy."

Hook prickled a bit at the word "boy."

The Chief's eyes wandered to the black trees, the silvery ribbons of wind that slid through all of their limbs. "Something foreboding is waiting to happen. And I believe that, should I let you pass without explanation, it would be a foolish thing." He brought his hard gaze back to Hook.

Something shifted then, in Hook's heart and in his stance. "You mean to stand in my way?"

"I do not wish to fight with you," said the Chief. "But I do wish an explanation."

"Am I not allowed to roam the island as I please anymore? Have you instated a curfew for me?"

The Chief rolled his eyes. "Do not be a child."

Hook was beginning to feel less and less childish, and more and more angry. He was the captain of the *Spanish Main*. His name was known across Neverland and beyond that. Who was the Chief to question him?

Hook narrowed his eyes. "Mind what you say, Chief. Don't you know who I am?"

"I do." The Chief stood taller then, made his voice deeper, more resonant. "You are the mighty Captain Hook. A man so great that he spends his life attacking weaker men and taking their treasure, and so wonderful that he beds women and leaves them cold in the morning, and so fierce that he shudders at the sight of a crocodile. I know who you are, James, and who you have chosen to become. And there is a grave disparity between them."

Hook felt the wind as it was knocked from his lungs, and he stood before the Chief, blinking silently. For a moment, he was unable to form a sentence. After the shock of the man's words wore off, he steeled himself.

"Let me by." His voice cracked when he said it.

The Chief caught him by the shoulder as he made a move to pass. "You mean to kill the Pan tonight."

Hook turned back to the Chief; in a low voice laced with ferocity, he said, "I do."

"I cannot let you do it. I am bound to do everything in my power to stop you."

Hook's face turned to a scowl, but it was composed purely of raw pain.

"Let me pass, Chief." He held up his hook, and his voice shook when he said, "Or I will not hesitate to kill you. I and all my men will set your people to running and we will soak the ground with their blood. I swear it."

The Chief looked down, sadness washing over his countenance. Hook saw a shred of disappointment, and it nearly stopped his heart.

After a minute of tense silence, the Chief stepped aside. Hook did not feel a bit of elation at this, only seething, simmering anger. But the captain walked past, looking stone and proud, and led his band of men with him.

Then, Hook froze. For there was a tap, and a whoosh of air, and the sickening sound of metal connecting with flesh. He turned to see one of his men with an arrow sticking out of his back.

THIRTY-FOUR

The man fell forward, blood seeping from the wound out onto his back, and when Hook looked closely at the skinny fellow, he recognized him as Flintwise. Jukes roared and dropped to his knees beside the man.

Hook jumped back, his face a mask of shock. He whirled around, long curls flying past his face, and his gaze fell upon the single bow among them that was raised and readied.

He slowly let his eyes travel from the bow to the fingers clasped around it to the dainty wrist and up the slender arm, lingering for a moment on the neck. He was petrified of seeing the face that sat atop it, for he knew without a doubt to whom it belonged. And when he could stop himself no more, his eyes flicked up, and there she was.

Tiger Lily was trembling, holding the bow. She had already nocked another arrow. He breathed in and out, desperate for air, eyes torrid pools of hurt. Hers mirrored his. Hook stared back at her, unblinking, shaking everywhere. Without breaking the look, he cocked his head, twitched it, really. Starkey appeared instantly at his side.

Hook said, in a voice that was both a growl and a whisper at once, "Kill them."

Starkey backed away into the crowd of ruffians and a clamor broke out. Jukes let Flintwise's lolling head drop to the ground and stared up at the Indians, murder in his eyes. He screamed out and drew his sword, the size of Jukes himself, then ran and began to carve.

Hook felt a great nausea boiling up in his gut, and he was compelled to cry out, "Leave Tiger Lily! And the Chief!"

The first Indian came at him, brandishing a weapon that was sharp and nicked in several places. It had survived a good number of battles.

Hook struck out with his sword, meeting his attacker across the middle, slicing through his stomach like a hot knife through butter. The man fell to the ground with a guttural cry and Hook shut his eyes. The forest was alive with gunshots and bellows and the clink of metal against metal.

He hacked through the throng of men, slashing at one with his sword and gutting another with his hook, spilling the blood of another with the hook's point across his jugular. He pretended that the warm spray across his face was something other than blood. Pretended that he was back in his room as a boy, playing at battles with no one—that hurt no one, killed no one.

There was no piece of him that desired to be massacring the Indians. And a massacre it was. Several pirates fell in the fray, some of whom Hook knew personally and some of whom he did not. But, the Chief's tribe was shrinking at a dramatic rate. Hook himself was responsible for the majority of the carnage. He wielded the hook like a piece of him, slicing and stabbing with horrible precision.

He came up from a particularly brutal stroke and drew back his hook, power coursing through his veins, quaking his muscles, and stopped, stumbling back. Tiger Lily was staring back at him, eyes wide, arrow drawn on her bow. He wondered momentarily if she would shoot at him. There was a horrible, charged silence between them that to Hook lasted for an age. But probably, it was no longer than an instant. And at the end of it, she turned away just a fraction, and he left as well, shaken to his core.

Minutes passed, and more and more of the Chief's men fell until Hook noticed that the Indians were backing away and starting to run off. Hook raised his sword and yelled out to his men, who were giving them chase, "Stop!"

His crew ended the pursuit in an instant.

"The night is won. Let them be."

The forest floor was soaked and sticky, coated crimson and black. Hook gagged once, not so much from the carnage or the blood, but from the guilt.

The Chief stared solemnly at Hook, eyes dead with sorrow and disbelief, as he and his tribe turned to leave. This was nothing like the wars the Indians had had with Pan and the Lost Boys so long ago. And neither was the Chief's face. The lines around his mouth, etched into his forehead, were deeper, his eyes dark and wet, and filled to the brim with regret and surrender.

"After the suns have risen, come back and collect your dead," Hook said, voice rough and worn from battle. The Chief's mouth was a thin, grim line, and he gave Hook a single nod, then jerked his head and beckoned his men to follow.

Tiger Lily caught Hook's eye across the way, and the look on her face was one he would never forget. Her lips were parted, her skin so pale it was barely brown. In her eyes was a grave accusation, and a feeling of betrayal, and a deep, bone-chilling sadness.

He held her gaze for as long as he could, trying to ignore the blood of his men sprayed across her face, knowing that the blood of hers was on his. After what seemed a terrible, silent age, she left, and Hook turned to his men.

"What are you doing just standing around?" he snarled. "Get back on the trail, men. Pan will not come delivered to us on a platter."

The men who were still alive hopped up and rambled on down through the forest, tearing a path through the woods, Bill Jukes leading them. Hook, looking horribly fierce and war-torn, stalked on behind them.

Soon, the terrain became familiar, and Hook grinned. They were getting closer; he could feel it. He could feel Peter's life emanating through the trees, illuminating everything, and it drove him onward faster, faster. The leaves on the trees here were nearly glowing, and the taste on the air was sickeningly sweet, mingling with the metallic flavor of blood sprinkled across Hook's lips. He made his way to the front of the wicked crew, trusting himself, now, to lead the onslaught.

Suddenly, he stopped and grabbed the sleeve of the man nearest him, who happened to be Smee.

"This is it, Smee. I can feel it. We're nearly atop it."

"Indeed, Captain. Pan is right close, to be sure."

Hook turned slowly around, then dropped to his hands and knees, feeling for fungus of unusual temperatures. It smelled like dirt and moisture and rot down there, but he did not care. It was certainly undignified, the captain rooting around in the soil, mussing up his jacket and pants and scuffing his boots nearly beyond repair. But at this juncture, dignity was not Hook's chief concern.

His slender fingers crept along the ground as he crawled, hook dragging a thin line, splitting the foliage. He held up the hook, signaling his men to stop. Each man in the company froze immediately, even going so far as to halt their breathing. Hook smirked and continued the slow line forward. Then he stopped. Beneath his hand, he felt a warmth that did not fit with the rest of the earth. He rose just slightly, face to face with a rather large mushroom. This was it.

He mouthed a silent command for the men to stay put, then rose slowly from the ground, pushing his hands out at them. Starkey was the first to interpret the gesture, and he began to back away. The rest of the crew followed his lead, until Hook was satisfied. He stood, walked softly over to his line of fellows, and leaned over to Starkey's ear. He spoke in quick, hushed tones. "We'll take all of them. I want every Lost Boy in our possession. Until I have Peter on my hook, none goes free."

"And after you have the Pan?"

"I need them no further. We'll let them go."

Starkey nodded.

"Spread the men out. I want them a meter apart. You see those trees over there? That's where the boys will be coming from. I want no space left unmanned, no chance for escape."

Starkey stepped back into the crowd and the men dispersed. When they stilled, there was a semi-circle around the trees. For the Lost Boys, there was very little chance of making it out of the night unscathed if they fought. Hook smiled wickedly and drew out his sword, then set his chin upon the round piece of his hook, waiting.

The minutes (or something like minutes) rolled along, the silence threatening to choke him. He cursed it, for the longer they waited, the more he began to doubt himself. But, finally, there was a rustle in one of the trees.

Hook perked up his head and signaled to his men to be silent, and to be ready. Smee shifted his weight nervously, and Jukes lowered his chin, eyes blazing. Then, out of one of the smaller trees, a boy Hook did not recognize descended. He had curly, auburn hair that fairly flashed in the moonlight. Starkey took hold of him, clapping his huge hand over the child's mouth, and flung him across the circle to Smee, who did the same and held the child captive, but in an almost genial way so that, cushioned against the roundness of the pirate's belly, the child barely looked frightened.

One by one, the children slid out onto the ground, and the second they hit the earth, each of them was snatched up by one pirate or another. Hook was no longer crouching. He was strutting around the circle, menacing from the blood still on his face, dashing from all the rest of him. He was both greatly anticipating and greatly fearing the arrival of Peter Pan, knowing that his own glorious moment would finally come, and almost wishing it wouldn't.

At long last, all the boys had vacated their trees, and there was a break in the commotion. The captain drew nearer to the little grove, brandishing his horribly lustrous hook. And when the last person came from the tree, he smiled and reached out and grabbed the child's arm. But, when he saw the eyes, he drew back.

"A girl," he said, only just now remembering the girl he had seen at the lagoon.

She stared up at him, eyes wide and unblinking and astonishingly blue. There was a light spray of freckles across her cream face, and her mouth hung open. She was mesmerized by him, just as Tiger Lily had been mesmerized by Peter when she was little, so long ago.

"Who are you, girl?"

The girl just kept staring at his eyes, blonde curls shrinking against her chest.

Smee tossed his boy to another pirate and scampered over.

"It's his Wendy, Captain."

He frowned. "His what?"

Smee flashed a somewhat embarrassed smile at the girl, then turned back to Hook. "His Wendy."

"*His* Wendy?" Wendy huffed.

Hook ignored her. "Explain to me, Smee."

"Well, I've heard tell that Peter Pan had got himself a mother, called a Wendy. He's terribly attached to her, I believe."

Wendy turned up a corner of her mouth at that.

"Is he?" Hook said, raising a perfectly shaped eyebrow. "Indeed."

At this point, Hook was satisfied that Peter would not be vacating the house. He looked back at Wendy and released her arm, taking her by her tiny hand instead. He was resolved to be a gentleman to the lady, even under these circumstances.

"Tie the boys," he said, and the pirates hopped to, tying rope around each of the boy's arms and faces and midsections. "Leave the Wendy. She shall remain unharmed."

The tying went smoothly, he suspected, because Wendy was not putting up much of a fight; she was too intent on staring at him. So the boys were surprisingly unresisting. When it came to Slightly, however, the plan hitched a bit. He was a rotund sort of boy, just as he'd always been, and there was barely enough rope to go around him. Hook pursed his lips. How on earth could a boy get so round when Pan never fed them anything but make-believe food?

Hook narrowed his eyes and looked back at Slightly's tree. It was decidedly larger than all the rest; it had to be. In fact, the tree was nearly man-sized. Hook whipped his face back to eye Slightly. The boy caught his gaze and paled, eyes as wide as dinner plates.

Hook handed Wendy to Smee without a word and returned to examining Slightly's tree. None of the others was close to large enough for the captain, but this one, this was no twig. This particular entrance to Pan's hideout, Hook could almost certainly fit through. Herein was the way to the Pan.

"Take them back to the ship, and leave me be."

His tone of voice was such that none of his men dared question him. They simply took the strange order and, boys (and girl) in hand, they left. And Captain Hook was alone with the trees and the aggressive blackness in his heart.

THIRTY-FIVE

WHEN THE NIGHT WAS STILL, HOOK REMOVED HIS jacket and hat, leaving himself in nothing but his boots and pants and threadbare linen shirt. His skin was chilled, and so was his blood, but he doubted that came from the weather.

Hook approached Slightly's tree and ran his fingers over the rough edges, fingernails scraping against the glimmering bark. He stepped with one foot into the tree, crouched, and smiled. It was indeed large enough to accommodate him, though barely so. He shimmied down the hollow trunk, glad that he'd chosen to abandon his hat and jacket aboveground. The splinters in the wood tore at his pants and shirt, fraying them and ripping small holes in the fabric. He continued his decidedly uncomfortable descent, until he landed with a muffled *thump* on the ground. Hook drew his sword immediately upon exiting the trunk and his eyes darted around the room. He gripped the handle harder and his heart began to crash wildly against his ribcage. Pan was in the room.

There was a small creak from one of the house's shadowy recesses, and he jumped and held the blade out in front of him. Then, Hook saw him. Peter was lying there, in bed, defenseless, asleep. The candles glowing softly beside the bed gave him a kind of unearthly glow, and Hook's heart jumped up into his windpipe. The picture of Peter, mouth open, hair frayed and mussed on the pillow, was disgustingly idyllic.

He took a step toward Peter, holding his hook in front of his face, hiding behind it. The closer he got, the more the doubt in him took over, until he was right at the boy's face, and the uncertainty was overwhelming. He had some difficult breathing as he stared at Peter, taking in the peace on his face, his small relaxed body, and the hint of sweetness buried beneath the wickedness.

Then, Hook noted the mouth, which was twitched up in a smirk and laced with arrogance. He narrowed his eyes and looked over the rest of the boy once more, the cocky smirk tainting his view. Peter was relaxed, arm and leg both bent in such a way that even his body exuded conceit. That hardened the captain.

It was that easy pride, the unthinking narcissism that had caused Hook to lose everything. The self-centered arrogance had caused Peter to forget that the boy James had wished to go home, had taken his parents, his life, the only woman he'd ever loved.

He drew back his hook, gazing intently at the pulse in the boy's throat. But his eyes forced him to stop. They would not allow him to pierce the skin or the veins of Peter Pan. It was too brutal, too inhuman, too intentional. And, most of all, he heard his father's voice admonishing him.

"Bad form, James."

Hook bit his lower lip, teeth raking over it harshly. The incarnation of his father was right, though he hated to admit it. Killing a boy or a man while he was sleeping was the epitome of bad form.

It was a quandary, to be sure. He could not slay the boy while he was unconscious. If he did that, he would be letting go of every thread of Eton man left in him, and he was unwilling to kill that man completely.

The obvious solution, then, was to wake Pan and then duel him. But in his heart he knew that if he chose to do the honorable thing and wake him, it would be no different from committing suicide.

Suicide. Hook cocked his head, and his thoughts turned to a third option, one he could not believe he hadn't thought of already. He set his sword down gently and reached into his jacket pocket, closing his fingers around the vial. This was it, the way to marry his honor with his desire to live.

There was a little cup on Peter's bedside table, and it was filled with something Hook did not recognize. He left the cup on the table then knelt beside it, jumping when Pan jerked in his sleep. Hook held his breath. After several seconds, he let it out again and returned to the task at hand.

He held the vial in one hand, and with his hook, he pierced the cork in the top of it and slid it out. He felt uneasy just being this close to the open vessel, and his hand trembled just a bit. Despite the heat that scattered from his cheeks to his neck, begging for him to stop, he pressed forward and tipped the glass. Five fat drops fell from the vial into the cup, spreading out, discoloring the liquid just slightly.

He was sure, despite the attempt not to think about it, that he'd just descended into a level of villainy he'd never wanted to know, at least not so intimately. But the deed was done.

He clawed his way up the tree, and reached the top, skin burning from splinters, conscience burning from something else entirely. The cold did nothing to soothe either. He draped his jacket across his back and set his hat atop his head, brim shadowing his brooding face, and he walked off into the night.

Neverland seemed less confused, now, less frenetic. The leaves were slow, along with the stars. And the forest was dark, but at least now it was committed to it—deep and black and decisive. The world was just sort of holding its breath.

Alone with his thoughts, he wondered if Pan would drink the poison upon waking, or if he would disregard it entirely. And if he did drink it at all, would he even die, or would Neverland cook him up an antidote? Could Peter even *be* killed?

As was nearly always the case with Hook, there were two sides of him dueling on the issue. One said that no, Neverland belonged to Peter and loved him, and Peter was the beating heart of the place. Since Neverland could never really be destroyed, neither could its heart. But, the other side concluded that Peter, though certainly fantastical and imbued with defense beyond reason, was but a boy, and could be killed like any other boy. Somehow, Hook believed both.

When he came to the clearing he and Tiger Lily had claimed for their own, he lost his breath instantly. He hadn't intended to go there.

He snarled and pressed on through the meadow without bothering to stop.

"Will he drink that poison? Will he die tonight?" Hook muttered aloud, evidence that he was beginning to lose it completely. No sooner had he said it than he heard a faint tinkling of bells. He stopped and looked up.

There was a little light bobbing overhead, and it tinkled again. Blasted fairies; he never had been able to interpret the language. He shooed the thing away and continued on toward the *Main*, keeping his mumblings to himself.

When the ship entered his view, no smile played on his lips. Aboard the vessel, he knew, was a group of children.

A group he'd no idea how to handle. It depended greatly on Pan, whether he was alive or dead. He supposed he had no choice but to wait it out.

Tonight sometime, or tomorrow morning, all of Neverland would be in its usual state, or it would be mourning the death of Peter Pan.

THIRTY-SIX

HOOK FLIPPED A DOUBLOON OVER AND OVER ACROSS his hook, staring darkly out the window. In the night, it was difficult to make out the weather. It did not feel especially cold or especially warm, and it simply looked black. No hint of Pan's being, well or otherwise.

If Pan were to die, he'd decided to release the children. No question lingered in Hook's mind on that anymore. Granted, that left a score of children out in the Neverwoods without a Pan to lead them, but it was preferable to death. If the boy were to live, therein lay the problem.

Most of him expected Peter to survive. He doubted the boy could truly be felled by poison, no matter how deadly it was. Something would conspire with some other dreadful thing to save the boy, he was sure of it. And so, though he did not wish to, he was forced to consider what happened when Pan flitted up to his boat. *If* Pan flitted up to his boat.

Perhaps the way to bait him was to threaten the deaths of his Lost Boys. He was sure Pan would know if the boys were in danger. More likely than not, Pan would appear before he had to lay a hook on any of them. Hook bit the inside of his cheek and pondered.

Then, he gazed once again out the window. The air was gloomy, and there was a light coating of ice on the edges of the glass. *Gloom. Ice.* He leapt up, letting the doubloon fall to the floor.

The cold and the dark outside could only mean one thing.

Pan was dead.

Hook burst out of his cabin, grinning into the biting wind. It stung his face and his hands and every bit of him that was uncovered. He splayed his fingers and threw out his arms, basking in the delicious cold. Tiny grey snowflakes started to fall, swirling around in the wind, resting in his hair, and he laughed out loud.

It was a dark, pained sort of laugh, the kind that makes listeners question whether it is truly a laugh. And in the black of the night, it was even harder to tell. The laughing devolved into something even more insane than it already was, and slowly, each head on the boat turned toward Hook.

"Captain?" Smee said, toddling up to him.

Hook's laughter faded out until it was nothing more than a spark of absurdity in his eyes.

"Are you all right, sir?"

Hook glanced around, at the grey-brown leaves on the trees that had shriveled into themselves, and ran his tongue over his teeth, tasting in the air nothing at all. "Of course I'm all right, Smee. I am marvelous, wonderful, spectacular. You're standing outside with me, aren't you?"

"Well, I, yes. I am," Smee blustered.

"Then you know. I am quite, quite all right." He smiled widely with his teeth, little dimples from his boyhood showing.

Smee frowned, cheeks rosy from the cold, and possibly from embarrassment that he somehow *didn't* know. Smee walked off, stopping beside the pile of children, who had the ropes still tied around them to prevent them flying away. The tying, however, was rather abysmal—loose and drapey and hardly knotted. Hook wondered for a moment how all of them hadn't wriggled out yet. Several had freed most of their body parts.

The smallest one, whom Hook recognized as Tootles, reached out and grabbed Smee's shirttail, and one Hook did not recognize grabbed Smee's spectacles and put them on his own face, magnifying his little eyes. Smee hopped back and nearly fell over, sending the little captives into fits of laughter. Hook shook his head.

The interaction betwixt Smee and the children did pierce Hook in the heart a bit, and gave him a hollow feeling. Smee was flashing his blade about, trying to look menacing. Generally, the children would all shriek and shrink back when he did, but it was in the way children shrink back from frightening stories and beg their parents to tell them again.

Hook felt a great disquiet, watching all of them. When any of them dared to glance his way, it was with the same look on their faces that came over his when he saw the crocodile. Was that was he was now? A predator? When was it, he wondered, that the last piece of childhood had fled from him entirely?

None of the boys, including those he'd once called his friends, would look him in the eye now. With that last little glimmer of innocence snuffed out, he reckoned, there was nothing left for any of the children to love.

"No little children love me," he said quietly, to himself.

"What was that, Captain?" Starkey asked, approaching him with two rums in hand.

Hook took one from him and brought the glittering goblet to his lips, closing his eyes as the spice warmed his mind.

"Nothing, Starkey. Nothing of any consequence."

Starkey said nothing. But he watched the captain watching the children, and Hook thought that Starkey was more perceptive than he let on. It was not so much the play that bothered Hook, or the fact that they seemed to be inexplicably enjoying Smee's company. It was the innocence, that elusive trait he'd lost so long ago. Without an ounce of boyhood left, children were bound to hate him, and he was bound to become the villain, no matter which story he chose to be a part of. He tilted his head back and drained the cup in a single motion, then looked away.

"Smee, ye can't be doin' such things with those children," Starkey called.

"Doing what?"

"Playin' about. It's not a piratin' way to behave."

Smee scoffed. "Playing? I've got them shaking in their boots."

Hook raised an eyebrow. The shaking was from laughter, no doubt. He stole another glance at the group and noted, with curiosity, that Wendy was bound separately and sitting a good deal away from the rest. It reminded him of himself somehow, and he was stirred.

He made his way toward her and pulled up a chair, scraping its worn legs across the deck.

"Good evening, lady."

"Darling," she said, and she shivered.

Hook frowned. "What?"

"Lady Darling. Wendy Moira Angela Darling."

"My apologies."

She looked at him from the corners of her big eyes then looked away. But because it seemed she could not help herself, she mumbled, "Good evening."

"Why, my dear, are you sitting so far away from your boys?"

"Because I'm tired. And I'd rather not play in their childish games. I'm not in the mood for them."

She had a haughty tone of voice, which, if it had come from the mouth of an older woman, would have annoyed Hook greatly. But, because Wendy was a child, he was amused.

He leaned back and crossed his boots. "You don't fancy Smee?"

"Well, it's not that I don't like him. I just don't believe that now is the time for games and laughing and silliness." She shifted, and Hook could see that behind her back, she'd withdrawn her little fingers into the sleeves of her frilly nightgown.

"And why not?"

"Because, I expect you'll try to kill us soon." Her mouth was flat, her eyes carefully devoid of expression. She was afraid of him too, perhaps. But Hook noticed that she did not avoid his eyes like the rest.

He feigned shock and drew his hook to his breast. "Heaven forbid James Hook would kill a lady in cold blood."

"I don't believe that."

"Why not? You've heard tales of me murdering women and girls for fun?"

Wendy pursed her lips then looked up at him. "Well, no. I suppose I haven't."

Hook smiled, then glanced briefly over her shoulder, at the sea that was blue-black and raging, waves tipped with ice. The sky was growling and seemed ready to cave in on itself.

"I *have* heard of all the pirates you've killed," she said, ripping his gaze away from the sea and the sky. "And I know of all the places you've plundered, and I've told Michael and John all about the times you savagely tried to fell Peter Pan."

Hook's smile widened. Generally, that smile would have been a comforting thing. But the black clouds and striking lightning and rumbling waves gave it a decidedly different effect.

"Ah. A storyteller, are you?"

She nodded proudly. "I am."

Hook leaned forward in his chair, exuding villainy, but trying to come off as friendly. It was a tragic endeavor, because it seemed he'd forgotten how. When Tiger Lily had gone, she'd stolen the last childish piece of his heart, and he was left nothing but a knave, trying desperately to bring out something that did not exist anymore.

Wendy, however, gave him a look that cut to his soul. It was a look she should not have given him, not reasonably. It was so out of place with the ice falling from the sky, the terrible roar of the ocean, the frightening, wicked sea, and band of men surrounding her. She stared at him with admiration, not curdled with fear. Just itself, pure and childlike and innocent. He choked and sat back in his chair.

He stared at her as goose bumps rose on his skin and dead, black crackles of the dying trees surrounding the beach fluttered around them. And he noted the brave regality in her face, the blue in her lips, the pure, sweet youth in her eyes. Perhaps Pan was truly dead, and if he was, Hook did not know that he could leave this enchanting little girl to her fate in the Never Woods. Perhaps Neverland would let him go, and he would sail away on the sea, and lead Wendy and the Lost Boys back to London. Then it would be as though none of this fool adventure had ever happened.

He knew enough to know that this was unlikely. Nonetheless, a spark of hope was kindled in him.

"Would you like to know something about your stories, Wendy Darling?" he asked.

She pursed her lips and gave him an appraising look, evaluating him from the tip of his hat down to his boots, and came to rest back on his eyes.

"They call them stories," Hook said. "They call them pretend. But your make-believe, your games, the little heroes they would drum up for you. Your Peter Pan. They're all false. A story is just another word for a lie."

Wendy smiled bravely back at him, a little wrinkle in her small, pointed nose, and her eyes were sad, and much too old. "I know."

"Do you?"

"Peter isn't everything I tell him to be in my stories. I know very well."

Hook narrowed his eyes. "Then why do you tell them?"

Wendy glanced back at the Lost Boys, Slightly who was detaining the redhead by smashing the boy's face into his armpit, the new set of twins, who were both quite small, playing some sort of finger game with each other despite the dark situation. "Little children need things to believe in," she said, and Hook felt the words like a knife to his throat. His eyelids fluttered for a moment, and he looked away, the thought having only just occurred to him that he'd never had a thing to believe in. Not even Peter Pan.

Wendy's sugar-sweet voice brought him back to her. "What about you, Captain Hook?"

"What about me?" he said, quiet, chilly breeze letting little pieces of his hair rise and fall around his face.

"Are you real? Are my stories about you a lie?"

He looked at her curiously. "*You*, Peter's Wendy, tell stories about me?"

"Yes," she said, staring right through him, harder and with less fear than any pirate captain he'd ever faced. "When we play pretend, I'm always you."

He blinked and lay back, staring up at the cold, whirling, twirling sky.

He did not wish to consider her initial query, either. Was he the man she told stories about? The merciless, cold, murderous pirate captain? Dread of the Never Sea?

Without thinking, without allowing himself to convince him otherwise, he whispered, "I am not a lie, Wendy girl."

"Good," Wendy said, and Hook looked down from the sky and frowned. "The captain I play at wouldn't murder us. Not like this, in cold blood. No, the very soul of Captain James Hook is composed of good form."

Hook cocked his head, then, and Wendy gave him a little specter of a smile.

For a stupid moment, he very briefly considered untying her, the lot of them. He even felt himself rise to do it. But just then, the thunder crashed so loudly that all the children but Wendy covered their ears.

Hook jumped up from the chair, eyes dark and angry. "Do not manipulate me, Wendy Darling."

"I'm not," she said calmly, but her eyes held a spark of fire. "I'm only saying what you already know. If you do this thing, if you murder us all with our hands tied 'round our backs, then you lose. Peter wins, James Hook."

He slammed his hook into the chair and yanked it back out, sending splinters flying everywhere.

"I hate to disappoint you, my dear. But that is simply not the case."

Wendy stared at him, eyes steely, too defiant for a girl her age.

Hook's nostrils flared. "He cannot win if he is dead. Your Pan is dead, Wendy. I killed him myself."

Wendy shut her eyes and shook her head. Hook rushed over to her, face less than an inch from hers, and set his hook beneath her chin.

"Open your eyes. Look around. Can't you see the storm?"

Wendy did open her eyes. And when she did, the landscape around them changed. The black of the clouds faded to grey, and then to white. The sea calmed, until it was glass once again, and the suns beamed brightly in the blue. Vanilla in the air.

"No," Hook said, releasing the girl's smiling face.

"No," he repeated, and he strode across the deck, yanking at his hair.

"No," he screamed, the peace in the air like an awful racket in his head.

His crewmen scrambled about, drawing their weapons and loading the cannons, sprinting about in a clamor.

"I was finally going to leave, Starkey. I was going to do it."

Hook's words were running together, and he was out of breath. Starkey clapped him on the shoulder.

"Ye won't be doin' so any time soon, Captain. Pan is alive."

THIRTY-SEVEN

T HE CAPTAIN TAPPED HIS HOOK NERVOUSLY ON THE mast beside him and pulled his jacket around his arms, wishing to shield himself from the abominable warmth.

"Pan is alive. Of course he is. Blast the boy."

Wendy looked indignant, bringing a scowl to Hook's countenance.

He stared out at the sky, disdaining it wholly. If Pan was truly alive, and it seemed there was no other explanation for the weather, then he would have to use the tools at his disposal to bring him there. Those tools, he knew, were the children.

Were Pan's Lost Boys, and especially his Wendy, in imminent danger, Peter would know just as soon as he'd known about his flute and his Tiger Lily, and the *Spanish Main* would call to him like a beacon.

"Starkey," he said, voice on the edge of apathy, which was where it was the most frightening.

"Aye, Captain."

Hook felt a drop of guilt in the pit of his stomach when he said, "Bind the children more tightly. Free their legs, but I want the hands behind their backs. There can be no chance that they will fly off. And then, you bring them all to me."

Starkey nodded, and he made his way to the children, enlisting the help of several of the other pirates. Smee was included in the retying, but this time, the children were not delighted by him. For whatever reason, this gladdened the captain a bit.

When it was done, the pirate marched the captives to the captain, and they stood in a solemn line, looking grim, as though they were being forced to drink castor oil. It was appropriate.

"Six of you will walk the plank today, boys."

Jukes came to stand beside him and crossed his massive arms, muscles bulging, mouth hard and angry. He'd been nothing but hard and angry since Flintwise had died in the battle with the Indians. Hook nodded at him.

He very intentionally ignored Wendy and tried to ignore the voice in his head that said, *"Peter wins. Peter wins. Peter wins."*

Several of the boys puffed up their chests at the claim, but a couple of them slouched and cast their eyes downward. It made Hook rather sad to see the fear in them, particularly in Tootles and Slightly. Slightly had been his friend once, hadn't he? And Tootles was the small one, the one he still, inexplicably, felt an obligation to protect. But, unless they truly believed it, he had no doubt that Pan would not come.

"I've room on my vessel, however, for two cabin boys."

After he said it, he felt foolish. But he was so guilt-stricken over the looks on the children's faces that he was compelled to offer them some glimmer of hope. Besides, perhaps the thought of his boys defecting to piracy would be more drawing to Peter than the threat of their deaths.

The boys looked at each other, heads whipping about, dancing with nervous energy.

Hook shifted his weight from one foot to the other. "Well, hop to, boys. It's not often that you get an offer such as this from the dreadful Captain Hook."

Tootles stepped forward, and Hook smiled with relief. Tootles had always been one of his favorites. When the child looked up into his face, Hook realized that Tootles did not recognize him in the slightest. That wiped the smile from him.

"The problem, Mister Captain, is that it doesn't seem proper to be a pirate. My mother would faint."

"And who is your mother?"

"Wendy, Mister Captain, sir."

Slightly piped in. "It's true. She'd have us for dinner. She's awfully strict for a mother."

Slightly didn't know him either. Had he truly changed so much?

Hook narrowed his eyes and looked back at Wendy, who was smiling softly. She looked older in this light, silhouetted by the blue sky and the light of the suns, and Hook saw her for a moment as the children saw her. She did remind him a bit of his mother back home in England. The hint of a smile, the wisdom behind the eyes, the softness in her face. It was nonsense, of course. Peter had fooled the boys into believing that she was their mother, nothing more. But it was a clever ruse.

He followed her gaze to two boys, two he did not recognize. One was tall and lanky and proud. The other was tiny with delicately angled little features, and he had a mischievous spark in his eye. Hook looked at Wendy out of the corner of his eyes and back to the boys, and he grinned.

"You, boy," he said, pacing over to stand in front of the little one. He knelt in front of him and lowered his voice. "What's your name?"

"Michael Darling."

Darling. A brother of Wendy's then, no doubt.

The child looked at his feet.

"Michael, can you really tell me you've never dreamed of becoming a pirate?"

Michael screwed up his face in the way of little boys and peered up at Hook. "Well, I've played at it. I've always wanted to be called, to be called…"

"Called what?" Hook said, stooping a bit more, tilting his ear toward the boy.

Michael leaned in very close to the captain, so his voice was only a whisper. "Red-Handed Jack."

Hook raised his eyebrows and stood then set his hand on Michael's shoulder. "Red-Handed Jack. I truly believe I've never heard a fiercer name for a pirate."

It beat Captain Bloodheart. That was for certain.

Michael smiled, though he looked a bit bashful. And he turned to the boy beside him, who looked deep in thought.

"What would my name be?" said the taller boy.

"What's your name now?"

"John Darling. But I won't be known as the pirate Darling."

Another brother. Hook scraped his teeth across his lower lip. Starkey saw his hesitation and stepped forward. "We've been sorely needin' a Blackbeard Joe."

"You haven't got one already?" said John.

"No. We're fresh out."

John looked content with this and nodded.

"Boys!" came the shriek from Wendy. Both brothers jumped out of their skins. "How can you consider it? Think for a moment. You know what our real mother would say, don't you? If you became pirates? You're not fiends. I know it."

John and Michael both stepped back at once and hung their heads.

"You'd truly choose to die rather than sail under my flag?"

The brothers peeked up at him, eyes large and woeful, then looked over at Wendy.

"Of course they will," she piped in. "They will die like English gentlemen. With good form."

She locked eyes with Hook, and he was struck again at how like his mother she seemed. He stared at her until the shame welled up in his gut, and he could take it no longer. Hook looked away from the group and out at the bright, calm sea. Pan had not yet come. He frowned. How was it that he wasn't here yet, with all his boys so close to meeting their deaths? Pan had always been cavalier about death anyway, and perhaps Hook's plan would fail and Peter would never show up. He sighed, and then turned back to his crew. The plan was in motion. Despite his misgivings, there was no stopping it now.

"Set up the plank," he ordered to Thatcher. Thatcher and Cecco disappeared below deck and Hook surveyed the waters. He felt a vague stirring in himself when he gazed upon the faces of the children. None looked at him; all their eyes were fixed upon the plank. Their faces had all drained of color, and Hook wondered if his had as well. Pan was still out, gallivanting in Neverland. Of course he was. And very soon, Hook would be forced to send eight children hurtling into the ocean.

Cecco and Thatcher hoisted the rough plank between them and brought it out to the edge of the ship. They secured it slowly, or it seemed slow to Hook. There were several moments wherein both Hook and the Lost Boys shared looks of terror, the boys because they knew they would soon meet their doom, and Hook because he was dreading that he would have to be the one to introduce them.

Hook removed his hat and shivered, then looked away. The suns beat down upon him, warming his head until it burned. It was getting warmer. Did that mean that Pan was getting closer? Or did it mean that he was distracting himself with some happy adventure? Hook made an exasperated noise. It was impossible to know.

"Captain?" Thatcher said.

In Hook's voice was a great weariness when he answered, "Aye."

"The plank is ready."

Hook did not answer. He ran his hand through his hair, releasing several tangles from it, and stood slowly up. He put his hat back atop his head and tipped it at a rakish angle, still turned away from the solemn little crew. He polished his hook on his jacket until it gleamed. When he knew he could stall no longer, he turned around, looking more elegant and more menacing than any of the crew had ever seen him, and he looked one by one over the children.

"Which of you desires to lead the band?"

Not a child raised his hand. Hook met the eyes of the tallest one, John. How had he not been killed yet? He was nearly as tall as Peter. It didn't matter much, did it? Strange thoughts go through a man's head in the instant before he does something despicable.

"You there. *Blackbeard Joe*," he said, sneering.

John looked up at him, eyes shining with fear, but face stubborn and collected. An Eton man, that one. Or at least with the heart of one.

"You may have the honor of walking first."

John drew in a breath then stood, struggling to get fully upright, being that his hands were still bound. His skinny legs wobbled, and everyone could see it. Hook felt a great pang in him as John approached the plank. Where was Peter? Was he truly going to force him to send a child into the ocean?

John walked slowly over to the spot where the plank met the *Main*, and he looked, long and doleful, over the band of Lost Boys.

Hook made a sudden, panicked move toward him, unwilling for him to plunge into the water with his hands tied behind his back. John jumped, and he fell backward onto the plank, which vibrated heavily beneath his weight.

"Wait, boy."

John sat up and hung each of his legs over the rough wooden beam, wincing momentarily. Hook cringed when he saw a spot of blood appear on the child's leg.

"You won't die with your hands bound like that. I will allow you to die with dignity."

Out of the corner of his eye, he saw a flash of surprise on Wendy's face. He smiled to himself. Then, he approached the plank and held out his hook.

John eyed it, suspicion written plainly all over him. But the captain remained steady, and John held out a shaky hand and took the hook. He pulled John back onto the ship and turned him around.

"I thought you'd slash me for sure," John said.

"That would be terrible form, boy. And I am nothing if not a man of good form."

He took John's bound hands in his and drew back his hook to cut the rope, when he froze. A sound came, first from the sea and then from the side of the boat. It turned his insides and made him white at the gills. He forgot completely about John and left him tied, then backed away, trembling from head to toe.

Tick-tock tick-tock tick-tock.

THIRTY-EIGHT

Hook shrank back up against the wall of his cabin, pale and shaking.

"Captain?" Starkey said, looking at him strangely.

"Do you not hear it?" Hook was next to breathless. The ticking of the clock had changed him wholly in a matter of seconds.

"Hear what, sir?"

A sweat broke out over Hook's brow and he hissed, "Listen."

Starkey cocked his head toward the edge of the boat, and his eyes widened. "The crocodile."

In an instant, Starkey was by Hook's side, brandishing his sword in one hand and a gun in the other. Smee came to him as well, and most of the rest of the crew followed—Cecco, Noodler, Thatcher, Jukes, all of them. Despite the fear paralyzing him, Hook was touched by this. The men all looked terribly fierce and aggressive, ready to defend him in a blink.

Hook breathed in and out, in and out, then drew his weapon. He refused to play the coward while the rest of his band looked able to fell the creature with their bare hands. The boldness started to dissipate when the ticking grew louder.

"He's coming up the side of the boat," Hook whispered, and Starkey drew a bit closer to him, and stared, unblinking, out over the ship's edge.

How was it that a mindless creature terrified him so, when the thought of fighting a cunning knave like Pan did not chill his blood, but boiled it? Perhaps it was the mindlessness itself. A cunning person, he could predict. A fellow with a brain had strategies and thoughts and precaution and weakness. But a reptile, one that lusted after his blood, he could not hope to understand. A reptile would stop at nothing to get what it was after, even if it was foolish. Though he hated to admit his fear, he could not stop himself imagining the thing ripping at him and biting into him and consuming him whole.

He allowed himself to consider the possibility and to collapse into his own mind, give in to the panic, only for a moment. After he'd exhausted every possible feeling he could have about the brutal death he so dreaded, there was nothing to do but stand up straight. So, he did.

Hook blinked quickly several times, then straightened to his full height. He controlled his breathing until it was even and low. And he ran his fingers through the hair that hung by his chin and brushed his hook across his lips.

If he was to meet his death at the jaws of this awful creature, he was resolved to do it, as Wendy had said, an English gentleman, a captain. He flipped the sword once over in his hand and stepped in front of his men, steeling his features, staring out into the blue, resolved not to be afraid.

In that moment, as he faced the deepest fear he'd ever held, he felt a profound sense of peace. That could have had to do with the instant change in him, or it could have had to do with the sudden lack of ticking.

Hook frowned and let his sword drop just a bit. "Do you hear that? The quiet?"

"Aye. Seems to me the beast is gone, sir," said Starkey.

Hook was uneasy and shifted his weight. It seemed odd behavior, even for a mindless creature, to simply swim off in the midst of a pursuit. He turned around and faced his crew, then opened his mouth to speak. But as he did, he there was a tiny *thump* behind him. He whirled around. Nothing. Perhaps he was finally going mad.

Hook ground his teeth and took several paces toward the children, who were all still safely bound and sitting in a huddle. One of them was grinning a little.

"Why are you smiling, boy?" he asked Slightly.

Slightly's grin left his face quite quickly. "I'm not."

Hook shook his head. The entire ship was going batty. Hook paced back and forth in front of the group for a moment, trying to calm his rapidly fraying nerves.

"Cecco," he said.

"Aye, aye," said the man, running up to the captain, dark curls flying behind him.

"Fetch me a glass of wine from the main cabin. Red."

"Wine, Sir?"

Hook's nostril flared. "Do not question me."

Cecco gave him a strange look and headed off toward the cabin.

Hook was aware that alcohol was a strange thing to be requesting, especially at this moment. But, without it, he would be a paranoid mess if Pan ever did come to call. And without it, he feared he would not truly be able to send any of the children overboard.

Minutes passed. Hook furrowed his brow. "Blast that Cecco. Where is he?"

Slightly said solemnly, "One."

"What?" he said, peering at his old friend.

Slightly shut his mouth and stared defiantly up at him, seeing him fully as a pirate, and not at all as James. He would get no answer from the boy.

Hook rolled his eyes and made off toward the cabin.

"Cecco! What could possibly be taking this long?"

Cecco did not answer.

He stepped closer and stared into the dark. There were no lights in this cabin, which seemed strange. It contrasted completely with the warm brightness outside. Hook felt a chill course through him. And then, he furrowed his brow and lifted his boot. Pooling around it was a circle of dark red liquid that was not wine. The blood stuck to his shoe when he stumbled backward.

"Cecco!" he called, voice holding no malice now, but fear.

Several of his crewmen rallied around him, and they all looked on into the black.

"Show yourself."

There was no response.

"I said, show yourself or be known as a coward!"

There was a second of silence, and then, "I am no coward."

Out of the cabin shot a boy, the one Hook had been baiting. He was ticking and tocking and laughing. He'd come after all. A little light shot out with him. A fairy. Pan's fairy. Of course—the one he'd seen in the woods. Pan went through fairies like he did Lost Boys. Hook had never had the time to learn the difference between Pan's fairy and the myriad of others, particularly since he'd had a difficult time telling fairies apart anyway. She'd warned him, no doubt. Hook scowled; he hated this fairy more than any other he'd had the pleasure of hating.

Peter did not come at Hook, not at first. Instead, he went for Wendy. Of course he went for Wendy. He slit her bonds easily, before any of the pirates could react. Then, he freed several of the boys. There was no detaining them now. Each of the ones who was freed was hastily untying another, and it was a useless cause.

Though Hook could focus on no one but Pan, the boy was darting around, totally scattered, poking at a pirate here, kicking another there, laughing. His little dagger was flashing in the sunlight, sending flares into Hook's eyes. Hook squinted up at him, and his vision distorted. Peter darted in and out among the pirates and back into the cabin before any of them could move. He came back out in a blur, arms full of weaponry, and dropped the treasure trove of daggers and tomahawks beside the Lost Boys, who gathered them up immediately.

Hook brandished his sword as the whole lot of the children scrambled toward him and his crew, weapons flailing. It put him in a position he desperately did not want to hold, one where he was forced to slash out at the children who were more or less playing war games and dress-up. Most of the rest of his crew was on the defensive as well, all pirates, but none villainous enough to seek the blood of children.

Despite the chaotic nature of the swordplay, the battle itself was not terribly frightening. Children with knives were decidedly less threatening than many of the other foes he had faced. So, he found that as he swung his sword and hook this way and that, he did it in an easy manner, almost relaxed, until a loud cry sounded to his right. He turned his face over his shoulder to see a large body, covered in tattoos, falling to the floor. Blood coated Bill Jukes's back and seeped out onto the waistband of his pants. Hook stifled a cry.

The Lost Boy standing nearest Jukes was Slightly, and he was grinning wickedly, his knife coated red and shiny.

"Two," said the boy. And then Hook understood. It was a body count.

He felt a horrible hollow in his stomach. Hook had lost men before, of course, but not this way. Not to a Lost Boy, and not a man he truly knew. Hook was stuck looking at the hulking, dying man. In the midst of that paralyzing, silent moment, he felt a large force crash into him.

"Captain, look out!"

There was a blur of color and arms and legs twisting together and a crash as Hook's body hit the deck. And there was Peter above him, laughing and spinning and flying off, his little dagger slick with blood. Hook felt sick, for whoever was lying on top of him had taken the blow for him.

He only felt sicker when he heard the man's voice.

"Captain, don't ye be concerned. 'Tis barely a scratch."

When Hook detected a bit of wetness seeping onto his own shirt, soaking onto it from the other man, he nearly lost the contents of his stomach. Starkey.

Hook slid out from under his first mate and stared at him, willing it not to be him. But, of course, it was.

"Starkey, why did you do it?"

Starkey coughed, color draining from the leathery skin of his face. "It's my job, sir. Protectin' the captain."

"You shouldn't have, you shouldn't have," Hook said, barely able to come up with full sentences. He was desperate, grabbing at Starkey's shirt, pressing his hand into the pool of blood.

"I'll stop it. We can stop the blood. Of course we can. Don't you worry, Starkey. Don't you worry."

"Careful, Captain," he choked, bits of blood spraying out onto his lips. And he smiled. "Don't go usin' the wrong hand. That hook won't do a whole lot to help me, will it?"

"Don't joke, Starkey. Don't waste your breath."

"Don't have much of it left anyway."

Hook was frantic, eyes darting around, searching for anything he could use to stop the flow. He could not lose Starkey. Anyone but him. And not to Pan.

"Don't speak that way. I am your captain. That is an order."

Starkey grinned and leaned his head back, staring up into the sky.

"Don't you just lie back and die. I'll have none of it."

Hook's voice was unnecessarily aggressive, hoarse with fear and sorrow mixed. He kept pressing at the wound until Starkey reached out and grabbed his hand.

"Leave me be, Captain. Worry about the *Main*. This isn't the first time I been stabbed, and it won't be the last."

The dullness in Starkey's eyes suggested otherwise. He was dying, and the sparkle of Neverland was leaving his skin.

Starkey pushed Hook in the shoulder. "Go. Three more've died since you been sittin' here."

Hook clenched his jaw, eyes stinging.

Starkey blinked slowly, eyes clearer than they'd ever been as his gaze shifted to Pan, like a fog was drifting away from them. Then he looked directly into Hook's eyes. "Kill the boy, Captain Hook."

THIRTY-NINE

STARKEY BACKED UP AND LEANED AGAINST THE CABIN, breathing heavily, clutching his torso, fingers stained red. Hook rose to a kneeling position, hair falling into his face, and pulled his sword slowly up. His hand and hook were covered in Starkey's blood. The visual darkened his eyes until only rage spat out of them.

He took in a deep breath, then bellowed, "Pan!"

His voice echoed across the ship, and Pan turned to look at him and flashed him an arrogant smile. Then, Peter darted down and slit Thatcher across the throat. Hook was overcome with violent, deep, vibrating wrath, and strode toward the child. Waves of malice poured off him as he got closer, clearing a clean path to the boy.

Tootles stepped bravely in front of the captain, holding out his needle of a blade. Usually, this would have stirred something in Hook. But not today. Not now. Hook did not even look the little one in the face. He drew back his sword and smashed it across Tootles's dagger. It was to his credit that he did not injure the child, but the force of the blow was enough to knock the boy on his bottom. Hook continued, without stopping, toward Pan, and he flinched when Peter felled another of his men.

"Twelve!" Slightly called out.

Hook was silent, his brow shadowing his features, and in his eyes was a fierce determination. He brought up his sword and pointed the tip at Peter. Despite the weight, his hand was steady. The captain did not so much as blink; he simply held out the blade, a dark challenge.

"You," he said.

Peter floated down, that horrible smirk still marring his face, and he turned to his Lost Boys. "Stand down. This *man* is mine."

They stared at one another for a long, tense moment, each of them pouring loathing into the other.

"Proud and insolent youth," said Hook, voice threaded with hate, "prepare to meet thy doom."

"Dark and sinister man, have at thee."

Pan struck first, true to form. But the little dagger was no match for Hook's long blade. He parried with ease and counter-struck, throwing all of his weight behind the sword, knocking Pan backward. Pan's eyebrows shot up, and he flew back at Hook.

Hook could feel the Lost Boys' eyes on him, and very few of the pirates'. Most of them were dead or dying now. Pan lunged at him again, and he dodged the blow, then they circled each other. Perhaps it was best not to focus on casualties at that particular moment.

The captain jumped out at Peter, distracting him with the sword, lashing out with the hook. Hook caught him in the cheek. Peter gasped and stepped back, then put a hand to his face. When he pulled it away, his fingers were red. Peter frowned. Hook was filled with a fleeting elation and grinned broadly.

"Ah, so the Pan is not so indestructible after all."

Peter gritted his teeth, looking like a child who has not gotten his way. He burst toward Hook and slashed at his neck, tearing open his long red coat. The top fell apart, and his throat was bare. Hook could feel the air tingling against his scar, and his cheeks flushed crimson.

When Peter saw it, something flashed in his eyes. Almost recognition, but not exactly.

"How did you get that?"

"A villain gave it to me, long ago."

Peter smiled. "And I shall give you another."

He made good on that promise immediately and flew into Hook's rib, knife out, drawing blood. Hook lost his grip on the sword, and it clattered to the ground.

Hook blanched. This was it.

Peter approached him, holding out the little blade. To Hook's surprise, though, rather than stabbing at him, he knelt to pick up the sword. Then, he handed it up to Hook. He wished, in that moment, that Peter had run him through. It would have been preferable to the shame that overwhelmed him.

But he hadn't. The captain shook as he reached for his blade, and then he grabbed hold of it, and Peter returned immediately to the battle.

There were no more interludes after that, no more moments of peaceful introspection or witty banter. There was only the hook and the dagger and the sword, and they beat against one another with a powerful vengeance. Hook swung again and again, trying in vain to so much as nick the boy. Peter flitted back and forth in the air above him effortlessly.

To Hook's utter distress, he found that he was tiring. He was no longer a child, no longer able to move endlessly for days on end and not suffer for it. He was breathing hard and swinging at Pan with all his might. Hadn't he thought less of Blackbeard for fighting in such a way not so long ago? But here was Pan, forcing him into maneuvers he so despised. Pan barely breathed at all, unless he was laughing. The boy struck and struck again, with no effort, and swam through the air above Hook, doing a backstroke, and then breast.

Peter was toying with him.

The second Hook realized it, his energy drained. The child was not even trying. And if that was so, there was no escaping this, not for him. Perhaps for some of his fellows. Starkey hadn't quite died yet, and Smee had a chance; he doubted any of the boys could truly lay a hand on the man. But, for him, this would be the last hurrah. So, in the midst of the little war, he stood up straight and he adjusted his hat, and he stared at Peter so regally, so dashingly, that Peter himself had to stop for a moment and stare.

James drew in a long breath and grinned, the grin of a man who knows he is at his end.

"Forget James, the child I was, and forget your fairies and forget your Lost Boys. Forget everyone you ever knew, Peter Pan. But you will never, never forget me."

With that, the taste of metal flared through the air, and Peter barreled into him. James was knocked over the edge of the ship. *Bad form,* he thought as he hit the ocean.

The water was like ice, pricking at him everywhere, lapping at his chest, his neck. He treaded water, wondering if he could possibly make it to shore. That question was answered when he turned to find the blasted crocodile behind him. It was curious, he thought, that no *tick-tocking* accompanied the beast this time. The clock in its belly had finally run out, it seemed. Irony of ironies.

It smiled, and James smiled grimly back. He started to swim away, knowing it was futile, but paddling anyway. It was not dignified to give up all hope, was it? To stop fighting altogether?

In the midst of the swim for his life, he was distracted by a sound. It was far off at first, distant and echoing and quiet. But it got louder as the croc got closer. And then, he realized what it was. It was the sound of the bells, and the chiming of the grand clock that stood in the middle of London. The chimes were hollow and loud, ringing in his ears, and when he looked up at the purple sky, behind the clouds and the suns, he could nearly see it.

There was Big Ben, face looking right at him, and there was the smell of something burning, something his mother was failing at making edible. Then there was the sea smell of his father, the one that matched his own now. He smiled, and an unexpected peace overtook him. Bibble had been right. The sky did look strange.

Had anyone seen him, they would have thought it odd that, with a crocodile snapping at his heels, he smiled. But James did not care much for what imaginary people would have thought. So, smile he did. For there was a shred of James that would forever be a Lost Boy. And as he paddled in the icy water, that piece grew until Lost Boy was all that was left in the shell of the pirate. The Pan crowed, and the crocodile snapped its awful teeth behind him.

To die, thought the Lost Boy in place of the Captain, *will be an awfully big adventure.*

ACKNOWLEDGEMENTS

So, I think we pretty much know that getting a book out in the world involves a whole lot more than a solitary, bearded author pounding out a tale on a typewriter in an isolated cabin, swilling some gin, and calling it a day. No, making a whole book takes so much more than that.

First and foremost, I want to thank God, for giving me the opportunity to do something I truly love for a living.

The incredible Bree Ogden, for championing this book and me, and for loving James Hook when he and his story hadn't yet grown up. I am so, so grateful for you. And to her assistant at the time, Maria Vicente, for really loving my story. My editors at Spencer Hill, Danielle Ellison and Patricia Riley, thank you so much for taking a chance on my strange little book, and for pushing it to be so much more than it was. My lovely and tireless publicist Meredith Maresco, for doing so much amazingness. Hafsah, for designing a cover that still makes me want to cry a little when I see it (in happiness, I promise). To the rest of the team at Spencer Hill, THANK YOU for everything you did and continue to do.

My critique partners, some of my closest friends: Tabitha Martin, you are a solid rock of support, and willing to listen to me neurotically freak out over my characters for hours like they're real people, and not hang up on me when we start into hour number three. Nazarea Andrews, thanks so much for...just, everything. Your insight into my stories, your unwavering belief in them and in me, and your constant preparedness to send me gifs of cute boys and tequila. (Who can write a book without gifs of cute boys and tequila??) Dan Malossi, my New Yorkahhh CP, for always being there to support me, to be a sounding board, and to eye-rollingly tolerate my phone shattering into oblivion every six months. (I know. Six months is generous.)

Thank you so much to everyone who read this book, in any of its ten million incarnations, and loved it, critiqued it, wrote fanfic of it that still makes me cry just a little (*ahem* looking at you, Darci). Rachel O'Laughlin, Darci Cole, and Rachel Solomon, massive group tacklehug because EVERYTHING. You guys are wonderful. James and I love your faces. The fizztacular Summer Heacock, for picking me out of your slush and flailing over James. This book would not be here without you and Brenda Drake. Team Fizzy: Carol Pavliska and Samantha Bohrman, for reading, critiquing, and always being there with a slightly (or not-so-slightly) dirty joke and virtual drink.

To all of my super-awesome online peeps, who make this sometimes lonely profession totally un-lonely for an extrovert. Some writerly friends who have been extra supportive and freaking wonderful: Christine Tyler, Liz Lincoln, and Rachel Simon. All you bloggers and writers and ALL you readers who have spared a thought or a post or a review or some change or anything for my book and me, THANK YOU.

Thanks so much to my wonderful friends, who have been totally cool when I'm all emotional over people I created in my head, when I had to pass on a hangout because I had to write, all of you who have been excited with me, I love you guys. Special thanks to Nicole Silvano, for being my person for over a decade now, and for reading everything I write, even when it's in its messy awkward phase, and still managing to love it. Rachel Chase, my amazing friend and a shining light of support. Love you, lady. To Luke Chase, for being there, being writerly, being nerd-tastic, being awesome.

My family. Every single one of you (some of you blood, some of you not) has been so supportive and wonderful throughout me pursuing this dream of mine. I am truly blessed to have so many amazing people in my corner. Papa and Nana, thank you for teaching me to love words, and for believing not only in this story, but in me. Mom and Dad, thank you for teaching me that I could do anything, and believing that I really could. Chase, Makenzie, and Taylor…for brainstorming, jumping up and down when you saw my cover, for caring about this and me and all those awesome sibling-y things, thanks, guys. My little boys (one of whom is legit angry-crying and assaulting my shirt as I write these), you guys are everything. You are everything.

And last, thank you to my husband, Harry (and you know I really mean Chrumby Face). Thank you for being willing to stay up with crying kids and clean the kitchen while I was revising into the wee hours of the morning. For listening to every idea I've ever had (in WAY too much detail) 'til midnight, and staying up even later to play video games with me. For supporting me in this crazy dream. I couldn't have done this if it weren't for you, my Someone.

About the Author

BRIANNA SHRUM LIVES IN COLORADO WITH HER high-school-sweetheart-turned-husband, two boys, and two big, floppy hound dogs. She thinks chai tea is proof of magic in the world, and loves all things kissy, magical, and strange. She'd totally love to connect with you, so you can find her online at briannashrum.com or saying ridiculous things on Twitter @briannashrum

CPSIA information can be obtained at www.ICGtesting.com
Printed in the USA
LVOW11s2026120116

469371LV00003B/5/P